THE CASEBOOK OF
MR. CARRINGTON

THE CASEBOOK OF MR. CARRINGTON

Simon Carrington's Cases

J. STORER CLOUSTON

COACHWHIP PUBLICATIONS
Greenville, Ohio

The Casebook of Mr. Carrington, by J. Storer Clouston
Joseph Storer Clouston (1870-1944)
Simon, first published 1919.
Carrington's Cases, first published 1920.
© 2013 Coachwhip Publications
No claims made on public domain material.

CoachwhipBooks.com

ISBN 1-61646-172-1
ISBN-13 978-1-61646-172-0

CONTENTS

CARRINGTON'S CASES

SIMON

1

THE SOLITARY PASSENGER

The train had come a long journey and the afternoon was wearing on. The passenger in the last third class compartment but one, looking out of the window sombrely and intently, saw nothing now but desolate brown hills and a winding lonely river, very northern looking under the autumnal sky.

He was alone in the carriage, and if any one had happened to study his movements during the interminable journey, they would have concluded that for some reason he seemed to have a singularly strong inclination for solitude. In fact this was at least the third compartment he had occupied, for whenever a fellow traveller entered, he unostentatiously descended, and in a moment had slipped, also unostentatiously, into an empty carriage. Finally he had selected one at the extreme end of the train, a judicious choice which had ensured privacy for the last couple of hours.

When the train at length paused in the midst of the moorlands and for some obscure reason this spot was selected for the examination of tickets, another feature of this traveller's character became apparent. He had no ticket, he confessed, but named the last station as his place of departure and the next as his destination. Being an entirely respectable looking person, his statement was accepted and he slipped the change for half a crown into his pocket; just as he had done a number of times previously in the course of his journey. Evidently the passenger was of an economical as well as of a secretive disposition.

As the light began to fade and the grey sky to change into a deeper grey, and the lighted train to glitter through the darkening moors, and he could see by his watch that their distant goal was now within an hour's journey, the man showed for the first time signs of a livelier interest. He peered out keenly into the dusk as though recognising old landmarks, and now and then he shifted in his seat restlessly and a little nervously.

He was a man of middle age or upwards, of middle height, and thickset. Round his neck he wore a muffler, so drawn up as partially to conceal the lower part of his face, and a black felt hat was drawn down over his eyes. Between them could be seen only the gleam of his eyes, the tip of his nose, and the stiff hairs of a grizzled moustache.

Out of his overcoat pocket he pulled a pipe and for a moment looked at it doubtfully, and then, as if the temptation were irresistible, he took out a tobacco pouch too. It was almost flat and he jealously picked up a shred that fell on the floor, and checked himself at last when the bowl was half filled. And then for a while he smoked very slowly, savouring each whiff.

When they stopped at the last station or two, the reserved and exclusive disposition of this traveller became still more apparent. Not only was he so muffled up as to make recognition by an unwelcome acquaintance exceedingly difficult, but so long as they paused at the stations he sat with his face resting on his hand, and when they moved on again, an air of some relief was apparent.

But a still more remarkable instance of this sensitive passion for privacy appeared when the train stopped at the ticket platform just outside its final destination. Even as they were slowing down, he fell on his knees and then stretched himself at full length on the floor, and when the door was flung open for an instant, the compartment was to all appearances empty. Only when they were well under way again did this retiring traveller emerge from beneath the seat.

And when he did emerge, his conduct continued to be of a piece with this curious performance. He glanced out of the window for an instant at the lights of the platform ahead, and the groups under them, and the arch of the station roof against the night sky, and then swiftly stepped across the carriage and gently opened the door on the wrong side. By the time the train was fairly at rest, the door had been as quietly closed again and the man was picking his way over the sleepers in the darkness, past the guard's van and away from the station and publicity. Certainly he had succeeded in achieving a singularly economical and private journey.

For a few minutes he continued to walk back along the line, and then after a wary look all round him, he sprang up the low bank at the side, threw his leg over a wire fence, and with infinite care began to make his way across a stubble field. As he approached the wall on the further side of the field his precautions increased. He listened intently, crouched down once or twice, and when at last he reached the wall, he peered over it very carefully before he mounted and dropped on the other side.

"Well," he murmured, "I'm here, by God, at last!"

He was standing now in a road on the outskirts of the town. On the one hand it led into a dim expanse of darkened country; on the other the lights of the town twinkled. Across the road, a few villas stood back amidst trees, with gates opening on to a footpath, the outlying houses of the town; and the first lamp-post stood a little way down this path. The man crossed the road and turned townwards, walking slowly and apparently at his ease. What seemed to interest him now was not his own need for privacy but the houses and gates he was passing. At one open gate in particular he half paused and then seemed to spy something ahead that altered his plans. Under a lamp-post a figure appeared to be lingering, and at the sight of this, the man drew his hat still more closely over his face and moved on.

As he drew near the lamp the forms of two youths became manifest, apparently loitering there idly. The man kept his eyes on the ground, passed them at a brisk walk and went on his way into town.

"Damn them!" he muttered.

This incident seemed to have deranged his plans a little for his movements during the next half hour were so purposeless as to suggest that he was merely putting in time. Down one street and up another he walked, increasing his pace when he had to pass any fellow walkers, and then again falling slow at certain corners and looking round him curiously as though those dark lanes and half-lit streets were reminiscent.

Even seen in the light of the infrequent lamps and the rays from thinly blinded windows, it was evidently but a small country town of a hard, grey stone, northern type. The ends of certain lanes seemed to open into the empty country itself, and one could hear the regular cadence of waves hard by upon a shore.

"It doesn't seem to have changed much," said the man to himself.

He worked his way round, like one quite familiar with the route he followed, till at length he drew near the same quiet country road whence he had started. This time he stopped for a few minutes in the thickest shadow and scanned each dim circle of radiance ahead. Nobody seemed now to be within the rays of the lamps or to be moving in the darkness between. He went on warily till he had come nearly to the same open gate where he had paused before, and then there fell upon his ears the sound of steps behind him and he stopped again and looked sharply over his shoulder.

Somebody was following, but at a little distance off, and after hesitating for an instant, he seemed to make up his mind to risk it, and turned swiftly and stealthily through the gates. A short drive of some pretentions ran between trees and then curved round towards the house, but there was no lodge or any sign of a possible watcher, and the man advanced for a few yards swiftly and confidently enough. And then he stopped abruptly. Under the shade of the trees the drive ahead was pitch dark, but footsteps and voices were certainly coming from the house. In an instant he had vanished into the belt of plantation along one side of the drive.

The footsteps and voices ceased, and then the steps began again, timidly at first and then hurriedly. The belt of shrubs and trees was just thick enough to hide a man perfectly on a moonless cloudy night like this. Yet on either side the watcher could see enough of what was beyond to note that he stood between the dark drive on one hand and a lighter space of open garden on the other, and he could even catch a glimpse of the house against the sky. Light shone brightly from the fanlight over the front door, and less distinctly from one window upstairs and through the slats of a blind in a downstairs room. For a moment he looked in that direction and then intently watched the drive.

The footsteps by this time were almost on the run. The vague forms of two women passed swiftly and he could see their faces dimly turned towards him as they hurried by. They passed through the gates and were gone, and then a minute later men's voices in the road cried out a greeting. And after that the silence fell profound.

2

THE PROCURATOR FISCAL

The procurator fiscal breakfasted at 8.30, punctually, and at 8.30 as usual he entered his severely upholstered dining-room and shut the door behind him. The windows looked into a spacious garden with a belt of trees leading up to the house from the gate, and this morning Mr. Rattar, who was a machine for habit, departed in one trifling particular from his invariable routine. Instead of sitting straight down to the business of breakfasting, he stood for a minute or two at the window gazing into the garden, and then he came to the table very thoughtfully.

No man in that northern county was better known or more widely respected than Mr. Simon Rattar. In person, he was a thick-set man of middle height and elderly middle age, with cold steady eyes and grizzled hair. His clean shaved face was chiefly remark-able for the hardness of his tight-shut mouth, and the obstinacy of the chin beneath it. Professionally, he was lawyer to several of the larger landowners and factor on their estates, and lawyer and ad-viser also to many other people in various stations in life. Offi-cially, he was procurator fiscal for the county, the setter in motion of all criminal processes, and generalissimo, so to speak, of the police; and one way and another, he had the reputation of being a very comfortably well off gentleman indeed.

As for his abilities, they were undeniably considerable, of the hard, cautious, never-caught-asleep order; and his taciturn man-ner and way of drinking in everything said to him while he looked at you out of his steady eyes, and then merely nodded and gave a significant little grunt at the end, added immensely to his reputation for profound wisdom. People were able to quote few definite opinions uttered by "Silent Simon," but any that could be quoted were shrewdness itself.

He was a bachelor, and indeed, it was difficult for the most fanciful to imagine Silent Simon married. Even in his youth he had not been attracted by the other sex, and his own qualities certainly did not attract them. Not that there was a word to be said seriously against him. Hard and shrewd though he was, his respectability was extreme and his observance of the conventions scrupulous to a fault. He was an elder of the Kirk, a non-smoker, an abstemious drinker (to be an out and out teetotaler would have been a little too remarkable in those regions for a man of Mr. Rattar's conventional tastes), and indeed in all respects he trod that sober path that leads to a semi-public funeral and a vast block of granite in the parish kirkyard.

He had acquired his substantial villa and large garden by a very shrewd bargain a number of years ago, and he lived there with just the decency that his condition in life enjoined, but with not a suspicion of display beyond it. He kept a staff of two competent and respectable girls, just enough to run a house of that size, but only just; and when he wanted to drive abroad he hired a conveyance exactly suitable to the occasion from the most respectable hotel. His life, in short, was ordered to the very best advantage possible.

Enthusiastic devotion to such an extremely exemplary gentleman was a little difficult, but in his present housemaid, Mary MacLean, he had a girl with a strong Highland strain of fidelity to a master, and an instinctive devotion to his interests, even if his person was hardly the chieftain her heart demanded. She was a soft voiced, anxious looking young woman, almost pretty despite her nervous high strung air, and of a quiet and modest demeanour.

Soon after her master had begun breakfast, Mary entered the dining-room with an apologetic air, but a conscientious eye.

"Begging your pardon, sir," she began, "but I thought I ought to tell you that when cook and me was going out to the concert last night we thought we saw *something* in the drive."

Mr. Rattar looked up at her sharply and fixed his cold eyes on her steadily for a moment, never saying a word. It was exactly his ordinary habit, and she had thought she was used to it by now, yet this morning she felt oddly disconcerted. Then it struck her that perhaps it was the red cut on his chin that gave her this curious feeling. Silent Simon's hand was as steady as a rock and she never remembered his having cut himself shaving before; certainly not as badly as this.

"Saw 'something'?" he repeated gruffly. "What do you mean?"

"It looked like a man, sir, and it seemed to move into the trees almost as quick as we saw it!"

"Tuts!" muttered Simon.

"But there was two friends of ours meeting us in the road," she hurried on, "and they thought they saw a man going in at the gate!"

Her master seemed a little more impressed.

"Indeed?" said he.

"So I thought it was my duty to tell you, sir."

"Quite right," said he.

"For I felt sure it couldn't just be a gentleman coming to see you, sir, or he wouldn't have gone into the trees."

"Of course not," he agreed briefly. "Nobody came to see me."

Mary looked at him doubtfully and hesitated for a moment.

"Didn't you even hear anything, sir?" she asked in a lowered voice.

Her master's quick glance made her jump.

"Why?" he demanded.

"Because, sir, I found footsteps in the gravel this morning— where it's soft with the rain, sir, just under the library window."

Mr. Rattar looked first hard at her and then at his plate. For several seconds he answered nothing, and then he said:

"I did hear some one."

There was something both in his voice and in his eye as he said this that was not quite like the usual Simon Rattar. Mary began to feel a sympathetic thrill.

"Did you look out of the window, sir?" she asked in a hushed voice.

Her master nodded and pursed his lips.

"But you didn't see him, sir?"

"No," said he.

"Who could it have been, sir?"

"I have been wondering," he said, and then he threw a sudden glance at her that made her hurry for the door. It was not that it was an angry look, but that it was what she called so "queer-like."

Just as she went out she noted another queer-like circumstance. Mr. Rattar had stretched out his hand towards the toast rack while he spoke. The toast stuck between the bars, and she caught a glimpse of an angry twitch that upset the rack with a clatter. Never before had she seen the master do a thing of that kind.

A little later the library bell called her. Mr. Rattar had finished breakfast and was seated beside the fire with a bundle of legal papers on a small table beside him, just as he always sat, absorbed in work, before he started for his office. The master's library impressed Mary vastly. The furniture was so substantial, new-looking, and conspicuous for the shininess of the wood and the brightness of the red morocco seats to the chairs. And it was such a tidy room—no litter of papers or books, nothing ever out of place, no sign even of pipe, tobacco jar, cigarette or cigar. The only concession to the vices were the ornate ash tray and the massive globular glass match box on the square table in the middle of the room, and they were manifestly placed there for the benefit of visitors merely. Even they, Mary thought, were admirable as ornaments, and she was concerned to note that there was no nice red-headed bundle of matches in the glass match box this morning. What had become of them she could not imagine, but she resolved to repair this blemish as soon as the master had left the house.

"I don't want you to go gossiping about this fellow who came into the garden, last night," he began.

"Oh, no, sir!" said she.

Simon shot her a glance that seemed compounded of doubt and warning.

"As procurator fiscal, it is my business to inquire into such affairs. I'll see to it."

"Oh, yes, sir; I know," said she. "It seemed so impudent like of the man coming into the fiscal's garden of all places!"

Simon grunted. It was his characteristic reply when no words were absolutely necessary.

"That's all," said he, "don't gossip! Remember, if we want to catch the man, the quieter we keep the better."

Mary went out, impressed with the warning, but still more deeply impressed with something else. Gossip with cook of course was not to be counted as gossip in the prohibited sense, and when she returned to the kitchen, she unburdened her Highland heart.

"The master's no himsel'!" she said. "I tell you, Janet, never have I seen Mr. Rattar look the way he looked at breakfast, nor yet the way he looked in the library!"

Cook was a practical person and apt to be a trifle unsympathetic.

"He couldna be bothered with your blethering most likely!" said she.

"Oh, it wasna that!" said Mary very seriously. "Just think yoursel' how would you like to be watched through the window at the dead of night as you were sitting in your chair? The master's feared of yon man, Janet!"

Even Janet was a little impressed by her solemnity.

"It must have taken something to make silent Simon feared!" said she.

Mary's voice fell.

"It's my opinion, the master knows more than he let on to me. The thought that came into my mind when he was talking to me was just—'The man feels he's being *watched*!'"

"Oh, get along wi' you and your Hieland fancies!" said cook, but she said it a little uncomfortably.

3
THE HEIR

At 9.45 precisely Mr. Rattar arrived at his office, just as he had arrived every morning since his clerks could remember. He nodded curtly as usual to his head clerk, Mr. Ison, and went into his room. His letters were always laid out on his desk and from twenty minutes to half an hour were generally spent by him in running through them. Then he would ring for Mr. Ison and begin to deal with the business of the day. But on this morning the bell went within twelve minutes, as Mr. Ison (a most precise person) noted on the clock.

"Bring the letter book," said Mr. Rattar. "And the business ledger."

"Letter book and business ledger?" repeated Mr. Ison, looking a little surprised.

Mr. Rattar nodded.

The head clerk turned away and then paused and glanced at the bundle of papers Mr. Rattar had brought back with him. He had expected these to be dealt with first thing.

"About this Thomson business—" he began.

"It can wait."

The lawyer's manner was peremptory and the clerk fetched the letter book and ledger. These contained, between them, a record of all the recent business of the firm, apart from public business and the affairs of one large estate. What could be the reason for such a comprehensive examination, Mr. Ison could not divine, but Mr. Rattar never gave reasons unless he chose, and the clerk who would venture to ask him was not to be found on the staff of Silent Simon.

In a minute or two the head clerk returned with the books. This time he was wearing his spectacles and his first glance through them at Mr. Rattar gave him an odd sensation. The lawyer's mouth was as hard set and his eyes were as steady as ever. Yet something about his expression seemed a little unusual. Some unexpected business had turned up to disturb him, Mr. Ison felt sure; and indeed, this seemed certain from his request for the letter book and ledger. He now noticed also the cut on his chin, a sure sign that something had interrupted the orderly tenor of Simon Rattar's life, if ever there was one. Mr. Ison tried to guess whose business could have taken such a turn as to make Silent Simon cut himself with his razor, but though he had many virtues, imagination was not among them and he had to confess that it was fairly beyond James Ison.

And yet, curiously enough, his one remark to a fellow clerk was not unlike the comment of the imaginative Mary MacLean.

"The boss has a kin' of unusual look to-day. There was something kin' of suspicious in that eye of his—rather as though he thought someone was watching him."

Mr. Rattar had been busy with the books for some twenty minutes when his head clerk returned.

"Mr. Malcolm Cromarty to see you, sir," he said.

Silent Simon looked at him hard, and it was evident to his clerk that his mind had been extraordinarily absorbed, for he simply repeated in a curious way:

"Mr. *Malcolm* Cromarty?"

"Yes, sir," said Mr. Ison, and then as even this seemed scarcely to be comprehended, he added, "Sir Reginald's cousin."

"Ah, of course!" said Mr. Rattar. "Well, show him in."

The young man who entered was evidently conscious of being a superior person. From the waviness of his hair and the studied negligence of his tie (heliotrope with a design in old gold), it seemed probable that he had literary or artistic claims to be superior to the herd. And from the deference with which Mr. Ison had

pronounced his name and his own slightly condescending manner, it appeared that he felt himself in other respects superior to
Mr. Rattar. He was of medium height, slender, and dark-haired. His
features were remarkably regular, and though his face was somewhat small, there could be no doubt that he was extremely good
looking, especially to a woman's eye, who would be more apt than
a fellow man to condone something a little supercilious in his smile.

The attire of Mr. Malcolm Cromarty was that of the man of fashion dressed for the country, with the single exception of the tie
which intimated to the discerning that here was no young man of
fashion merely, but likewise a young man of ideas. That he had
written, or at least was going to write, or else that he painted or
was about to paint, was quite manifest. The indications, however,
were not sufficiently pronounced to permit one to suspect him of
fiddling, or even of being about to fiddle.

This young gentleman's manner as he shook hands with the
lawyer and then took a chair was on the surface cheerful and politely condescending. Yet after his first greeting, and when he was
seated under Simon's inscrutable eye, there stole into his own a
hint of quite another emotion. If ever an eye revealed apprehension it was Malcolm Cromarty's at that instant.

"Well, Mr. Rattar, here I am again, you see," said he with a little
laugh; but it was not quite a spontaneous laugh.

"I see, Mr. Cromarty," said Simon laconically.

"You have been expecting to hear from me before, I suppose,"
the young man went on, "but the fact is I've had an idea for a story
and I've been devilish busy sketching it out."

Simon grunted and gave a little nod. One would say that he
was studying his visitor with exceptional attention.

"Ideas come to one at the most inconvenient times," the young
author explained with a smile, and yet with a certain hurried ut-
terance not usually associated with smiles, "one just has to shoot
the bird when he happens to come over your head, don't you know,
you can't send in beaters after that kind of fowl, Mr. Rattar. And
when he does come out, there you are! You have to make hay while
the sun shines."

Again the lawyer nodded, and again he made no remark. The apprehension in his visitor's eye increased, his smile died away, and suddenly he exclaimed:

"For God's sake, Mr. Rattar, say something! I meant honestly to pay you back—I felt sure I could sell that last thing of mine before now, but not a word yet from the editor I sent it to!"

Still there came only a guarded grunt from Simon and the young man went on with increasing agitation.

"You won't give me away to Sir Reginald, will you? He's been damned crusty with me lately about money matters, as it is. If you make me desperate—!" He broke off and gazed dramatically into space for a moment, and then less dramatically at his lawyer.

Silent Simon was proverbially cautious, but it seemed to his visitor that his demeanour this morning exceeded all reasonable limits. For nearly a minute he answered absolutely nothing, and then he said very slowly and deliberately:

"I think it would be better, Mr. Cromarty, if you gave me a brief, explicit statement of how you got into this mess."

"Dash it, you know too well—" began Cromarty.

"It would make you realise your own position more clearly," interrupted the lawyer. "You want me to assist you, I take it?"

"Rather—if you will!"

"Well then, please do as I ask you. You had better start at the beginning of your relations with Sir Reginald."

Malcolm Cromarty's face expressed surprise, but the lawyer's was distinctly less severe, and he began readily enough:

"Well, of course, as you know, my cousin Charles Cromarty died about 18 months ago and I became the heir to the baronetcy—" he broke off and asked, "Do you mean you want me to go over all that?"

Simon nodded, and he went on:

"Sir Reginald was devilish good at first—in his own patronising way, let me stay at Keldale as often and as long as I liked, made me an allowance and so on; but there was always this fuss about my taking up something a little more conventional than literature. Ha, ha!" The young man laughed in a superior way and then looked apprehensively at the other. "But I suppose you agree with Sir Reginald?"

Simon pursed his lips and made a non-committal sound.

"Well, anyhow, he wanted me to be called to the Bar or something of that kind, and then there was a fuss about money—his ideas of an allowance are rather old fashioned, as you know. And then you were good enough to help me with that loan, and—well, that's all, isn't it?"

Mr. Rattar had been listening with extreme attention. He now nodded, and a smile for a moment seemed to light his chilly eyes.

"I see that you quite realise your position, Mr. Cromarty," he said.

"Realise it!" cried the young man. "My God, I'm in a worse hole—" he broke off abruptly.

"Worse than you have admitted to me?" said Simon quickly and again with a smile in his eye.

Malcolm Cromarty hesitated, "Sir Reginald is so damned narrow! If he wants to drive me to the devil—well, let him! But I say, Mr. Rattar, what are you going to do?"

For some moments Simon said nothing. At length he answered:

"I shall not press for repayment at present."

His visitor rose with a sigh of relief and as he said good-bye his condescending manner returned as readily as it had gone.

"Good morning and many thanks," said he, and then hesitated for an instant. "You couldn't let me have a very small cheque, just to be going on with, could you?"

"Not this morning, Mr. Cromarty."

Mr. Cromarty's look of despair returned.

"Well," he cried darkly as he strode to the door, "people who treat a man in my position like this are responsible for—er—!" The banging of the door left their precise responsibility in doubt.

Simon Rattar gazed after him with an odd expression. It seemed to contain a considerable infusion of complacency. And then he rang for his clerk.

"Get me the Cromarty estate letter book," he commanded.

The book was brought and this time he had about ten minutes to himself before the clerk entered again.

"Mr. Cromarty of Stanesland to see you, sir," he announced.

This announcement seemed to set the lawyer thinking hard. Then in his abrupt way he said:

"Show him in."

4

THE MAN FROM THE WEST

Mr. Rattar's second visitor was of a different type. Mr. Cromarty of Stanesland stood about 6 feet two and had nothing artistic in his appearance, being a lean strapping man in the neighbourhood of forty, with a keen, thin, weather-beaten face chiefly remarkable for its straight sharp nose, compressed lips, reddish eye-brows, puckered into a slight habitual frown, and the fact that the keen look of the whole was expressed by only one of his eyes, the other being a good imitation but unmistakably glass. The whole effect of the face, however, was singularly pleasing to the discerning critic. An out of door, reckless, humorous, honest personality was stamped on every line of it and every movement of the man. When he spoke his voice had a marked tinge of the twang of the wild west that sounded a little oddly on the lips of a country gentleman in these northern parts. He wore an open flannel collar, a shooting coat, well cut riding breeches and immaculate leather leggings, finished off by a most substantial pair of shooting boots. Unlike Mr. Malcolm Cromarty, he evidently looked upon his visit as expected.

"Good morning, Mr. Rattar," said he, throwing his long form into the clients' chair as he spoke. "Well, I guess you've got some good advice for me this morning."

Simon Rattar was proverbially cautious, but to-day his caution struck his visitor as quite remarkable.

"Um," he grunted. "Advice, Mr. Cromarty? Umph!"

"Don't trouble beating about the bush," said the tall man. "I've been figuring things out myself and so far as I can see, it comes to

27

this:—that loan from Sir Reginald put me straight in the meantime, but I've got to cut down expense all round to keep straight,
and I've got to pay him back. Of course you know his way when it's
one of the clan he's dealing with. 'My dear Ned, no hurry whatever. If you send my heir a cheque some day after I'm gone it will
have the added charm of surprise!' Well, that's damned decent,
but hardly business. I want to get the whole thing off my chest.
Got the statement made up?"

Simon shook his head.

"Very sorry, Mr. Cromarty. Haven't had time yet."

"Hell!" said Mr. Cromarty, though in a cheerful voice, and then
added with an engaging smile, "Pardon me, Mr. Rattar. I'm trying
to get educated out of strong language, but, Lord, at my time of
life it's not so damned—I mean dashed easy!"

Even Simon Rattar's features relaxed for an instant into a smile.

"And who is educating you?" he enquired.

Mr. Cromarty looked a little surprised.

"Who but the usual lady? Gad, I've told you before of my sister's
well meant efforts. It's a stiff job making a retired cow puncher
into a high grade laird. However, I can smoke without spitting now,
which is a step on the road towards being a Lord Chesterfield."

He smiled humorously, stretched out his long legs and added:

"It's a nuisance, your not having that statement ready. When
I've got to do business I like pushing it through quick. That's an
American habit I don't mean to get rid of, Mr. Rattar."

Mr. Rattar nodded his approval.

"Certainly not," said he.

"I've put down my car," his visitor continued. "Drive a buggy
now—beg its pardon, a trap, and a devilish nice little mare I've got
in her too. In fact, there are plenty of consolations for whatever
you have to do in this world. I'm only sorry for my sister's sake
that I have to draw in my horns a bit. Women like a bit of a splash—
at least judging from the comparatively little I know of 'em."

"Miss Cromarty doesn't complain, I hope?"

"Oh, I think she's beginning to see the necessity for reform.
You see, when both my civilised elder brothers died—" he broke
off, and then added: "But you know the whole story."

"I would—er—like to refresh my memory," said Simon; and there seemed to be a note of interest and almost of eagerness in his voice that appeared to surprise his visitor afresh.

"First time I ever heard of your memory needing refreshing!" laughed his visitor. "Well, you know how I came back from the wild and woolly west and tried to make a comfortable home for Lilian. We were neither of us likely to marry at our time of life, and there were just the two of us left, and we'd both of us knocked about quite long enough on our own, and so why not settle down together in the old place and be comfortable? At least that's how it struck me. Of course, as you know, we hadn't met for so long that we were practically strangers and she knew the ways of civilisation better than me, and I gave her a pretty free hand in setting up the establishment. I don't blame her, mind you, for setting the pace a bit too fast to last. My own blamed fault entirely. However, we aren't in a very deep hole, thank the Lord. In fact if I hadn't got to pay Sir Reginald back the £1,200 it would be all right, so far I can figure out. But I want your exact statement, Mr. Rattar, and as quick as you can let me have it."

Simon nodded and grunted.

"You'll get it." And then he added: "I think I can assure you there is nothing to be concerned about."

Ned Cromarty smiled and a reckless light danced for a moment in his one efficient eye.

"I guess I almost wish there were something to be concerned about! Sir Reginald is always telling me I'm the head of the oldest branch of the whole Cromarty family and it's my duty to live in the house of my ancestors and be an ornament to the county, and all the rest of it. But I tell you it's a damned quiet life for a man who's had his eye put out with a broken whisky bottle and hanged the man who did it with his own hands!"

"Hanged him!" exclaimed the lawyer sharply.

"Oh, it wasn't merely for the eye. That gave the performance a kind of relish it would otherwise have lacked, being a cold-blooded ceremony and a little awkward with the apparatus we had. We hanged him for murder, as a matter of fact. Now, between ourselves, Mr. Rattar, we don't want to crab our own county, but you must confess that real good serious crime is devilish scarce here, eh?"

Cromarty's eye was gleaming humorously, and Simon Rattar might have been thought the kind of tough customer who would have been amused by the joke. He seemed, however, to be affected unpleasantly and even a little startled.

"I—I trust we don't," he said.

"Well," his visitor agreed, "as it means that something or somebody has got to be sacrificed to start the sport of man-hunting, I suppose there's something to be said for the quiet life. But personally I'd sooner be after men than grouse, from the point of view of getting thorough satisfaction while it lasts. My sister says it means I haven't settled down properly yet—calls me the bold bad bachelor!"

Through this speech Simon seemed to be looking at his visitor with an attention that bordered on fascination, and it was apparently with a slight effort that he asked at the end:

"Well, why don't you marry?"

"Marry!" exclaimed Ned Cromarty. "And where will you find the lady that's to succumb to my fascinations? I'm within a month of forty, Mr. Rattar, I've the mind, habits, and appearance of a backwoodsman, and I've one working eye left. A female collector of antique curiosities, or something in the nature of a retired wardress might take on the job, but I can't think of any one else!"

He laughed as he spoke, and yet something remarkably like a sigh followed the laugh, and for a moment after he had ceased speaking his eye looked abstractedly into space.

Before either spoke again, the door opened and the clerk, seeing Mr. Rattar was still engaged, murmured a "beg pardon" and was about to retire again.

"What is it?" asked the lawyer.

"Miss Farmond is waiting to see you, sir."

"I'll let you know when I'm free," said Simon.

Had his eye been on his visitor as his clerk spoke, he might have noticed a curious commentary on Mr. Cromarty's professed lack of interest in womankind. His single eye lit up for an instant and he moved sharply in his chair, and then as suddenly repressed all sign of interest.

A minute or two later the visitor jumped up.

"Well," said he, "I guess you're pretty busy and I've been talking too long as it is. Let me have that statement as quick as you like. Good morning!"

He strode to the door, shut it behind him, and then when he was on the landing, his movements became suddenly more leisurely. Instead of striding downstairs he stood looking curiously in turn at each closed door. It was an old fashioned house and rather a rabbit warren of an office, and it would seem as though for some reason he wished to leave no door unwatched. In a moment he heard the lawyer's bell ring and very slowly he moved down a step or two while a clerk answered the call and withdrew. And then he took a cigar from his case, bit off the end, and felt for matches; all this being very deliberately done, and his eye following the clerk. Thus when a girl emerged from the room along a passage, she met, apparently quite accidentally, Mr. Cromarty of Stanesland.

At the first glance it was quite evident that the meeting gave more pleasure to the gentleman than to the lady. Indeed, the girl seemed too disconcerted to hide the fact.

"Good morning, Miss Farmond," said he with what seemed intended for an air of surprise; as though he had no idea she had been within a mile of him. "You coming to see Simon on business too?" And then taking the cue from her constrained manner, he added hurriedly, and with a note of dejection he could not quite hide, "Well, good-bye."

The girl's expression suddenly changed, and with that change the laird of Stanesland's curious movements became very explicable, for her face was singularly charming when she smiled. It was a rather pale but fresh and clear-skinned face, wide at the forehead and narrowing to a firm little chin, with long-lashed expressive eyes, and a serious expression in repose. Her smile was candid, a little coy and irresistibly engaging, and her voice was very pleasant, rather low, and most engaging too. She was of middle height and dressed in mourning. Her age seemed rather under than over twenty.

"Oh," she said, with a touch of hesitation at first, "I didn't mean—" She broke off, glanced at the clerk, who being a discreet young man was now in the background, and then with lowered voice confessed, "The fact is, Mr. Cromarty, I'm not really supposed to be here at all. That's to say nobody knows I am."

Mr. Cromarty looked infinitely relieved.

"And you don't want anybody to know?" he said in his outspoken way. "Right you are. I can lie low and say nothing, or lie hard and say what you like; whichever you choose."

"Lying low will do," she smiled. "But please don't think I'm doing anything very wrong."

"I'll think what you tell me," he said gallantly. "I *was* thinking Silent Simon was in luck's way—but perhaps you're going to wig him?"

She laughed and shook her head.

"Can you imagine me daring to wig Mr. Simon Rattar?"

"I guess he needs waking up now and then like other people. He's been slacking over my business. In fact, I can't quite make him out this morning. He's not quite his usual self for some reason. Don't be afraid to wig him if he needs it!"

The clerk in the background coughed and Miss Cicely Farmond moved towards the door of the lawyer's room, but Ned Cromarty seemed reluctant to end the meeting so quickly.

"How did you come?" he asked.

"Walked," she smiled.

"Walked! And how are you going back?"

"Walk again."

"I say," he suggested eagerly, "I've got my trap in. Let me drive you!"

She hesitated a moment.

"It's awfully good of you to think of it—"

"That's settled then. I'll be on the look out when you leave old Simon's den."

He raised his cap and went downstairs this time without any hesitation. He had forgotten to light his cigar, and it was probably as a substitute for smoking that he found himself whistling.

Miss Cicely Farmond's air as she entered Simon Rattar's room seemed compounded of a little shyness, considerable trepidation, and yet more determination. In her low voice and with a fleeting smile she wished him good morning, like an acquaintance with whom she was quite familiar, and then with a serious little frown, and fixing her engaging eyes very straight upon him, she made the surprising demand:

"Mr. Rattar, I want you to tell me honestly who I am."

For an instant Simon's cold eyes opened very wide, and then he was gazing at her after his usual silent and steadfast manner.

"Who you are?" he repeated after a few seconds' pause.

"Yes. Indeed, Mr. Rattar, I *insist* on knowing!"

Simon smiled slightly.

"And what makes you think I can assist you to—er—recover your identity, Miss Farmond?"

"To discover it, not recover it," she corrected. "Don't you really know that I am honestly quite ignorant?"

Mr. Rattar shook his head cautiously. "It is not for me to hazard an opinion," he answered.

"Oh please, Mr. Rattar," she exclaimed, "don't be so dreadfully cautious! Surely you can't have thought that I knew all the time!"

Again he was silent for a moment, and then enquired:

"Why do you come to me now?"

"Because I *must* know! Because—well, because it is so unsatisfactory not knowing—for various reasons."

"And why are you so positive that I can tell you?"

"Because all my affairs and arrangements went through your hands, and of course you know!"

Again he seemed to reflect for a moment.

"May I ask, Miss Farmond," he enquired, "why, in that case, you think I shouldn't have told you before, and why—also in that case—I should tell you now?"

This enquiry seemed to disconcert Miss Farmond a little.

"Oh, of course I presume Sir Reginald and you had some reasons," she admitted.

"And don't you think then we have them still?"

"I can't honestly see why you should make such a mystery of it—especially as I can guess the truth perfectly easily!"

"If you can guess it—" he began.

"Oh please don't answer me like that! Why won't you tell me?"

He seemed to consider the point for a moment, and then he said:

"I am not at all sure that I am at liberty to tell you, Miss Farmond, without further consultation."

"Has Sir Reginald really any good reasons for not telling me?"

"Have you asked him that question?"

"No," she confessed. "He and Lady Cromarty have been so frightfully kind, and yet so—so reserved on that subject, that I have never liked to ask them direct. But they know that I have guessed, and they haven't done anything to prevent me finding out more for myself, which means that they really are quite willing to let me find out if I can."

He shook his head.

"I am afraid I shall require more authority than that."

She pursed her lips and looked at the floor in silence, and then she rose.

"Well, if you absolutely refuse to tell me *anything*, Mr. Rattar, I suppose—"

A dejected little shrug completed her sentence, and as she turned towards the door her eloquent eyes looked at him for a moment beneath their long lashes with an expression in them that

might have moved a statue. Although Simon Rattar had the reputation of being impervious to woman's wiles, he may have been
moved by this unspoken appeal. He certainly seemed struck by
something, for even as her back was turning towards him, he said
suddenly, and in a distinctly different voice:

"You say you can guess yourself?"

She nodded, and added with a pathetic coaxing note in her low
voice:

"But I want to *know*!"

"Supposing," he suggested, "you were to tell me precisely how
much you do know already, and then I could judge whether the
rest might or might not be divulged."

Her face brightened and she returned to her chair with a promp-
titude that suggested she was not unaccustomed to win a lost battle
with these weapons.

"Well," she said, "it was only six months ago—when mother
died—that I first had the least suspicion there was any mystery
about me—anything to hide. I knew she hadn't always been happy
and that her trouble had something to do with my father, simply
because she hardly ever mentioned him. But she lived at
Eastbourne just like plenty of other widows and we had a few
friends, though never very many, and I was very happy at school,
and so I never troubled much about things."

"And knew nothing up till six months ago?" asked Simon, who
was following her story very attentively.

"Nothing at all. Then, about a month after mother's death, I
got a note from you asking me to go up to London and meet Sir
Reginald Cromarty. I had never even heard of him before! Well, I
went and he was simply as kind as—well, as he always is to everybody, and said he was a kind of connection of my family and asked
me to pay them a long visit to Keldale."

"How long ago precisely was that?"

She looked a little surprised.

"Oh, you know exactly. Almost just four months ago, wasn't it?"

He nodded, but said nothing, and she went on:

"From the very first it had seemed very strange that I had never heard a word about the Cromartys from mother, and as soon as I got to Keldale and met Lady Cromarty, I felt sure there was something wrong. I mean that I wasn't an ordinary distant relation. For one thing they never spoke of our relationship and exactly what sort of cousins we were, and considering how keen Sir Reginald is on his pedigree and all his relations and everybody, that alone made me certain I wasn't the ordinary kind. That was obvious, wasn't it?"

"It seems so," the lawyer admitted cautiously.

"Of course it was! Well, one day I happened to be looking over an old photograph album and suddenly I saw my father's photograph! Mother had a miniature of him—I have it still, and I was certain it was the same man. I pulled myself together and asked Sir Reginald in a very ordinary voice who that was, and I could see that both he and Lady Cromarty jumped a little. He had to tell me it was his brother Alfred and I discovered he had long been dead, but I didn't try to get any more information from them. I applied to Bisset."

She gave a little laugh and looked at him with a touch of defiance. His inscrutable countenance appeared to annoy her.

"Well?" he remarked.

"Perhaps you think I oughtn't to have gone to a butler about such a thing, but Bisset is practically one of the family and I didn't give him the least idea of what I was after. I simply drew him on the subject of the Cromarty family history and among other things—that didn't so much interest me—I found that Mr. Alfred Cromarty was never married and seemed to have had rather a gay reputation."

She looked at him with an expression that would have immediately converted any susceptible man into a fellow conspirator, and asked in her most enticing voice:

"Need you ask what I guessed? What is the use in not telling me simply whether I have guessed right!"

Silent Simon's face remained a mask.

"What precisely did you guess?"

"That my mother wasn't married," she said, her voice falling very low, "and I am really Sir Reginald's niece though he never can acknowledge it—and I don't want him to! But I do want to be sure. Dear Mr. Rattar, won't you tell me?"

Dear Mr. Rattar never relaxed a muscle.

"Your guess seems very probable," he admitted.

"But tell me definitely."

"Why?" he enquired coldly.

"Oh, have you no *curiosity* yourself—especially about who your parents were; supposing you didn't know?"

"Then it's only out of curiosity that you enquired?"

"Only!" she repeated with a world of woman's scorn. "But what sort of motives did you expect? I have walked in the whole way this morning just to end the suspense of wondering! Of course, I'll never tell a soul you told me."

She threw on him a moving smile.

"You needn't actually tell me outright. Just use some legal word—'Alibi' if I am right and 'forgery' if I'm wrong!"

Silent Simon's sudden glance chilled her smile. She evidently felt she had been taking the law in vain.

"I only meant—" she began anxiously.

"I must consult Sir Reginald," he interrupted brusquely.

She made no further effort. That glance seemed to have subdued her spirit.

"I am sorry I have bothered you," she said as she went.

As the door closed behind her, Mr. Rattar took out his handkerchief and wiped his brow and his neck. And then he fell to work again upon the recent records of the firm. Yet, absorbed though he seemed, whenever a door opened or shut sharply or a step sounded distinctly outside his room, he would look up quickly and listen, or that expression would come into his eye which both Mary MacLean and Mr. Ison had described as the look of one who was watched.

6

AT NIGHT

When Simon Rattar came to his present villa, he brought from his old house in the middle of the town (which had been his father's before him) a vast accumulation of old books and old papers. Being a man who never threw away an opportunity or anything else, and also a person of the utmost tidyness, he compromised by keeping this litter in the spare rooms at the top of the house. In fact Simon was rather pleased at discovering this use for his superfluous apartments, for he hated wasting anything.

On this same morning, just before he started for his office, he had again called his housemaid and given her particular injunctions that these rooms were not to be disturbed during the day. He added that this was essential because he expected a gentleman that evening who would be going through some of the old papers with him.

Perhaps it was the vague feeling of disquiet which possessed Mary MacLean this morning that made his injunction seem a little curious. She had been with the master three years and never presumed or dreamt of presuming to touch his papers. He might have known that, thought she, without having to tell her not to. Indeed, she felt a little aggrieved at the command, and in the course of the morning she made a discovery that seemed to her a further reflection on her discretion.

When she came to dust the passage in which these rooms opened her eye was at once caught by a sheet of white paper pinned to each of the three doors. On each of these sheets was written in her master's hand the words "This room not to be entered. Papers to be undisturbed." The result was a warning to those who take superfluous precautions. Under ordinary circumstances Mary would never have thought of touching the handles of those doors. Now, she looked at them for a few moments and then tried the handle nearest to her. The door was locked. She tried the second and the third, and they stood locked too. And the three keys had all been removed.

"To think of the master locking the doors!" said she to herself after failing at each in turn. "As if I'd have tried to open them!"

That top storey was of the semi-attic kind, with roofs that sloped and a sky-light in one of them and the slates close overhead. It was a grey windy morning, and as she stood there, alone in that large house save for the cook far away in the kitchen, with a loose slate rattling in the gusts, and a glimpse of clouds driving over the sky-light, she began all at once to feel uncomfortable. Those locked doors were uncanny—something was not as it should be; there was a sinister moan in the wind; the slate did not rattle quite like an ordinary slate. Tales of her childhood, tales from the superstitious western islands, rushed into her mind. And then, all at once, she heard another sound. She heard it but for one instant, and then with a pale face she fled downstairs and stood for a space in the hall trembling and wondering.

She wondered first whether the sound had really come from behind the locked doors, and whether it actually was some one stealthily moving. She wondered next whether she could bring herself to confide in cook and stand Janet's cheerful scorn. She ended by saying not a word, and waiting to see what happened when the master came home.

He returned as usual in time for a cup of tea. It was pretty dark by then and Mary was upstairs lighting the gas (but she did not venture up to the top floor). She heard Mr. Rattar come into the hall, and then, quite distinctly this time, she heard overhead a dull sound, a kind of gentle thud. The next moment she heard the master running upstairs, and when he was safely past she ran even more swiftly down and burst into the kitchen.

"There's something in yon top rooms!" she panted.

"There's something in your top storey!" snapped cook; and poor Mary said no more.

When she brought his tea in to Mr. Rattar, she seemed to read in his first glance at her the same expression that had disturbed her in the morning, and yet the next moment he was speaking in his ordinary grumpy, laconic way.

"Have you noticed rats in the house?" he asked.

"Rats, sir!" she exclaimed. "Oh, no, sir, I don't think there are any rats."

"I saw one just now," he said. "If we see it again we must get some rat poison."

So it had only been a rat! Mary felt vastly relieved; and yet not altogether easy. One could not venture to doubt the master, but it was a queer-like sound for a rat to make.

Mr. Rattar had brought back a great many papers to-day, and sat engrossed in them till dinner. After dinner he fell to work again, and then about nine o'clock he rang for her and said:

"The gentleman I expect this evening will probably be late in coming. Don't sit up. I'll hear him and let him in myself. We shall be working late and I shall be going upstairs about those papers. If you hear anybody moving about, it will only be this gentleman and myself."

This was rather a long speech for silent Simon, and Mary thought it considerate of him to explain any nocturnal sounds beforehand; unusually considerate, in fact, for he seldom went out of his way to explain things. And yet those few minutes in his presence made her uncomfortable afresh. She could not keep her eyes away from that red cut on his chin. It made him seem odd-like, she thought. And then as she passed through the hall she heard faintly from the upper regions that slate rattling again. At least it was either the slate or—she recalled a story of her childhood, and hurried on to the kitchen.

She and the cook shared the same bedroom. It was fairly large with two beds in it, and along with the kitchen and other back premises it was shut off from the front part of the house by a door at the end of the hall. Cook was asleep within ten minutes. Mary could hear her heavy breathing above the incessant droning and whistling of the wind, and she envied her with all her Highland heart. In her own glen people would have understood how she felt, but here she dared not confess lest she were laughed at. It was such a vague and nameless feeling, a sixth sense warning her that all was not well; that *something* was in the air. The longer she lay awake the more certain she grew that evil was afoot; and yet what could be its shape? Everything in that quiet and respectable household was going on exactly as usual; everything that any one else would have considered material. The little things she had noticed would be considered absurd trifles by the sensible. She knew that as well as they.

She thought she had been in bed about an hour, though the time passed so slowly that it might have been less, when she heard, faintly and gently, but quite distinctly, the door from the hall into the back premises being opened. It seemed to be held open for nearly a minute, as though some one were standing there listening. She moved a little and the bed creaked; and then, as gently as it had been opened, the door was closed again.

Had the intruder come through or gone away? And could it only be the master, doing this curious thing, or was it some one—or something—else? Dreadful minutes passed, but there was not a sound of any one moving in the back passage, or the kitchen, and then in the distance she could hear the grating noise of the front door being opened and the rush of wind that accompanied it. It was closed sharply in a moment and she could catch the sound of steps in the hall and the master's voice making some remark. Another voice replied, gruff and muffled and indistinct, and then again the master spoke. Evidently the late caller had arrived, and a moment later she heard the library door shut, and it was plain that he and Mr. Rattar were closeted there.

They seemed to remain in the library about a quarter of an hour before the door opened again, and in a moment the stairs were creaking faintly. Evidently one or both were going up for the old papers.

All this was exactly what she had been led to expect, and ought to have reassured her, yet, for no reason at all, the conviction remained as intense and disturbing as ever, that something unspeakable was happening in this respectable house. The minutes dragged by till quite half an hour must have passed, and then she heard the steps descending. They came down very slowly this time, and very heavily. The obvious explanation was that they were bringing down one of those boxes filled with dusty papers which she had often seen in the closed rooms; yet though Mary knew perfectly that this was the common sense of the matter, a feeling of horror increased till she could scarcely refrain from crying out. If cook had not such a quick temper and such a healthy contempt for this kind of fancy, she would have rushed across to her bed; but as it was, she simply lay and trembled.

The steps sounded still heavy but more muffled on the hall carpet, though whether they were the steps of one man or two she could not feel sure. And then she heard the front door open again and then close; so that it seemed plain that the visitor had taken the box with him and gone away. And with this departure came a sense of relief, as devoid of rational foundation as the sense of horror before. She felt at last that if she could only hear the master going upstairs to bed, she might go to sleep.

But though she listened hard as she lay there in the oppressive dark, she heard not another sound so long as she kept awake, and that was for some time, she thought. She did get off at last and had been asleep she knew not how long when she awoke drowsily with a confused impression that the front door had been shut again. How late it was she could but guess—about three or four in the morning her instinct told her. But then came sleep again and in the morning the last part of her recollections was a little uncertain.

At breakfast the master was as silently formidable as ever and he never said a word about his visitor. When Mary went to the top floor later the papers were off the doors and the keys replaced.

Under the grey autumnal sky Miss Cicely Farmond drove out of the town wrapped in Ned Cromarty's overcoat. He assured her he never felt cold, and as she glanced a little shyly up at the strapping figure by her side, she said to herself that he certainly was the toughest looking man of her acquaintance, and she felt a little less contrition for the loan. She was an independent young lady and from no one else would she have accepted such a favour, but the laird of Stanesland had such an off-hand authoritative way with him that, somewhat to her own surprise, she had protested—and submitted.

The trap was a high dog cart and the mare a flier.

"What a splendid horse!" she exclaimed as they spun up the first hill.

"Isn't she?" said Ned. "And she can go all the way like this, too."

Cicely was therefore a little surprised when at the next hill this flier was brought to a walk.

"I thought we were going all the way like that!" she laughed.

Ned glanced down at her.

"Are you in a hurry?" he enquired.

"Not particularly," she admitted.

"No more am I," said he, and this time he smiled down at her in a very friendly way.

So far they had talked casually on any indifferent subject that came to hand, but now his manner grew a little more intimate.

"Are you going to stay on with the Cromartys long?" he asked.

"I am wondering myself," she confessed.

"I hope you will," he said bluntly.

"It is very kind of you to say so," she said smiling at him a little shyly.

"I mean it. The fact is, Miss Farmond, you are a bit of a treat."

The quaintness of the phrase was irresistible and she laughed outright.

"Am I?"

"It's a fact," said he, "you see I live an odd lonely kind of life here, and for most of my career I've lived an odd lonely kind of life too, so far as girls were concerned. It may sound rum to you to hear a backwood hunks of my time of life confessing to finding a girl of your age a bit of a treat, but it's a fact."

"Yes," she said. "I should have thought I must seem rather young and foolish."

"Lord, I don't mean that!" he exclaimed. "I mean that *I* must seem a pretty uninteresting bit of elderly shoe-leather."

"Uninteresting? Oh no!" she cried in protest, and then checked herself and her colour rose a little.

He smiled humorously.

"I can't see you out of this glass eye unless I turn round, so whether you're pulling my leg or not I don't know, but I was just saying to old Simon that the only kind of lady likely to take an interest in me was a female collector of antique curiosities, and you don't seem that sort, Miss Farmond."

She said nothing for a moment, and then asked:

"Were you discussing ladies then with Mr. Rattar?"

He also paused for a moment before replying.

"Incidentally in the course of a gossip, as the old chap hadn't got my business ready for me. By the way, did you get much change out of him?"

She shook her head a little mournfully.

"Nothing at all. He just asked questions instead of answering them."

"So he did with me! Confound the man. I fancy he has made too much money and is beginning to take it easy. That's one advantage of not being too rich, Miss Farmond; it keeps you from waxing fat."

"I'm not likely to wax fat then!" she laughed, and yet it was not quite a cheerful laugh.

He turned quickly and looked at her sympathetically.

"That your trouble?" he enquired in his outspoken way.

Cicely was not by way of giving her confidences easily, but this straight-forward, friendly attack penetrated her reserve.

"It makes one so dependent," she said, her voice even lower than usual.

"That must be the devil," he admitted.

"It is!" said she.

He whipped up the mare and ruminated in silence. Then he remarked:

"I'm just wondering."

Cicely began to smile.

"Wondering what?"

"What the devil there can be that isn't utterly uninteresting about me—assuming you weren't pulling my leg."

"Oh," she said, "no man can be uninteresting who has seen as much and done as much as you have."

"The Lord keep you of that opinion!" he said, half humorously, but only half, it seemed. "It's true I've knocked about and been knocked about, but I'd have thought you'd have judged more by results."

She laughed a little low laugh.

"Do you think yourself the results are very bad?"

"Judging by the mirror, beastly! Judging by other standards— well, one can't see one's self in one's full naked horror, thank Heaven for it too! But I'm not well read, and I'm not—but what's the good in telling you? You're clever enough to see for yourself."

For a man who had no intention of paying compliments, Ned Cromarty had a singular gift for administering the pleasantest— because it was so evidently the most genuine—form of flattery. In fact, had he but known it, he was a universal favourite with women, whenever he happened to meet them; only he had not the least suspicion of the fact—which made him all the more favoured.

"I don't know very many men," said Cicely, with her serious expression and a conscientious air, "and so perhaps I am not a good judge, but certainly you seem to me quite unlike all the others."

"I told you," he laughed, "that the female would have to be a bit of a collector."

"Oh," she cried, quite serious still, "I don't mean that in the least. I don't like freaks a bit myself. I only mean—well, people do differ in character and experience, don't they?"

"I guess you're pretty wise," said he simply. "And I'm sized up right enough. However, the trouble at present is this blamed mare goes too fast!"

On their left, the chimneys and roof of a large mansion showed through the surrounding trees. In this wind-swept seaboard country, its acres of plantation were a conspicuous landmark and marked it as the seat of some outstanding local magnate. These trees were carried down to the road in a narrow belt enclosing an avenue that ended in a lodge and gates. At the same time that the lodge came into view round a bend in the road, a man on a bicycle appeared ahead of them, going in the same direction, and bent over his handle-bars against the wind.

"Hullo, that's surely Malcolm Cromarty!" said Ned.

"So it is!" she exclaimed, and there was a note of surprise in her voice. "I wonder where he has been."

The cyclist dismounted at the lodge gates a few moments before the trap pulled up there too, and the young man turned and greeted them. Or rather he greeted Miss Farmond, for his smile was clearly aimed at her alone.

"Hullo! Where have you been?" he cried.

"Where have you?" she retorted as she jumped out and let him help her off with the driving coat.

They made a remarkably good-looking young couple standing together there on the road and their manner to one another was evidently that of two people who knew each other well. Sitting on his high driving seat, Ned Cromarty turned his head well round so as to bring his sound eye to bear and looked at them in silence. When she handed him his coat and thanked him afresh, he merely laughed, told her, in his outspoken way, that all the fun had been his, and whipped up his mare.

"That's more the sort of fellow!" he said to himself gloomily, and for a little the thought seemed to keep him depressed. And then as he let the recollections of their drive have their own way undisturbed, he began to smile again, and kept smiling most of the way home.

The road drew ever nearer to the sea, trees and hedgerows grew even rarer and more stunted, and then he was driving through a patch of planting hardly higher than a shrubbery up to an ancient building on the very brink of the cliffs. The sea crashed white below and stretched grey and cold to the horizon, the wind whistled round the battlements and sighed through the stunted trees, and Ned (who had been too absorbed to remember his coat) slapped his arms and stamped his feet as he descended before a nail-studded front door with a battered coat of arms above it.

"Lord, what a place!" he said to himself, half critically, half affectionately.

The old castle of Stanesland was but a small house as castles, or even mansions, go, almost devoid of architectural ornament and evidently built in a sterner age simply for security, and but little embellished by the taste of more degenerate times. As a specimen of a small early 15th Century castle it was excellent; as a home it was inconvenience incarnate. How so many draughts found their way through such thick walls was a perennial mystery, and how to convey dishes from the kitchen to the dining room without their getting cold an almost insoluble problem.

The laird and his sister sat down to lunch and in about ten minutes Miss Cromarty remarked,

"So you drove Cicely Farmond home?"

Her brother nodded. He had mentioned the fact as soon as he came in, and rather wondered why she referred to it again.

Miss Cromarty smiled her own peculiar shrewd worldly little smile, and said:

"You are very silent, Ned."

Lilian Cromarty was a few years older than her brother; though one would hardly have guessed it. Her trim figure, bright eyes, vivacity of expression when she chose to be vivacious, and quick movements might have belonged to a woman twenty years younger. She had never been pretty, but she was always perfectly dressed and her smile could be anything she chose to make it. Until her youngest brother came into the property, the place had been let and she had lived with her friends and relations. She had had a good time, she always frankly confessed, but as frankly admitted that it was a relief to settle down at last.

"I was thinking," said her brother.

"About Cicely?" she asked in her frankly audacious way.

He opened his eyes for a moment and then laughed.

"You needn't guess again, Lilian," he admitted.

"Funny little thing," she observed.

"Funny?" he repeated, and his tone brought an almost imperceptible change of expression into his sister's eye.

"Oh," she said as though throwing the subject aside, "she is nice and quite pretty, but very young, and not very sophisticated; is she? However, I should think she would be a great success as a man's girl. That low voice and those eyes of hers are very effective. Pass me the salt, Ned."

Ned looked at her in silence, and then over her shoulder out through the square window set in the vast thickness of the wall, to the grey horizon line.

"I guess you've recommended me to marry once or twice, Lilian," he observed.

"Don't 'guess' please!" she laughed, "or I'll stick my bowie knife or gun or something into you! Yes, I've always advised you to marry—if you found the right kind of wife."

She took some credit to herself for this disinterested advice, since, if he took it, the consequences would be decidedly disconcerting to herself; but she had never pointed out any specific lady yet, or made any conspicuous effort to find one for him.

"Well—" he began, and then broke off.

"You're not thinking of Cicely, are you?" she asked, still in the same bright light way, but with a quick searching look at him.

"It seems a bit absurd. I don't imagine for an instant she'd look at me."

"Wouldn't look—!" she began derisively, and then pulled herself up very sharply, and altered her tactics on the instant. "She might think you a little too old for her," she said in a tone of entire agreement with him.

"And also that I've got one too few eyes, and in fact several other criticisms."

His sister shrugged her shoulders.

"A girl of that age might think those things," she admitted, "but it seems to me that the criticism ought to be on the other side. Who is she?"

Ned looked at her and she broke into a laugh.

"Well," she said, "I suppose we both have a pretty good idea. She's somebody's something—Alfred Cromarty's, I believe; though of course her mother may have fibbed, for she doesn't look much like the Cromartys. Anyhow that pretty well puts her out of the question."

"Why?"

"If you were a mere nobody, it mightn't make so much difference, but your wife must have some sort of a family behind her. One needn't be a snob to think that one mother and a guess at the father is hardly enough!"

"After all, that's up to me. I wouldn't be wanting to marry her great-mothers, even if she had any."

She shrugged her shoulders again.

"My dear Ned, I'm no prude, but there's always some devilment in the blood in these cases."

"Rot!" said he.

"Well, rot if you like, but I know more than one instance."

He said nothing for a moment and as he sat in silence, a look of keen anxiety came into her eye. She hid it instantly and compressed her lips, and then abruptly her brother said:

"I wonder whether she's at all taken up with Malcolm Cromarty!"

She ceased to meet his eye, and her own became expressionless.

"They have spent some months in the same house. At their age the consequences seem pretty inevitable."

She had contrived to suggest a little more than she said, and he started in his chair.

"What do you know?" he demanded.

"Oh, of course, there would be a dreadful row if anything was actually known abroad. Sir Reginald has probably other ideas for his heir."

"Then there *is* something between them?"

She nodded, and though she still did not meet his eye, he accepted the nod with a grim look that passed in a moment into a melancholy laugh.

"Well," he said, rising, "it was a pretty absurd idea anyhow. I'll go and have a look at myself in the glass and try to see the funny side of it!"

His sister sat very still after he had left the room.

Cicely Farmond and Malcolm Cromarty walked up the avenue together, he pushing his bicycle, she walking by his side with a more
than usually serious expression.

"Then you won't tell me where you've been?" said he.

"You won't tell me where you've been!"

He was silent for a moment and then said confidentially:

"We might as well say we've been somewhere together. I mean,
if any one asks."

"Thank you, I don't need to fib," said she.

"I don't mean I need to. Only—" he seemed to find it difficult
to explain.

"I shall merely say I have been for a walk, and you need only
say you have been for a ride—if you don't want to say where you
have really been."

"And if you don't want to mention that you were driving with
Ned Cromarty," he retorted.

"He only very kindly offered me a lift!"

She looked quickly at him as she spoke and as quickly away
again. The glint in her eye seemed to displease him.

"You needn't always be so sharp with me, Cicely," he complained.

"You shouldn't say stupid things."

Both were silent for a space and then in a low mournful voice
he said:

"I wish I knew how to win your sympathy, Cicely. You don't absolutely hate me, do you?"

"Of course I don't hate you. But the way to get a girl's sympathy is not always to keep asking for it."

He looked displeased again.

"I don't believe you know what I mean!"

"I don't believe you do either."

He grew tender.

"*Your* sympathy, Cicely, would make all the difference to my life!"

"Now, Malcolm—" she began in a warning voice.

"Oh, I am not asking you to love me again," he assured her quickly. "It is only sympathy I demand!"

"But you mix them up so easily. It isn't safe to give you anything."

"I won't again!" he assured her.

"Well," she said, though not very sympathetically, "what do you want to be sympathised with about now?"

"When you offer me sympathy in that tone, I can't give you my confidence!" he said unhappily.

"Really, Malcolm, how can I possibly tell what your confidence is going to be beforehand? Perhaps it won't deserve sympathy."

"If you knew the state of my affairs!" he said darkly.

"A few days ago you told me they were very promising," she said with a little smile.

"So they would be—so they are—if—if only you would care for me, Cicely!"

"You tell me they are promising when you want me to marry you, and desperate when you want me to sympathise with you," she said a little cruelly. "Which am I to believe?"

"Hush! Here's Sir Reginald," he said.

The gentleman who came through a door in the walled garden beside the house was a fresh-coloured, white-haired man of sixty; slender and not above middle height, but very erect, and with the carriage of a person a little conscious of being of some importance.

Sir Reginald Cromarty was, in fact, extremely conscious of his position in life, and the rather superior and condescending air he was wont to assume in general society made it a little difficult for a stranger to believe that he could actually be the most popular person in the county; especially as it was not hard to discover that his temper could easily become peppery upon provocation. If, however, the stranger chanced to provide the worthy baronet with even the smallest opening of exhibiting his extraordinary kindness of heart—were it only by getting wet in a shower or mislaying a walking stick, he would quickly comprehend. And the baronet's sympathy never waited to be summoned; it seemed to hover constantly over all men and women he met, spying for its chance.

He himself was totally unconscious of this attribute and imagined the respect in which he was held to be due to his lineage, rank, and superior breeding and understanding. Indeed, few people in this world can have cut a more dissimilar figure as seen from his own and from other men's eyes; though as both parties were equally pleased with Sir Reginald Cromarty, it mattered little.

At the sight of Cicely his smile revealed the warmth of his feelings in that direction.

"Ah, my dear girl," said he, "we've been looking for you. Where have you been?"

"I've been having a walk."

She smiled at him as she answered, and on his side it was easy to see that the good gentleman was enraptured, and that Miss Farmond was not likely to be severely cross-examined as to her movements. Towards Malcolm, on the other hand, though his greeting was kindly enough, his eye was critical. The young author's tie seemed to be regarded with particular displeasure.

"My God, Margaret, imagine being found dead in such a thing!" he had exclaimed to his wife, after his first sight of it; and time had done nothing to diminish his distaste for this indication of a foreign way of life.

Lady Cromarty came out of the garden a moment later; a dark thin-faced lady with a gracious manner when she spoke, but with lips that were usually kept very tight shut and an eye that could easily be hard.

"Nearly time for lunch," she said. "You two had better hurry up!"

The young people hurried on to the house and the baronet and his lady walked slowly behind.

"So they have been away all morning together, Reginald," she remarked.

"Oh, I don't think so," said he. "He had his bicycle and she has been walking."

"You are really too unsuspicious, Reggie!"

"A woman, my dear, is perhaps a little too much the reverse where a young couple is concerned. I have told you before, and I repeat it now emphatically, that neither Cicely nor Malcolm is in a position to contemplate matrimony for an instant."

"He is your heir—and Cicely is quite aware of it."

"I assure you, Margaret," he said with great conviction, "that Cicely is not a girl with mercenary motives. She is quite charming—"

"Oh, I know your opinion of her, Reggie," Lady Cromarty broke in a trifle impatiently, "and I am fond of her too, as you know. Still, I don't believe a girl who can use her eyes so effectively is quite as simple as you think."

Sir Reginald laughed indulgently.

"Really, my love, even the best of women are sometimes a trifle uncharitable! But in any case Malcolm has quite enough sense of his future position to realise that his wife must be somebody without the blemish on her birth, which is no fault of dear Cicely's, but—er—makes her ineligible for this particular position."

"I wish I could think that Malcolm is the kind of young man who would consult anything but his own wishes. I have told you often enough, Reggie, that I don't think it is wise to keep these two young people living here in the same house for months on end."

"But what can one do?" asked the benevolent baronet. "Neither of them has any home of their own. Hang it, I'm the head of their family and I'm bound to show them a little hospitality."

"But Malcolm has rooms in town. He needn't spend months on end at Keldale."

The baronet was silent for a moment. Then he said:

"To tell the truth, my dear, I'm afraid Malcolm is not turning out quite so well as I had hoped. He certainly ought to be away doing something. At the same time, hang it, you wouldn't have me turn my own kinsman and heir out of my house, Margaret; would you?"

Lady Cromarty sighed, and then her thin lips tightened.

"You are hopeless, Reggie. I sometimes feel as though I were here merely as matron of a home for lost Cromartys! Well, I hope your confidence won't be abused. I confess I don't feel very comfortable about it myself."

"Well, well," said Sir Reginald. "My own eyes are open too, I assure you. I shall watch them very carefully at lunch, in the light of what you have been saying."

The baronet was an old Etonian, and as his life had been somewhat uneventful since, he was in the habit of drawing very largely on his recollections of that nursery of learning. Lunch had hardly begun before a question from Cicely set him going, and for the rest of the meal he regaled her with these reminiscences.

After luncheon he said to his wife:

"Upon my word, I noticed nothing whatever amiss. Cicely is a very sensible as well as a deuced pretty girl."

"I happened to look at Malcolm occasionally," said she.

Sir Reginald thought that she seemed to imply more than she said, but then women were like that, he had noticed, and if one took all their implications into account, life would be a troublesome affair.

9
A PHILOSOPHER

During luncheon an exceedingly efficient person had been moving briskly behind the chairs. His face was so expressionless, his mouth so tightly closed, and his air of concentration on the business in hand so intense, that he seemed the perfect type of the silent butler. But as soon as lunch was over, and while Cicely still stood in the hall listening with a dubious eye to Malcolm's suggestion of a game of billiards, Mr. James Bisset revealed the other side of his personality. He came up to the young couple with just sufficient deference, but no more, and in an accent which experts would have recognised as the hall mark of the western part of North Britain, said:

"Excuse me, miss, but I've mended your bicycle and I'll show it you if ye like, and just explain the principle of the thing."

There was at least as much command as invitation in his tones. The billiard invitation was refused, and with a hidden smile Cicely followed him to the bicycle house.

Expert knowledge was James Bisset's foible. Of some subjects, such as buttling, carpentry, and mending bicycles, it was practical; of others, such as shooting, gardening, and motoring, it was more theoretical. To Sir Reginald and my lady he was quite indispensable, for he could repair almost anything, knew his own more particular business from A to Z, and was ready at any moment to shoulder any responsibility. Sir Reginald's keeper, gardener, and chauffeur were apt however to be a trifle less enthusiastic, Mr. Bisset's passion for expounding the principles of their professions sometimes exceeding his tact.

In person, he was an active, stoutly built man (though far too energetic to be fat), with blunt rounded features, eyes a little protruding, and sandy hair and a reddish complexion which made his age an unguessable secret. He might have been in the thirties or he might have been in the fifties.

"With regard to these ladies' bicycles, miss—" he began with a lecturer's air.

But by this time Cicely was also an expert in side-tracking her friend's theoretical essays.

"Oh, how clever of you!" she exclaimed rapturously. "It looks as good as ever!"

The interruption was too gratifying to offend.

"Better in some ways," he said complacently. "The principle of these things is—"

"I did miss it this morning," she hurried on. "In fact I had to have quite a long walk. Luckily Mr. Cromarty of Stanesland gave me a lift coming home."

"Oh, indeed, miss? Stanesland gave ye a lift, did he? An interesting gentleman yon."

This time she made no effort to divert Mr. Bisset's train of thought.

"You think Mr. Cromarty interesting, then?" said she.

"They say he's hanged a man with his ain hands," said Bisset impressively.

"What!" she cried.

"For good and sufficient reason, we'll hope, miss. But whatever the way of it, it makes a gentleman more interesting in a kin' of way than the usual run. And then looking at the thing on general principles, the theory of hanging is—"

"Oh, but surely," she interrupted, "that isn't the only reason why Mr. Cromarty—I mean why you think he is interesting?"

"There's that glass eye, too. That's very interesting, miss."

She still seemed unsatisfied.

"His glass eye! Oh—you mean it has a story?"

"Vera possibly. He says himself it was done wi' a whisky bottle, but possibly that's making the best of it. But what interests me, miss, about yon eye is this—"

He paused dramatically and she enquired in an encouraging voice:

"Yes, Bisset?"

"It's the principle of introducing a foreign substance so near the man's brain. What's glass? What's it consist of?"

"I—I don't know," confessed Cicely weakly.

"Silica! And what's silica? Practically the same as sand! Well now if ye put a handful of sand into a man's brain—or anyhow next door to it, it's bound to have some effect, bound to have some effect!"

Bisset's voice fell to a very serious note, and as he was famous for the range of his reading and was generally said to know practically by heart *The People's Self-Educator in Science and Art*, Cicely asked a little apprehensively:

"But what effect can it possibly have?"

"It might take him different ways," said the philosopher cautiously though sombrely. "But it's a good thing, anyway, Miss Farmond, that the laird of Stanesland is no likely to get married."

"Isn't he?" she asked, again with that encouraging note.

Bisset replied with another question, asked in an ominous voice:

"Have ye seen yon castle o' his, miss?"

Cicely nodded.

"I called there once with Lady Cromarty."

"A most interesting place, miss, illustrating the principle of thae castles very instructively."

Mr. Bisset had evidently been studying architecture as well as science, and no doubt would have given Miss Farmond some valuable information on the subject. But she seemed to lack enthusiasm for it to-day.

"But will the castle prevent him marrying?" she enquired with a smile.

"The lady in it will," said the philosopher with a sudden descent into worldly shrewdness.

"Miss Cromarty! Why?"

"She's mair comfortable there than setting off on her travels again. That's a fac', miss."

"But—but supposing he—" Cicely began and then paused.

"Oh, the laird's no the marrying sort anyhow. He says to me himself one day when I'd taken the liberty of suggesting that a lady would suit the castle fine—we was shooting and I was carrying his cartridges, which I do for amusement, miss, whiles—'Bisset,' says he, 'the lady will have to be a damned keen shot to think me worth a cartridge. I'm too tough for the table,' says he, 'and not ornamental enough to stuff. They've let me off so far, and why the he—' begging your pardon, miss, but Stanesland uses strong expressions sometimes. 'Why the something,' says he, 'should they want to put me in the bag now? I'm happier free—and so's the lady.' But he's a grand shot and a vera friendly gentleman, vera friendly indeed. It's a pity, though, he's that ugly."

"Ugly!" she exclaimed. "Oh, I don't think him ugly at all. He's very striking looking. I think he is rather handsome."

Bisset looked at her with a benevolently reproving eye.

"Weel, miss, it's all a matter of taste, but to my mind Stanesland is a fine gentleman, but the vera opposite extreme from a Venus." He broke off and glanced towards the house. "Oh, help us! There's one of thae helpless women crying on me. How this house would get on wanting me—!"

He left Miss Farmond to paint the gloomy picture for herself.

10

THE LETTER

It was a few days later that Cicely looked up from the local paper she was reading and asked:

"Who was George Rattar?"

Sir Reginald laid down his book and looked at her in some surprise.

"George Rattar? What do you know about him?"

"I see the announcement of his death. 'Son of the late John Simon Rattar' he's called."

"That's Silent Simon's brother!" exclaimed Sir Reginald. "Where did he die?"

"In New York, it says."

Sir Reginald turned to his wife.

"We can hardly send our sympathies to Simon on this bereavement!"

"No," she said significantly. "I suppose congratulations would be more appropriate."

The baronet took the paper from Cicely and studied it himself.

"Died about a fortnight ago, I see," he observed. "I wonder whether Simon put this announcement in himself, or whether brother George arranged it in his will? It would be quite like the fellow to have this posthumous wipe at Simon. George had a certain sense of humour—which Simon lacks. And there was certainly no love lost between them!"

"Why should it annoy Mr. Rattar?" asked Cicely.

"Because brother George was not a member of his family he would care to be reminded of. Though on the other hand, Simon is as hard as whinstone and has as much sentiment as this teapot, and he may have put the notice in himself simply to show the world he was rid of the fellow."

"What was George Rattar then?" enquired Cicely.

"He was once Simon Rattar's partner, wasn't he, Reginald?" said Lady Cromarty. "And then he swindled him, didn't he?"

"Swindled several other people as well," said Sir Reginald, "myself included. However, the thing was hushed up, and brother George disappeared. Then he took to forgery on his own account and among other people's signatures he imitated with remarkable success was Simon's. This let old Simon in for it again and there was no hushing it up a second time. Simon gave evidence against him without mercy, and since then George has been his Majesty's guest for a number of years. So if you meet Mr. Simon Rattar, Cicely, you'd better not tell him how sorry you are to hear of poor George's decease!"

"I wish I could remember him more distinctly," said Lady Cromarty. "I'm afraid I always mix him up with our friend Mr. Simon."

"It's little wonder," her husband replied. "They were twins. George was the one with a moustache; one knew them apart by that. Extraordinary thing, it has always seemed to me, that their natures should have been so different."

"Perhaps," suggested Cicely compassionately, with her serious air, "it was only that George was tempted."

Sir Reginald laughed heartily.

"You little cynic!" he cried. "You mean to insinuate that if you tempted Simon, he'd be as bad a hat as his brother?"

"Oh, no!" cried Cicely. "I meant—"

"Tempt him and see!" chuckled the baronet. "And we'll have a little bet on the result!" He was glancing at the paper as he laughed, and now he suddenly stopped laughing and exclaimed, "Hullo! Here's a much more serious loss for our friend. Would you like to earn £1, Cicely?"

"Very much," said she.

"Well then if you search the road very carefully between Mr. Simon Rattar's residence and his office you may find his signet ring and obtain the advertised, and I may say princely, reward of one pound."

"Only a pound!" exclaimed Lady Cromarty, "for that handsome old ring of his?"

"If he had offered a penny more, I should have taken my business out of his hands!" laughed Sir Reginald. "It would have meant that Silent Simon wasn't himself any longer. A pound is exactly his figure; a respectable sum, but not extravagant."

"What day did he lose it?" asked Cicely.

"The advertisement doesn't say."

"He wasn't wearing it—" Cicely pulled herself up sharply.

"When?" asked Lady Cromarty.

"Where can I have seen him last?" wondered Cicely with an innocent air.

"Not for two or three weeks certainly," said Lady Cromarty decisively. "And he can't have lost it then if this advertisement is only just put in."

"No, of course not," Cicely agreed.

"Well," said Sir Reginald, "he'll miss his ring more than his brother! And remember, Cicely, you get a pound for finding the ring, and you win a pair of gloves if you can tempt Simon to stray from the paths of honesty and virtue! By Jingo, I'll give you the gloves if you can even make him tell a good sporting lie!"

When the good baronet was in this humour no man could excel him in geniality, and, to do him justice, a kindly temper and hearty spirits were the rule with him six days out of seven. On the other hand, he was easily ruffled and his tempers were hot while they lasted. Upon the very next morning there arose on the horizon a little cloud, a cloud that seemed at the moment the merest fleck of vapour, which upset him, his family thought, quite unduly.

It took the form of a business letter from Mr. Simon Rattar, a letter on the surface perfectly innocuous and formally polite. Yet Sir Reginald seemed considerably disturbed.

"Damn the man!" he exclaimed as he cast it on the breakfast table.

"Reggie!" expostulated his wife gently. "What's the matter?"

"Matter?" snapped her husband. "Simon Rattar has the impudence to tell me he is letting the farm of Castleknowe to that fellow Shearer after all!"

"But why not? You meant to some time ago, I know."

"Some time ago, certainly. But I had a long talk with Simon ten days ago and told him what I'd heard about Shearer and said I wouldn't have the fellow on my property at any price. I don't believe the man is solvent, in the first place; and in the second place he's a socialistic, quarrelsome, mischievous fellow!"

"And what did Mr. Rattar think?"

"He tried to make some allowances for the man, but in the end when he saw I had made up my mind, he professed to agree with me and said he would look out for another tenant. Now he tells me that the matter is settled as per my instructions of the 8th. That's weeks ago, and not a word does he say about our conversation cancelling the whole instructions!"

"Then Shearer gets the farm?"

"No, he doesn't! I'm dashed if he does! I shall send Mr. Simon a letter that will make him sit up! He's got to alter the arrangement somehow."

He turned to Malcolm and added:

"When your time comes, Malcolm, beware of having a factor who has run the place so long that he thinks it's his own property! By Gad, I'm going to tell him a bit of my mind!"

During the rest of breakfast he glanced at the letter once or twice, and each time his brows contracted, but he said nothing more in presence of Cicely and Malcolm. After he had left the dining room, however, Lady Cromarty followed him and said:

"Don't be too hasty with Mr. Rattar, Reggie! After all, the talk may have slipped his memory."

"Slipped his memory? If you had heard it, Margaret, you'd know better. I was a bit cross with him for a minute or two then, which I hardly ever am, and that alone would make him remember it, one would think. We talked for over an hour on the business and the upshot was clear and final. No, no, he has got a bit above himself and wants a touch of the curb."

"What are you going to do?" she asked.

"I'm going to send in a note by car and tell him to come out and see me about the business at once."

"Let me see the letter before you send it, Reggie."

He seemed to growl assent, but when she next saw him the letter had gone; and from the baronet's somewhat crusty explanation, she suspected that it was a little sharper than he knew she would have approved.

When the car returned his annoyance was increased again for a space. Mr. Rattar had sent a brief reply that he was too busy to come out that afternoon, but he would call on Sir Reginald in the morning. For a time this answer kept Sir Reginald in a state of renewed irritation, and then his natural good humour began to prevail, till by dinner time he was quite calm again, and after dinner in as genial humour as he had been in the day before.

He played a game of pyramids with Cicely and Malcolm in the billiard room, and then he and Cicely joined Lady Cromarty in the drawing room while the young author went up to his room to work, he declared. He had a large bedroom furnished half as a sitting room where he retired each night to compose his masterpieces as soon as it became impossible to enjoy Miss Farmond's company without having to share it in the drawing room with his host and hostess. At least, that was the explanation of his procedure given by Lady Cromarty, whose eye was never more critical than when it studied her husband's kinsman and heir.

Lady Cromarty's eye was not uncritical also of Cicely at times, but to-night she was so relieved to see how Sir Reginald's temper improved under her smiles and half shy glances, that she let her stay up later than usual. Then when she and the girl went up to bed, she asked her husband if he would be late.

"The magazines came this morning," said he. "I'd better sleep in my dressing room."

The baronet was apt to sit up late when he had anything to read that held his fancy, and the procedure of sleeping in his dressing room was commonly followed then.

He bade them good-night and went off towards the library, and a few minutes later, as they were going upstairs, they heard the library door shut.

When they came to Lady Cromarty's room, Cicely said good-night to her hostess and turned down the passage that led to her own bedroom. A door opened quietly as she passed and a voice whispered:

"Cicely!"

She stopped and regarded the young author with a reproving eye.

"Is anything the matter?" she asked.

"I just wanted to speak to you!" he pleaded.

"Now, Malcolm," she said severely, "you know quite well that Lady Cromarty trusts us *not* to do this sort of thing!"

"She's in her room, isn't she?"

"What does that matter?"

"And where's Sir Reginald?"

"Still in the library."

"Sitting up late?"

"Yes, but that doesn't matter either. Good night!"

"Wait just one minute, Cicely! Come into my room—I won't shut the door!"

"Certainly not!" she said emphatically.

"Well then, don't speak so loudly! I must confide in you, Cicely; I'm getting desperate. My position is really serious. Something's got to happen! If you would only give me your sympathy—"

"I thought you were writing," she interrupted.

"I've been trying to, but—"

"Well, write all this down and read it to me to-morrow," she smiled. "Good night!"

"The blame be on your head!" began the author dramatically, but the slim figure was already moving away, throwing him a parting smile that seemed to wound his sensitive soul afresh.

11

NEWS

Even in that scattered countryside of long distances by windy roads, with scarcely ever a village as a focus for gossip, news flew fast. The next morning Ned Cromarty had set out with his gun towards a certain snipe marsh, but while he was still on the high road he met a man on a bicycle. The man had heard strange news and stopped to pass it on, and the next moment Ned was hurrying as fast as his long legs could take him back to the castle.

He saw his sister only for a moment.

"Lilian!" he cried, and the sound of his voice made her start and stare at him. "There's a story that Sir Reginald was murdered last night."

"Murdered!" she repeated in a low incredulous voice. "Ridiculous, Ned! Who told you?"

"I only know the man by sight, but he seemed to believe it right enough."

"But how—who did it?"

Her brother shook his head.

"Don't know. He couldn't tell me. My God, I hope it's not true! I'm off to see."

A few minutes later he was driving his mare headlong for his kinsman's house. It had begun to rain by this time, and the mournful wreaths of vapour that swept over the bare, late autumnal country and drove in fine drops against his face sent his spirits down ever lower as the mare splashed her way along the empty miles of road. The melancholy thrumming of the telegraph wires droned by his side all the while, and as this dirge waxed for the moment as they passed each post, his eye would glance grimly at those gaunt poles. Very suitable and handy for a certain purpose, they struck him—if by any possibility this tale were true.

He knew the worst when he saw Bisset at the door.

"Thank God, you've come, sir," said the butler devoutly. "The master would have expected it of you."

"How did it happen? What does it mean? Do you mean to say it's actually *true*?"

Bisset shook his head sombrely.

"Ower true," said he. "But as to how it happened, come in to the library, sir. It was in his ain library he was killed! The Fiscal and Superintendent is there now and we've been going into the circumstantial evidence. Most extraordinary mystery, sir—most extraordinary!"   -

In the library they found Simon Rattar and Superintendent Sutherland. The Superintendent was a big burly red-moustached man; his face a certificate of honesty, but hardly of the intellectual type. Ned looked round him apprehensively for something else, but Bisset said:

"We've taken him upstairs, sir."

For a moment as he looked round that spacious comfortable room with its long bookcases and easy chairs, and on the tables and mantel-piece a hundred little mementoes of its late owner, the laird of Stanesland was unable to speak a word, and the others respected his silence. Then he pulled himself together sharply and asked:

"How did it happen? Tell me all about it!"

Perhaps there might have been for a moment in Simon's eye a hint that this demand was irregular, but the superintendent evidently took no exception to the intrusion. Besides being a considerable local magnate and a kinsman of the dead baronet, Stanesland had a forcible personality that stood no gainsaying.

"Well, sir," said the superintendent, "Mr. Rattar could perhaps explain best—"

"Explain yourself, Sutherland," said Simon briefly.

The superintendent pointed to a spot on the carpet a few paces from the door.

"We found Sir Reginald lying there," he said. "His skull had been fairly cracked, just over the right eye, sir. The blow would have been enough to kill him I'd think myself, but there were marks in his neck too, seeming to show that the murderer had strangled him afterwards to make sure. However, we'll be having the medical evidence soon. But there's no doubt that was the way of it, and Mr. Rattar agrees with me."

The lawyer merely nodded.

"What was it done with?"

The superintendent pursed his lips and shook his head.

"That's one of the mysterious things in the case, sir. There's no sign of any weapon in the room. The fire irons are far too light. But it was an unco' heavy blow. There was little bleeding, but the skull was fair cracked."

"Was anything stolen?"

"That's another mystery, sir. Nothing was stolen anywhere in the house and there was no papers in a mess like, or anything."

"When was he found?" asked Ned.

"Seven-fifty this morning, sir," said Bisset. "The housemaid finding the door lockit came to me. I knew the dining-room key fitted this door too, so I opened it—and there he lay."

"All night, without any one knowing he hadn't gone to bed?"

"That's the unfortunate thing, sir," said the superintendent. "It seems that Sir Reginald had arranged to sleep in his dressing room as he was going to be sitting up late reading."

"Murderer must have known that," put in Simon.

"Almost looks like it," agreed the superintendent.

"And nobody in the house heard or saw anything?"

"Nobody, sir," said the superintendent.

"That's their statement," added the lawyer in his driest voice.

"Was anybody sitting up late?"

"Nobody admits it," said the lawyer, again very drily.

"Thirteen," said Bisset softly.

They turned towards him, but it seemed that he was talking to himself. He was, in fact, quietly taking measurements with a tape.

"Go on," said Cromarty briefly.

"Well, sir," said the superintendent. "The body was found near the door as I was pointing out, but it's a funny thing that a small table had been upset apparently, and Bisset tells us that that table stood near the window."

"Humph," grunted Simon sceptically.

"I'm quite sure of it, Mr. Rattar," said Bisset confidently, looking round from his work of measurement.

"No positive proof it was upset," said the lawyer.

"Did you find it upset?" asked Ned.

The lawyer shook his head emphatically and significantly, and the superintendent agreed.

"No, it was standing just where it is now near the wall."

"Then why do you think it was upset?"

"I picked up yon bits of sealing wax and yon piece of India rubber," said Bisset, looking round again. "I know they were on the wee table yesterday and I found them under the curtain in the morning and the table moved over to the wall. It follows that the table has been cowpit and then set up again in another place, and the other things on it put back. Is that not a fair deduction, sir?"

Ned nodded thoughtfully.

"Seems to me so," he said.

"It seems likely enough," the superintendent also agreed. "And if that's the case there would seem to have been some kind of ongoings near the window."

The Procurator Fiscal still seemed unconvinced.

"Nothing to go on. No proper evidence. It leads nowhere definitely," he said.

"Well now," continued the superintendent, "the question is— how did the murderer get into the room? The door was found locked and the key had been taken away, so whether he had locked it from the inside or the outside we can't tell. There's small chance of finding the key, I doubt, for a key's a thing easy hidden away."

"So he might have come in by the door and then left by the door and locked it after him," said Ned. "Or he might have come in by the window, locked the door and gone out by the window. Or he might have come in by the window and gone out by the door, locking it after him. Those are all the chances, aren't they?"

"Indeed, that seems to be them all," said the superintendent with a note of admiration for this clear exposition that seemed to indicate he was better himself at details than deductions.

"And now what about the window? Was that open or shut or what?"

"Shut but not snibbed, sir."

Ned turned to Bisset.

"Did Sir Reginald ever forget to snib the windows, supposing one happened to be open?"

"Practically never, sir."

"Last thing before he left the room, I suppose?" said the lawyer.

The butler hesitated.

"I suppose so, sir," he admitted, "but of course I was never here to see."

"Exactly!" said Simon. "Therefore one can draw no conclusions as to whether the window had been standing all the time just as it is now, or whether it had been opened and shut again from the outside; seeing that Sir Reginald was presumably killed before his usual time for looking to the windows."

"Wait a bit!" said Ned. "I was assuming a window had been open. But were the windows fastened before Sir Reginald came in to sit here last thing?"

"Certainly they were that," said the butler emphatically.

"It was a mild night, he might have opened one himself," replied the Procurator Fiscal. "Or supposing the man had come in and left again by the door, what's more likely than that he unsnibbed the window to make people think he had come that way?"

"He would surely have left it wide open," objected Ned.

"Might have thought that too obvious," replied the lawyer, "or might have been afraid of the noise. Unsnibbing would be quite enough to suggest entry that way."

Ned turned his keen eye hard on him.

"What's your own theory then?"

"I've none," grunted Simon. "No definite evidence one way or the other. Mere guesses are no use."

Ned walked to the window and looked at it carefully. Then he threw it up and looked out into the garden.

"Of course you've looked for footsteps underneath?" he asked.

"Naturally," said Simon. "But it's a hard gravel path and grass beyond. One could fancy one saw traces, but no definite evidence."

The window was one of three together, with stone mullions between. They were long windows reaching down nearly to the level of the floor, so that entrance that way was extremely easy if one of them were open. Cromarty got out and stood on the sill examining the middle sash.

Simon regarded him with a curious caustic look for a moment in his eye.

"Looking for finger marks?" he enquired.

"Yes," said Ned. "Did you look for them?"

For a single instant the Procurator Fiscal seemed a little taken aback. Then he grunted with a half laugh:

"Don't believe much in them."

"Experienced criminals, that's been convicted before, frequently wears gloves for to prevent their finger prints being spotted," said the learned Bisset.

Mr. Rattar shot him a quick ambiguous glance, and then his eyes assumed their ordinary cold look and he said:

"No evidence anybody ever opened that window from the outside. If they had, Sir Reginald would have heard them."

"Well," said Ned, getting back into the room, "there are no finger marks anyhow."

"The body being found near the door certainly seems to be in favour of Mr. Rattar's opinion," observed the superintendent.

"I thought Mr. Rattar had formed no opinion yet," said Cromarty.

"No more I have," grunted the lawyer.

The superintendent looked a trifle perplexed.

"Before Mr. Cromarty had come in, sir, I understood you for to say everything pointed to the man having come in by the door and hit Sir Reginald on the head as he came to see who it was when he heard him outside."

"I merely suggested that," said Simon Rattar sharply. "It fits the facts, but there's no definite evidence yet."

Ned Cromarty had turned and was frowning out of the window. Now he wheeled quickly and exclaimed:

"If the murderer came in through the window while Sir Reginald was in the room, either the window was standing open or Sir Reginald opened it for him! Did Sir Reginald ever sit with his window open late at night at this time of year?"

"Never once, sir," said Bisset confidently. "He likit fresh air outside fine but never kept his windies open much unless the weather was vera propitious."

"Then," said Ned, "why should Sir Reginald have opened the window of his own accord to a stranger at the dead of night?"

"Exactly!" said Mr. Rattar. "Thing seems absurd. He'd never do it."

"That's my own opinion likewise, sir," put in Bisset.

"It's only common sense," added the superintendent.

"Then how came the window to be unfastened?" demanded Ned.

"I've suggested a reason," said Simon.

"As a blind? Sounds to me damned thin."

Simon Rattar turned away from him with an air that suggested that he thought it time to indicate distinctly that he was in charge of the case and not the laird of Stanesland.

"That's all we can do just now, Sutherland," he said. "No use disturbing the household any longer at present."

Cromarty stepped up to him suddenly and asked:

"Tell me honestly! Do you suspect anybody?"

Simon shook his head decidedly.

"No sufficient evidence yet. Good morning, Mr. Cromarty."

Ned was following him to the door, his lips compressed and his eyes on the floor, when Bisset touched his arm and beckoned him back.

"Excuse me, sir," said he, "but could you not manage just to stop on for a wee bit yet?"

Ned hesitated.

"They won't be wanting visitors, Bisset."

"They needn't know if you don't want them to, sir. Lady Cromarty is shut up in her room, and the others are keeping out of the way. If you wouldn't mind my giving you a little cold luncheon in my sitting room, sir, I'd like to have your help. I'm making a few sma' bits of investigation on my own. You're one of the family, sir, and I know you'll be wanting to find out who killed the master."

Ned's eye flashed suddenly.

"By God, I'll never rest in this world or the next till I do! All right, I'll wait for a bit."

12

CICELY

Ned Cromarty waited in the hall while Bisset went to the door with the Procurator Fiscal and Superintendent of Police. As he stood there in the darkened silence of the house, there came to his ears for an instant the faint sound of a voice, and it seemed to be a woman's. With that the current of his thoughts seemed to change, and when Bisset returned he asked, though with marked hesitation:

"Do you think, Bisset, I could do anything for any of them, Mr. Malcolm Cromarty, or—er—Miss Farmond?"

Bisset considered the point judicially. It was clear he felt that the management of the household was in his hands now.

"I am sure Miss Farmond would be pleased, sir—poor young lady!"

"Do you really think so?" said Ned, and his manner brightened visibly. "Well, if she won't mind—"

"I think if you come this way, sir, you will find her with Sir Malcolm."

"*Sir* Malcolm!" exclaimed Ned. "My God, so he is!"

To himself he added:

"And she will soon be Lady Cromarty!"

But the thought did not seem to exhilarate him.

He was led towards the billiard room, an addition to the house which lay rather apart. The door was half open and through it he could see that the blinds had been drawn down, and he could hear a murmur of voices.

"They are in there, sir," said Bisset, and he left him.

As Ned Cromarty entered he caught the words, spoken by the new baronet:

"My dear Cicely, I depend on your sympathy—"

He broke off as he heard a footstep, and seemed to move a little apart from the chair where Cicely was sitting.

The two young people greeted their visitor, Cicely in a voice so low that it was scarcely audible, but with a smile that seemed, he thought, to welcome him; Sir Malcolm with a tragic solemnity which no doubt was quite appropriate to a bereaved baronet. The appearance of a third party seemed, however, to afford him no particular gratification, and after exchanging a sentence or two, he begged, in a very serious tone, to be excused, and retired, walking softly and mournfully. Ned noticed then that his face was extraordinarily pale and his eye disturbed.

"I was afraid of disturbing you," said Ned. He was embarrassed, a rare condition with him, which, when it did afflict him, resulted in an impression of intimidating truculence.

Cicely seemed to shrink a little, and he resolved to leave instantly.

"Oh no!" she said shyly.

"I only wanted to say that if I could do anything for you—well, you've only to let me know."

"It's awfully kind of you," she murmured.

There was something so evidently sincere in this murmur that his embarrassment forthwith left him.

"Thank Heaven!" he said after his outspoken habit. "I was afraid I was putting my foot in it. But if you really don't mind my seeing you for a minute or two, I'd just like to say—"

He broke off abruptly, and she looked up at him questioningly.

"Dash it, I can't say it, Miss Farmond! But you know, don't you?"

She murmured something again, and though he could not quite hear what it was, he knew she understood and appreciated.

Leaning against the corner of the shrouded billiard table, with the blinds down and this pale slip of a girl in deep mourning sitting in a basket chair in the dim light, he began suddenly to realise the tragedy.

"I've been too stunned till now to grasp what's happened," he said in a moment. "Our best friend gone, Miss Farmond!"

He had said exactly the right thing now.

"He certainly was mine!" she said.

"And mine too. We may live to be a brace of Methuselahs, but I guess we'll never see his like again!"

His odd phrase made her smile for a moment despite herself. It passed swiftly and she said:

"*I* can't believe it yet."

Again there was silence, and then he said abruptly:

"It's little wonder you can't believe it. The thing is so extraordinary. It's incredible. A man without an enemy in the world—no robbery attempted—sitting in his own library—in just about the most peaceful and out of the way county in Scotland—not a sound heard by anybody—not a reason that one can possibly imagine—and yet murdered!"

"But it must have been a robber surely!"

"Why didn't he rob something then?"

"But how else—?"

"How indeed! You've not a suspicion of any one yourself, Miss Farmond? Say it right out if you have. We don't lynch here. At least," he corrected himself as he recalled the telegraph posts, "it hasn't been done yet."

"I *can't* suspect any one!" she said earnestly. "I never met any one in my life that I could possibly imagine doing such a thing!"

"No," he said. "I guess our experiences have been pretty different. I've met lots, but then there are none of those boys here. Who is there in this place?"

He paused and stared into space.

"It must have been a tramp—some one who doesn't belong here!"

"I was trying to think whether there are any lunatics about," he said in a moment. "But there aren't any."

There was silence for some minutes. He was thinking; she never moved. Then he heard a sound, and looking down saw that she had her handkerchief in her hand. He had nearly bent over her before he remembered Sir Malcolm, and at the recollection he said abruptly:

"Well, I've disturbed you too long. If I can do anything—anything whatever, you'll let me know, won't you?"

"You are very, very kind," she murmured, and a note in her voice nearly made him forget the new baronet. In fact, he had to retire rather quickly to be sure of himself.

The efficiency of James Bisset was manifest at every conjuncture. Businesslike and brisk he appeared from somewhere as Cromarty reached the hall, and led him from the front regions to the butler's sitting room.

"I will bring your lunch in a moment, sir," he murmured, and vanished briskly.

The room looked out on a courtyard at the back, and through the window Ned could see against the opposite buildings the rain driving in clouds. In the court the wind was eddying, and beneath some door he could hear it drone insistently. Though the toughest of men, he shivered a little and drew up a wicker chair close in front of the fire.

"It's incredible!" he murmured, and as he stared at the flames this thought seemed to haunt him all the time.

Bisset laid the table and another hour passed. Ned ate a little lunch and then smoked and stared at the fire while the wind droned and blustered without ceasing, and occasionally a cross gust sent the rain drops softly pattering on the panes.

"I'm damned if I see a thing!" he suddenly exclaimed half aloud, and jumped to his feet.

Before he had time to start for the door, Bisset's mysterious efficiency was made manifest again. Precisely as he was wanted, he appeared, and this time it was clear that his own efforts had not been altogether fruitless. He had in fact an air of even greater complacency than usual.

"I have arrived at certain conclusions, sir," he announced.

13

THE DEDUCTIVE PROCESS

Bisset laid on the table a sheet of note paper.

"Here," said he, "is a kin' of bit sketch plan of the library. Observing this plan attentively, you will notice two crosses, marked A and B. A is where yon wee table was standing—no the place against the wall where it was standing this morning, but where it was standing before it was knocked over last night. B is where the corp was found. You follow that, sir?"

Ned nodded.

"I follow," said he.

"Now, the principle in a' these cases of crime and detection," resumed the philosopher, assuming his lecturer's air, "is noticing such sma' points of detail as escape the eye of the ordinar' observer, taking full and accurate measurements, making a plan with the principal sites carefully markit, and drawing, as it were, logical conclusions. Applying this method now to the present instance, Mr. Cromarty, the first point to observe is that the room is twenty-six feet long, measured from the windie, which is a bit recessed or set back, as it were, to the other end of the apartment. Half of 26 is 13, and if you take the half way line and draw approximate perpendiculars to about where the table was standing and to as near as one can remember where the middle of the corp roughly was lying, you get exactly six feet ten and five-eighths inches, in both cases."

"An approximate perpendicular to roughly about these places gives this exact measurement?" repeated Cromarty gravely. "Well, what next?"

"Well, sir, I'll not insist too much on the coincidence, but it seems to me vera remarkable. But the two significant features of this case seem to me yon table being upset over by the windie and the corp being found over by the door."

"You're talking horse sense now," murmured Ned.

"Now, yon table was upset by Sir Reginald falling on it!"

Ned looked at him keenly.

"How do you know?"

"Because one of the legs was broken clean off!"

"What, when we saw it this morning?"

"We had none of us noticed it then, sir; but I've had a look at it since, and there's one leg broken fair off at the top. The break was half in the socket, as it were, leaving a kind of spike, and if you stick that into the socket you can make the table look as good as new. It's all right, in fac', until you try to move it, and then of course the leg just drops out."

"And it wasn't like that yesterday?"

"I happened to move it myself not so long before Sir Reginald came into the room, and that's how I know for certain where it was standing and that it wasn't broken. And yon wee light tables dinna lose their legs just with being cowped, supposing there was nothing else than that to smash them. No, sir, it was poor Sir Reginald falling on top of it that smashed yon leg."

"Then he was certainly struck down near the window!"

"Well, we'll see that in a minute. It's no in reason, Mr. Cromarty, to suppose he deliberately opened the windie to let his ain murderer in. And it's a' just stuff and nonsense to suggest Sir Reginald was sitting on a winter's night—or next door to winter onyhow, with his windie wide open. I'm too well acquaint with his habits to believe that for a minute. And it's impossible the man can have opened a snibbed windie and got in, with some one sitting in the room, and no alarm given. So it's perfectly certain the man must have come in at the door. That's a fair deduction, is it not, sir?"

Ned Cromarty frowned into space in silence. When he spoke it seemed to be as much to himself as to Bisset.

"How did the window get unsnibbed? Everything beats me, but that beats me fairly."

"Well, sir, Mr. Rattar may no be just exac'ly as intellectual as me and you, but I think there's maybe something in his idea it was done to put us off the scent."

"Possibly—but it strikes me as a derned feeble dodge. However, what's your next conclusion?"

"My next conclusion is, sir, that Simon Rattar may not be so vera far wrong either about Sir Reginald hearing some one at the door and starting to see who it was. Then—bang!—the door would suddenly open, and afore he'd time to speak, the man had given him a bat on the heid that finished him."

"And where does the table come in?"

"Well, my explanation is just this, that Sir Reginald suspected something and took the wee table as a kind of weapon."

"Rot!" said Ned ruthlessly. "You think he left the fireplace and went round by the window to fetch such a useless weapon as that?"

James Bisset was not easily damped.

"That's only a possibility, sir. Excluding that, what must have happened? For that's the way, Mr. Cromarty, to get at the fac's; you just exclude what's not possible and what remains is the truth. If you'd read—"

"Well, come on. What's your theory now?"

"Just that Sir Reginald backed away from the door with the man after him, till he got to the table. And then down went him and the table together."

"And why didn't he cry out or raise the alarm in some way while he was backing away?"

"God, but that fits into my other deductions fine!" cried Bisset. "I hadna thought of that. Just wait, sir, till you see how the case is going to hang together in a minute."

"But how did Sir Reginald's body come to be lying near the door?"

The philosopher seemed to be inspired afresh.

"The man clearly meant to take it away and hide it somewhere—that'll be just it! And then he found it ower heavy and decided to leave it after all."

"And who was this man?"

"That's precisely where proper principles, Mr. Cromarty, lead to a number of vera interesting and instructive discoveries, and I think ye'll see, sir, that the noose is on the road to his neck already. I've not got the actual man, mind! In fac' I've no idea who he is, but I can tell you a good few things about him—enough, in fac', to make escape practically impossible. In the first place, he was one well acquaint with the ways of the house. Is that not a fair deduction, sir?"

"Sure!" said Ned. "I've put my bottom dollar on that already."

"He came from inside this house and not outside it. How long he'd been in the house, that I cannot say, but my own deductions are he'd been in the house waiting for his chance for a good while before the master heard him at yon door. Is that not a fair deduction too, sir?"

"It's possible," said Ned, though not with great conviction.

"And now here's a point that accounts for Sir Reginald giving no alarm—Sir Reginald knew the man and couldna believe he meant mischief!"

Ned looked at him quickly and curiously.

"Well?" said he.

"Is that not a fair deduction, Mr. Cromarty?"

"Seems to fill the bill."

"And now, here's a few personal details. Yon man was a fair active strong man to have dealt with the master the way he did. But he was not strong enough to carry off the corp like a sack of potatoes; he was no a great muckle big giant, that's to say. And finally, calculating from the distance the body was from the door and the number of steps he would be likely to take to the door, and sae arriving at his stride and deducing his height accordingly, he'd be as near as may be five feet nine inches tall. Now, sir, me and you ought to get him with a' that known!"

Ned Cromarty looked at him with a curious gleam in his eye.

"What's your own height, Bisset?" he enquired.

"Five feet nine inches," said the reasoner promptly, and then suddenly his mouth fell open but his voice ceased.

"And now," pursued Ned with a grimly humorous look, "can you not think of a man just that height, pretty hefty but not a giant, who was certainly in the house last night, who knew all the ways of it, and who would never have been suspected by Sir Reginald of meaning mischief?"

"God!" exclaimed the unfortunate reasoner. "I've proved it was mysel'!"

"Well, and what shall I do—string you up now or hand you over to the police?"

"But, Mr. Cromarty—you don't believe that's right surely?"

Tragic though the occasion was, Ned could not refrain from one brief laugh. And then his face set hard again and he said:

"No, Bisset, I do not believe it was you. In fact, I wouldn't believe it was you if you confessed to it. But I'd advise you not to go spreading your deductions abroad! Deduction's a game that wants a bit more practice than you or I have had."

It is possible that James Bisset had never looked quite so crestfallen in his life.

"Then that's all nonsense I've been talking, sir?" he said lugubriously.

"No," said Ned emphatically. "I'll not say that either. You've brought out some good points—that broken table, the place the body was found, the possible reason why Sir Reginald gave no alarm; seems to me those have something to them. But what they mean—what to conclude; we're as far off that, Bisset, as ever!"

The philosopher's self esteem was evidently returning as fast as it had gone.

"Then you wouldn't think there would be any harm, sir, in my continuing my investigations?"

"On your present lines, the only harm is likely to be to yourself. Keep at it—but don't hang yourself accidentally. And let me know if you discover anything else—mind that."

"I'll mind on it, no fears, Mr. Cromarty!"

Ned left him with an expression on his countenance which indicated that the deductive process had already been resumed.

Till he arrived at his own door, the laird of Stanesland was unconscious of a single incident of his drive home. All the way his eye stared straight into space. Sometimes a gleam would light it for an instant, and then he would shake his head and the gleam would fade away.

"I can see neither a damned head nor a damned tail to it!" he said to himself as he alighted.

14

THE QUESTION OF MOTIVE

Two days later Mr. Ison entered Mr. Simon Rattar's room and informed him that Mr. Cromarty of Stanesland wished to see him on particular business. The lawyer was busy and this interruption seemed for the moment distinctly unwelcome. Then he grunted:

"Show him in."

In the minute or two that passed before the laird's entrance, Simon seemed to be thinking intently and finally to come to a decision, which, to judge from his reception of his client, was on rather different lines from his first thoughts when Mr. Cromarty's name was announced. To describe Simon Rattar at any time as genial would be an exaggeration, but he showed his nearest approach to geniality as he bade his client good-morning.

"Sorry to interrupt you," said Ned, "but I can't get this business out of my head, night or day. Whether you want me or not, I've got to play a hand in this game; but it's on your side, Mr. Rattar, and maybe I might be able to help a little if I could get something to go on."

The lawyer nodded.

"I quite understand. Glad to have your help, Mr. Cromarty. Dreadful affair. We're all trying to get to the bottom of it, I can assure you."

"I believe you," said Ned. "There never was a man better worth avenging than Sir Reginald."

"Quite so," said Simon briefly, his eyes fixed on the other's face. "Any fresh facts?"

Simon drew a sheet of paper from his desk.

"Superintendent Sutherland has given me a note of three—for what they are worth, discovered by the butler. The first is about that table. It seems a leg has been broken."

"Bisset told me that before I left the house."

"And thought it was an important fact, I suppose?"

"What its importance is, it's hard to say, but it's a fact, and seems to me well worth noting."

"It is noted," said the Procurator Fiscal drily. "But I can't see that it leads anywhere."

"Bisset maintains it implies Sir Reginald fell over it when he was struck down; and that seems to me pretty likely."

Simon shook his head.

"How do we know Sir Reginald hadn't broken it himself previously and then set it up against the wall—assuming it ever stood anywhere else, which seems to want confirmation?"

"A dashed thin suggestion!" said Ned. "However, what are the other discoveries?"

"The second is that one or two small fragments of dried mud were found under the edge of the curtain, and the third is that the hearth brush was placed in an unusual position—according to Bisset."

"And what are Bisset's conclusions?"

"That the man, whoever he was, had brought mud into the room and then swept it up with the hearth brush; these fragments being pieces that he had swept accidentally under the curtain and so overlooked."

"Good for Bisset!" exclaimed Ned. "He has got there this time, I do believe."

Simon smiled sceptically.

"Sir Reginald was in the library in his walking boots that afternoon. Naturally he would leave mud, and quite likely he swept it up himself then, though the only evidence of sweeping is Bisset's statement about the brush. And what proof is that of anything? Does your hearth brush always stay in the same position?"

"Never noticed," said Ned.

"And I don't believe anybody notices sufficiently closely to make their evidence on such a point worth a rap!" said Simon.

"A servant would."

"Well, Mr. Cromarty, make the most of the hearth brush then."

There seemed for an instant to be a defiant note in the Procurator Fiscal's voice that made Ned glance at him sharply. But he saw nothing in his face but the same set and steady look.

"We're on the same side in this racket, Mr. Rattar," said Ned. "I'm only trying to help—same as you."

Simon's voice seemed now to have exactly the opposite note. For him, his tone of acquiescence was even eager.

"Quite so; quite so, Mr. Cromarty. We are acting together; exactly."

"That's all the new evidence then?"

Simon nodded, and a few moments of silence followed.

"Tell me honestly," demanded Ned at last, "have you actually no clue at all? No suspicion of any kind? Haven't you got on the track of any possible reason for the deed?"

"Reason?" repeated Simon. "Now we come to business, Mr. Cromarty. What's the motive? That's the point."

"Have you found one?"

Simon looked judicially discreet.

"At this moment all I can tell you is to answer the question: 'Who benefits by Sir Reginald Cromarty's death?'"

"Well—who did? Seems to me every one who knew him suffered."

"Sentimentally perhaps—but not financially."

Ned looked at him in silence, as if an entirely new point of view were dawning on his mind. But he compressed his lips and merely asked:

"Well?"

"To begin with, nothing was stolen from the house. Therefore no outside thief or burglar gained anything. I may add also that the police have made enquiries throughout the whole county, and no bad characters are known to be in the place. Therefore there is no ground for supposing the deed was the work of a robber, and to my mind, no evidence worth considering to support that view. The only people that gained anything, Mr. Cromarty, are those who will benefit under Sir Reginald's will."

Cromarty's expression did not change again. This was evidently the new point of view.

Simon opened a drawer and took from it a document.

"In the ordinary course of events Sir Reginald's will would not be known till after his funeral to-morrow, but if I may regard this conversation as confidential, I can tell you the principal facts so far as they affect this case."

"I don't want you to do anything you shouldn't," said Ned quickly. "If it's not the proper game to read the will now, don't."

But Silent Simon seemed determined to oblige this morning.

"It is a mere matter of form delaying till to-morrow, and I shall not read it now; merely tell you the pertinent facts briefly."

"Fire away then. The Lord knows I want to learn every derned pertinent fact—want to badly!"

"In the first place," the lawyer began, "Lady Cromarty is life rented in the mansion and property, less certain sums to be paid to other people, which I am coming to. She therefore lost her husband and a certain amount of income, and gained nothing that we know of."

"That's a cold-blooded way of putting it," said Ned with something like a shiver. "However, what next?"

"Sir Malcolm gets £1,000 a year to support him during the life time of Lady Cromarty, and afterwards falls heir to the whole estate. He therefore gains a baronetcy and £1,000 a year immediately, and the estate is brought a stage nearer him. Miss Farmond gets a legacy of £2,000. She therefore gained £2,000."

"Not that she'll need it," said Ned quickly. "That item doesn't count."

Simon looked at him curiously.

"Why not?" he enquired.

Ned hesitated a moment.

"Perhaps I oughtn't to have said anything," he said, "but this conversation is confidential, and anyhow the fact will be known soon enough now, I guess. She is engaged to Sir Malcolm."

For a moment Simon continued to look at him very hard. Then he merely said:

"Indeed?"

"Of course you won't repeat this till they care to make it known themselves. I told you so that you'd see a legacy of two thousand pounds wouldn't count much. It only means an income of—what?"

"One hundred pounds at five per cent; eighty pounds at four."

"Well, that will be neither here nor there now."

Again Simon stared in silence for a moment, but rather through than at his visitor, it seemed. Then he glanced down at the document again.

"James Bisset gets a legacy of three hundred pounds. There are a few smaller legacies to servants, but the only two that might have affected this case do not actually do so. One is John Robertson, Sir Reginald's chauffeur, but on the night of the crime he was away from home and an alibi can be established till two in the morning. The other is Donald Mackay, the gardener, but he is an old man and was in bed with rheumatism that night."

"I see," observed Ned, "you are giving everybody mentioned in the will credit for perhaps having committed the murder, supposing it was physically possible?"

"I am answering the question—who that could conceivably have committed it, had a motive for doing so? And also, what was that motive?"

"Is that the whole list of them?"

Mr. Rattar glanced at the will again.

"Sir Reginald has cancelled your own debt of twelve hundred pounds, Mr. Cromarty."

"What!" exclaimed Ned, and for a moment could say no more. Then he said in a low voice: "It's up to me more than ever!"

"That is the full list of persons within the vicinity two nights ago who gained by Sir Reginald's death," said Simon in a dry voice, as he put away the will.

"Including me?" said Ned. "Well, all I've got to say is this, Mr. Rattar, that my plain common sense tells me that those are no motives at all. For who knew what they stood to gain by this will?

Or that they stood to gain any blessed thing at all? I hadn't the foggiest notion Sir Reginald meant to cancel that debt!"

"You may not have known," said Simon still very drily, "and it is quite possible that Bisset may not have known of his legacy. Though, on the other hand, it is likely enough that Sir Reginald mentioned the fact that he would be remembered. But Lady Cromarty presumably knew his arrangements. And it is most un-likely that he should have said nothing to his heir about his inten-tion to make him an adequate allowance if he came into the title and Lady Cromarty was still alive and life rented in the place. Also, it is highly probable that either Sir Reginald or Lady Cromarty told Miss Farmond that some provision would be made for her."

Ned Cromarty said nothing for a few moments, but he seemed to be thinking very hard. Then he rose from his chair and remarked:

"Well, I guess this has all got to be thought over."

He moved slowly to the door, while Simon gazed silently into space. His hand was on the handle when the lawyer turned in his chair and asked:

"Why was nothing said about Sir Malcolm's engagement to Miss Farmond?"

"Well," said Ned, "the whole thing is no business of mine, but Sir Reginald had pretty big ideas in some ways and probably one of them was connected with his heir's marriage."

"A clandestine engagement then?"

Ned Cromarty seemed to dislike the term.

"It's none of my business," he said shortly. "There was no blame on anyone, anyhow; and mind you, this is absolutely confidential."

The door closed behind him and Simon was left still apparently thinking.

15

TWO WOMEN

On the day after the funeral Lady Cromarty for the first time felt able to see the family lawyer. Simon Rattar came out in the morning in a hired car and spent more than a couple of hours with her. Then for a short time he was closeted with Sir Malcolm, who, referring to the interview afterwards, described him as "infernally close and unsatisfactory"; and finally, in company with the young baronet and Cicely Farmond, he ate a hurried lunch and departed.

Ever since the fatal evening, Lady Cromarty had been shut up in her own apartments and the two young people had taken their meals together. Sir Malcolm at his brightest and best had been capricious company. He was now moody beyond all Cicely's experience of him. His newborn solemnity was the most marked feature of his demeanour, but sometimes it dissolved into pathetic demands for sympathy, and then again froze into profound and lugubrious silence. He said that he was sleeping badly, and the pallor of his face and the darkness beneath his eyes seemed to confirm this. Several times he appeared to be on the point of some peculiarly solemn disclosure of his feelings or his symptoms, but always ended by upbraiding his fellow guest for her lack of sympathy, and then relapsing into silence.

Every now and then on such occasions Cicely caught him staring at her with an expression she had never seen before, and then looking hurriedly away; a disconcerting habit that made her own lot none the easier. So far as the observant Bisset could judge, the baronet seemed, indeed, to be having so depressing an effect upon the young lady that as her friend and counsellor he took the liberty of advising a change of air.

"We'll miss you vera much, Miss Farmond," he was good enough to say, "but I'm thinking that what you want is a seaside resort."

She smiled a little sadly.

"I shall have to make a change very soon, Bisset," she said. "Indeed, perhaps I ought to have let Lady Cromarty know already that I was ready to go the moment I was sure I could do nothing more for her."

She began her packing on the morning of Simon's visit. At lunch her air was a little livelier at first, as if even Simon Rattar were a welcome variety in a régime of undiluted baronet. Sir Malcolm, too, endeavoured to do the honours with some degree of cheerfulness; but short though the meal was, both were silent before the end and vaguely depressed afterwards.

"I can't stand the old fellow's fishy eye!" declared Sir Malcolm. "I'd as soon lunch with a cod-fish, dash it! Didn't you feel it too, Cicely?"

"He seemed to look at one so uncomfortably," she agreed. "I couldn't help feeling he had something on his mind against me, though I suppose he really doesn't trouble his head about my existence."

"I'm hanged if I like the way he looks at me!" muttered the baronet, and once again Cicely caught that odd expression in his eye.

That afternoon Bisset informed Miss Farmond that her ladyship desired to see her. Lady Cromarty's face looked thinner than ever and her lips more tightly compressed. In her deep mourning and with her grave air, she seemed to Cicely a monumental figure of tragedy. Her thinness and pallor and tight lips, she thought only natural, but there was one note that seemed discordant with pure desolation. The note was sounded by Lady Cromarty's eyes. At all times they had been ready to harden upon an occasion, but Cicely thought she had never seen them as hard as they were now.

"What are your plans, Cicely?" she asked in a low, even voice that showed no feeling one way or the other.

"I have begun to pack already," said the girl. "I don't want to leave so long as I can be of any use here, but I am ready to go at any time."

She had expected to be asked where she was going, but Lady Cromarty instead of putting any question, looked at her for a few moments in silence. And it was then that a curious uncomfortable feeling began to possess the girl. It had no definite form and was founded on no reason, beyond the steady regard of those hard dark eyes.

"I had rather you stayed."

Cicely's own eyes showed her extreme surprise.

"Stayed—here?"

"Yes."

"But are you sure? Wouldn't you really rather be alone? It isn't for my sake, is it? because—"

"It is for mine. I want you to remain here and keep me company."

She spoke without a trace of smile or any softening of her face, and Cicely still hesitated.

"But would it really be convenient? You have been very kind to me, and if you really want me here—"

"I do," interrupted Lady Cromarty in the same even voice. "I want you particularly to remain."

"Very well then, I shall. Thank you very much—"

Again she was cut short.

"That is settled then. Perhaps you will excuse me now, Cicely."

The girl went downstairs very thoughtfully. At the foot the young baronet met her.

"Have you settled where to go?" he asked.

"Lady Cromarty has asked me to stay on with her."

His face fell.

"Stay on in this house of mourning? Oh, no, Cicely!"

"I have promised," she said.

The young man grew curiously agitated.

"Oh, don't stay here!" he besought her. "It keeps me in such dreadful suspense!"

"In suspense!" she exclaimed. "Whatever do you mean, Malcolm?"

Again she saw that look in his eye, and again he raised a sympathy-beseeching wail. Cicely's patience began to give way.

"Really, Malcolm!" she cried tartly, "if you have anything to say, say it, but don't go on like a baby!"

"Like a baby!" repeated the deeply affronted baronet. "Heavens, would you liken me to *that*, of all things! I had meant to confide in you, Cicely, but you have made it impossible. Impossible!" he repeated sombrely, and stalked to the door.

Next morning, Sir Malcolm left for London, his confidence still locked in his breast, and Cicely was alone with Lady Cromarty.

16

RUMOUR

One windy afternoon a man on a bicycle struggled up to the door of Stanesland Castle and while waiting for an answer to his ring, studied the front of that ancient building with an expression which would at once have informed his intimates that he was meditating on the principles of Scottish baronial architecture. A few minutes later Mr. Bisset was shown into the laird of Stanesland's smoking room and addressed Mr. Cromarty with a happy blend of consciousness of his own importance and respect for the laird's.

"I have taken the liberty of calling, sir, for to lay before you a few fresh datas."

"Fire away," said the laird.

"In the first place, sir, I understand that you have been making enquiries through the county yourself, sir; is that not so?"

"I've been through this blessed county, Bisset, from end to end to see whether I could get on the track of any suspicious stranger. I've been working both with the police and independent of the police, and I've drawn blank."

Bisset looked distinctly disappointed.

"I've heard, sir, one or two stories which I was hoping might have something in them."

"I've heard about half a dozen and gone into them all, and there's nothing in one of them."

"Half a dozen stories?" Bisset's eye began to look hopeful again. "Well, sir, perhaps if I was to go into some of them again in the light of my fresh datas, they might wear, as it were, a different aspect."

"Well," said Ned. "What have you found? Have a cigar and let's hear what you've been at."

The expert crackled the cigar approvingly between his fingers, lit it with increased approval, and began:

"Yon man was behind the curtains all the time."

"The devil he was! How do you know?"

"Well, sir, it's a matter of deduction. Ye see supposing he came in by the door, there are objections, and supposing he came in by the windie there are objections. Either way there are objections which make it difficult for to accept those theories. And then it struck me—the man must have been behind the curtains all the while!"

"He must have come either by the door or window to get there."

"That's true, Mr. Cromarty. But such minor points we can consider in a wee while, when we have seen how everything is otherwise explained. Now supposing we have the murderer behind the curtains; that brings him within six feet of where the wee table was standing. How did he get Sir Reginald to come to the table? He made some kind of sound. What kind of sound? Some imitation of an animal; probably of a cat. How did Sir Reginald not cry out when he saw the man? Because he never did see the man! How did he not see him?"

"Man was a ventriloquist and made a sound in the other direction," suggested Ned with extreme gravity.

"God, but that's possible, Mr. Cromarty! I hadna thought of that! Well, it'll fit into the facts all right, you'll see. My theory was that either the man threw something at the master and knocked him down that way, or he was able to reach out and give him a bat on the heid without moving from the curtains."

"He must have been an awkward customer."

"He was that! A great tall man with long arms. And what had he at the end of them? Either a club such as savages use or something to throw like a boomerang. And he could imitate animals, and as you say, he was probably a ventriloquist. And he was that active and strong he could get into the house through one of the windies, just like a great monkey. Now what's the history of that man?"

"Pretty wild, I guess."

"Ah, but one can say more than that, sir. He was not an ordinary Englishman or Scotchman. He was from the Colonies or America or one of thae wild places! Is that not a fair deduction, sir?"

"It all points to that," said Ned, with a curious look.

"It points to that indeed, sir. Now where's he hidden himself? It should not be difficult to find him with all that to go on."

"A tall active strong man who has lived in the Colonies or America; one ought to get him. Has he only one eye, by any chance?"

The reasoner gazed petrified at his counsellor.

"God, but I've just described yoursel', sir!" he cried in an unhappy voice.

"You're determined to hang one of us, Bisset."

For a moment Bisset seemed to find conversation difficult. Then he said miserably:

"So it's no good, and all the alternatives just fa' to pieces."

The extreme dejection of his voice struck the other sharply.

"Alternatives to what?" he asked.

For a few seconds Bisset did not answer.

"What's on your mind, man?" demanded Cromarty.

"The reason, sir, I've got that badly off the rails with my deductions is just that I *had* to find some other theory than the story that's going about."

"What story?"

"You've no heard it, sir?"

Ned shook his head.

"I hardly like to repeat it, sir; it's that cruel and untrue. They're saying Sir Malcolm and Miss Farmond had got engaged to be married."

"Well?" said Ned sharply, and he seemed to control his feelings with an effort.

"A secret engagement, like, that Sir Reginald would never have allowed. But there I think they're right, sir. Sir Reginald was unco' taken up with Miss Farmond, but he'd have looked higher for his

heir. And so as they couldn't get married while he was alive—neither of them having any money, well, sir, this story says—"

He broke off and neither spoke for an instant.

"Good God!" murmured Cromarty. "They actually accuse
Malcolm Cromarty and Miss Cicely of—?"

He paused too, and Bisset nodded.

"Who is saying this?"

"It seems to be the clash of the haill country by this time, sir."

He seemed a little frightened at the effect of his own words;
and it was small wonder. Ned Cromarty was a nasty looking customer at that moment.

"Who started the lie?"

"It's just ignorance and want of education of the people, I'm
thinking, Mr. Cromarty. They're no able to grasp the proper principles—"

"Lady Cromarty must be told! She could put a stop to it—"

Something in Bisset's look pulled him up sharply.

"I'm afraid her ladyship believes it herself, sir. Maybe you have
heard she has keepit Miss Farmond to stay on with her."

"I have."

"Well, sir," said Bisset very slowly and deliberately, "I'm thinking—it's just to watch her."

Ned Cromarty had been smoking a pipe. There was a crack now
as his teeth went through the mouthpiece. He flung the pipe into
the fire, jumped up, and began pacing the room without a word or
a glance at the other. At last he stopped as abruptly as he had
started.

"This slander has got to be stopped!"

And then he paced on.

"Just what I was saying to myself, sir. It was likely a wee thing
of over anxiety to stop it that made me think o' the possibility of a
wild man from America, which was perhaps a bit beyond the limits of what ye might call, as it were, scientific deduction."

"When did Lady Cromarty begin to take up this attitude?"

"Well, the plain truth is, sir, that her ladyship has been keeping sae much to herself that it's not rightly possible to tell what's

been in her mind. But it was the afternoon when Mr. Rattar had been at the house that she sent for Miss Farmond and tellt her then she was wanting her to stop on."

"That would be after she knew the contents of the will! I wonder if the idea had entered her head before, or if the will alone started it? Old Simon would never start such a scandal himself about his best client. He knows too well which side his bread is buttered for that! But he might have talked his infernal jargon about the motive and the people who stood to gain by the death. That might have been enough to set her suspicions off."

"Or I was thinking maybe, sir, it was when her ladyship heard of the engagement."

"Ah!" exclaimed Ned, stopping suddenly again, "that's possible. When did she hear?"

Bisset shook his head.

"That beats me again, sir. Her own maid likely has been telling her things the time we've not been seeing her."

"Did the maid—or did you know about the engagement?"

"Servants are uneducated creatures," said Bisset contemptuously. "And women at the best have just the ae' thought—who's gaun to be fool enough to marry next? They were always gossiping about Mr. Malcolm and Miss Cicely, but there was never what I should call a data to found a deduction on; not for a sensible person. I never believed it myself, but it's like enough her ladyship may have suspected it for a while back."

"I suppose Lady Cromarty has been nearly distracted?"

"Very near, sir."

"That's her only excuse. But the story is such obvious nonsense, Bisset, that surely no one in their proper senses really believes it?"

The philosopher shook a wise head.

"I have yet to learn, Mr. Cromarty, what folks will not believe."

"They've got to stop believing this!" said Ned emphatically.

Next morning Simon Rattar was again informed that Mr. Cromarty of Stanesland wished to see him, and again the announcement seemed to be unwelcome. He was silent for several seconds before answering, and when he allowed Mr. Cromarty to be shown in, it was with an air which suggested the getting over a distasteful business as soon as possible.

"Well, Mr. Cromarty?" he grunted brusquely.

Mr. Cromarty never beat about the bush.

"I've come to see you about this scandalous story that's going round."

The lawyer glanced at the papers he had been busy with, as if to indicate that they were of more importance than scandals.

"What story?" he enquired.

"That Sir Malcolm and Miss Farmond were concerned in Sir Reginald's murder."

There was something compelling in Ned's directness. Simon pushed aside the papers and looked at him fixedly.

"Oh," he said. "They say that, do they?"

"Haven't you heard?"

Simon's grunt was non-committal.

"Well anyway, this derned story is going about, and something's got to be done to stop it."

"What do you suggest?"

"Are you still working the case for all you know how?"

Simon seemed to resent this enquiry a little.

"I am the Procurator Fiscal. The police make the actual enquiries. They have done everything they could."

"'They have done'? Do you mean that they have stopped looking for the murderer?"

"Certainly not. They are still enquiring; not that it is likely to be much further use."

There seemed to be a sardonic note in his last words that deepened Cromarty's frown and kindled his eye.

"You mean to suggest that any conclusion has been reached?"

"Nothing is absolutely certain," said Simon.

Again the accent on the "absolutely" seemed to rouse his visitor's ire.

"You believe this story, do you?"

"If I *believed* it, I should order an arrest. I have just told you nothing is absolutely certain."

"Look here," said Cromarty, "I don't want to crab Superintendent Sutherland or his men, but you want to get somebody better than them on to this job."

Though the Procurator Fiscal kept his feelings well in hand, it was evident that this suggestion struck him more unfavourably than anything his visitor had said yet. He even seemed for one instant to be a little startled by its audacity.

"I disagree," he muttered.

"Now don't you take offence, Mr. Rattar," said Ned with a sudden smile. "I'm not aiming this at you, but, hang it, you know as well as I do that Sutherland is no great shakes at detection. They are all just country bobbies. What we want is a London detective."

Simon seemed to have recovered his equanimity during this speech. He shook his head emphatically, but his voice was as dispassionately brusque as ever.

"London detective? Much over-rated people, I assure you. No use in a case of this kind."

"The very kind of case a real copper-bottomed expert would be some use in!"

"You are thinking of detectives in stories, Mr. Cromarty. The real men are no better than Sutherland—not a bit. I believe in

Sutherland. Better man than he looks. Very shrewd, most pains-
taking. Couldn't have a better man. Useless expense getting a man
from London."

"Don't you trouble about the expense, Mr. Rattar. That can be
arranged all right. I want a first class man engaged."

The sudden glance which the lawyer shot at him, struck Ned as
unusual in his experience of Simon Rattar. He appeared to be
startled again, and yet it was not mere annoyance that seemed to
show for the fraction of a second in his eye. And then the next instant the man's gaze was as cold and steady as ever. He pursed his
lips and considered his answer in silence before he spoke.

"You are a member of the family, Mr. Cromarty; the actual head
of it, in fact, I believe."

"Going by pedigrees, I believe I am, but being a member is reason enough for my wanting to get daylight through this business—
and seeing somebody swing for it!"

"What if you made things worse?"

"Worse! How could they be?"

"Mr. Cromarty, I am the Procurator Fiscal in charge of this case.
But I am also lawyer and factor to the Cromarty family, and my
father was before me. If there was evidence enough—clear and
proper evidence—to convict any person of this crime, it would be
my duty as Procurator Fiscal to convict them. But there is no definite evidence, as you know yourself. All we can do, if we push this
matter too far, is to make a family scandal public. Are you as the
head of the Cromarty family, and I as their factor, to do this?"

It was difficult to judge with what feelings Ned Cromarty heard
this deliberate statement and appeal. His mouth was as hard as
the lawyer's and his eye revealed nothing.

"Then you propose to hush the thing up?"

"I said nothing about hushing up. I propose to wait till I get
some *evidence*, Mr. Cromarty. It is a little difficult perhaps for a
layman to realise what evidence means, but I can tell you—and any
lawyer, or any detective, would tell you—we have nothing that can
be called evidence yet."

"And you won't get any till you call in somebody a cut above
Sutherland."

"The scent is too cold by this time—"

"Who let it cool?" interrupted Ned.

For a moment the lawyer's eyes looked unpleasant.

"Every effort was made to find a clue; by yourself as well as by the police. And let me tell you, Mr. Cromarty, that our efforts have not been as fruitless as you seem to think."

"What have we discovered?"

"In the first place that there was no robbery committed and no sign of anybody having entered the house from the outside."

Ned shook his head.

"That's a lot too strong. I believe the man *did* come in by the window."

"You admit there is no proof?"

"Sure," said Ned candidly. "I quite admit there is no proof of anything—yet."

"No robbery, no evidence of anyone having come in by the window—"

"No proof," corrected Ned. "I maintain that the window being unsnibbed and that mud on the floor and the table near the window being upset is evidence; but not proof positive."

Simon's patience had by this time become exemplary. His only wish seemed to be to convince by irresistible argument this obstinate objector. It struck the visitor, moreover, that in this effort the lawyer was displaying a fluency not at all characteristic of silent Simon.

"Well, let us leave it at that. Suppose there be a possibility that entry was actually made by the window. It is a bare possibility against the obvious and easy entrance by the door,—near which, remember, the body was found. Then, as I have pointed out, there was no robbery, and not a trace has been found of anybody outside that house with a motive for the crime."

"Except me."

"Unless you care to except yourself. But neither you nor the police have found any bad characters in the place."

"That's true enough," Ned admitted reluctantly.

"On the other hand, there were within the house two people with a very strong motive for committing the crime."

"I deny that!" cried Ned with a sudden gleam of ferocity in his eye that seemed to disconcert the lawyer.

"Deny it? You can scarcely deny that two young people, in love with one another and secretly engaged, with no money, and no chance of getting married, stood to gain everything they wanted by a death that gave them freedom to marry, a baronetcy, a thousand a year, and two thousand in cash besides?"

"Damn it, Mr. Rattar, is the fact that a farmer benefits by a shower any evidence that he has turned on the rain?"

"I have repeatedly said, Mr. Cromarty, that there is no definite evidence to convict anybody. But nothing would have been easier than making an end of Sir Reginald Cromarty, to anybody inside that house whom he would never suspect till they struck the blow. All the necessary conditions are fulfilled by this view of the case, whereas every other view—every other view, mind you, Mr. Cromarty—is confronted with these difficulties:—no robbery, no definite evidence of entry, no explanation of Sir Reginald's extraordinary silence when the man appeared, no bad characters in the neighbourhood, and, above all, no motive."

At the end of this speech Simon shut his mouth tight and leaned back in his chair. For a moment it seemed as though Ned Cromarty was impressed by the lawyer's view of the case. But when he replied, his voice, though deliberate had a fighting ring in it, and his single eye, a fighting light.

"Then you propose to leave this young couple under the most damnable cloud of suspicion that a man and a woman could lie under—simply leave 'em there, and let that be the end of it?"

Simon seemed to be divided between distaste for this way of putting the case, and anxiety still to convince his visitor.

"I propose to avoid the painful family scandal which further disclosures and more publicity would almost certainly bring about; so long as I am justified as Procurator Fiscal in taking this course. And until I get more evidence, I am not only justified but forced to take this course."

Ned suddenly jumped to his feet.

"I'm no lawyer," said he, "but to me you seem to be arguing in the damnedest circle I ever met. You won't do anything because you can't get more evidence. And you won't look for more evidence because you don't want to do anything."

There was more than a hint of temper in Simon's eye and his answer was rapped out sharply.

"I certainly do not *want* to cause a family scandal. I haven't said all I could say about Sir Malcolm if I were pressed."

"Why not?"

"I've told you. Suspicion is not evidence, but if I do get evidence, those who will suffer by it had better beware!"

Ned turned at the door and surveyed him with a cool and caustic eye.

"That's talk," he said, "and something has got to be *done*."

He was gone, and Simon Rattar was left frowning at the closed door behind him. The frown remained, but became now rather thoughtful than indignant. Then he sprang up and began to pace the floor, deliberately at first, and then more rapidly and with increasing agitation.

18

£1200

Ned Cromarty had returned home and was going upstairs, when he heard a voice cry:

"Ned!"

The ancient stone stair, spiralling up round the time-worn pillar that seemed to have no beginning or end, gave at intervals on to doors which looked like apertures in a cliff. Through one of these he turned and at the end of a brief passage came to his sister's sitting room. In that mediæval setting of ponderous stone, it looked almost fantastic in its daintiness. It was a small room of many cushions and many colours, its floor covered with the softest rugs and its walls with innumerable photographs, largely of country houses where Miss Cromarty had visited.

Evidently she was a lady accustomed to a comfortable life in her roving days, and her sitting room seemed to indicate very distinctly that she proposed to live up to this high standard permanently.

"Oh Neddy dear, I want to talk to you about something," she began in her brisk way and with her brightest smile.

Her brother, though of a simple nature, was by this time aware that when he was termed "Neddy dear" the conversation was apt to turn on Miss Cromarty's requirements.

"Well," said he, "how much is the cheque to be this time?"

"How clever you're getting!" she laughed. "But it isn't a cheque I want this time. It's only a motor car."

He looked at her doubtfully for a moment.

"Pulling my leg; or a real car?"

"Real car of course—nice one too!"

"But, my dear girl, we've just put down our car. You agreed it was necessary."

"I agreed then; but it isn't necessary now."

"Have you come into a fortune? I haven't!"

"You've come into £1200."

Again he looked at her, and this time his expression changed.

"That's only a debt wiped out."

"Well, and your great argument for economy was that you had to pay back that debt. Now you haven't. See, Neddy dear?"

Her brother began to shake his head, and her smile became a little less bright.

"I don't want to get my affairs into a tangle again just yet."

"But they weren't in a bad tangle. Cancelling that debt makes us absolutely all right again. It's absurd for people like us not to have a car! Look at the distances from our neighbours! One can't go anywhere. I'll undertake to keep down the household expenses if you get the car."

Her brother frowned out of the window.

"No," he said, "it's too soon to get a car again."

"But you told me you had got part of that £1200 in hand and hoped to make up the rest very soon. What are you going to do with the money now?"

He glanced at her over his shoulder for an instant and then his mouth assumed a grim and obstinate look she knew too well.

"I may need the money," he said briefly. "And I'm not much in the mood at this moment for buying things."

Behind his back Lilian made a little grimace. Then in a tone of sisterly expostulation she said:

"You are worrying too much over this affair, Ned. You've done all you can—"

He interrupted her brusquely:

"And it's dashed little! What have I actually done? Nothing! One needs a better man than me."

"Well, there's your friend Silent Simon, and all the police—"

"A fat lot of good they are!" said Ned.

His sister looked a little surprised at his unusual shortness of temper. To her he was very rarely like this.

"You need a good day's shooting to take your mind off it for a little," she suggested.

He turned upon her hotly.

"Do you know the story that's going about, Lilian?"

"Sir Malcolm and the Farmond girl? Oh, rather," she nodded.

"Is that how it strikes you?"

Lilian Cromarty jumped. There was something very formidable in her brother's voice.

"My dear Ned, don't frighten me! Eat me if you like, but eat me quietly. I didn't say I believed the story."

"I hope not," he said in the same grim tone, "but do you mean to say it doesn't strike you as the damnedest slander ever spread?"

"Between myself I hadn't called it the 'damnedest' anything. But how do I know whether it's a slander?"

"You actually think it might conceivably be true?"

She shrugged her well-gowned shoulders.

"I never could stand Malcolm Cromarty—a conceited little jackanapes. He hasn't a penny and he was head over ears in debt."

It was his turn to start.

"Was he?"

"Oh, rather! Didn't you know? Owed money everywhere."

"But such a crime as that!"

"A man with ties and hair like his is capable of anything. You know quite well yourself he is a rotter."

"Anyhow you can't believe Cicely Farmond had anything to do with it?"

Again she shrugged her shoulders.

"My dear Ned, I'm not a detective. A pretty face is no proof a woman is a saint. I told you before that there was generally something in the blood in those cases."

As he stared at her, it seemed as though her words had indeed rushed back to his memory, and that they hit him hard.

"People don't say that, do they?" he asked in a low voice.

"Really, Ned, I don't know everything people say: but they are not likely to overlook much in such a case."

He stood for a moment in silence.

"She—I mean they've both got to be cleared!" he said, and strode out of the room.

It was on this same evening that Superintendent Sutherland was almost rewarded for his vigilance by having something distinctly suspicious to report. As it happened, it proved a disappointing incident, but it gave the superintendent something to think about.

He was going a few stations down the line to investigate a rumour of a suspicious person seen in that neighbourhood. It was a vague and improbable rumour and the superintendent was setting out merely as a matter of form, and to demonstrate his vigilance and almost abnormal sense of duty. Darkness had already fallen for an hour or two when he strode with dignified gait down the platform, exchanging a greeting with an acquaintance or two, till he came to the front carriage of the train. He threw open the door of the rear compartment, saw that it was empty, and was just going to enter when glancing over his shoulder he perceived his own cousin Mr. MacAlister upon the platform. Closing the door, he stepped down again and greeted him.

Mr. MacAlister hailed him with even more than usual friendliness, and after a few polite preliminaries drew him insidiously towards the far side of the platform. An intelligent, inveterate and persevering curiosity was Mr. MacAlister's dominating characteristic, and as soon as he had got his distinguished kinsman out of earshot of the herd, he inquired in a hushed voice:

"And what's doing aboot the murder noo, George?"

The superintendent pursed his lips and shook his head.

"Aye, man, yon's a proper puzzle," said he.

"But you'll have gotten a guid idea whae's din it by noo, George?" said Mr. MacAlister persuasively.

"Weel," admitted the superintendent, "we maybe have our notions, but there's no evidence yet, Robbie; that's the fair truth. As the fiscal says, there's no evidence."

"I'd like fine to hae a crack wi' you aboot it, George," sighed Mr. MacAlister. "I may tell you I've notions of ma own; no bad notions either."

"Well," said the superintendent, moving off, "I'd have enjoyed a crack myself if it wasna that I've got to be off by this train—"

"Man!" cried his kinsman, "I'm for off by her mysel'! Come on, we'll hae our crack yet."

The tickets had already been taken and the doors were closed as the two recrossed the platform.

"This carriage is empty," said the superintendent, and threw open the door of the same compartment he had almost entered before.

But it was not empty now. In one of the further corners sat a man wrapped in a dark coloured ulster. A black felt hat was drawn down over his eyes, and his muffled face was resting on his hand. So much the superintendent saw in the brief moment during which he stood at the open door, and it struck him at once that the man must be suffering from toothache. And then his cousin caught him by the arm and drew him back.

"Here, man, the carriage next door is empty!" cried he, and the superintendent closed the door and followed him.

It was scarcely more than a minute later when the whistle blew and they were off, and Mr. MacAlister took out his pipe and prepared himself to receive official confidences. But the miles went by, and though he plied his questions incessantly and skilfully, no confidences were forthcoming. The superintendent, in fact, had something else to think about. All at once he asked abruptly:

"Robbie, did ye see yon man next door sitting with his face in his hands?"

"Aye," said Mr. MacAlister, "I noticed the man."

"Did ye ken who he was?"

"No," said Mr. MacAlister, "I did not."

"Had ye seen him on the platform?"

"No," said Mr. MacAlister, "I had not."

"I didna see him myself," said the superintendent musingly. "It seems funny-like a man dressed like yon and with his face wrapped up too—and a man forbye that's a stranger to us both, coming along the platform and getting into that carriage, and me not noticing him. I'm not used not to notice people, Robbie."

"It's your business, George," said Mr. MacAlister, and then as he gazed at his cousin's thoughtful face, his own grew suddenly animated.

"You're not thinking he's to dae wi' the murder, are you!" he cried.

"I'm not sure what to think till I've had another look into yon carriage," said the superintendent cautiously.

"We're slowing doon the noo!" cried Mr. MacAlister, "God, George, I'll come and hae a look wi' you!"

The train was hardly in the platform before the superintendent was out, with Mr. MacAlister after him, and the door of the next compartment was open almost as soon as the train was at rest. Never had the superintendent been more vigilant; and never had his honest face looked blanker.

"God! It's empty!" he murmured.

"God save us!" murmured Mr. MacAlister, and then he was visited by an inspiration which struck his relative afterwards as one of the unhappiest he had ever suffered from. "This canna be the richt carriage!" he cried. "Come on, Geordie, let's hae a look in the ithers!"

By the time they had looked into all the compartments of the carriage, the guard was waving his flag and the two men climbed hurriedly in again. The brooding silence of the superintendent infected even Mr. MacAlister, and neither spoke for several minutes. Then the superintendent said bitterly:

"It was you hurrying me off to look in thae other carriages, Robbie!"

"What was?" inquired Mr. MacAlister a little nervously.

"I ought to have stopped and looked under the seats!"

Mr. MacAlister shook his head and declared firmly:

"There was naething under the seats. I could see that fine. And onyhow we can hae a look at the next stop."

"As if he'll be waiting for us, now he kens we're looking for him!"

"But there was naething there!" persisted Mr. MacAlister.

"Then what's come over the man? Here were we sitting next the platform. He can't have got out afore we started, or we'd have seen him. Folks don't disappear into the air! I'll try under the seats, though I doubt the man will have been up and out while we were wasting our time in yon other carriages."

At the next station they searched that mysterious compartment earnestly and thoroughly, but there was not a sign of the muffled stranger, under the seats or anywhere else. Again the superintendent was silent for a space, and then he said confidentially:

"I'm just wondering if it's worth while reporting the thing, Robbie. The fiscal might have a kin' of unpleasant way of looking at it. Besides, there's really naething to report. Anyhow I'll think it over. And that being the case, the less said the better. I can tell ye all that's known about the case, Robbie; knowing that you'll be discreet."

"Oh, you can trust me," said Mr. MacAlister earnestly,—"I'll no breathe a word o' yon man. Weel, now, you were saying you'd tell me the haill story."

By this judicious arrangement Mr. MacAlister got his money's worth of sensational disclosures, and the superintendent was able to use his discretion and think the incident over. He thought over it very hard and finally decided that he was demonstrating his vigilance quite sufficiently without mentioning the trifling mystery of the empty compartment.

In summer and autumn, visitors were not uncommon in this re-
mote countryside; mostly shooting or fishing people who rented
the country houses, raised the local prices, and were described by
the tradesmen as benefiting the county greatly. But in late autumn
and winter this fertilising stream ceased to flow, and when the
trains from the south crawled in, the porters and the boots from
the hotels resigned themselves to welcoming a merely commercial
form of traveller.

It was therefore with considerable pleasure and surprise that
they observed one afternoon an unmistakably sporting gentleman
descend from a first class compartment and survey them with a
condescending yet affable eye.

"Which is the best of these hotels?" he demanded with an amiable smile, as he surveyed through a single eyeglass the names on
the caps of the various boots.

His engaging air disarmed the enquiry of embarrassment, and
even when he finally selected the Kings Arms Hotel, the other boots
merely felt regret that they had not secured so promising a client.
His luggage confirmed the first favourable impression. It included
a gun case, a bag of golf clubs, and one or two handsome leather
articles. Evidently he meant to make more than a passing visit,
and as he strolled down the platform, his leisurely nonchalant air
and something even in the way in which he smoked his cigarette in
its amber holder, suggested a gentleman who, having arrived here,

was in no hurry to move on. On a luggage label the approving boots noted the name of "F. T. Carrington."

When he arrived at the Kings Arms, Mr. Carrington continued to produce favourable impressions. He was a young man, apparently a little over thirty, above middle height, with a round, ingenuous, very agreeable face, smooth fair hair, a little, neatly trimmed moustache, and a monocle that lent just the necessary touch of distinction to what might otherwise have been a too good-humoured physiognomy. His tweed suit was fashionably cut and of a distinctly sportive pattern, and he wore a pair of light spats. In short, there could be no mistaking him for anything but a gentleman of position and leisure with strong sporting proclivities, and his manner amply confirmed this. It was in fact almost indolent in its leisurely ease.

Miss Peterkin, the capable manageress of the Kings Arms, was at first disposed to think Mr. Carrington a trifle too superior, and, as she termed it, "la-de-da," but a very few minutes' conversation with the gentleman completely reassured her. He was so polite and so good-humoured and so ready to be pleased with everything he saw and anything she suggested, that they became firm friends within ten minutes of his arrival, and after Mr. Carrington had disposed of his luggage in the bedroom and private sitting room which he engaged, and partaken of a little dinner, she found herself welcoming him into her own sitting room where a few choice spirits nightly congregated.

It is true that these spirits, though choice, were hardly of what she called Mr. Carrington's "class," but then in all her experience she had never met a gentleman of such fashion and such a superior air, who adapted himself so charmingly to any society. In fact, "charming" was the very adjective for him, she decided.

About his own business he was perfectly frank. He had heard of the sporting possibilities of the county and had come to look out for a bit of fishing or shooting; preferably fishing, for it seemed he was an enthusiastic angler. Of course, it was too late in the season for any fishing this year, but he was looking ahead as he preferred to see things for himself instead of trusting to an agent's description. He had brought his gun just on the chance of getting a day somewhere, and his club in case there happened to be a golf links. In short, he seemed evidently to be a young man of means who lived for sport; and what other question could one ask about such a satisfactory type of visitor? Absolutely none, in Miss Peterkin's opinion.

As a matter of fact, she found very early in the evening, and continued to find thereafter, that the most engaging feature of Mr. Carrington's character was the interest he took in other people's business, so that the conversation very quickly strayed away from his own concerns—and remained away. It was not that he showed any undue curiosity; far from it. He was simply so sympathetic and such a good listener and put questions that showed he was following everything you said to him in a way that really very few people did. And, moreover, in spite of his engaging frankness, there was an indefinable air of discretion about him that made one feel safe to tell him practically everything. She herself told him the sad story of her brother in Australia (a tale which, as a rule, she told only to her special intimates) before he had been in her room half an hour.

But with the arrival of three or four choice spirits, the conversation became more general, and it was naturally not long before it turned on the greatest local sensation and mystery within the memory of man—the Cromarty murder. Mr. Carrington's surprise was extreme when he realised that he was actually in the county where the tragedy had occurred, within a very few miles of the actual spot, in fact. Of course, he had read about it in the papers, but only cursorily, it seemed, and he had no idea he was coming into the identical district that had acquired such a sinister notoriety.

"By Jove!" he exclaimed more than once when he had made this discovery, "I say, how interesting!"

"Oh," said Miss Peterkin with becoming pride, "we are getting quite famous, I can assure you, Mr. Carrington."

"Rather so!" cried he, "I've read quite a lot about this Carnegie case—"

"Cromarty," corrected one of the spirits.

"Cromarty, of course, I mean! I'm rather an ass at names, I'm afraid." The young man smiled brightly and all the spirits sympathised. "Oh yes, I've seen it reported in the papers. And now to think here I am in the middle of it, by George! How awfully interesting! I say, Miss Peterkin, what about these gentlemen having another wee droppie with me, all round, just to celebrate the occasion?"

With such an appreciative and hospitable audience, Miss Peterkin and the choice spirits spent a long and delightful evening in retailing every known circumstance of the drama, and several that were certainly unknown to the authorities. He was vastly interested, though naturally very shocked, to hear who was commonly suspected of the crime.

"Do you mean to say his own heir—and a young girl like that—? By Jove, I say, how dreadful!" he exclaimed, and, in fact, he would hardly believe such a thing conceivable until all the choice spirits in turn had assured him that there was practically no doubt about it.

The energetic part played by Mr. Simon Rattar in unravelling the dark skein, or at least in trying to, was naturally described at some length, and Mr. Carrington showed his usual sympathetic, and, one might almost say, entranced appreciation of the many facts told him concerning that local celebrity.

Finally Miss Peterkin insisted on getting out the back numbers of the local paper giving the full details of the case, and with many thanks he took these off to read before he went to bed.

"But mind you don't give yourself the creeps and keep yourself from going to sleep, Mr. Carrington!" she warned him with the last words.

"By Jove, that's an awful thought!" he exclaimed, and then his eyes twinkled. "Send me up another whisky and soda to cure the creeps!" said he.

Miss Peterkin thought he was quite one of the pleasantest, and promised to be one of the most profitable gentlemen she had met for a very long time.

Next morning he assured her he had kept the creeps at bay sufficiently to enjoy an excellent night's sleep in a bed that did the management credit. In fact, he had thoroughly enjoyed reading the mystery and had even begun to feel some curiosity to see the scene of the tragedy. He proposed to have a few walks and drives through the neighbouring country, he said, looking at its streams and lochs with an eye to sporting possibilities, and it would be interesting to be able to recognise Keldale House if he chanced to pass near it.

Miss Peterkin told him which road led to Keldale and how the house might be recognised, and suggested that he should walk out that way this very morning. He seemed a little doubtful; spoke of his movements as things that depended very much on the whim of the moment, just as such an easy-going young man would be apt to do, and rather indicated that a shorter walk would suit him better that morning.

And then a few minutes later she saw him saunter past her window, wearing a light gray felt hat at a graceful angle and apparently taking a sympathetic interest in a small boy trying to mount a bicycle.

21

MR. CARRINGTON'S WALK

Mr. Carrington's easy saunter lasted till he had turned out of the street on which the Kings Arms stood, when it passed into an easy walk. Though he had seemed, on the whole, disinclined to go in the Keldale direction that morning, nevertheless he continued to head that way till at last he was on the high road with the little town behind him; and then his pace altered again. He stepped out now like the sportsman he was, and was doing a good four miles an hour by the time he was out of sight of the last houses.

For a man who had come out to gather ideas as to the sporting possibilities of the country, Mr. Carrington seemed to pay singularly little attention to his surroundings. He appeared, in fact, to be thinking about something else all the time, and the first sign of interest he showed in anything outside his thoughts was when he found himself within sight of the lodge gates of Keldale House, with the avenue sweeping away from the road towards the roofs and chimneys amid the trees. At the sight of this he stopped, and leaning over the low wall at the roadside gazed with much interest at the scene of the tragedy he had heard so much of last night. The choice spirits, had they been there to see, would have been gratified to find that their graphic narratives had sent this indolent looking gentleman to view the spot so swiftly.

From the house and grounds his eye travelled back to the road and then surveyed the surrounding country very attentively. He even stood on top of the wall to get a wider view; and then all of a sudden he jumped down again and adopted the reverse procedure, bending now so that little more than his head appeared above the wall. And the reason for this change of plan appeared to be a figure which had emerged from the trees and began to move along a path between the fields.

Mr. Carrington studied this figure with concentrated attention, and as it drew nearer and became more distinct, a light leapt into his eye that gave him a somewhat different expression from any his acquaintances of last night had observed. He saw that the path followed a small stream and ran at an angle to the high road, joining it at last at a point some little distance back towards the town. He looked quickly up and down the road. Not a soul was in sight to see his next very curious performance. The leisurely Mr. Carrington crossed to the further side, where he was invisible from the path, and then set out to run at a rapid pace till he reached the junction of path and road. And then he turned down the path.

But now his bearing altered again in a very extraordinary way. His gait fell once more to a saunter and his angling enthusiasm seemed suddenly to have returned, for he frequently studied the burn as he strolled along, and there was no sign of any thoughtfulness on his ingenuous countenance. There were a few willows beside the path, and the path itself meandered, and this was doubtless the reason why he appeared entirely unconscious of the approach of another foot passenger till they were within a few yards of one another. And then Mr. Carrington stopped suddenly, seemed to hesitate, pulled out his watch and glanced at it, and then with an apologetic air raised his hat.

The other foot passenger was face to face with him now, a slim figure in black, with a sweet, serious face.

"Excuse me," said Mr. Carrington, "but can you tell me where this path leads?"

He was so polite and so evidently anxious to give no offence, and his face was such a certificate to his amiable character that the girl stopped too and answered without hesitation:

"It leads to Keldale House."

"Keldale House?" he repeated, and then the idea seemed to arouse associations. "By Jove!" he exclaimed. "Really? I'm an utter stranger here, but isn't that the place where the murder took place?"

Had Mr. Carrington been a really observant man, one would think he would have noticed the sudden change of expression in the girl's face—as if he had aroused painful thoughts. He did seem to look at her for an instant as he asked the question, but then turned his gaze towards the distant glimpse of the house.

"Yes," she murmured and looked as though she wanted to pass on; but Mr. Carrington seemed so excited by his discovery that he never noticed this and still stood right in her path.

"How very interesting!" he murmured. "By Jove, how very interesting!" And then with the air of passing on a still more interesting piece of news, he said suddenly, "I hear they have arrested Sir Malcolm Cromarty."

This time he kept his monocle full on her.

"Arrested him!" she cried. "What for?"

This question, put with the most palpable wonder, seemed to disconcert Mr. Carrington considerably. He even hesitated in a very unusual way for him.

"For—for the murder, of course."

Her eyes opened very wide.

"For Sir Reginald's murder? How ridiculous!"

Again Mr. Carrington seemed a little disconcerted.

"Er—why is it ridiculous?" he asked. "Of course, I—I know nothing about the gentleman."

"Evidently!" she agreed with reproach in her eyes. "If Sir Malcolm really has been arrested, it can only have been for something quite silly. He couldn't commit a murder!"

The fact that this tribute to the baronet's innocence was not wholly devoid of a flavour of criticism seemed to strike Mr. Carrington, for his eye twinkled for an instant.

"You are acquainted with him then?" said he.

"I am staying at Keldale; in fact, I am a relation."

There was no doubt of her intention to rebuke the too garrulous gentleman by this information, and it succeeded completely. He passed at once to the extreme of apology.

"Oh! I beg your pardon!" he exclaimed. "I had no idea. Really, I hope you will accept my apologies, Miss—er—Cromarty."

"Miss Farmond," she corrected.

"Miss Farmond, I mean. It was frightfully tactless of me!"

He said it so nicely and looked so innocently guilty and so contrite, that her look lost its touch of indignation.

"I still can't understand what you mean about Sir Malcolm being arrested," she said. "How did you hear?"

"Oh, I was very likely misinformed. An old fellow at the hotel last night was saying so."

Her eye began to grow indignant again.

"What old fellow?"

"Red hair, shaky knees, bit of a stammer, answers to the name of Sandy, I believe."

"Old Sandy Donaldson!" she exclaimed. "That drunken old thing! He was simply talking nonsense as usual!"

"He seemed a little in liquor," he admitted, "but you see I am a mere stranger. I didn't realise what a loose authority I quoted. There is nothing in the report, I am certain. And this path leads only to Keldale House? Thank you very much. Good morning!"

How Mr. Carrington had obtained this erroneous information from a person whose back he had merely seen for a couple of minutes the night before, as the reprobate in question was being ejected from the Kings Arms, he did not stop to explain. In fact, at this point he showed no inclination to continue the conversation, but bowing very politely, continued his stroll.

But the effect of the conversation on him remained, and a very marked effect it appeared to be. He took no interest in the burn any longer, but paced slowly on, his eyes sometimes on the path and sometimes staring upwards at the Heavens. So far as his face revealed his sensations, they seemed to be compounded of surprise and perplexity. Several times he shook his head as though some very baffling point had cropped up in his thoughts, and once he murmured:

"I'm damned!"

When the path reached the policies of the house, he stopped and seemed to take some interest in his surroundings once more. For a moment it was clear that he was tempted to enter the plantations, and then he shook his head and turned back.

All the way home he remained immersed in thought and only recovered his nonchalant air as he entered the door of the Kings Arms. He was the same easy-going, smiling young man of fashion as he passed the time of day with Miss Peterkin; but when he had shut the door of his private sitting room and dropped into an easy chair over the fire, he again became so absorbed in thought that he had to be reminded that the hour of luncheon had passed.

Thought seemed to vanish during lunch, but when he had retired to his room again, it returned for another half hour. At the end of that time he apparently came to a decision, and jumping up briskly, repaired to the manageress' room. And when Miss Peterkin was taken into his confidence, it appeared that the whole problem had merely concerned the question of taking either a shooting or a fishing for next season.

"I have been thinking," said he, "that my best plan will perhaps be to call upon Mr. Simon Rattar and see whether he knows of anything to let. I gather that he is agent for several estates in the county. What do you advise?"

Miss Peterkin decidedly advised this course, so a few minutes later Mr. Carrington strolled off towards the lawyer's office.

22

MR. CARRINGTON AND THE FISCAL

The card handed in to Mr. Simon Rattar contained merely the name "Mr. F. T. Carrington" and the address "Sports Club." Simon gazed at it cautiously and in silence for the better part of a minute, and when he glanced up at his head clerk to tell him that Mr. Carrington might be admitted, Mr. Ison was struck by the curious glint in his eye. It seemed to him to indicate that the fiscal was very wide awake at that moment; it struck him also that Mr. Rattar was not altogether surprised by the appearance of this visitor.

The agreeable stranger began by explaining very frankly that he thought of renting a place for next season where he could secure good fishing and a little shooting, and wondered if any of the properties Mr. Rattar was agent for would suit him. Simon grunted and waited for this overture to develop.

"What about Keldale House?" the sporting visitor suggested. "That's the place where the murder was committed, isn't it?" and then he laughed. "Your eye betrays you, Mr. Rattar!" said he.

The lawyer seemed to start ever so slightly.

"Indeed?" he murmured.

"Look here," said Carrington with a candid smile, "let's put our cards on the table. You know my business?"

"Are you a detective?" asked the lawyer.

Mr. Carrington smiled and nodded.

"I am; or rather I prefer to call myself a private enquiry agent. People expect so much of a detective, don't they?"

Simon grunted, but made no other comment.

"In a case like this," continued Carrington, "when one is called in weeks too late and the household broom and scrubbing brush and garden rake have removed most of the possible clues, and witnesses' recollections have developed into picturesque legends, it is better to rouse as few expectations as possible, since it is probably impossible to find anything out. However, in the capacity of a mere enquiry agent I have come to pick up anything I can. May I smoke?"

He asked in his usual easy-going voice and with his usual candid smile, and then his eye was arrested by an inscription printed in capital letters, and hung in a handsome frame upon the office wall. It ran:

"MY THREE RULES OF LIFE,
1. I DO NOT SMOKE.
2. I LAY BY A THIRD OF MY INCOME.
3. I NEVER RIDE WHEN I CAN WALK."

Beneath these precepts appeared the lithographed signature of an eminent philanthropist, but it seemed reasonable to assume that they also formed the guiding maxims of Mr. Simon Rattar.

His visitor politely apologised for his question.

"I had not noticed this warning," said he.

"Smoke if you like. My clients sometimes do. I don't myself," said the lawyer.

His visitor thanked him, placed a cigarette in his amber holder, lit it, and let his eyes follow the smoke upwards.

Mr. Rattar, on his part, seemed in his closest, most taciturn humour. His grunt and his nod had, in fact, seldom formed a greater proportion of his conversation. He made no further comment at all now, but waited in silence for his visitor to proceed.

"Well," resumed Carrington, "the simple facts of the case are these. I have been engaged through a certain firm of London lawyers, whose name I am not permitted to mention, on behalf of a person whose name I don't know."

At this a flash of keen interest showed for an instant in Simon's eye; and then it became as cold as ever again.

"Indeed?" said he.

"I am allowed to incur expense," continued the other, "up to a certain figure, which is so handsome that it gives me practically a free hand, so far as that is concerned. On the other hand, the arrangement entails certain difficulties which I daresay you, Mr. Rattar, as a lawyer, and especially as a Procurator Fiscal accustomed to investigate cases of crime, will readily understand."

"Quite so; quite so," agreed Mr. Rattar, who seemed to be distinctly relaxing already from his guarded attitude.

"I arrived last night, put up at the Kings Arms—where I gathered beforehand that the local gossip could best be collected, and in the course of the evening I collected enough to hang at least two people; and in the course of a few more evenings I shall probably have enough to hang half a dozen—if one can believe, say, a twentieth of what one hears. This morning I strolled out to Keldale House and had a look at it from the road, and I learned that it was a large mansion standing among trees. That's all I have been able to do so far."

"Nothing more than that?"

Mr. Carrington seemed to have a singularly short memory.

"I think that's the lot," said he. "And what is more, it seems to me the sum total of all I am likely to do without a little assistance from somebody in possession of rather more authentic facts than my friend Miss Peterkin and her visitors."

"I quite understand," said the lawyer; and it was plain that his interest was now thoroughly enlisted.

"Well," continued Mr. Carrington, "I thought things over, and rightly or wrongly, I came to this decision. My employer, whoever he is, has made it an absolute condition that his name is not to be known. His reasons may have been the best imaginable, but it obviously made it impossible for me to get any information out of *him*. For my own reasons I always prefer to make my enquiries in these cases in the guise of an unsuspected outsider, whenever it is possible; and it happens to be particularly possible in this case, since nobody here knows me from Adam. But I must get facts—as distinguished from the Kings Arms' gossip, and how was I to get them without giving myself away? That was the problem, and I soon realised that it was insoluble. I saw I must confide in somebody, and so I came to the decision to confide in you."

Simon nodded and made a sound that seemed to indicate distinctly his opinion that Mr. Carrington had come to a sensible decision.

"You were the obvious person for several reasons," resumed Carrington. "In the first place you could pretty safely be regarded as above suspicion yourself—if you will pardon my associating even the word suspicion with a Procurator Fiscal." He smiled his most agreeable smile and the Fiscal allowed his features to relax sympathetically. "In the second place you know more about the case than anybody else. And in the third place, I gather that you are—if I may say so, a gentleman of unusual discretion."

Again he smiled pleasantly, and again Mr. Rattar's features relaxed.

"Finally," added Carrington, "I thought it long odds that you were either actually my employer or acting for him, and therefore I should be giving nothing away by telling you my business. And when I mentioned Keldale House and the murder I saw that I was right!"

He laughed, and Simon permitted himself to smile. Yet his answer was as cautious as ever.

"Well, Mr. Carrington?" said he.

"Well," said Carrington, "if you actually are my employer and we both lay our cards on the table, there's much to be gained, and—if I may say so—really nothing to be lost. I won't give you away if you won't give me."

The lawyer's nod seemed to imply emphatic assent, and the other went on:

"I'll keep you informed of everything I'm doing and anything I may happen to discover, and you can give me very valuable information as to what precisely is known already. Otherwise, of course, one could hardly exchange confidences so freely. Frankly then, you engaged me to come down here?"

Even then Simon's caution seemed to linger for an instant. The next he answered briefly but decidedly:

"Yes."

"Very well, now to business. I got a certain amount of literature on the case before I left town, and Miss Peterkin gave me some
very valuable additions in the shape of the accounts in the local
papers. Are there any facts known to you or the police beyond those
I have read?"

Simon considered the question and then shook his head.

"None that I can think of, and I fear the local police will be
able to add no information that can assist you."

"They are the usual not too intelligent country bobbies, I suppose?"

"Quite so," said Simon.

"In that case," asked Mr. Carrington, still in his easy voice, but
with a quick turn of his eyeglass towards the lawyer, "why was no
outside assistance called in at once?"

For a moment Simon Rattar's satisfaction with his visitor
seemed to be diminished. He seemed, in fact, a little disconcerted,
and his reply again became little more than a grunt.

"Quite satisfied with them," seemed to be the reading of his
answer.

"Well," said Carrington, "no doubt you knew best, Mr. Rattar."

His eyes thoughtfully followed the smoke of his cigarette upwards for a moment, and then he said:

"That being so, my first step had better be to visit Keldale House
and see whether it is still possible to find any small point the local
professionals have overlooked."

Mr. Rattar seemed to disapprove of this.

"Nothing to discover," said he. "And they will know what you
have come about."

Mr. Carrington smiled.

"I think, Mr. Rattar, that, on the whole, my appearance pro-
vokes no great amount of suspicion."

"Your appearance, no," admitted Simon, "but—"

"Well, if I go to Keldale armed with a card of introduction from
you, to make enquiry about the shootings, I think I can undertake
to turn the conversation on to other matters without exciting suspicion."

"Conversation with whom?" enquired the lawyer sceptically.

"I had thought of Mr. Bisset, the butler."

"Oh—" began Mr. Rattar with a note of surprise, and then pulled himself up.

"Yes," smiled Mr. Carrington, "I have picked up a little about the household. My friends of last night were exceedingly communicative—very gossipy indeed. I rather gather that omniscience is Mr. Bisset's foible, and that he is not averse from conversation."

The look in Simon's eye seemed to indicate that his respect for this easy-going young man was increasing; though whether his liking for him was also increased thereby was not so manifest. His reply was again a mere grunt.

"Well, that can easily be arranged," said Carrington, "and it is obviously the first thing to do."

He blew a ring of smoke from his lips, skilfully sent a second ring in chase of it, and then turning his monocle again on the lawyer, enquired (though not in a tone that seemed to indicate any very acute interest in the question):

"Who do you think yourself murdered Sir Reginald Cromarty?"

"Well," said Mr. Rattar deliberately, "I think myself that the actual evidence is very slight and extremely inclusive."

"You mean the direct evidence afforded by the unfastened window, position of the body, table said to have been overturned, and so forth?"

"Exactly. That evidence is slight, but so far as it goes it seems to me to point to entry by the door and to the man having been in the house for some little time previously."

"Well?" said Carrington in an encouraging voice.

"So much for the direct evidence. I may be wrong, but that is my decided opinion. No bad characters are known to the police to have been in the county at that time, and there was no robbery."

"Apparently confirming the direct evidence?"

"Decidedly confirming it—or so it seems to me."

"Then you think there is something in the popular theory that the present baronet and Miss Farmond were the guilty parties?"

Simon was silent for a moment, but his face was unusually expressive.

"I fear it looks like it."

"An unpleasant conclusion for you to come to," observed Mr. Carrington. "You are the family lawyer, I understand."

"Very unpleasant," Mr. Rattar agreed. "But, of course, there is no absolute proof."

"Naturally; or they'd have been arrested by now. What sort of a fellow is Sir Malcolm?"

"My own experience of him," said the lawyer drily, "is chiefly confined to his visits to my office to borrow money of me."

"Indeed?" said Carrington with interest. "That sort of fellow, is he? He writes, I understand."

Simon nodded.

"Any other known vices?"

"I know little about his vices except that they cost him considerably more than he could possibly have paid, had it not been for Sir Reginald's death."

"So the motive is plain enough. Any evidence against him?"

Simon pursed his lips and became exceedingly grave.

"When questioned next morning by the superintendent of police and myself, he led us to understand that he had retired to bed early and was in no position to hear or notice anything. I have since found that he was in the habit of sitting up late."

"'In the habit,'" repeated Carrington quickly. "But you don't suggest he sat up that night in particular?"

"Undoubtedly he sat up that night."

"But merely as he always did?"

"He might have been waiting for his chance on the previous nights."

Carrington smoked thoughtfully for a moment and then asked:

"But there is no evidence that he left his room or was heard moving about that night, is there?"

"There is not yet any positive evidence. But he was obviously in a position to do so."

"Was his room near or over the library?"

"N—no," said the fiscal, and there seemed to be a hint of reluctance in his voice.

Carrington glanced at him quickly and then gazed up at the ceiling.

"What sort of a girl is Miss Farmond?" he enquired next.

"She is the illegitimate daughter of a brother of the late Sir Reginald's."

Carrington nodded.

"So I gathered from the local gossips. But that fact is hardly against her, is it?"

"Why not?"

Carrington looked a little surprised.

"Girls don't generally murder their uncles for choice, in my own experience; especially if they are also their benefactors."

"This was hardly the usual relationship," said the lawyer with a touch of significance.

"Do you suggest that the irregularity is apt to breed crime?"

Simon's grunt seemed to signify considerable doubt as to the morals of the type of relative.

"But what sort of girl is she otherwise?"

"I should call Miss Farmond the insinuating type. A young man like yourself would probably find her very attractive—at first anyhow."

Mr. Carrington seemed to ponder for a moment on this suggestive description of Miss Farmond's allurements. And then he asked:

"Is it the case that she is engaged to Sir Malcolm?"

"Certainly."

"You are sure?"

Something in his voice seemed to make the lawyer reflect.

"Is it called in question?" he asked.

Carrington shook his head.

"By nobody who has spoken to me on the subject. But I understand that it has not yet been announced."

"No," said Simon. "It was a secret engagement; and marriage would have been impossible while Sir Reginald lived."

"So there we get the motive on her part. And you yourself, Mr. Rattar, *know* both these young people, and you believe that this accusation against them is probably well founded?"

"I believe, Mr. Carrington, that there is no proof and probably never will be any; but all the evidence, positive and negative, together with the question of motive, points to nobody else. What alternative is possible?"

"That is the difficulty, so far," agreed Carrington, but his thoughts at the moment seemed to be following his smoke rings up towards the ceiling. For a few moments he was silent, and then he asked:

"What other people benefited by the will and to what extent?"

The lawyer went to his safe, brought out the will, and read through the legacies to the servants, mentioning that the chauffeur and gardener were excluded by circumstances from suspicion.

"That leaves Mr. Bisset," observed Carrington. "Well, I shall be seeing him to-morrow. Any other legatees who might conceivably have committed the crime?"

Simon looked serious and spoke with a little reluctance that he seemed to make no effort to conceal.

"There is a relative of the family, a Mr. Cromarty of Stanesland, who certainly benefited considerably by the will and who certainly lives in the neighbourhood—if one once admitted the possibility of the crime being committed by some one outside the house. And I admit that it is a possibility."

"Ah!" said Carrington. "I heard about him last night, but so far suspicion certainly hasn't fastened on him. What sort of a fellow is he?"

"He has lived the greater part of his life in the wilder parts of America—rather what one might call a rough and ready customer."

It was apparent that Mr. Carrington, for all his easy-going air, was extremely interested.

"This is quite interesting!" he murmured. "To what extent did he benefit by the will?"

"£1,200."

"£1,200!" Carrington repeated the words with an odd intonation and stared very hard at the lawyer. There was no doubt that his interest was highly excited now, and yet it seemed to be rather a different quality of interest this time.

"A considerable sum," said Simon.

"That is the only point about it which strikes you?"

Simon was manifestly puzzled.

"What else?" he enquired.

"No coincidence occurs to you?"

The lawyer's puzzled look remained, and the next instant Carrington broke into a hearty laugh.

"I beg your pardon, Mr. Rattar," he cried. "What an owl I am! I have just been dealing lately with a case where that sum of money was involved, and for the moment I mixed the two up together!" He laughed again, and then resuming his businesslike air, asked: "Now, what else about this Mr. Cromarty? You say he is a relation. Near or distant?"

"Oh, quite distant. Another branch altogether."

"Younger branch, I presume."

"Poorer but not younger. He is said to be the head of the family."

"Really!" exclaimed Mr. Carrington, and this information seemed to have set him thinking again. "He is the head of the family, and I hear he took up the case with some energy."

Simon's grunt seemed to be critical.

"He got in our way," he said.

"Got in your way, did he?"

Carrington was silent for a few moments, and then said:

"Well I am afraid I have taken up a great deal of your time. May I have a line of introduction to Mr. Bisset before I go?"

While the line was being written he walked over to the fire and cleared the stump of his last cigarette out of the holder. This operation was very deliberately performed, and through it his eyes seemed scarcely to note what his hands were doing.

He put the note in his pocket, shook hands, and then, just as he was going, he said:

"I want to understand the lie of the land as exactly as possible. Your own attitude, so far has been, I take it—no proof, therefore no arrest; but a nasty family scandal left festering, so you decided to call me in. Now, I want to know this—is there anybody else in the neighbourhood who knows that I have been sent for?"

Mr. Rattar replied with even more than his usual deliberation, and after what is said by foreigners to be the national habit, his reply consisted of another question.

"You say that your employer made a particular point of having his identity concealed?"

"Yes, a particular point."

"Doesn't that answer your question, Mr. Carrington?"

"No," said Carrington, "not in the least. I am asking now whether there is any other employer in this neighbourhood besides yourself. And I may say that I ask for the very good reason that it might be awkward for me if there were and I didn't know him, while if I did know him, I could consult with him if it happened to be advisable. Is there any one?"

He seemed to hang on the lawyer's answer, and Simon to dislike making the answer.

Yet when he did make it, it was quite emphatic.

"No," he replied.

"That's all right then," said Mr. Carrington with his brightest smile. "Good afternoon, Mr. Rattar."

The smile faded from his ingenuous face the moment the door had closed behind him, and it was a very thoughtful Mr. Carrington who slowly went downstairs and strolled along the pavement. If his morning's interview had puzzled him, his afternoon's interview seemed to have baffled him completely. He even forgot to relapse into the thoughtless young sportsman when he entered the hotel, and his friend the manageress, after eyeing him with great surprise, cried archly:

"A penny for your thoughts, Mr. Carrington! About shooting or fishing, I'm sure!"

Mr. Carrington recovered his pleasant spirits instantly.

"Quite right," said he. "I was thinking about fishing—in very deep waters."

MR. BISSET'S ASSISTANT

At eleven o'clock next morning a motor car drove up to Keldale House and an exceedingly affable and pleasing stranger delivered a note from Mr. Simon Rattar to Mr. James Bisset. Even without an introduction, Mr. Carrington would have been welcome, for though Mr. Bisset's sway over Keldale House was by this time almost despotic, he had begun to find that despotism has its lonely side, and to miss "the gentry." With an introduction, Mr. Carrington quickly discovered that Mr. Bisset and the mansion he supervised were alike entirely at his disposal.

The preliminary discussion on the sporting possibilities of the estate and the probability of its being let next season impressed Mr. Bisset very favourably indeed with his visitor; and then when the conversation had passed very naturally to the late tragedy in the house, he was still further delighted to find that Mr. Carrington not only shared his own detective enthusiasm, but was vastly interested in his views on this particular mystery.

"Come along here, sir," said he, "we can just have a look at the library and I'll explain to you the principles of the thing."

"I'd like to see the actual scene of the crime immensely!" cried Mr. Carrington eagerly. "You are sure that Lady Cromarty won't object?"

"Not her," said Bisset. "She's never in this part of the house now. She'll be none the wiser anyhow."

This argument seemed to assure Mr. Carrington completely, and they went along to the library.

"Now," began Bisset, "I'll just explain to you the haill situation. Here where I'm laying this sofie cushion was the corp. Here where I'm standing the now was the wee table, and yon's the table itself."

To the disquisition that followed, Mr. Carrington listened with the most intelligent air. Bisset had by this time evolved quite a number of new theories, but the one feature common to them all was the hypothesis that the murderer must have come in by the window and was certainly not an inmate of the household. His visitor said little till he had finished, and then he remarked:

"Well, Bisset, you don't seem to put much faith in the current theory, I see."

"Meaning that Sir Malcolm and Miss Farmond were concerned?" said Bisset indignantly. "That's just the ignorance of the uneducated masses, sir! The thing's physically impossible, as I've just been demonstrating!"

Carrington smiled and gently shook his head.

"I don't know much about these things," said he, "but I'm afraid I can't see the physical impossibility. It was very easy for any one in the house to come downstairs and open that door, and if Sir Reginald knew him, it would account for his silence and the absence of any kind of a struggle."

"But yon table and the windie being unfastened! And the mud I picked up myself—and the hearth brush!"

"They scarcely make it impossible," said Carrington.

"Well, sir," demanded the butler, "what's your own theory?"

Carrington said nothing for several minutes. He strolled up and down the room, looked at the table and the window, and at last asked:

"Do you remember quite distinctly what Sir Reginald looked like when you found him—the position of the body—condition of the clothes—and everything else?"

"I see him lying there every night o' my life, just as plain as I see you now!"

"The feet were towards the door, just as though he had been facing the door when he was struck down?"

"Aye, but then my view is the body was moved—"

He was interrupted by a curious performance on Mr. Carrington's part. His visitor was in fact stretching himself out on the floor on the spot where Sir Reginald was found.

"He lay like this?" he asked.

"Aye, practically just like that, sir."

"Now, Bisset," said the recumbent visitor, "just have a very good look at me and tell me if you notice any difference between me and the body of Sir Reginald."

Bisset looked for a few seconds and then exclaimed:

"Your clothes are no alike! The master's coat was kind of pulled up like about his shoulders and neck. Oh, and I mind now the tag at the back for hanging it up was broken and sticking out."

Carrington sprang to his feet with a gleam in his eye.

"The tag was not broken before he put on the coat?"

"It certainly was not that! But what's your deduction, sir?"

Carrington smiled at him.

"What do you think yourself, Bisset? You saw how I threw myself down quite carelessly and yet my coat wasn't pulled up like that."

"God, sir!" cried the butler. "You mean the corp had been pulled along the floor by the shoulders!"

Carrington nodded.

"Then he had been killed near the windie!"

"Not too fast, not too fast!" smiled Carrington. "Your own first statement which I happened to read in a back number of the newspaper the other day said that the windows were all fastened when Sir Reginald came into the room."

"Ah, but I've been altering my opinion on that point, sir."

Carrington shook his head.

"I'm afraid because a fastened window doesn't suit your theory."

"But the master might have opened it to him, thinking it was some one he knew."

"Sounds improbable," said Carrington thoughtfully.

"But not just absolutely impossible."

"No," said Carrington, still very thoughtfully, "not impossible."

"Sir Reginald might never have seen it was a stranger till the man was fairly inside."

Carrington smiled and shook his head.

"Thin, Bisset; very thin. Why need the man have been a stranger at all?"

Bisset's face fell.

"But surely you're not believing yon story that it was Sir Malcolm and Miss Farmond after a'?"

His visitor stood absolutely silent for a full minute. Then he seemed suddenly to banish the line of thought he was following.

"Is it quite certain that those two are engaged?" he asked.

Bisset's face showed his surprise at the question.

"They all say so," said he.

"Have either of them admitted it?"

"No, sir."

"Why don't they acknowledge it now and get married?"

"They say it's because they daurna for fear of the scandal."

"'They' say again!" commented Carrington. "But, look here, Bisset, you have been in the house all the time. Did you think they were engaged?"

"Honestly, sir, I did not. There's nae doubt Sir Malcolm was sweet on the young lady, but deil a sign of sweetness on him did I ever see in her!"

"Do they correspond now?"

Bisset shook his head.

"Hardly at a'. But of course folks just say they are feared to now."

"Has anybody asked either of them if they are—or ever were—engaged?"

"No, sir. But if they denied it now, folks would just say the same thing."

"Yes. I see—naturally. Lady Cromarty believes it and is keeping Miss Farmond under her eye, the gossips tell me. Is that so?"

"Oh, that's true right enough, sir."

"Who told Lady Cromarty?"

"That I do not know, sir."

Again the visitor seemed to be thinking, and again to cast his thoughts aside and take up a new aspect of the case.

"Supposing," he suggested, "we were to draw the curtains and light these candles for a few minutes? It might help us to realise the whole thing."

This suggestion pleased Mr. Bisset greatly and in a minute or two the candles were lit and the curtains drawn.

"Put the table where it stood," said Carrington. "Now which was Sir Reginald's chair? This?"

He sat in it and looked slowly round the darkened, candle-lit library.

"Now," said he, "suppose I was Sir Reginald, and there came a tap at that window, what would I do?"

"If you were the master, sir, you'd go straight to the windie to see who it was."

"I wouldn't get in a funk and ring the bell?"

"No fears!" said Bisset confidently.

"And any one who knew Sir Reginald at all well could count on his not giving the alarm then if they tapped at the window?"

"They could that."

Carrington looked attentively towards the window.

"Those curtains hang close against the window, I see," he observed. "A very slight gap in them would enable any one to get a good view of the room, if the blinds were not down. Were the blinds down that night?"

Bisset slapped his knee.

"The middle blind wasn't working!" he cried. "What a fool I've been not to think on the extraordinar' significance of that fac'! My, the deductions to be drawn! You've made it quite clear now, sir. The man tappit at that windie—"

"Steady, steady!" said Carrington, smiling and yet seriously. "Don't you go announcing that theory! If there's anything in it— mum's the word! But mind you, Bisset, it's only a bare possibility. There's no good evidence against the door theory yet."

"Not the table being cowpit and the body moved?"

"They might be explained."

He was thoughtful for a moment and then said deliberately:

"I want—I mean you want certain evidence to exclude the door theory. Without that, the window theory remains a guess. Sir Malcolm is in London, I understand?"

"Yes, sir."

"Likely to be coming north soon?"

"No word of it, sir."

Mr. Carrington reflected for a moment and then rose and went towards the window.

"We can draw back the curtains now," said he.

He drew them as he spoke and on the instant stepped involuntarily back and down went the small table. Miss Cicely Farmond was standing just outside, evidently arrested by the drawn curtains. Her eyes opened very wide indeed at the sight of Mr. Carrington suddenly revealed. Her lips parted for an instant as though she would cry out, and then she hurried away.

Mr. Carrington seemed more upset by this incident than one would expect from such a composed, easy-going young man.

"What will they think of me!" he exclaimed. "You must be sure to tell Miss Farmond—and Lady Cromarty too if she hears of this—that I came solely to enquire about the shootings and not to poke my nose into their library! Make that very explicit, Bisset."

Even though assured by Bisset that the young lady was the most amiable person imaginable, he was continuing to lay stress on the point when his attention was abruptly diverted by the sight of another lady in deep black walking slowly away from the house.

"Is that Lady Cromarty?" he asked, and no sooner had Bisset said "yes" than the window was up and Mr. Carrington stepping out of it.

"I really must explain and apologise to her ladyship," said he.

"Her ladyship will never know—!" began Bisset, but the surprising visitor was already hastening after the mourning figure. Had the worthy man been able to hear the conversation which ensued he would have been more surprised still.

"Lady Cromarty, I believe?" said the stranger in a deferential voice.

She turned quickly, and her eyes searched him with that hard glance they wore always nowadays.

"Yes, I am Lady Cromarty," she said.

"Pardon me for disturbing you," said he. "It is a mere brief matter of business. I represent an insurance company to which Sir Malcolm Cromarty has made certain proposals. We are not perfectly satisfied with his statements, and from other sources learn that he is engaged to be married. I have come simply to ascertain whether that is the case."

Lady Cromarty was (as Mr. Carrington had shrewdly divined) no better versed in the intricate matter of insurance than the majority of her sex, and evidently perceived nothing very unusual in this enquiry. It may be added in her excuse that the manner in which it was put by the representative of the company was a perfect example of how a business man should address a lady.

"It is the case," said she.

"May I ask your ladyship's authority—in strict confidence of course?" enquired the representative firmly, but very courteously.

"I learned it from my own man of business," said she.

"Thank you," said the insurance representative. "I beg that your ladyship will say nothing of my call, and I shall undertake not to mention the source of my information," and with an adequate bow he returned to the house.

Before disappearing through her library window, Mr. Carrington saw that her ladyship's back was turned, and he then gave this candid, if somewhat sketchy, account of his interview to her butler.

"It suddenly struck me," said he, "that Lady Cromarty might think it somewhat unseemly of me to come enquiring about shooting so soon after her bereavement; so I gave her a somewhat different explanation. She is not likely to make any further enquiries about me and so you need say nothing about my visit."

He was careful however to impress on his friend Mr. Bisset that he actually had come from purely sporting motives. In fact he professed some anxiety to get in touch with Sir Malcolm on the subject, even though assured that the young baronet had nothing to do with the shootings.

"Ah, but it will gratify him, Bisset," said he, "and I think it is the nice thing to do. Could you give me his London address?"

He jotted this down in his pocket book, and then as he was leaving he said confidentially:

"You tell me that you think Sir Malcolm is interested in Miss Farmond, though she seemed not so keen on him?"

"That was the way of it to my thinking," said Bisset. "And what deduction would you draw from that, sir?"

"I should deduce," said this sympathetic and intelligent visitor, "the probable appearance of certain evidence bearing on our theories, Bisset."

Mr. Bisset thought he had seldom met a pleasanter gentleman or a more helpful assistant.

The car took Mr. Carrington straight back to the town and dropped him at the door of Mr. Rattar's office.

"I shall want you again at two o'clock sharp," he said to the chauffeur, and turned in to the office.

He caught the lawyer just before he went out to lunch and said at once:

"I want to see Sir Malcolm Cromarty. Can you arrange for him to run up here for a day?"

Simon stared at him hard, and there seemed to be even more caution than usual in his eye; almost, indeed, a touch of suspicion. The lawyer was not looking quite as well as usual; there was a drawn look about the upper part of the face and a hint of strain both in eyes and mouth.

"Why do you want to see Sir Malcolm?" he enquired.

"Well," said Carrington, "the fact of the matter is, Mr. Rattar, that, as you yourself said, the direct evidence is practically nil, and one is forced to go a good deal by one's judgment of the people suspected or concerned."

Simon grunted sceptically.

"Very misleading," he said.

"That depends entirely on one's judgment, or rather on one's instinct for distinguishing bad eggs from good. As a matter of observation I don't find that certain types of men and women commit certain actions, and I do find that they are apt to commit others. And contrariwise with other types."

"Very unsafe doctrine," said Simon emphatically.

"Extremely—in the hands of any one who doesn't know how to apply it. On the other hand, it can be made a short and common-sense cut to the truth in many cases. For instance, the man who suspected Mr. Bisset of committing the crime would simply be wasting his time and energy, even if there seemed to be some evidence against him."

"Any man can commit any crime," said Simon dogmatically.

Carrington smiled and shook his head.

"Personally," said he, "if you had a young and pretty wife, I am capable of running away with her, and possibly even of letting her persuade me to abscond with some of your property, but I am not capable of laying you out in cold blood and rifling that safe. And a good judge of men ought to be able to perceive this and not waste his time in trying to convict me of an offence I couldn't commit. On the other hand, if the crime was one that my type is apt to commit he would be a fool to acquit me off-hand, even if there was next to no evidence against me."

"Then you simply go by your impressions of people?"

"Far from it. A complete absence of motive would force me to acquit even the most promising looking blackguard, unless of course there were some form of lunacy in his case. One must have motive and one must have evidence as well, but character is the short cut—if the circumstances permit you to use it. Sometimes of course they don't, but in this case they force me to depend on it very largely. Therefore I want to see Sir Malcolm Cromarty."

The lawyer shook his head.

"No, no, Mr. Carrington," he said, "I can't bring him down here on such trivial grounds."

"But you yourself suspect him!"

For a moment the lawyer was silent.

"I think suspicion points to him; but what is wanted is *evidence.* You can't get evidence merely by bringing him here. You don't suppose he will confess, do you?"

"Have you ever studied the French methods of getting at the truth?" enquired Carrington, and when Simon shook his head contemptuously, he added with some significance: "We can learn a good deal from our neighbours."

"Trivial grounds!" muttered Simon. "No, no!"

Carrington became unusually serious and impressive.

"I am investigating this case, Mr. Rattar, and I want to see Sir Malcolm. Will you send for him or not?"

"He wouldn't come."

"It depends on the urgency of the message."

"I can't invent bogus urgent messages to my clients."

Carrington smiled.

"I might do the inventing for you."

Again the lawyer stared at him and again there was the same extreme caution in his eye, mingled with a hint of suspicion.

"I'll think about it," he said.

"I want to see him immediately."

"Call again to-morrow morning."

Carrington's manner altered at once into his usual easy-going air.

"Very well, then, Mr. Rattar," said he as he rose.

"By the way," said Simon, "you have been out at Keldale this morning, I presume?"

"Yes," said Carrington carelessly, "but there is really nothing new to be found."

Simon looked at him hard.

"No fresh evidence?"

Carrington laughed.

"Not likely, after you and your sleuth hounds had been over the ground!"

He went to the door, and there Simon again spoke.

"What are you doing next?"

"Upon my word, I am rather wondering. I must think about it. Good morning."

For a man who was rather wondering, Mr. Carrington's next movements were remarkably prompt. He first went straight to the Post Office and dispatched a wire. It was addressed to Sir Malcolm Cromarty and it ran—"Come immediately urgent news don't answer please don't delay." The only thing that seemed to indicate a wondering and abstracted mind was the signature to this message. Instead of "Carrington" he actually wrote "Cicely Farmond."

He then hurried to the hotel, which he reached at one-fifty. In ten minutes he had bolted a hasty lunch and at two o'clock was sitting in the car again.

"To Stanesland Castle," he commanded. "And be as quick as you can."

Mr. Carrington's interview with the laird of Stanesland began on much the same lines as his talk with Bisset. The amiable visitor was shown into the laird's smoking room—an apartment with vast walls like a dungeon and on them trophies from the laird's adventurous days, and proceeded to make enquiry whether Mr. Cromarty was disposed to let his shootings for next season, or, if not, whether he could recommend any others.

As the visitor was in no hurry, he declared, to fix anything up, it was very natural that this conversation, like the morning's, should eventually turn on to the subject of the great local mystery. Through it all Mr. Carrington's monocle was more continually fixed on the other than usual, but if he were looking for peculiarities in the laird's manner or any admissions made either by tongue or eye, he was disappointed. Cromarty was as breezy and as direct as ever, but even when his visitor confessed his extreme interest in such cases of remarkable crime, he (to all seeming) scented nothing in this beyond a not uncommon hobby. There was no doubt, however, of his keenness to discuss the subject. Carrington gave him an entertaining account of his efforts to assist Mr. Bisset, and then Ned asked:

"Well, what do you think of his theory that the man came in by the window?"

Carrington smiled.

"Bisset is evidently extremely anxious to save the credit of the family."

Ned Cromarty was aroused now.

"Good God!" he cried. "But do you mean to say that you think that story will hold water?"

"What story?" enquired Carrington mildly.

"You know what I mean—the scandal that Sir Malcolm and—and a lady were concerned in the murder."

"They are said to have actually committed it, aren't they?"

Ned's eye began to look dangerous.

"Do you think it's credible?" he asked brusquely.

"You know them better than I. Do you think it is?"

"Not for an instant!"

"I haven't met Sir Malcolm," said Carrington, wiping his eyeglass on his handkerchief. "I can't judge of him. What sort of a fellow is he?"

"A bit of a young squirt," said Ned candidly. "But I'll not believe he's a murderer till I get some proof of it."

"And Miss Farmond? Is she at all a murderous lady?"

He fixed his monocle in his eye just in time to see his host control himself after what seemed to have been a somewhat violent spasm.

"I'll stake my life on her innocence!" said Ned, and it was hard to know whether his manner as he said this should be termed fierce or solemn.

For the space of perhaps two seconds Carrington's eyeglass stared very straight at him, and immediately afterwards was taken out for cleaning again, while its owner seemed to have found some new food for thought. The silence was broken by Ned asking brusquely:

"Don't you believe me?"

Again his visitor fixed the monocle in his eye, and he answered now very quietly and deliberately:

"I happened to meet a young lady one afternoon, whom I discovered to be Miss Farmond. My own impression—for what it is worth—is that it would be a mere waste of time to investigate the suspicion against her, supposing, that is, that one were a detective or anything of that kind engaged in this case."

"You think she is innocent?" asked Ned eagerly.

"I am quite certain of it, so far as I am any judge."

Ned heaved a sigh of relief, and for an instant a smile flitted across Carrington's face. It seemed as though he were amused at such a tribute to the opinion of a mere chance visitor.

"And Sir Malcolm?" enquired Ned.

Carrington shook his head.

"I have no means of judging—yet."

Ned glanced at him quickly.

"Do you expect to get hold of a means?"

Carrington's smile was his only answer to the question. And then, still smiling, he said:

"I rather wonder, Mr. Cromarty, that you who have taken so much interest in this case, and who are, I am told, the head of the family, don't get some professional assistance to help you to get at the bottom of it."

Ned's mouth shut hard and his eyes turned to the fire. He said nothing for a moment and then remarked:

"Well, I guess that's worth thinking over."

Carrington's shoulders moved in an almost imperceptible shrug, but he made no comment aloud. In a moment Ned said:

"Supposing those two are scored out, there doesn't seem to be anybody else inside the house who could have committed the crime, does there? You wouldn't suspect Lady Cromarty or Bisset, would you?"

"Lady Cromarty is physically incapable of giving her husband the blow he must have received. Besides, they were a very devoted couple, I understand, and she gained nothing by his death—lost heavily, in fact. As for Bisset—" Carrington let his smile finish the sentence.

"Then it must have been some one from outside—but who?"

"Can you think of any one?" asked Carrington.

Ned shook his head emphatically.

"Can you?" he asked.

"Me?" said his visitor with an innocent air, and yet with a twinkle for an instant in his eye. "I am a mere stranger to the place, and if you and Mr. Rattar and the police are baffled, what can I suggest?"

Ned seemed for a moment a trifle disconcerted. Then he said:

"That's so, of course, Mr. Carrington. But since we happen to be talking about it—well, I guess I'm quite curious to know if any ideas have just happened to occur to you."

"Well," said the other, "between ourselves, Mr. Cromarty, and speaking quite confidentially, one idea has struck me very forcibly."

"What's that?" asked Ned eagerly.

"Simply this, that though it *might* be conceivable to think of somebody or other, the difficulty that stares me in the face is— motive!"

Ned's face fell.

"Well, that's what has struck all of us."

"Sir Reginald was a popular landlord, I hear."

"The most popular in the county."

"This isn't Ireland," continued Carrington. "Tenants don't lay out their landlords on principle, and in this particular instance they would simply stand to lose by his death. Then take his tradesmen and his agent and so on, they all stand to lose too. An illicit love affair and a vengeful swain might be a conceivable theory, if his character gave colour to it; but there's not a hint of that, and some rumour would have got about for certain if that had been the case."

"You may dismiss that," said Ned emphatically.

"Then there you are—what's the motive?"

"If one could think of a possible man, one could probably think of a possible motive."

On Carrington's face a curious look appeared for an instant.

"I only wish one could," he murmured.

A gong sounded and Ned rose.

"That means tea," said he. "I always have it in my sister's room. Come up."

They went up the stone stair and turned into Miss Cromarty's boudoir. On her, Mr. Carrington produced a favourable impression that was evident at once. At all times she liked good-looking and agreeable gentlemen, and lately she had been suffering from a dearth of them. She had been suffering also from her brother's pig-headed refusal to reconsider his decision not to buy a car; and finally from the lack of some one to sympathise with her in this matter. In the opulent-looking and sportingly attired Mr. Carrington she quickly perceived a kindred spirit, and having a tongue that was not easily intimidated even by the formidable looking laird, she launched into her grievance. They had been talking about the long distances that separated most of the mansions in the county.

"Isn't it ridiculous, Mr. Carrington," said she, "we haven't got a car!"

"Absurd," agreed Mr. Carrington, helping himself to cake.

"Do you know, this brother of mine here has actually come into a fortune, and yet he won't buy me even one little motor car!"

Ned frowned and muttered something that might have checked their visitor's reply, had he noticed the laird's displeasure, but for the moment he seemed to have become very unobserving.

"Come into a fortune?" said he. "What a bit of luck! How much— a million—two million?"

"Oh, not as much as that, worse luck! But quite enough to buy at least three decent cars if he was half a sportsman! And he won't get one!"

Mr. Carrington was now trying to balance his cake in his saucer and was evidently too absorbed in his efforts to notice his host's waxing displeasure.

"In my experience," said he, "you can't get a decent car much under four hundred."

"Well," said she, "that's just the figure it would bring it to."

"Lilian!" muttered her brother wrathfully.

But at that moment Mr. Carrington coughed, evidently over a cake crumb, and failed to hear the expostulation.

"But perhaps he is going to buy you something even handsomer instead," he suggested.

"Is he!" she scoffed, with a defiant eye on her brother. "I believe he's going to blue it in something too scandalous to talk about in mixed society! Anyhow it's something too mysterious to tell me!"

By this time Ned's face was a thundercloud in which lightning was clearly imminent, but Mr. Carrington now recovered his wonted tact as suddenly as he had lost it.

"That reminds me of a very curious story I heard at my club the other day," he began, and in a few minutes the conversation was far away from Miss Cromarty's grievances. And then, having finished his cup of tea, he looked at his watch with an exclamation and protested that he must depart on the instant.

As he lay back in his car he murmured with a satisfied smile: "That's settled anyhow!"

And then for the whole drive home he fell very thoughtful indeed. Only one incident aroused him, and that but for a moment. It was quite dark by this time, and somewhere between the Keldale House lodge and the town, the lamps of the car swept for an instant over a girl riding a bicycle in the opposite direction. Carrington looked round quickly and saw that she was Miss Cicely Farmond.

On the morning after his visit from Mr. Carrington, Ned Cromarty took his keeper with him and drove over to shoot on a friend's estate. He stayed for tea and it was well after five o'clock and quite dark when he started on his long drive home. The road passed close to a wayside station with a level crossing over the line, and when they came to this the gates were closed against them and the light of the signal of the up line had changed from red to white.

"Train's up to time," said Ned to the keeper. "I thought we'd have got through before she came."

There was no moon, a fine rain hung in the air, and the night was already pitch dark. Sitting there in the dogcart before the closed gates, behind the blinding light of the gig lamps, they were quite invisible themselves; but about thirty yards to their left they saw the station platform plainly in the radiance of its lights, and, straight before them in the radiance of their own, they could see less distinctly the road beyond the line.

At first, save for the distant rumble of the southward bound train, there was no sign of life or of movement anywhere, and then all at once a figure on a bicycle appeared on the road, and in a moment dismounted beside the station. It was a girl in black, and at the sight of her, Ned bent forward suddenly in his driving seat and stared intently into the night. He saw her unstrap a small suitcase from the bicycle and lead the bicycle into the station. A minute or two passed and then she emerged from the ticket office on to the platform carrying the suitcase in her hand. The bicycle she had evidently left in the station, and it seemed manifest that she was going by this train.

"That's Miss Farmond, sir, from Keldale House!" exclaimed the keeper.

His master said nothing but kept his eye intently fixed on the girl. One of the platform lamps lit her plainly, and he thought she looked the most forlorn and moving sight that had ever stirred his heart. There was something shrinking in her attitude, and when she looked once for a few moments straight towards him, there seemed to be something both sad and frightened in her face. Not another soul was on the platform, and seen in that patch of light against an immensity of dark empty country and black sky, she gave him such an impression of friendlessness that he could scarcely stay in his seat. And all the while the roar of the on-coming train was growing louder and ever louder. In a few minutes she would be gone—"Where?" he asked himself.

"I'm wondering where she'll be going at this time o' night with nae mair luggage than yon," said the keeper.

That decided it.

"Take the trap home and tell Miss Cromarty not to expect me to-night," said his master, quickly. "Say I've gone—oh, anywhere you derned well like! There's something up and I'm going to see what it is."

He jumped quietly on the road just as the engine thundered between the gates in front. By the time the train was at rest, he was over the gate and making his way to the platform. He stopped in the darkness by the rear end of the train till he saw the figure in black disappear into a carriage, and then he stepped into a compartment near the guard's van.

"Haven't got a ticket, but I'll pay as I go along," he said to the guard as he passed the window.

The guard knew Mr. Cromarty well and touched his cap, and then the train started and Mr. Cromarty was embarked upon what he confessed to himself was the blindest journey he had ever made in all his varied career.

Where was she going—and why was she going? He asked himself these questions over and over again as he sat with a cigar between his teeth and his long legs stretched out on the opposite seat,
and the train drove on into an ever wilder and more desolate land.
It would be very many miles and a couple of hours or more before
they reached any sort of conceivable destination for her, and as a
matter of fact this train did not go beyond that destination. Then
it struck him sharply that up till the end of last month the train
had continued its southward journey. The alteration in the timetable was only a few days old. Possibly she was not aware of it and
had counted on travelling to—where? He knew where she had got
to stop, but where had she meant to stop? Or where would she go
to-morrow? And above all, why was she going at all, leaving her
bicycle at a wayside station and with her sole luggage a small suitcase? Ned shook his head, tried to suck life into his neglected
cigar, and gave up the problem in the meanwhile.

As to the question of what business he had to be following Miss
Farmond like this, he troubled his head about it not at all. If she
needed him, here he was. If she didn't, he would clear out. But
very strong and very urgent was the conviction that she required a
friend of some sort.

The stations were few and far between and most desolate, improbable places as endings for Cicely Farmond's journey. He looked
out of the window at each of them, but she never alighted.

"She's going to find herself stuck for the night. That's about
the size of it," he said to himself as they left the last station before
the journey ended.

Though their next stop was the final stop, he did not open the
carriage door when the train pulled up. He did not even put his
head far out of the window, only just enough to see what passed
on the platform ahead.

"I'm not going to worry her if she doesn't need me," he said to
himself.

He saw the slip of a figure in black talking to the stationmaster,
and it was hardly necessary to hear that official's last words in
order to divine what had happened.

"Weel, miss," he overheard the stationmaster say, "I'm sorry ye're disappointed, but it's no me that has stoppit the train. It's aff for the winter. If ye turn to the left ye'll fin' the hotel."

The girl looked round her slowly and it seemed to Ned that the way she did it epitomised disappointment and desolation, and then she hurried through the station buildings and was gone.

He was out of the carriage and after her in an instant. Beyond the station the darkness was intense and he had almost passed a road branching to the left without seeing it. He stopped and was going to turn down it when it struck him the silence was intense that way, but that there was a light sound of retreating footsteps straight ahead.

"She's missed the turning!" he said to himself, and followed the footsteps. In a little he could see her against the sky, a dim hurrying figure, and his own stride quickened. He had never been in this place before, but he knew it for a mere seaboard village with an utterly lonely country on every inland side. She was heading into a black wilderness, and he took his decision at once and increased his pace till he was overhauling her fast.

At the sound of his footsteps he could see that she glanced over her shoulder and made the more haste till she was almost running. And then as she heard the pursuing steps always nearer she suddenly slackened speed to let him pass.

"Miss Farmond!" said he.

He could hear her gasp as she stopped short and turned sharply. She was staring hard now at the tall figure looming above her.

"It's only me—Ned Cromarty," he said quietly.

And then he started in turn, for instead of showing relief she gave a half smothered little cry and shrank away from him. For a moment there was dead silence and then he said, still quietly, though it cost him an effort.

"I only mean to help you if you need a hand. Are you looking for the hotel?"

"Yes," she said in a low frightened voice.

"Well," said he, "I guess you'd walk till morning before you reached an hotel along this road. You missed the turning at the station. Give me your bag. Come along!"

She let him take the suitcase and she turned back with him, but it struck him painfully that her docility was like that of a frightened animal.

"Where are you bound for?" he enquired in his usual direct way.

She murmured something that he could not catch and then they fell altogether silent till they had retraced their road to the station and turned down towards a twinkling light or two which showed where the village lay.

"Now, Miss Farmond," said he, "we are getting near this pub and as we've both got to spend the night there, you'll please observe these few short and simple rules. I'm your uncle—Uncle Ned. D'you see?"

There was no laugh, or even a smile from her. She gave a little start of surprise and in a very confused voice murmured:

"Yes, I see."

"My full name is Mr. Ned Dawkins and you're Louisa Dawkins my niece. Just call me 'Uncle Ned' and leave me to do the talking. We are touring this beautiful country and I've lost my luggage owing to the derned foolishness of the railroad officials here. And then when we've had a little bit of dinner you can tell me, if you like, why you've eloped and why you've got a down on me. Or if you don't like to, well, you needn't. Ah, here's the pub at last."

He threw open the door and in a loud and cheerful voice cried:

"Well, here we are, Louisa. Walk right in, my dear!"

28

THE RETURN

His friends would scarcely have picked out Mr. Ned Cromarty of Stanesland as likely to make a distinguished actor, but they might have changed their opinion had they heard him breezily announce himself as Mr. Dawkins from Liverpool and curse the Scottish railways which had lost his luggage for him. It is true that the landlord looked at him a trifle askance and that the landlady and her maid exchanged a knowing smile when he ordered a room for his niece Louisa, but few people shut up in a little country inn with such a formidable looking, loud voiced giant, would have ventured to question his statements openly, and the equanimity of Mr. Dawkins remained undisturbed.

"Sit right down, Louisa!" he commanded when dinner was served; and then, addressing the maid, "You needn't wait. We'll ring when we need you."

But the moment she had gone he checked a strong expression with an effort.

"Damn—confound it!" he cried. "I ought to have remembered to say grace! That would have given just the finishing touch to the Uncle Ned business. However, I don't think they've smelt any rats."

Cicely smiled faintly and then her eyes fell and she answered nothing. Their only other conversation during dinner consisted in his expostulations on her small appetite and her low-voiced protests that she wasn't hungry. But when it was safely over, he pushed back his chair, crossed his knees, and began:

"Now, Louisa, I'm going to take an uncle's privilege of lighting my pipe before I begin to talk, if you don't mind."

He lit his pipe, and then suddenly dropping the rôle of uncle altogether, said gently:

"I don't want to press you with any questions that you don't want to answer, but if you need a friend of any sort, size, or description, here I am." He paused for a moment and then asked still more gently: "Are you afraid of me?"

For the first time she let her long-lashed eyes rest full on his face and in her low voice, she answered:

"Partly afraid."

"And partly what else?"

"Partly puzzled—and partly ashamed."

"Ashamed!" he exclaimed with a note of indignant protest. "Ashamed of what?"

"The exhibition I've made of myself," she said, her voice still very low.

"Well," he smiled, "that's a matter of opinion. But why are you afraid?"

"Oh," she exclaimed. "You know of course!"

He stared at her blankly.

"I pass; I can't play to that!" he replied. "I honestly do not know, Miss Farmond."

Her eyes opened very wide.

"That's what I meant when I said I was puzzled. You *must* know—and yet—!"

She broke off and looked at him doubtfully.

"Look here," said he, "some one's got to solve this mystery, and I'll risk a leading question. Why did you run away?"

"Because of what you have been doing!"

"*Me* been doing! And what have I been doing?"

"Suspecting me and setting a detective to watch me!"

Ned's one eye opened wide, but for a moment he said not a word. Then he remarked quietly:

"This is going to be a derned complicated business. Just you begin at the beginning, please, and let's see how things stand. Who told you I was setting a detective on to you?"

"I found out myself I was being watched."

"How and when?"

She hesitated, and the doubtful look returned to her eyes.

"Come, Louisa!" he said. "No nonsense this time! We've got to have this out—or my name's Dawkins!"

For the first time she smiled spontaneously, and the doubtful look almost vanished. Just a trace was left, but her voice, though still very low, was firmer now.

"I only discovered for the first time the wicked suspicion about poor Malcolm," she said, "when I met a gentleman a few days ago who told me he had heard Malcolm was arrested for the murder of Sir Reginald."

"But that's not true!" cried Ned.

"No, and he admitted it was only a story he had heard at the hotel, but it suddenly seemed to throw light on several things I hadn't been able to understand. I spoke to Lady Cromarty about it, and then I actually found that I was suspected too!"

"Did she tell you so?"

"Not in so many words, but I knew what was in her mind. And then the very next day I caught the same man examining the library with Bisset and I saw him out of the window follow Lady Cromarty and speak to her, and then I knew he was a detective!"

"How did you know?"

"Oh, by instinct, and I was right! The position was so horrible— so unbearable, that I went in to see Mr. Rattar about it."

"Why Rattar?"

"Because he is the family lawyer and he's also investigating the case, and I thought of course he was employing the detective. And Mr. Rattar told me you were really employing him. Are you?"

There was a pleading note in this question—a longing to hear the answer "No" that seemed to affect Ned strangely.

"It's all right, Miss Farmond!" he said. "Don't you worry! I got that man down here to clear you—just for that purpose and no other!"

"But—" she exclaimed, "Mr. Rattar said you suspected Malcolm and me and were determined to prove our guilt!"

"Simon Rattar said that!"

There was something so menacing in his voice that Cicely involuntarily shrank back.

"Do you mean to tell me, honour bright, that Simon Rattar told you that lie in so many words?"

"Yes," she said, "he did indeed. And he said that this Mr. Carrington was a very clever man and was almost certain to trump up a very strong case against us, and so he advised me to go away."

He seemed almost incapable of speech at this.

"He actually advised you to bolt?"

She nodded.

"To slip away quietly to London and stay in an hotel he recommended till I heard from him. He said you had sworn to track down the criminals and hang them with your own hands, and so when I saw you suddenly come up behind me in that dark road to-night—oh, you've no idea how terrified I was! Mr. Rattar had frightened away all the nerve I ever had, and then when I thought I was safely away, you suddenly came up behind me in that dark road!"

"You poor little—" he began, laying his hand upon hers, and then he remembered Sir Malcolm and altered his sentence into: "You know now that was all one infernal pack of lies, don't you?"

Though he took away his hand, she had not moved her own, and she gave him now a look which richly rewarded him for his evening's work.

"I believe every word you tell me," she said.

"Well then," said Ned, "I tell you that I got this fellow Carrington down to take up the case so that I could clear you in the first place and find the right man in the second. So as to give him an absolutely clear field, he wasn't told who was employing him, and then he could suspect me myself if he wanted to. As a matter of fact, I rather think he has guessed who's running him. Anyhow, yesterday afternoon he told me straight and emphatically that he knew you were innocent. So you've run away a day too late!"

She laughed at last, and then fell serious again.

"But what did Mr. Rattar mean by saying you had engaged the detective because you suspected Malcolm and me?"

"That's precisely what I want to find out," said Ned grimly. "He could guess easy enough who was employing Carrington, because

I had suggested getting a detective, only Simon wouldn't rise to it. But as to saying I suspected you, he knew that was a lie, and I can only suspect he's getting a little tired of life!"

They talked on for a little longer, still sitting by the table, with her eyes now constantly smiling into his, until at last he had to remind himself so vigorously of the absent and lucky baronet that the pleasure began to ebb. And then they said good-night and he was left staring into the fire.

Next morning they faced one another in a first class carriage on a homeward bound train.

"What shall I say to Lady Cromarty?" she asked, half smiling, half fearfully.

He reflected for a few minutes.

"Tell her the truth. Lies don't pay in the long run. I can bear witness to this part of the story, and to the Carrington part if necessary, though I don't want to give him away if I can help it."

"Oh no!" she said, "we mustn't interfere with him. But supposing Lady Cromarty doesn't believe—"

"Come straight to Stanesland! Will you?"

"Run away again?"

"It's the direction you run in that matters," said he. "Now, mind you, that's understood!"

She was silent for a little and then she said:

"I can't understand why these horrible stories associate Malcolm and me. Why should we have conspired to do such a dreadful thing?"

He stared at her, and then hesitated.

"Because—well, being engaged to him—"

"Engaged to Malcolm!" she exclaimed. "Whatever put that into people's heads?"

"What!" he cried. "Aren't you?"

"Good gracious no! Was *that* the reason then?"

He seemed too lost in his own thoughts to answer her; but they were evidently not unhappy thoughts this time.

"Who can have started such a story?" she demanded.

"Who started it?" he repeated and then was immersed in thought again; only now there was a grim look on his face.

"Well anyhow," he cried, in a minute or two, "we're out of that wood! Aren't we, Louisa?"

"Yes, Uncle Ned," she smiled back.

He stirred impulsively in his seat and then seemed to check himself, and for the rest of the journey he appeared to be divided between content with the present hour and an impulse to improve upon it. And then before he had realised where they were, they had stopped at a station, and she was exclaiming:

"Oh, I must get out here! I've left my bike in the station!"

"Look here," said he, with his hand on the door handle, "before you go you've got to swear that you'll come straight to Stanesland if there's another particle of trouble. Swear?"

"But what about Miss Cromarty?" she smiled.

"Miss Cromarty will say precisely the same as I do," he said with a curiously significant emphasis. "So now, I don't open this door till you promise!"

"I promise!" said she, and then she was standing on the platform waving a farewell.

"I half wish I'd risked it!" he said to himself with a sigh as the train moved on, and then he ruminated with an expression on his face that seemed to suggest a risk merely deferred.

29

BROTHER AND SISTER

Ned Cromarty found his sister in her room.

"Well, Ned," she asked, "where on earth have you been?"

He shut the door before he answered, and then came up to the fireplace, and planted himself in front of her.

"Who told you that Cicely Farmond was engaged to Malcolm Cromarty?" he demanded.

She made a little grimace of comic alarm, but her eye was apprehensive.

"Don't eat my head off, Neddy! How can I remember?"

"You've got to remember," said her brother grimly. "And you'd better be careful what you tell me, for I'll go straight to the woman, or man, you name."

She looked at him boldly enough.

"I don't know if you are aware of it, but this isn't the way I'm accustomed to be talked to."

"It's the way you're being talked to now," said he. "Who told you?"

"I absolutely refuse to answer if you speak to me like that, Ned!"

"Then we part company, Lilian."

There was no doubt about the apprehension in her eye now. For a moment it seemed to wonder whether he was actually in earnest, and then to decide that he was.

"I—I don't know who told me," she said in an altered voice.

"Did anybody tell you, or did you make it up?"

"I never actually said they were engaged."

He looked at her in silence and very hard, and then he spoke deliberately.

"I won't ask you why you deceived me, Lilian, but it was a low down trick to play on me, and it has turned out to be a damned cruel trick to play on that girl. I mentioned the engagement as a mere matter of course to somebody, and though I mentioned it confidentially, it started this slander about Malcolm Cromarty and Cicely Farmond conspiring to murder—to *murder*, Lilian!—the man of all men they owed most to. That's what you've done!"

By this time Lilian Cromarty's handkerchief was at her eyes.

"I—I am very sorry, Ned," she murmured.

But he was not to be soothed by a tear, even in the most adroit lady's eye.

"The latest consequence has been," he said sternly, "that through a mixture of persecution and bad advice she has been driven to run away. Luckily I spotted her at the start and fetched her back, and I've told her that if there is the least little bit more trouble she is to come straight here and that you will give her as good a welcome as I shall. Is that quite clear?"

"Yes," she murmured through her handkerchief.

"Otherwise," said he, "there's no room for us both here. One single suggestion that she isn't welcome—and you have full warning now of the consequences!"

"When is she coming?" she asked in an uncertain voice.

"When? Possibly never. But there's some very fishy—and it looks to me, some very dirty business going on, and this port stands open in case of a storm. You fully understand?"

"Of course I do," she said, putting away her handkerchief. "I'm not quite a fool!"

And indeed, none of her friends or acquaintances had ever made that accusation against Lilian Cromarty.

"Well, that's all," said Ned, and began to move across the room.

But now the instinct for finding a scapegoat began to revive.

"Who did you tell it to, Ned?" she asked.

"Simon Rattar."

"Then *he* has spread this dreadful story!" she exclaimed with righteous indignation.

Her brother stopped and slowly turned back.

"By heaven, I've scarcely had time to think it all out yet—but it looks like it!"

"It *must* be that nasty grumpy old creature! If you told nobody else—well, it can't be anybody else!"

"But why should he go and spread such a story?"

"Because he wants to shelter some one else!"

"Who?"

"Ah, that's for the police to find out. But I'm quite certain, Ned, that that pig-headed old Simon with his cod-fish eyes and his everlasting grunt is at the bottom of it all!"

He stared thoughtfully into space.

"Well," he said slowly, "he has certainly been asking for trouble in one or two ways, and this seems another invitation. But he'll get it, sure! At the same time—what's his object?"

His sister had no hesitation.

"Either to make money or hide something disgraceful. You really must enquire into this, Ned!"

He dropped into a chair and sat for a few minutes with his face in his hands. At last he looked up and shook his head.

"I'm out of my depth," he said. "I guess I'd better see Carrington."

"Mr. Carrington?" she exclaimed.

"I had a long talk with him," he explained. "He seems an uncommon shrewd fellow. Yes, that's the proper line!"

She looked at him curiously but evidently judged it tactful in the present delicate situation to ask no more. He rose now and went, still thoughtful, to the door.

"What a dreadful thing of Simon Rattar to do! Wasn't it, Ned?" she said indignantly, her eyes as bright as ever again.

He turned as she went out.

"The whole thing has been damnable!"

As the door closed behind him she made a little grimace again and then gave a little shrug.

"He's going to marry her!" she said to herself, and acting immediately on a happy inspiration, sat down to write a long and affectionate letter to an old friend whose country house might, with judicious management, be considered good for a six months' visit.

30

A MARKED MAN

The unexpected energy displayed by her charming guest in bustling all over the country had surprised and a little perplexed Miss Peterkin, but she now decided that it was only a passing phase, for on the day following his visits to Keldale and Stanesland he exhibited exactly the same leisurely calm she had admired at first. He sought out the local golf course and for an hour or two his creditable game confirmed his reputation as a sportsman, and for the rest of the time he idled in a very gentlemanly manner.

In the course of the afternoon he strolled out and gradually drifted through the dusk towards the station. Finding the train was, as usual, indefinitely late, he strolled out again and finally drifted back just as the signals had fallen at last. It was quite dark by this time and the platform lamps were lit, but Mr. Carrington chanced to stand inconspicuously in a background of shadows. As the engine hissed ponderously under the station roof and the carriage doors began to open, he still stood there, the most casual of spectators. A few passengers passed him, and then came a young man in a fur coat, on whom some very curious glances had been thrown when he alighted from his first class compartment. Mr. Carrington, however, seemed to take no interest either in him or anybody else till the young man was actually passing him, and then he suddenly stepped out of the shadows, touched him on the shoulder and said in a much deeper and graver voice than usual:

"Sir Malcolm Cromarty, I believe!"

The young man started violently and turned a pale face.

"Ye—es, I am," he stammered.

"May I have a word with you?" said Carrington gravely.

With a dreadfully nervous air Sir Malcolm accompanied him out into the dark road, neither speaking, and then the young man demanded hoarsely:

"What do you want with me?"

Carrington's voice suddenly resumed its usual cheerful note.

"Forgive me," he said, "for collaring you like this, but the fact is I am very keen to see you about the Keldale shootings."

Sir Malcolm gave a gasp of relief.

"Thank Heaven!" he exclaimed. "Good Lord, what a fright you gave me!"

"I say I'm awfully sorry!" said Carrington anxiously. "How frightfully stupid I must have been!"

The young man looked at him, and, like most other people, evidently found his ingenuous face and sympathetic manner irresistibly confidence inspiring.

"Oh, not at all," he said. "In fact you must have wondered at my manner. The fact is Mr.—er—"

"Carrington."

"Mr. Carrington, that I'm in a most awful position at present. You know of course that I'm suspected of murder!"

"No!" exclaimed Carrington, with vast interest. "Not really?"

"It's an absolute fact—suspected of murder! Good God, just imagine it!"

The young baronet stopped and faced his new acquaintance dramatically. In spite of his nervousness, it was evident that his notoriety had compensations.

"Yes," he said, "I—the head of an ancient and honourable house—am actually suspected of having murdered my cousin, Sir Reginald Cromarty!"

"What, that murder!" exclaimed Carrington. "By Jove, of course, I've heard a lot about the case. And you are really suspected?"

"So much so," said the baronet darkly, "that when you touched me on the shoulder I actually thought you were going to arrest me!"

Carrington seemed equally astounded and penitent at this unfortunate reading of his simple and natural action in stepping suddenly out of the dark and tapping a nervous stranger on the shoulder.

"How very tactless of me!" he repeated more than once. "Really, I must be more careful another time!"

And then he suddenly turned his monocle on to the baronet and enquired:

"But how do you know you are suspected?"

"How do I know! My God, all fingers are pointing at me! Even in my club in London I feel I am a marked man. I have discussed my awful position with all my friends, and by this time they tell me that everybody else knows too!"

"That is—er—not unnatural," said Carrington drily. "But how did you first learn?"

The young man's voice fell almost to a whisper and he glanced apprehensively over his shoulder as he spoke.

"I knew I should be suspected the moment I heard of the crime! The very night before—perhaps at the actual moment when the deed was being done—I did a foolish thing!"

"You don't say so!" exclaimed his new friend with every appearance of surprise.

"Yes, you may not believe me, but I acted like a damned silly ass. Mind you, I am not as a rule a silly ass," the baronet added with dignity, "but that night I actually confided in a woman!"

"What woman?"‘

"My relative Miss Cicely Farmond—a charming girl, I may mention; there was every excuse for me, still it was a rotten thing to do, I quite admit. I told her that I was hard up and feeling desperate, and I even said I was going to sit up late! And on top of that Sir Reginald was murdered that very night. Imagine my sensations for the next few days, living in the same house with the woman who had heard me say *that*! She held my fate in her hands, but, thank God, she evidently had such faith in my honour and humanity that she forebore to—er—"

"Peach," suggested Carrington, "though as a matter of fact, I fancy she had forgotten all about the incident."

"Forgotten my words!" exclaimed the baronet indignantly. "Impossible! I can never forget them myself so long as I live!"

"Well," said Carrington soothingly, "let us suppose she remembered them. Anyhow she said nothing, and, that being so, how did you first actually know that you were suspected?"

"My own man of business thought it his duty to drop me a hint!" cried the baronet.

This piece of information seemed to produce quite as much impression on his new acquaintance as his first revelation, though he took it rather more quietly.

"Really!" said he in a curious voice. "And what course of action did he advise?"

"He advised me to keep away from the place. In fact he even suggested I should go abroad—and, by Gad, I'm going too!"

To this, Carrington made no reply at all. His thoughts, in fact, seemed to have wandered entirely away from Sir Malcolm Cromarty. The baronet seemed a trifle disappointed at his lack of adequate interest.

"Don't you sympathise with me," he enquired.

"I beg your pardon," said Carrington, "my thoughts were wandering for the moment. I do sympathise. By the way, what are you going to do now?"

The baronet started.

"By Gad, my own thoughts are wandering!" said he, "though I certainly have some excuse! I must get down to the Kings Arms and order a trap to take me out to Keldale House as quickly as I can." And then he added mysteriously, "I only came down here because I was urgently wired for by some one who—well, I couldn't refuse."

"I'm going to the Kings Arms, too. We'll walk down together, if you don't mind."

"Delighted," said the baronet, "if you don't mind being seen with such a marked man."

"I rather like them marked," smiled Carrington.

All the way to the hotel the notorious Sir Malcolm pursued what had evidently become his favourite subject:—the vast sensation he was causing in society and the pain it gave a gentleman of title and

position to be placed in such a predicament. When they reached
the Kings Arms, his new acquaintance insisted in a very friendly
and confident way that there was no immediate hurry about starting for Keldale, and that the baronet must come up to his sitting
room first and have a little refreshment.

The effect of a couple of large glasses of sloe gin was quickly
apparent. Sir Malcolm became decidedly happier and even more
confidential. He was considerably taken aback, however, when his
host suddenly asked, with a disconcertingly intense glance:

"Are you quite sure you are really innocent?"

"Innocent!" exclaimed the baronet, leaping out of his chair. "Do
you mean to tell me you doubt it? Do you actually believe I am
capable of killing a man in cold blood? Especially the honoured
head of my own house?"

Carrington seemed to suppress a smile.

"No," said he, "I don't believe it."

"Then, sir," said the baronet haughtily, "kindly do not question my honour!"

This time Carrington allowed his smile to appear.

"Sit down, Sir Malcolm," he said, "pull yourself together, and
listen to a few words."

Sir Malcolm looked extremely surprised, but obeyed.

"What I am going to say is in the strictest confidence and you
must give me your word not to repeat one single thing I tell you."

His serious manner evidently impressed the young man.

"I give you my word, sir," said he.

"Well then, in the first place, I am a detective."

For a few seconds Sir Malcolm stared at him in silence and then
burst into a hearty laugh.

"Good egg, sir!" said he. "Good egg! If I had not finished my
sloe gin I should drink to your health!"

It was Carrington's turn to look disconcerted. Recovering himself he said with a smile:

"You shall have another glass of sloe gin when you have grasped
the situation. I assure you I am actually a detective—or, rather, a
private enquiry agent."

Sir Malcolm shook a knowing head.

"My dear fellow," said he, "you can't really pull my leg like that. I can see perfectly well you are a gentleman."

"I appreciate the compliment," said Carrington, "but just let me tell you what was in the telegram which has brought you here. It ran—'Come immediately urgent news don't answer please don't delay. Cicely Farmond.'"

Sir Malcolm's mouth fell open.

"How—how do you know that?" he asked.

"Because I wrote it myself. Miss Farmond is quite unaware it was sent."

The baronet began to look indignant.

"But—er—why the devil, sir—"

"Because I am a detective," interrupted Carrington, "and I wished to see you."

Sir Malcolm evidently began to grasp the situation at last.

"What about?" he asked, and his face was a little paler already.

"About this murder. I wanted to satisfy myself that you were— or were not—innocent."

"But—er—how?"

"By your actions, conversation, and appearance. I am now satisfied, Sir Malcolm."

"That I am innocent."

"Yes."

"Then will this be the end of my—er—painful position?"

"So far as your own anxiety goes; yes. You need no longer fear arrest."

The first look of relief which had rushed to the young man's face became clouded with a suggestion of chagrin.

"But won't people then—er—talk about me any longer?"

"I am afraid I can't prevent that—for a little longer."

The last of the baronet's worries seemed to disappear.

"Ah!" he said complacently. "Well, let them talk about me!"

Carrington rose and rang the bell.

"You deserve a third sloe gin!" said he.

While the third sloe gin was being brought, he very deliberately and very thoughtfully selected and lit a cigarette, and then
he said:

"You tell me specifically that Mr. Rattar was the first person to
inform you that suspicion was directed against you, and that he
advised you to keep away, and for choice to go abroad. There is no
doubt about that, is there?"

"Well," said Sir Malcolm, "he didn't specifically advise me to
go abroad, but certainly his letter seemed to suggest it."

"Ah!" said Carrington and gazed into space for a moment.

"I am now going to take the liberty of suggesting your best
course of action," he resumed. "In the first place, there is no object in your going out to Keldale House, so I think you had better
not. In the second place, you had better call on Mr. Rattar first
thing to-morrow and consult him about any point of business that
strikes you as a sufficient reason for coming so far to see him. I
may tell you that he has given you extremely bad advice, so you
can be as off-hand and brief with him as you like. Get out of his
office, in fact, as quick as you can."

"That's what I always want to do," said the baronet. "I can't
stick the old fellow at any price."

"If he asks you whether you have seen me, say you have just
seen me but didn't fancy me, and don't give him the least idea of
what we talked about. You can add that you left the Kings Arms
because you didn't care for my company."

"But am I to leave it?" exclaimed the young man.

Carrington nodded.

"It's better that we shouldn't stay in the same hotel. It will support your account of me. And finally, get back to London by the
first train after you have seen Mr. Rattar."

"Then aren't you working with old Simon?" enquired Sir
Malcolm.

"Oh, in a sense, I am," said Carrington carelessly, "but I daresay
you have found him yourself an arbitrary, meddlesome old boy,
and I like to be independent."

"By Gad, so do I," the baronet agreed cordially. "I am quite with you about old Silent Simon. I'll do just exactly as you suggest. He won't get any change out of me!"

"And now," said Carrington, "get your bag taken to any other hotel you like. I'll explain everything to Miss Peterkin."

Sir Malcolm by this time had finished his third sloe gin and he said farewell with extreme affability, while his friend Mr. Carrington dropped into the manageress' room and explained that the poor young man had seemed so nervous and depressed that he had advised his departure for a quieter lodging. He added with great conviction that as a sporting man he would lay long odds on Sir Malcolm's innocence, and that between Miss Peterkin and himself he didn't believe a word of the current scandals.

That evening Mr. Carrington joined the choice spirits in the manageress' room, and they had a very long and entertaining gossip. The conversation turned this time chiefly on the subject of Mr. Simon Rattar, and if by the end of it the agreeable visitor was not fully acquainted with the history of that local celebrity, of his erring partner, and of his father before him, it was not the fault of Miss Peterkin and her friends. Nor could it fairly be said to be the visitor's fault either, for his questions were as numerous as they were intelligent.

On the morning after Sir Malcolm's fleeting visit to the Kings Arms, the manageress was informed by her friend Mr. Carrington that he would like a car immediately after breakfast.

"I really must be a little more energetic, or I'll never find anything to suit me," he smiled in his most leisurely manner. "I am thinking of running out to Keldale to have another look at the place. It might be worth taking if they'd let it."

"But you've been to Keldale already, Mr. Carrington!" said Miss Peterkin. "I wonder you don't have a look at one of the other places."

"I'm one of those fellows who make up their minds slowly," he explained. "But when we cautious fellows do make up our minds, well, something generally happens!"

Circumstances, however, prevented this enthusiastic sportsman from making any further enquiry as to the letting of the Keldale shootings. When Bisset appeared at the front door consternation was in his face. It was veiled under a restrained professional manner, but not sufficiently to escape his visitor's eye.

"What's up?" he asked at once.

Bisset looked for a moment into his sympathetic face, and then in grave whisper said:

"Step in, sir, and I'll tell ye."

He led him into a small morning room, carefully closed the door, and announced,

"Miss Farmond has gone, sir!"

"Gone. When and how?"

"Run away, sir, on her bicycle yesterday afternoon and deil a sign of her since!"

"Any luggage?"

"Just a wee suit case."

"No message left, or anything of that kind?"

"Not a word or a line, sir."

"The devil!" murmured Carrington.

"That's just exac'ly it, sir!"

"No known cause? No difficulty with Lady Cromarty or anything?"

"Nothing that's come to my ears, sir."

Carrington stared blankly into space and remained silent for several minutes. Bisset watched his assistant with growing anxiety.

"Surely, sir," he burst forth at last, "you're not thinking this goes to indicate any deductions or datas showing she's guilty?"

"I'm dashed if I know what to think," murmured Carrington still lost in thought.

Suddenly he turned his eyeglass on the other.

"By Jove!" he exclaimed, "the day before yesterday I passed that girl riding on a bicycle towards Keldale House after dark! Do you know where she had been?"

"Into the town, sir. I knew she was out, of course, and she just mentioned afterwards where she had been."

"Have you any idea whom she saw or what she did?"

Bisset shook his head.

"I have no datas, sir, that's the plain fac'."

"But you can't think of any likely errand to take her in so late in the afternoon?"

"No, sir. In fact, I mind thinking it was funny like her riding about alone in the dark like yon, for she's feared of being out by hersel' in the dark; I know that."

Carrington reflected for a few moments longer and then seemed to dismiss the subject.

"By the way," he asked, "can you remember if, by any chance, Sir Reginald had any difficulty or trouble or row of any kind with anyone whatever during, say, the month previous to his death? I mean with any of the tenants, or his tradesmen—or his lawyer? Take your time and think carefully."

Carrington dismissed his car at Mr. Rattar's office. When he was shown into the lawyer's room, he exhibited a greater air of keenness than usual.

"Well, Mr. Rattar," said he, "you'll be interested to hear that I've got rather a new point of view with regard to this case."

"Indeed?" said Simon, and his lips twitched a little as he spoke. There was no doubt that he was not looking so well as usual. His face had seemed drawn and worried last time Carrington had seen him; now it might almost be termed haggard.

"I find," continued Carrington, "that Sir Reginald displayed a curious and unaccountable irritability before his death. I hear, for instance, that a letter from you had upset him quite unduly."

Carrington paused for an instant, and his monocle was full on Simon all the time, and yet he did not seem to notice the very slight but distinct start which the lawyer gave, for he continued with exactly the same confidential air.

"These seem to me very suggestive symptoms, Mr. Rattar, and I am wondering very seriously whether the true solution of his mysterious death is not—" he paused for an instant and then in a low and earnest voice said, "suicide!"

There was no mistake about the lawyer's start this time, or about the curious fact that the strain seemed suddenly to relax, and a look of relief to take its place. And yet Carrington seemed quite oblivious to anything beyond his own striking new theory.

"That's rather a suggestive idea, isn't it?" said he.

"Very!" replied Simon with the air of one listening to a revelation.

"How he managed to inflict precisely those injuries on himself is at present a little obscure," continued Carrington, "but no doubt a really expert medical opinion will be able to suggest an explanation. The theory fits all the other facts remarkably, doesn't it?"

"Remarkably," agreed Simon.

"This letter of yours, for instance, was a very ordinary business communication, I understand."

"Very ordinary," said Simon.

"Of course, you have a copy of it in your letter book—and also Sir Reginald's reply?"

There was a moment's pause and then Simon's grunt seemed to be forced out of himself. But he followed the grunt with a more assured, "Certainly."

"May I see them?"

"You—you think they are important?"

"As bearing on Sir Reginald's state of mind only."

Simon rang his bell and ordered the letter book to be brought in. While Carrington was examining it, his eyes never left his visitor's face, but they would have had to be singularly penetrating to discover a trace of any emotion there. Throughout his inspection, Carrington's air remained as imperturbable as though he were reading the morning paper.

"According to these letters," he observed, "there seems to have been a trifling but rather curious misunderstanding. In accordance with written instructions of a fortnight previously, you had arranged to let a certain farm to a certain man, and Sir Reginald then complained that you had overlooked a conversation between those dates in which he had cancelled these instructions. He writes with a warmth that clearly indicates his own impression that this conversation had been perfectly explicit and that your forgetfulness or neglect of it was unaccountable, and he proposes to go into this and one or two other matters in the course of a conversation with you which should have taken place that afternoon. You then reply that you are too busy to come out so soon, but will call on the following morning. In the meantime Sir Reginald is murdered, and so the conversation never takes place and no explanation passes between you. Those are the facts, aren't they?"

He looked up from the letter book as he spoke and there was no doubt he noticed something now. Indeed, the haggard look on Simon's face and a bead of perspiration on his forehead were so striking, and so singular in the case of such a tough customer, that the least observant—or the most circumspect—must have stared. Carrington's stare lasted only for the fraction of a second, and then he was polishing his eyeglass with his handkerchief in the most indifferent way.

A second or two passed before Simon answered, and then he said abruptly:

"Sir Reginald was mistaken. No such conversation."

"Do you mean to tell me literally that *no* such conversation took place? Was it a mere delusion?"

"Er—practically. Yes, a delusion."

"Suicide!" declared Carrington with an air of profound conviction. "Yes, Mr. Rattar, that is evidently the solution. The unfortunate man had clearly not been himself, probably for some little time previously. Well, I'll make a few more enquiries, but I fancy my work is nearly at an end. Good-morning."

He rose and was half way across the room, when he stopped and asked, as if the idea had suddenly occurred to him:

"By the way, I hear that Miss Farmond was in seeing you a couple of days ago."

Again Simon seemed to start a little, and again he hesitated for an instant and then replied with a grunt.

"Had she any news?" asked the other.

Simon grunted again and shook his head, and Carrington threw him a friendly nod and went out.

He maintained the same air till he had turned down a bye street and was alone, and only then he gave vent to his feelings.

"I'm dashed!" he muttered, "absolutely jiggered!"

All the while he shook his head and slashed with his walking stick through the air. There was no doubt that Mr. Carrington was thoroughly and genuinely puzzled.

Carrington's soliloquy was interrupted by the appearance of someone on the pavement ahead of him. He pulled himself together,
took out his watch, and saw that it was still only twenty minutes
past twelve. After thinking for a moment, he murmured:

"I might as well try 'em!"

And thereupon he set out at a brisk walk, and a few minutes
later was closeted with Superintendent Sutherland in the Police
Station. He began by handing the Superintendent a card with the
name of Mr. F. T. Carrington on it, but with quite a different address from that on the card he had sent up to Mr. Rattar. It was, in
fact, his business card, and the Superintendent regarded him with
respectful interest.

After explaining his business and his preference for not disclosing
it to the public, he went briefly over the main facts of the case.

"I see you've got them all, sir," said the Superintendent, when
he had finished. "There really seems nothing to add and no new
light to be seen anywhere."

"I'm afraid so," agreed Carrington. "I'm afraid so."

In fact he seemed so entirely resigned to this conclusion that
he allowed, and even encouraged, the conversation to turn to other
matters. The activity and enterprise of the Procurator Fiscal
seemed to have particularly impressed him, and this led to a long
talk on the subject of Mr. Simon Rattar. The Superintendent was
also a great admirer of the Fiscal and assured Mr. Carrington that
not only was Mr. Simon himself the most capable and upright of

men, but that the firm of Rattar had always conducted its business in a manner that was above reproach. Mr. Carrington had made one or two slightly cynical but perfectly good-natured comments on lawyers in general, but he got no countenance from the Superintendent so far as Mr. Rattar and his business were concerned.

"But hadn't he some trouble at one time with his brother?" his visitor enquired.

The Superintendent admitted that this was so, and also that Sir Reginald Cromarty had suffered thereby, but he was quite positive that this trouble was entirely a thing of the past. There was no doubt that this information had a somewhat depressing effect even on the good-humoured Mr. Carrington, and at last he confessed with a candid air:

"The fact is, Superintendent, that I have a theory Sir Reginald was worrying about something before his death, and as all his business affairs are conducted by Mr. Rattar, I was wondering whether he had any difficulties in that direction. Now about this bad brother of Mr. Rattar's—there couldn't be trouble still outstanding, you think?"

"Mr. George Rattar was out of the firm, sir, years ago," the Superintendent assured him. "No, it couldna be that."

"And Mr. George Rattar certainly died a short time ago, did he?"

"I can show you the paper with his death in it. I kept it as a kind of record of the end of him."

He fetched the paper and Carrington after looking at it for a few minutes, remarked:

"I see here an advertisement stating that Mr. Rattar lost a ring."

"Yes," said the Superintendent, "that was a funny thing because it's not often a gentleman loses a ring off his hand. I've half wondered since whether it was connected with a story of Mr. Rattar's maid that his house had been broken into."

"When was that?"

"Curiously enough it was the very night Sir Reginald was murdered."

Carrington's chair squeaked on the floor as he sat up sharply.

"The very night of the murder?" he repeated. "Why has this never come out before?"

The stolid Superintendent looked at him in surprise.

"But what connection could there possibly be, sir? Mr. Rattar thought nothing of it himself and just mentioned it so that I would know it was a mere story, in case his servants started talking about it."

"But you yourself seemed just now to think that it might not be a mere story."

"Oh, that was just a kind o' idea," said the Superintendent easily. "It only came in my mind when the ring was never recovered."

"What were the exact facts?" demanded Carrington.

"Oh," said the Superintendent vaguely, "there was something about a window looking as if it had been entered, but really, sir, Mr. Rattar paid so little attention to it himself, and we were that taken up by the Keldale case that I made no special note of it."

"Did the servants ever speak of it again?"

"Everybody was that taken up about the murder that I doubt if they've minded on it any further."

Carrington was silent for a few moments.

"Are the servants intelligent girls?" he enquired.

"Oh, quite average intelligent. In fact, the housemaid is a particular decent sort of a girl."

At this point, Mr. Carrington's interest in the subject seemed to wane, and after a few pleasant generalities, he thanked the Superintendent for his courtesy, and strolled down to the hotel for lunch. This time his air as he walked was noticeably brisker and his eye decidedly brighter.

About three o'clock that afternoon came a ring at the front door bell of Mr. Simon Rattar's commodious villa. Mary MacLean declared afterwards that she had a presentiment when she heard it, but then the poor girl had been rather troubled with presentiments lately. When she opened the front door she saw a particularly polite and agreeable looking gentleman adorned with that unmistakable mark of fashion, a single eyeglass; and the gentleman saw a pleasant looking but evidently high strung and nervous young woman.

"Is Mr. Simon Rattar at home?" he enquired in a courteous voice and with a soothing smile that won her heart at once; and on hearing that Mr. Rattar always spent the afternoons at his office and would not return before five o'clock, his disappointment was so manifest that she felt sincerely sorry for him.

He hesitated and was about to go away when a happy idea struck him.

"Might I come in and write a line to be left for him?" he asked, and Mary felt greatly relieved at being able to assist the gentleman to assuage his disappointment in this way.

She led him into the library and somehow or other by the time she had got him ink and paper and pen she found herself talking to this distinguished looking stranger in the most friendly way. It was not that he was forward or gallant, far from it; simply that he was so nice and so remarkably sympathetic. Within five minutes of making his acquaintance, Mary felt that she could tell him almost anything.

This sympathetic visitor made several appreciative remarks about the house and garden, and then, just as he had dipped his pen into the ink, he remarked:

"Rather a tempting house for burglars, I should think—if such people existed in these peaceable parts."

"Oh, but they do, sir," she assured him. "We had one in this very house one night!"

The sympathetic stranger almost laid down his pen, he was so interested by this unexpected reply.

"What!" he exclaimed. "Really a burglary in this house? I say,
how awfully interesting! When did it happen?"

"Well, sir," said Mary in an impressive voice, "it's a most extraordinary thing, but it was actually the very self same night of
Sir Reginald's murder!"

So surprised and interested was the visitor that he actually did
lay down his pen this time.

"Was it the same man, do you think?" he asked in a voice that
seemed to thrill with sympathetic excitement.

"Indeed I've sometimes wondered!" said she.

"Tell me how it happened!"

"Well, sir," said Mary, "it was on the very morning that we heard
about Sir Reginald—only before we'd heard, and I was pulling up
the blinds in the wee sitting room when I says to myself. 'There's
been some one in at this window!'"

"The wee sitting room," repeated her visitor. "Which is that?"

He seemed so genuinely interested that before she realised what
liberties she was taking in the master's house, she had led him into
a small sitting room at the end of a short passage leading out of
the hall. It had evidently been intended for a smoking room or study
when the villa was built, but was clearly never used by Mr. Rattar,
for it contained little furniture beyond bookcases. Its window
looked on to the side of the garden and not towards the drive, and

a grass lawn lay beneath it, while the room itself was obviously the most isolated, and from a burglarious point of view the most promising, on the ground floor.

"This is the room, sir," said Mary. "And look! You still can see the marks on the sash."

"Yes," said the visitor thoughtfully, "they seem to have been made by a tacketty boot."

"And forbye that, there was a wee bit mud on the floor and a tacket mark in that!"

"Was the window shut or open?"

"Shut, sir; and the most extraordinary thing was that it was snibbed too! That's what made the master say it couldna have been a burglar at all, or how did he snib the window after he went out again?"

"Then Mr. Rattar didn't believe it was a burglar?"

"N—no, sir," said Mary, a little reluctantly.

"Was anything stolen?"

"No, sir; that was another funny thing. But it must have been a burglar!"

"What about the other windows, and the doors? Were they all fastened in the morning?"

"Yes, sir, it's the truth they were," she admitted.

"And what did Mr. Rattar do with the piece of mud?"

"Just threw it out of the window."

The sympathetic stranger crossed to the window and looked out.

"Grass underneath, I see," he observed. "No footprints outside, I suppose?"

"No, sir."

"Did the police come down and make enquiries?"

"Well, sir, the master said he would inform the pollis, but then came the news of the murder, and no one had any thoughts for anything else after that."

The sympathetic visitor stood by the window very thoughtfully for a few moments, and then turned and rewarded her with the most charming smile.

"Thank you awfully for showing me all this," said he. "By the way, what's your name?" She told him and he added with a still nicer smile, "Thank you, Mary!"

They returned to the library and he sat down before the table again, but just as he was going to pick up the pen a thought seemed to strike him.

"By the way," he said, "I remember hearing something about the loss of a ring. The burglar didn't take that, did he?"

"Oh, no, sir, I remember the advertisement was in the paper before the night of the burglary."

He opened his eyes and then smiled.

"Brilliant police you've got!" he murmured, and took up the pen again.

"There was another burglar here and he might have taken it!" said Mary in a low voice.

The visitor once more dropped the pen and looked up with a start.

"Another burglar!" he exclaimed.

"Well, sir, this one didn't actually burgle, but—"

She thought of the master if he chanced to learn how she had been gossiping, and her sentence was cut short in the midst.

"Yes, Mary! You were saying?" cooed the persuasive visitor, and Mary succumbed again and told him of that night when a shadow moved into the trees and footprints were left in the gravel outside the library window, and the master looked so strangely in the morning. Her visitor was so interested that once she began it was really impossible to stop.

"How very strange!" he murmured, and there was no doubt he meant it.

"But about the master's ring, sir—" she began.

"You say he looked as though he were being *watched*?" he interrupted, but it was quite a polite and gentle interruption.

"Yes, sir; but the funny thing about losing the ring was that he never could get it off his finger before! I've seen him trying to, but oh, it wouldn't nearly come off!"

Again he sat up and gazed at her.

"Another mystery!" he murmured. "He lost a ring which wouldn't come off his finger? By Jove! That's very rum. Are there any more mysteries, Mary, connected with this house?"

She hesitated and then in a very low voice answered:

"Oh, yes, sir; there was one that gave me even a worse turn!"

By this time her visitor seemed to have given up all immediate thoughts of writing his note to Mr. Rattar. He turned his back to the table and looked at her with benevolent calm.

"Let's hear it, Mary," he said gently.

And then she told him the story of that dreadful night when the unknown visitor came for the box of old papers. He gazed at her, listening very attentively, and then in a soothing voice asked her several questions, more particularly when all these mysterious events occurred.

"And are these all your troubles now, Mary?" he enquired.

He asked so sympathetically that at last she even ventured to tell him her latest trouble. Till he fairly charmed it out of her, she had shrunk from telling him anything that seemed to reflect directly on her master or to be a giving away of his concerns. But now she confessed that Mr. Rattar's conduct, Mr. Rattar's looks, and even Mr. Rattar's very infrequent words had been troubling her strangely. How or why his looks and words should trouble her, she knew not precisely, and his conduct, generally speaking, she admitted was as regular as ever.

"You don't mean that just now and then he takes a wee drop too much?" enquired her visitor helpfully.

"Oh, no, sir," said she, "the master never did take more than what a gentleman should, and he's not a smoking gentleman either—quite a principle against smokers, he has, sir. Oh, it's nothing like that!"

She looked over her shoulder fearfully as though the walls might repeat her words to the master, as she told him of the curious and disturbing thing. Mr. Rattar had been till lately a gentleman of the most exact habits, and then all of a sudden he had taken to walking in his garden in a way he never did before. First she had noticed him, about the time of the burglary and the removal of the papers, walking there in the mornings. That perhaps was not so very disturbing, but since then he had changed this for a habit of slipping out of the house every night—every single night!

"And walking in the garden!" exclaimed Mr. Carrington.

"Sometimes I've heard his footsteps on the gravel, sir! Even when it has been raining I've heard them. Perhaps sometimes he goes outside the garden, but I've never heard of anyone meeting him on the road or streets. It's in the garden I've heard the master's steps, sir, and if you had been with him as long as I've been, and knew how regular his habits was, you'd know how I'm feeling, sir!"

"I do know, Mary; I quite understand," Mr. Carrington assured her in his soothing voice, and there could be no doubt he was wondering just as hard as she.

"What o'clock does he generally go out?" he asked.

"At nine o'clock almost exactly every night, sir!"

Mr. Carrington looked thoughtfully out of the window into the garden, and then at last looked down at the ink and paper and pen. Not a word was written on the paper yet.

"Look here, Mary," he said very confidentially. "I am a friend of Mr. Rattar's and I am sure you would like me to try and throw a little light on this. Perhaps something is troubling him and I could help you to clear it up."

"Oh, sir," she cried, "you are very kind! I wish you could!"

"Perhaps the best thing then," he suggested, "would be for me not to leave a note for him after all, and for you not even to mention that I have called. As he knows me pretty well he would be almost sure to ask you whether I had come in and if I had left any message and so on, and then he might perhaps find out that we had been talking, and that wouldn't perhaps be pleasant for you, would it?"

"Oh, my! No, indeed, it wouldn't!" she agreed. "I'm that feared of the master, sir, I'd never have him know I had been talking about him, or about anything that has happened in this house!"

So, having come to this judicious decision, Mr. Carrington wished Mary the kindest of farewells and walked down the drive again. There could be no question he had plenty to think about now, though to judge from his expression, it seemed doubtful whether his thoughts were very clear.

A CONFIDENTIAL CONVERSATION

The laird of Stanesland strode into the Kings Arms and demanded:

"Mr. Carrington? What, having a cup of tea in his room? What's his number? 27—right! I'll walk right up, thanks."

He walked right up, made the door rattle under his knuckles and strode jauntily in. There was no beating about the bush with Mr. Cromarty either in deed or word.

"Well, Mr. Carrington," said he, "don't trouble to look surprised. I guess you've seen right through me for some time back."

"Meaning—?" asked Carrington with his engaging smile.

"Meaning that I'm the unknown, unsuspected, and mysterious person who's putting up the purse. Don't pretend you haven't tumbled to that!"

"Yes," admitted Carrington, "I have tumbled."

"I knew my sister had given the whole blamed show away! I take it you put your magnifying glass back in your pocket after your trip out to Stanesland?"

"More or less," admitted Carrington.

"Well," said Ned, "that being so, I may as well tell you what my idea was. It mayn't have been very bright; still there was a kind of method in my madness. You see I wanted you to have an absolutely clear field and let you suspect me just as much as anybody else."

"In short," smiled Carrington, "you wanted to start with the other horses and not just drop the flag."

"That's so," agreed Ned. "But when my sister let out about that £1200, and I saw that you must have spotted me, there didn't seem much point in keeping up the bluff, when I came to think it over. And since then, Mr. Carrington, something has happened that you ought to know and I decided to come and see you and talk to you straight."

"What has happened?"

Ned smiled for an instant his approval of this prompt plunge into business, and then his face set hard.

"It's a most extraordinary thing," said he, "and may strike you as hardly credible, but here's the plain truth put shortly. Yesterday afternoon Miss Farmond ran away." Carrington merely nodded, and he exclaimed, "What! You know then?"

"I learned from Bisset this morning."

"Ah, I see. Did you know I'd happened to see her start and gone after her and brought her back?"

Carrington's interest was manifest.

"No," said he, "that's quite news to me."

"Well, I did, and I learnt the whole story from her. You can't guess who advised her to bolt?"

"I think I can," said Carrington quietly.

"Either you're on the wrong track, or you've cut some ice, Mr. Carrington. It was Simon Rattar!"

"I thought so."

"How the devil did you guess?"

"Tell me Miss Farmond's story first and I'll tell you how I guessed."

"Well, she spotted you were a detective—"

Carrington started and then laughed.

"Confound these women!" said he. "They're so infernally independent of reason, they always spot things they shouldn't!"

"Then she discovered she was suspected and so she got in a stew, poor girl, and went to see Rattar. Do you know what he told her? That I was employing you and meant to convict Sir Malcolm and her and hang them with my own hands!"

"The old devil!" cried Carrington. "Well, no wonder she bolted, Mr. Cromarty!"

"But even that was done by Simon's advice. He actually gave her an address in London to go to."

"Pretty thorough!" murmured Carrington.

"Now what do you make of that? And what ought one to do? And, by the way, how did you guess Simon was at the bottom of it?"

Carrington leaned back in his chair and thought for a moment before answering.

"We are in pretty deep waters, Mr. Cromarty," he said slowly. "As to what I make of it—nothing as yet. As to what we are to do— also nothing in the meantime. But as to how I guessed, well I can tell you this much. I had to get information from someone, and so I called on Mr. Rattar and told him who I was—in strict confidence, by the way, so that he had no business to tell Miss Farmond or anybody else. I had started off, I may say, with a wrong guess: I thought Rattar himself was probably either my employer or acting for my employer, and when I suggested this he told me I was right."

"What!" shouted Ned. "The grunting old devil told you that?" He stared at the other for a moment, and then demanded, "Why did he tell you that lie?"

"Fortune played my cards for me. Quite innocently and unintentionally. I tempted him. I said if I could be sure he was my employer I'd keep him in touch with everything I was doing. I had also let him know that my employer had made it an absolute condition that his name was not to appear. He evidently wanted badly to know what I was doing, and thought he was safe not to be given away."

"Then have you kept him in touch with everything you have done?"

Carrington smiled.

"I tell you, Mr. Cromarty, my cards were being played for me. Five minutes later I asked him who benefited by the will and I learned that you had scored the precise sum of £1200."

"I hadn't thought of that when I made my limit £1200!" exclaimed Ned. "Lord, you must have bowled me out at once! Of course, you spotted the coincidence straight off?"

"But Rattar didn't! I pushed it under his nose and he didn't see it! Inside of one second I'd asked myself whether it was possible for an astute man like that not to notice such a coincidence supposing he had really guaranteed me exactly that sum—an extraordinarily large and curious sum too."

"I like these simple riddles," said Ned with a twinkle in his single eye. "I guess your answer to yourself was 'No!'"

Carrington nodded.

"That's what I call having my cards played for me. I knew then that the man was lying; so I threw him off the scent, changed the subject, and did *not* keep Mr. Simon Rattar in touch with any single thing I did after that."

"Good for you!" said Ned.

"Good so far, but the next riddle wasn't of the simple kind—or else I'm even a bigger ass than I endeavour to look! What was the man's game?"

"Have you spotted it yet?"

Carrington shook his head.

"Mr. Simon Rattar's game is the toughest proposition in the way of puzzles I've ever struck. While I'm at it I'll just tell you one or two other small features of that first interview."

He lit a cigarette and leant over the arm of his chair towards his visitor, his manner growing keener as he talked.

"I happened to have met Miss Farmond that morning and my interview had knocked the bottom out of the story that she was concerned in the crime. I had satisfied myself also that she was not engaged to Sir Malcolm."

"How did you discover that?" exclaimed Ned.

"Her manner when I mentioned him. But I found that old Rattar was wrong on both these points and apparently determined to remain wrong. Of course, it might have been a mere error of judgment, but at the same time he had no evidence whatever against her, and it seemed to suggest a curious bias. And finally, I didn't like the look of the man."

"And then you came out to see me?"

"I went out to Keldale House first and then out to you. I next interviewed Sir Malcolm."

"Interviewed Malcolm Cromarty!" exclaimed Ned. "Where?"

"He came up to see me," explained Carrington easily, "and the gentleman had scarcely spoken six sentences before I shared your opinion of him, Mr. Cromarty—a squirt but not homicidal. He gave me, however, one very interesting piece of information. Rattar had advised him to keep away from these parts, and for choice to go abroad. I need hardly ask whether you consider that sound advice to give a suspected man."

"Seems to me nearly as rotten advice as he gave Miss Farmond."

"Exactly. So when I heard that Miss Farmond had flown and discovered she had paid a visit to Mr. Rattar the previous day, I guessed who had given her the advice."

Carrington sat back in his chair with folded arms and looked at his employer with a slight smile, as much as to say, "Tell me the rest of the story!" Cromarty returned his gaze in silence, his heaviest frown upon his brow.

"It seems to me," said Ned at last, "that Simon Rattar is mixed up in this business—sure! He has something to hide and he's trying to put people off the scent, I'll lay my bottom dollar!"

"What is he hiding?" enquired Carrington, looking up at the ceiling.

"What do you think?"

Carrington shook his head, his eyes still gazing dreamily upwards.

"I wish to Heaven I knew what to think!" he murmured; and then he resumed a brisker air and continued, "I am ready to suspect Simon Rattar of any crime in the calendar—leaving out petty larceny and probably bigamy. But he's the last man to do either good or evil unless he saw a dividend at the end, and where does he score by taking any part or parcel in conniving at or abetting or concealing evidence or anything else, so far as this particular crime is concerned? He has lost his best client, with whom he was on excellent terms and whose family he had served all his life, and he has now got instead an unsatisfactory young ass whom he suspects, or says he suspects, of murder, and who so loathes Rattar that, as far as I can judge, he will probably take his business away from him. To suspect Rattar of actually conniving at, or taking any part in the actual crime itself is, on the face of it, to convict either Rattar or oneself of lunacy!"

"I knew Sir Reginald pretty well," said Ned, "but of course I didn't know much about his business affairs. He hadn't been having any trouble with Rattar, had he?"

Carrington threw him a quick, approving glance.

"We are thinking on the same lines," said he, "and I have unearthed one very odd little misunderstanding, but it seems to have been nothing more than that, and, apart from it, all accounts agree that there was no trouble of any kind or description."

He took a cigarette out of his case and struck a match.

"There must be *some* motive for everything one does—even for smoking this cigarette. If I disliked cigarettes, knew smoking was bad for me, and stood in danger of being fined if I was caught doing it, why should I smoke? I can see no point whatever in Rattar's taking the smallest share even in diverting the course of justice by a hair's breadth. He and you and I have to all appearances identical interests in the matter."

"You are wiser than I am," said Ned simply, but with a grim look in his eye, "but all I can say is I am going out with my gun to look for Simon Rattar."

Carrington laughed.

"I'm afraid you'll have to catch him at something a little better known to the charge-sheets than giving bad advice to a lady client, before it's safe to fire!" said he.

"But, look here, Carrington, have you collected no other facts whatever about this case?"

Carrington shot him a curious glance, but answered nothing else.

"Oh well," said Ned, "if you don't want to say anything yet, don't say it. Play your hand as you think best."

"Mr. Cromarty," replied Carrington, "I assure you I don't want to make facts into mysteries, but when they *are* mysteries—well, I like to think 'em over a bit before I trust myself to talk. In the course of this very afternoon I've collected an assortment either of facts or fiction that seem to have broken loose from a travelling nightmare."

"Mind telling where you got 'em?" asked Ned.

"Chiefly from Rattar's housemaid, a very excellent but somewhat high-strung and imaginative young woman, and how much to believe of what she told me I honestly don't know. And the more one can believe, the worse the puzzle gets! However, there is one statement which I hope to be able to check. It may throw some light on the lady's veracity generally. Meantime I am like a man trying to build a house of what may be bricks or may be paper bags."

Ned rose with his usual prompt decision.

"I see," said he. "And I guess you find one better company than two at this particular moment. I won't shoot Simon Rattar till I hear from you, though by Gad, I'm tempted to kick him just to be going on with! But look here, Carrington, if my services will ever do you the least bit of good—in fact, so long as I'm not actually in the way—just send me a wire and I'll come straight. You won't refuse me that?"

Carrington looked at the six feet two inches of pure lean muscle and smiled.

"Not likely!" he said. "That's not the sort of offer I refuse. I won't hesitate to wire if there's anything happening. But don't count on it. I can't see any business doing just yet."

Ned held out his hand, and then suddenly said, "You don't see any business doing just yet? But you feel you're on his track, sure! Now, don't you?"

Carrington glanced at him out of an eye half quizzical, half abstracted.

"Whose track?" he asked.

Ned paused for a second and then rapped out:

"Was it Simon himself?"

"If we were all living in a lunatic asylum, probably yes! If we were living in the palace of reason, certainly not—the thing's ridiculous! What we are actually living in, however, is—" he broke off and gazed into space.

"What?" said Ned.

"A blank fog!"

It was a few minutes after half past eight when Miss Peterkin chanced to meet her friend Mr. Carrington in the entrance hall of the Kings Arms. He was evidently going out, and she noticed he was rather differently habited from usual, wearing now a long, light top coat of a very dark grey hue, and a dark coloured felt hat. They were not quite so becoming as his ordinary garb, she thought, but then Mr. Carrington looked the gentleman in anything.

"Are you going to desert us to-night, Mr. Carrington?" asked the manageress.

"I have a letter or two to post," said he, "they are an excuse for a stroll. I want a breath of fresh air."

He closed the glass door of the hotel behind him and stood for a moment on the pavement in the little circle of radiance thrown by the light of the hall. Mr. Carrington's leisurely movements undoubtedly played no small part in the unsuspecting confidence which he inspired. Out of the light he turned, strolling easily, down the long stretch of black pavement with its few checkers of lamplight here and there, and the empty, silent street of the little country town at his side. It was a very dark, moonless night, and the air was almost quite still. Looking upward, he could see a rare star or two twinkle, but all the rest of the Heavens were under cloud. Judging from his contented expression the night seemed to please him.

He passed the post office, but curiously enough omitted to drop any letters into the box. The breath of fresh air seemed, in fact, to be his sole preoccupation. Moving with a slightly quickened stride, but still easily, he turned out of that street into another even quieter and darker, and in a short time he was nearing the lights of the station. He gave these a wide birth, however, and presently was strolling up a very secluded road, with a few villas and gardens upon the one side, and black space on the other. There for a moment he stopped and transferred something from the pocket of his inner coat into the pocket of his top coat. It was a small compact article, and a ray of light from a lamp-post behind him gleamed for an instant upon a circular metal orifice at one end of it.

Before he moved on, he searched the darkness intently, before him and behind, but saw no sign of any other passenger. And then he turned the rim of his dark felt hat down over his face, stepped out briskly for some fifty yards further, and turned sharply through an open gate. Once again he stopped and listened keenly, standing now in the shadow of the trees beside the drive. In his dark top coat and with his hat turned over his face he was as nearly invisible as a man could be, but even this did not seem to satisfy him, for in a moment he gently parted the branches of the trees and pushed through the belt of planting to the lawn beyond.

The villa of Mr. Simon Rattar was now half seen beyond the curving end of the belt that bounded the drive. It was dim against the night sky, and the garden was dimmer still. Carrington kept on the grass, following the outside of the trees, and then again plunged into them when they curved round at the top of the drive. Pushing quietly through, he reached the other side, and there his expedition in search of fresh air seemed to have found its goal, for he leaned his back against a tree trunk, folded his arms, and waited.

He was looking obliquely across a sweep of gravel, with the whole front of the house full in view. A ray came from the fanlight over the front door and a faint radiance escaped through the slats of the library blinds, but otherwise the villa was a lump of darkness in the dark.

One minute after another passed without event and with scarcely even the faintest sound. Then, all at once, a little touch of breeze sprang up and sighed overhead through the tree tops, and from that time on, there was an alternation of utter silence with the sough of branches gently stirred.

From a church tower in the town came the stroke of a clock. Carrington counted nine and his eyes were riveted on the front door now. Barely two more minutes passed before it opened quietly; a figure appeared for an instant in the light of the hall, and then, as quietly, the door closed again. There was a lull at the moment, but Carrington could hear not a sound. The figure must be standing very still on the doorstep, listening—evidently listening. And then the thickset form of Simon Rattar appeared dimly on the gravel, crossing to the lawn beyond. The pebbles crunched a little, but not very much. He seemed to be walking warily, and when he reached the further side he stood still again and Carrington could see his head moving, as though he were looking all round him through the night.

But now the figure was moving again, coming this time straight for the head of the belt of trees. Carrington had drawn on a pair of dark gloves, and he raised his arm to cover the lower part of his face, looking over it through the branches, and facing the silent owner of the garden, till there were hardly three paces between them, the one on the lawn, the other in the heart of the plantation.

And then when Simon was exactly opposite, he stopped dead. Carrington's other hand slipped noiselessly into the pocket where he had dropped that little article, but otherwise he never moved a muscle and he breathed very gently. The man on the turf seemed to be doing something with his hands, but what, it was impossible to say. The hands would move into his pocket and then out again, till quite three or four minutes had passed, and then came a sudden flash of light. Carrington's right hand moved halfway out of his pocket and then was stayed, for by the light of the match he saw a very singular sight.

Simon Rattar was not looking at him. His eyes were focused just before his nose where the bowl of a pipe was beginning to glow. Carrington could hear the lips gently sucking, and then the aroma of tobacco came in a strong wave through the trees. Finally the match went out, and the glowing pipe began to move slowly along the turf, keeping close to the shelter of the trees.

For a space Carrington stood petrified with wonder, and then, very carefully and quite silently, he worked his way through the trees out on to the turf, and at once fell on his hands and knees. Had any one been there to see, they would have beheld for the next five minutes a strange procession of two slowly moving along the edge of the plantation; a thickset man in front smoking a pipe and something like a great gorilla stalking him from behind. This procession skirted the plantation nearly down to the gate; then it turned at right angles, following the line of trees that bordered the wall between the garden and the road; and then again at right angles when it had reached the further corner of Mr. Rattar's demesne. Simon was now in a secluded path with shrubs on either hand, and instead of continuing his tour, he turned at the end of this path and paced slowly back again. And seeing this, the ape behind him squatted in the shadow of a laurel and waited.

A steady breeze was now blowing and the trees were sighing continuously. The sky at the same time cleared, and more and more stars came out till the eyes of the man behind the bush could follow the moving man from end to end of the path. The wind made the pipe smoke quickly, and presently a shower of sparks showed that it was being emptied, and in a minute or two another match flashed and a second pipe glowed faintly.

Backwards and forwards paced the lawyer, and backwards and forwards again, but for the space of nearly an hour from his first coming out, that was everything that happened; and then at last came a tapping of the bowl and more sparks flying abroad in the wind. The procession was resumed, Simon in front, the ape-like form behind; but with a greater space between them this time as the night was clearer, and now they were heading for the house. The lawyer's steps crunched lightly on the gravel again, the front door opened and closed, and Carrington was alone in the garden.

Still crawling, he reached the shelter of the belt of trees and then rose and made swiftly for the gate, and out into the road. As he passed under a lamp, his face wore a totally new expression, compounded of wonder, excitement, and urgent thought. He was walking swiftly, and his pace never slackened, nor did the keenness leave his face, till he was back at the door of the Kings Arms Hotel. Before he entered, he took off his hat and turned up the brim again, and his manner when he tapped at the door of the manageress' room was perfectly sedate. He let it appear, however, that he had some slight matter on his mind.

"What is the name of Mr. Rattar's head clerk?" he enquired. "An oldish, prim looking man, with side whiskers."

"Oh, that will be Mr. Ison," said the manageress.

"I have just remembered a bit of business I ought to have seen about to-night," he continued. "I can't very well call on Mr. Rattar himself at this hour, but I was thinking of looking up Mr. Ison if I could discover his whereabouts."

"The boots will show you the way to his house," said she, and rang the bell.

While waiting for the boots, Mr. Carrington asked another casual question or two and learned that Mr. Ison had been in the office since he was a boy. No man knew the house of Rattar throughout its two generations better than Mr. Ison, said Miss Peterkin; and she remembered afterwards that this information seemed to give Mr. Carrington peculiar satisfaction. He seemed so gratified, indeed, that she wondered a little at the time.

And then the visitor and the boots set out together for the clerk's house, and at what hour her guest returned she was not quite sure. The boots, it seemed, had been instructed to wait up for him, but she had long gone to bed.

Had there been, next morning, any curious eyes to watch the conduct of the gentleman who had come to rent a sporting estate, they
would probably have surmised that he had found something to
please his fancy strangely, and yet that some perplexity still persisted. They would also have put him down as a much more excit-
able, and even demonstrative, young man than they had imagined.
On a lonely stretch of shore hard by the little town he paced for
nearly an hour, his face a record of the debate within, and his cane
gesticulating at intervals.

Of a sudden he stopped dead and his lips moved in a murmured
ejaculation, and then after standing stock still for some minutes,
he murmured again:

"Ten to one on it!"

His cane had been stationary during this pause. Now he raised
it once more, but this time with careful attention. It was a light
bamboo with a silver head. He looked at it thoughtfully, bent it
this way and that, and then drove it into the sand and pressed it
down. Though to the ordinary eye a very chaste and appropriate
walking stick for such a gentleman as Mr. Carrington, the result of
these tests seemed to dissatisfy him. He shook his head, and then
with an air of resolution set out for the town.

A little later he entered a shop where a number of walking sticks
were on view and informed the proprietor that he desired to purchase something more suitable for the country than the cane he
carried. In fact, his taste seemed now to run to the very opposite

extreme, for the points on which he insisted were length, stiffness, and a long and if possible somewhat pointed ferule. At last he found one to his mind, left his own cane to be sent down to the hotel, and walked out with his new purchase.

His next call was at Mr. Simon Rattar's villa. This morning he approached it without any of the curious shyness he had exhibited on the occasion of his recent visit. His advance was conducted openly up the drive and in an erect posture, and he crossed the gravel space boldly, and even jauntily, while his ring was firmness itself. Mary answered the bell, and her pleasure at seeing so soon again the sympathetic gentleman with the eyeglass was a tribute to his tact.

"Good morning, Mary," said he, with an air that combined very happily the courtesy of a gentleman with the freedom of an old friend, "Mr. Rattar is at his office, I presume."

She said that he was, but this time the visitor exhibited neither surprise nor disappointment.

"I thought he would be," he confessed confidentially, "and I have come to see whether I couldn't do something to help you to get at the bottom of these troublesome goings on. Anything fresh happened?"

"The master was out in the garden again last night, sir!" said she.

"Was he really?" cried Mr. Carrington. "By Jove, how curious! We really must look into that: in fact, I've got an idea I want you to help me with. By the way, it sounds an odd question to ask about Mr. Rattar, but have you ever seen any sign of a pipe or tobacco in the house?"

"Oh, never indeed!" said she. "The master has never been a smoking gentleman. Quite against smoking he's always been, sir."

"Ever since you have known him?"

"Oh, and before that, sir."

"Ah!" observed Mr. Carrington in a manner that suggested nothing whatever. "Well, Mary, I want this morning to have a look round the garden."

Her eyes opened.

"Because the master walks there at nights?"

He nodded confidentially.

"But—but if he was to know you'd been interfering, sir—I mean what he'd think was interfering, sir—"

"He shan't know," he assured her. "At least not if you'll do what I tell you. I want you to go now and have a nice quiet talk with cook for half an hour—half an hour by the kitchen clock, Mary. If you don't look out of the window, you won't know that I'm in the garden, and then nobody can blame you whatever happens. We haven't mentioned the word 'garden' between us—so you are out of it! Remember that."

He smiled so pleasantly that Mary smiled back.

"I'll remember, sir," said she. "And cook is to be kept talking in the kitchen?"

"You've tumbled to it exactly, Mary. If neither of you see me, neither of you know anything at all."

She got a last glimpse of his sympathetic smile as she closed the door, and then she went faithfully to the kitchen for her talk with cook. It was quite a pleasant gossip at first, but half an hour is a long time to keep talking, when one has been asked not to stop sooner, and it so happened, moreover, that cook was somewhat busy that morning and began at length to indicate distinctly that unless her friend had some matter of importance to communicate she would regard further verbiage with disfavour. At this juncture Mary decided that twenty minutes was practically as good as half an hour, and the conversation ceased.

Passing out of the kitchen regions, Mary glanced towards a distant window, hesitated, and then came to another decision. Mr. Carrington must surely have left the garden now, so there was no harm in peeping out. She went to the window and peeped.

It was only a two minutes' peep, for Mr. Carrington had not left the garden, and at the end of that space of time something very disturbing happened. But it was long enough to make her marvel greatly at her sympathetic friend's method of solving the riddle of the master's conduct. When she first saw him, he seemed to be smoothing the earth in one of the flower beds with his foot. Then he moved on a few paces, stopped, and drove his walking stick hard into the bed. She saw him lean on it to get it further in and apparently twist it about a little. And then he withdrew it again and was in the act of smoothing the place when she saw him glance sharply towards the gate, and the next instant leap behind a bush. Simultaneously the hum of a motorcar fell on her ear, and Mary was out of the room and speeding upstairs.

She heard the car draw up before the house and listened for the front door bell, but the door opened without a ring and she marvelled and trembled afresh. That the master should return in a car at this hour of the morning seemed surely to be connected with the sin she had connived at. It swelled into a crime as she held her breath and listened. She wished devoutly she had never set eyes on the insinuating Mr. Carrington.

But there came no call for her, or no ringing of any bell; merely sounds of movement in the hall below, heard through the thrumming of the waiting car. And then the front door opened and shut again and she ventured to the window. It was a little open and she could hear her master speak to the chauffeur as he got in. He was now wearing, she noticed, a heavy overcoat. A moment more and he was off again, down the drive, and out through the gates. When she remembered to look again for her sympathetic friend, he was quietly driving his walking stick once more into a flower bed.

About ten minutes afterwards the front door bell rang and there stood Mr. Carrington again. His eye seemed strangely bright, she thought, but his manner was calm and soothing as ever.

"I noticed Mr. Rattar return," he said, "and I thought I would like to make sure that it was all right, before I left. I trust, Mary, that you have got into no trouble on my account."

She thought it was very kind of him to enquire.

"The master was only just in and out again," she assured him.

"He came to get his overcoat, I noticed," he remarked.

Mr. Carrington's powers of observation struck her as very surprising for such an easy-going gentleman.

"Yes, sir, that was all."

"Well, I'm very glad it was all right," he smiled and began to turn away. "By the way," he asked, turning back, "did he tell you where he is going to now?"

"He didn't see me, sir."

"You didn't happen to overhear him giving any directions to the chauffeur, did you? I noticed you at an open window."

For the first time Mary's sympathetic friend began to make her feel a trifle uncomfortable. His eyes seemed to be everywhere.

"I thought I heard him say 'Keldale House,'" she confessed.

"Really!" he exclaimed and seemed to muse for a moment. In fact, he appeared to be still musing as he walked away.

Mary began to wonder very seriously whether Mr. Carrington was going to prove merely a fresh addition to the disquieting mysteries of that house.

The short November afternoon was fading into a gusty evening, as Ned Cromarty drew near his fortalice. He carried a gun as usual, and as usual walked with seven league strides. Where the drive passed through the scrap of stunted plantation it was already dusk and the tortured boughs had begun their night of sighs and tossings. Beyond them, pale daylight lingered and the old house stood up still clear against a broken sky and a grey waste with flitting whitecaps all the way to the horizon. He had almost reached the front door when he heard the sound of wheels behind him. Pausing there, he spied a pony and a governess' car, with two people distinct enough to bring a sudden light into his eye. The pony trotted briskly towards the door, and he took a stride to meet them.

"Miss Farmond!" he said.

A low voice answered, and though he could not catch the words, the tone was enough for him. And then another voice said:

"Aye, sir, I've brought her over."

"Bisset!" said he. "It's you, is it? Well, what's happened?"

He was lifting her out of the trap and not hesitating to hold her hand a little longer than he had ever held it before, now that he could see her face quite plainly and read what was in her eyes.

"I've dared to come after all!" she said, with a little smile, which seemed to hint that she knew the risk was over now.

"I advised her vera strongly, sir, to come over with me to Stanesland," explained her escort. "The young lady has had a trying experience at Keldale, and forby the fair impossibility of her stopping on under the unfortunate circumstances, I was of the opinion that the sea air would be a fine change and the architectural features remarkably interesting. In fac', sir, I practically insisted that Miss Farmond had just got to come."

"Good man!" said Ned. "Come in and tell me the unfortunate circumstances." He bent over Cicely and in a lowered voice added: "Personally I call 'em fortunate—so long as they haven't been too beastly for you!"

"It's all right now!" she murmured, and as they went up the steps he found, somehow or other, her hand for an instant in his again.

"If you'll stand by your pony for a moment, Bisset, I'll send out some one to take her," he said with happy inspiration.

But Mr. Bisset was not so easily shaken off.

"She'll stand fine for a wee while," he assured his host. "You'll be the better of hearing all about it from me."

They went into the smoking room and the escort began forthwith.

"The fact is, Mr. Cromarty, that yon man Simon Rattar is a fair discredit. Miss Farmond has been telling me the haill story of her running away, and your ain vera seasonable appearance and judicious conduct, sir; which I am bound to say, Mr. Cromarty, is neither more nor less than I'd have expectit of a gentleman of your intelligence. Weel, to continue, Miss Farmond acted on your advice—which would have been my own, sir, under the circumstances—and tellt her ladyship the plain facts. Weel then—"

"And what did Lady Cromarty say to you?" demanded Ned.

"Hardly a word. She simply looked at me and said she would send for Mr. Rattar."

Not a whit rebuffed, Mr. Bisset straightway resumed his narrative.

"A perfectly proper principle if the man was capable of telling the truth. I'm no blaming her ladyship at that point, but where she departit from the proper principles of evidence—"

"When did Rattar come?"

"This morning," said Cicely. "And—can you believe it?—he absolutely denied that he had ever advised me to go away!"

"I can believe it," said Ned grimly. "And I suppose Lady Cromarty believed him?"

"God, but you're right, sir!" cried Bisset. "Your deductions are perfectly correct. Yon man had the impudence to give the haill thing a flat denial! And then naturally Miss Farmond was for off, but at first her ladyship was no for letting her go. Indeed she went the length of sending for me and telling me the young lady was not to be permitted to shift her luggage out of the house or use any conveyance."

"But Bisset was splendid!" cried Cicely. "Do you know what the foolish man did? He gave up his situation and took me away!"

Bisset, the man, permitted a gleam of pleasure to illuminate his blunt features; but Bisset, the philosopher, protested with some dignity.

"It was a mere matter of principle, sir. Detention of luggage like yon is no legal. I tellt her ladyship flatly that she'd find herself afore the Shirra', and that I was no going to abet any such proceedings. I further informed her, sir, of my candid opinion of Simon Rattar, and I said plainly that he was probably meaning to marry her and get the estate under his thumb, and these were the kind o' tricks rascally lawyers took in foolish women wi'."

"You told Lady Cromarty that!" exclaimed Ned. "And what did she say?"

"We had a few disagreeable passages, as it were, sir," said the philosopher calmly. "And then I borrowed yon trap and having advised Miss Farmond to come to Stanesland and she being amenable, I just brought her along to you."

"Oh, it was on your advice then?"

"Yes, sir."

Cicely and her host exchanged one fleeting glance and then looked extremely unconscious.

"She's derned wise!" said he to himself.

He held out his hand to the gratified counsellor.

"Well done, Bisset, you've touched your top form to-day, and I may tell you I've been wanting some one like you badly for a long while, if you are willing to stay on with me. Put that in your pipe,

Bisset, and smoke over it! And now, you know your way, go and get yourself some tea, and a drink of the wildest poison you fancy!"

Hardly was the door closed behind him than the laird put his fate to the test as promptly and directly as he did most other things.

"I want you to stop on too, Cicely—for ever. Will you?"

Her eyes, shyly questioning for a moment and then shyly tender, answered his question before her lips had moved, and it would have been hard to convince them that the minutes which followed ever had a parallel within human experience.

A little later he confessed:

"Do you know, Cicely, I've always had a funky feeling that if I ever proposed my glass eye would drop out!"

The next event was the somewhat sudden entry of Lilian Cromarty, and that lady's self control was never more severely tested or brilliantly vindicated. One startled glance, and then she was saying, briskly, and with the old bright smile:

"A telegram for you, Ned."

"Thanks," said he. "By the way, here's the future Mrs. Ned— that's to say if she doesn't funk it before the wedding."

Lilian's welcome, Lilian's embrace, and Lilian's congratulations were alike perfect. Cicely wondered how people could ever have said the critical things of her which some of her acquaintances were unkind enough to say at times. As to Bisset's dictum regarding the lady in the castle, that was manifestly absurd on the face of it. Miss Cromarty was clearly overjoyed to hear of her brother's engagement.

"And now, Neddy dear!" cried the bright lady, "tell me how it all came about!"

Ned looked up from his telegram with a glint in his eye that was hardly a lover's glance.

"Cicely will tell you all about it," said he. "I'm afraid I've got to be off pretty well as quick as I can."

He handed them the wire and they read: "Meet me eight tonight Kings Arms urgent. Carrington."

"From Mr. Carrington!" exclaimed his sister.

Ned smiled.

"Cicely will explain him too," he said. "By Gad, I wonder if this is going to be the finishing bit of luck!"

In another twenty minutes the lights of his gig lamps were raking the night.

Cromarty and Carrington slipped unostentatiously out of the hotel a few minutes after eight o'clock.

"Take any line you like," said Carrington, "but as he knows now that you brought Miss Farmond back and have heard her version, he'll naturally be feeling a little uncomfortable about the place where one generally gets kicked, when he sees you march in. He will expect you to open out on that subject, so if I were you I'd take the natural line of country and do what he expects."

"Including the kicking?"

Carrington laughed.

"Keep him waiting for that. Spin it out; that's your job to-night."

"I wish it were more than talking!" said Ned.

"Well," drawled Carrington, "it may lead to something more amusing. Who knows? You haven't bought your own gun, I suppose? Take mine."

He handed him the same little article he had taken out the night before, and Ned's eye gleamed.

"What!" said he. "That kind of gun once more? This reminds me of old times!"

"It's a mere precaution," said the other. "Don't count on using it! Remember, you're going to visit the most respectable citizen of the town—perhaps on a wild goose errand."

"I guess not," said Ned quietly.

"We daren't assume anything. I don't want to make a fool of myself, and no more do you, I take it."

"I see," said Ned, with a nod. "Well, I'll keep him in his chair for you."

"That's it."

They were walking quickly through the silent town under the windy night sky. It was a dark boisterous evening, not inviting for strollers, and they scarcely passed a soul till they were in the quiet road where the villa stood. There, from the shadows of a gateway, two figures moved out to meet them, and Cromarty recognised Superintendent Sutherland and one of his constables. The two saluted in silence and fell in behind. They each carried, he noticed, something long-shaped wrapped up loosely in sacking.

"What have they got there?" he asked.

"Prosaic instruments," smiled Carrington. "I won't tell you more for fear the gamble doesn't come off."

"Like the sensation before one proposes, I suppose," said Ned. "Well, going by that, the omens ought to be all right."

They turned in through Simon's gates and then the four stopped.

"We part here," whispered Carrington. "Good luck!"

"Same to you," said Ned briefly, and strode up the drive.

As he came out into the gravel sweep before the house, he looked hard into the darkness of the garden, but beyond the tossing shapes of trees, there was not a sign of movement.

"Mr. Rattar in?" he enquired. "Sitting in the library I suppose? Take me right to him. Cromarty's my name."

"Mr. Cromarty to see you, sir," announced Mary, and she was startled to see the master's sudden turn in his chair and the look upon his face.

"Whether he was feared or whether he was angered, I canna rightly say," she told cook, "but anyway he looked fair mad like!"

"Good evening," said Ned.

His voice was restrained and dry, and as he spoke he strode across the room and seated himself deliberately in the arm chair on the side of the fire opposite to the lawyer.

Simon had banished that first look which Mary saw, but there remained in his eyes something more than their usual cold stare.

Each day since Carrington came seemed to have aged his face and changed it for the worse: a haggard, ugly, malicious face it seemed to his visitor looking hard at it to-night. His only greeting was a briefer grunt than ordinary.

"I daresay you can guess what's brought me here," said Ned.

The lawyer rapped out his first words jerkily.

"No. I can't."

"Try three guesses," suggested his visitor. "Come now, number one—?"

For a moment Simon was silent, but to-night he could not hide the working of that face which usually hid his thoughts so effectually. It was plain he hesitated what line to take.

"You have seen Miss Farmond, I hear," he said.

"You're on the scent," said his visitor encouragingly. "Have another go."

"You believe her story."

"I do."

"It's false."

Ned stared at him very hard and then he spoke deliberately.

"I'm wondering," said he.

"Wondering what?" asked Simon.

"Whether a horse whip or the toe of a shooting boot is the best cure for your complaint."

The lawyer shrank back into his chair.

"Do you threaten me?" he jerked out. "Be careful!"

"If I threatened you I'd certainly do what I threatened," said Ned. "So far I'm only wondering. Where did you learn to lie, Mr. Rattar?"

The lawyer made no answer at all. His mind seemed concentrated on guessing the other's probable actions.

"Out with it, man! I've met some derned good liars in my time, but you beat the lot. I'm anxious to know where you learned the trick, that's all."

"Why do you believe her more than me?" asked Simon.

"Because you've been found out lying before. That was a pretty stiff one about your engaging Carrington, wasn't it?"

Simon was quite unable to control his violent start, and his face turned whiter.

"I—I didn't say I did," he stammered.

"Well," said Ned, "I admit I wasn't there to hear you, but I know Carrington made you put your foot fairly in it just by way of helping him to size you up, and he got your size right enough too."

"Then—" began Simon, and stopped and changed it into: "What does Carrington suspect—er—accuse me of?"

Ned stared at him for several seconds without speaking, and this procedure seemed to disconcert the lawyer more than anything had done yet.

"What—what does Carrington mean?" he repeated.

"He means you've lied, and he believes Miss Farmond, and he believes Sir Malcolm, and he believes me, and he puts you down as a pretty bad egg. What did you expect to be accused of?"

Simon could no more hide his relief to-night than he could hide his fears.

"Only of what you have told me—only of course of what you say! But I can explain. In good time I can explain."

It was at that moment that the door opened sharply and the start the lawyer gave showed the state of his nerves after Mr. Cromarty's handling. Mary MacLean stood in the doorway, her face twitching.

"What's the matter?" snapped her master.

"Please, sir, there are men in the garden!" she cried.

The lawyer leapt to his feet.

"Men in the garden!" he cried, and there was a note in his voice which startled even tough Ned Cromarty. "What are they doing?"

"I don't know, sir. It sounded almost as if they was digging."

Simon swayed for an instant and grasped the back of his chair. Then in a muffled voice he muttered:

"I'm going to see!"

He had scarcely made a step towards the door when Cromarty was on his feet too.

"Steady!" he cried. "Get out there, and shut the door!"

The towering form and formidable voice sent Mary out with a shut door between them almost as the command was off his tongue. A couple of strides and he had got the lawyer by the shoulder and pulled him back.

"Sit down!" he commanded.

Simon turned on him with a new expression. The terror had passed away and he stood there now as the sheer beast at bay.

"Damn you!" he muttered, and turned his back for a moment.

The next, his hand rose and simultaneously Ned's arm shot out and got him by the wrist, while the shock of his onslaught drove the man back and down into his chair. Though Simon was tough and stoutly built, he was as a child in the hands of his adversary. A sharp twist of the wrist was followed by an exclamation of pain and the thud of something heavy on the floor. Ned stooped and picked up the globular glass matchbox that had stood on the table. For a few moments he stared at it in dead silence, balancing it in his hands. It was like a small cannon ball for concentrated weight. Then in a curious voice he asked:

"Is this the first time you have used this?"

Simon made no reply. His face was dead white now, but dogged and grim, and his mouth stayed tight as a trap. Ned replaced the matchbox on the table, and planted himself before the fire.

"Nothing to say?" he asked, and Simon said nothing.

They remained like this for minute after minute; not a movement in the room and the booming of the wind the only sound. And then came footsteps on the gravel and the ringing of a bell.

"We'll probably learn something now," said Ned, but the other still said nothing, and only a quick glance towards the door gave a hint of his thoughts.

There was no announcement this time. Superintendent Sutherland entered first, then the constable, and Carrington last. The superintendent went straight up to the lawyer, his large face preternaturally solemn. Touching him on the shoulder he said:

"I arrest you in the King's name!"

The man in the chair half started up and then fell back again.

"What for?" he asked huskily.

"The murder of Simon Rattar."

The lawyer took it as one who had seen the sword descending, but not so Ned Cromarty.

"Of Simon Rattar!" he shouted. "What the—then who the devil is this?"

Carrington answered. He spoke with his usual easy smile, but his triumphant eye betrayed his heart.

"The superintendent has omitted part of the usual formalities," he said. "This person should have been introduced as Mr. George Rattar."

"George!" gasped Ned. "But I thought he was dead!"

"So did I," said Carrington, "but he wasn't."

"What proof have you of this story?" demanded the man in the chair suddenly.

"We have just dug up your brother's body from that flower bed," said Carrington quietly. "Do you recognise his ring?"

He held up a gold signet ring, and the lawyer fell back in his chair.

"But look here!" exclaimed Ned, "what about Sir Reginald's murder? He did that too, I suppose!"

Carrington nodded.

"We hope to add that to his account in a day or two. This is enough to be going on with, but as a matter of fact we have nearly enough evidence now to add the other charge."

"I can add one bit," said Ned, picking up the matchbox. "He has just tried to do me in with this little thing, and I take it, it was the third time of using."

Carrington weighed it in his hand, and then said to the prisoner:

"You put it in the end of a stocking, I suppose?"

The man looked up at him with a new expression in his eye. If it were not a trace of grim humour, it was hard to say what else it could be.

"Get me a drink," he said huskily, nodding towards the tantalus on the side table, "and I'll tell you the whole damned yarn. My God, I'm dry as a damned bone!"

"Give me the key of the tantalus," said Carrington promptly.

But the superintendent seemed somewhat taken aback.

"Anything you say may be used against you," he reminded the prisoner.

"You know enough to swing me, anyhow," said Rattar, "but I'd like you to know that I didn't really mean to do it. I want that drink first though!"

He took the glass of whisky and water and as he raised it to his lips, that same curious look came back into his eye.

"Here's to the firm of S. and G. Rattar, and may their clients be as damned as themselves!" he said with a glance at Cromarty, and finished the drink at a draught.

39

THE YARN

"I needn't trouble you with my adventures before I came down here to visit brother Simon," began the prisoner, "for you know them well enough. It was about a month ago when I turned up at this house one night."

"How did you get here?" demanded the superintendent.

"I did the last bit under the seat of the carriage," grinned Rattar, "and when we got into the station I hopped out on the wrong side of the train. The way I paid my fare wasn't bad either, considering I hadn't half of the fare from London in my pocket when I started— or anything like it. However, the point is I got here and just as I'd come through the gates I had the luck to see both the maids going out. So the coast was clear.

"Well, I rang the bell and out came Simon—the man who'd got me convicted, and my own brother too, mind you!—looking as smug as the hard-hearted old humbug he was. He got the shock of his life when he saw who it was, but I began gently and I put a proposition to him. I'll bet none of you will guess what it was!"

He looked round the company, and Carrington answered:

"Blackmail of some sort."

"You may call it blackmail if you like, but what was the sort? Well, you'd never guess. I was wearing a beard and moustaches then, but I knew if I took them off I'd look so like Simon that no one meeting one of us would know which it was, supposing we were dressed exactly alike and I did Simon's grunting tricks and all that. And Simon knew it too.

"'Well, Simon, my dear brother,' I said to him, 'I'll make you a sporting proposition. My idea is to settle down in this old place, and I'm so fond of you I mean to shave, get an outfit just like yours, and give free rein to my affection for you. I'm so fond of you,' I said, 'that I know I shan't be able to keep more than five yards away from you whenever you are walking the streets, and I'll have to sit in church beside you, Simon. That's my present programme.'

"I let that sink in, and then I went on:

"'Supposing this programme embarrasses you, Simon, well there's one way out of it, and I leave it to your judgment to say what it is.'

"Now, mind you, I'd banked on this coming off, for I knew what a stickler Simon was for the respectable and the conventional and all that. Can't you see the two of us going through the streets together, five yards apart and dressed exactly alike! Wouldn't the small boys have liked it! That was my only idea in coming down here. I meant no more mischief, I'll swear to that! Unfortunately, though, I'd got so keen on the scheme that I hadn't thought of its weak spot.

"Simon said not a word, but just looked at me—exactly as I've been looking at people since I took his place in society. And then he asked me if I was really very hard up. Like a fool I told him the plain truth, that I had inside of five bob in my pockets and that was every penny I owned in the world.

"He grinned then—I can see him grinning now—and he said:

"'In that case you'll have a little difficulty in paying your board and lodging here, and still more in buying clothes. I tell you what I'll do,' he said, 'I'll buy a ticket back to London for you and leave it with the stationmaster, and that's every penny you'll ever get out of me!'

"I saw he had me, but I wasn't going off on those terms. I damned him to his face and he tried to shut the door on me. We were talking at the front door all this while, I may mention. I got my foot in the way, and as I was always a bit stronger than Simon, I had that door open after a tussle and then I followed him into the library.

"I knew the man was hard as flint and never showed mercy to any one in his life when he had them on toast, and I knew he had me on toast. How was I to get any change out of him? That was what I was wondering as I followed him, and then all at once something—the devil if you like—put the idea into my head. I'd *be* Simon!"

He looked round on his audience as though he still relished the memory of that inspiration.

"The beauty of the idea was that no one would ever dream of suspecting a man of not being himself! They might suspect him of a lot of things, but not of that. I hadn't thought of the scheme ten seconds before I realised how dead safe it was so long as I kept my head. And I have kept it. No one can deny that!"

His glance this time challenged a contradiction, but no one spoke. The circle of steadfast eyes and silent lips he seemed to take as a tribute to his address, for he smiled and then went on:

"Yes, I kept my head from the beginning. I stood talking to him in this very room, he refusing to answer anything except to repeat that he'd buy a ticket to London and leave it with the stationmaster, and I working out the scheme—what to do it with and how to manage afterwards. I knew it was a swinging risk, but against that was a starving certainty, and then I spied that matchbox and the thing was settled. I got him to look the other way for a moment—and then he was settled. Give me another drink!"

Carrington got him a drink and he gulped it down, and then turned suddenly on Ned Cromarty.

"Your damned glass eye has been getting on my nerves long enough!" he exclaimed. "My God, that eye and your habit of hanging people—I've had enough of them! Can't you turn it away from me?"

"Won't turn," said Ned coolly, "spring broken. Get on with your story!"

Even in his privileged position as prisoner, Rattar seemed disinclined to have trouble with his formidable ex-client. He answered nothing, but turned his shoulder to him and continued:

"After that was over I set about covering my tracks. The first part was the worst. Before the maids came back I had to get Simon stowed away for the night—no time to bury him then of course, and I had to get into his clothes, shave, and learn the lie of the house and all that. I did it all right and came down to breakfast next morning and passed muster with the servants, and never a suspicion raised!"

"There was a little," remarked Carrington, "but never enough."

"Not enough was good enough!"

"I am not quite certain of that," said Carrington. "However, go on. Your next bunker was the office."

The prisoner nodded.

"It took some nerve," he said complacently, "and I'm free to confess that to begin with I always had a beastly feeling that some one was watching me and spotting something that didn't look quite right, but, good Lord, keeping my head the way I kept it, there was nothing to worry about! Who would ever think that the Simon Rattar who walked into his office and grunted at his clerks on Wednesday morning, wasn't the same Simon Rattar who walked in and grunted on Tuesday morning? And then I had one tremendous pull in knowing all the ropes from old days. Simon was a conservative man, nothing was ever changed—not even the clerks, so I had the whole routine at my fingers. And he was an easy man to imitate too. That was where I scored again. I daresay I have inherited some of the same tricks myself. I know I found them come quite easy—the stare and the silence and the grunts and the rest of them. And then I always had more brains than Simon and could pick up business quicker. You should have heard me making that ass Malcolm Cromarty, and the Farmond girl, and this hangman with the glass eye tell me all about themselves and what their business was, without their ever suspecting they were being pumped! For, mind you, I'd never set eyes on Malcolm Cromarty or the Farmond girl before in my life! No, it wasn't at the office I had the nastiest time. It was burying the body that night."

The boastful smile died off his lips and for a moment he shivered a little.

"What happened about that?" enquired Carrington keenly.

Rattar's voice instinctively fell a little.

"When I got home that afternoon I found he wasn't quite dead after all!"

"That accounts for it!" murmured Carrington.

"For what?"

"Your maid heard him moving."

The prisoner seemed to have recovered from his passing emotion.

"And I told her it was a rat, and she swallowed it!" he laughed. "Well, he didn't move for long, and I had fixed up quite a good scheme for getting him out of the house. A man was to call for old papers. I even did two voices talking in the hall to make the bluff complete! Not being able to get his ring off his finger rather worried me, but I put that right by an advertisement in the paper saying I'd lost it!"

He was arrested by the look on Carrington's face.

"What happened?" he exclaimed. "Do you mean to say that gave me away?"

"Those superfluous precautions generally give people away."

"But how?"

"It doesn't matter now. You'll learn later. What next?"

"Next?" said Rattar. "Well, I just went on keeping my head and bluffing people—" he broke off, looked at Superintendent Sutherland, and gave a short laugh. "I only lost my nerve a bit once, and that was when the glass-eyed hangman butted in and said he was going to get down a detective. It struck me then it was time I was off—and what's more, I started!"

The superintendent's mouth fell open.

"You—you weren't the man—" he began.

"Yes," scoffed the prisoner, "I was the man with toothache in that empty carriage. I'd got in at the wrong side after the ticket collector passed and just about twenty seconds before you opened the door. But the sight of your red face made me change my plans, and I was out again before that train started! A bright policeman you are! After that I decided to stick it out and face the music; and I faced it."

His mouth shut tight and he sat back in his chair, his eyes travelling round the others as though to mark their unwilling admiration. He certainly saw it in the faces of the two open-eyed policemen, but Cromarty's was hard and set, and he seemed still to be waiting.

"You haven't told us about Sir Reginald yet," he said.

Rattar looked at him defiantly.

"No evidence there," he said with a cunning shake of his head, "you can go on guessing!"

"Would you like to smoke a pipe?" asked Carrington suddenly.

The man's eyes gleamed.

"By God, yes!"

"You can have one if you tell us about Sir Reginald. We've got you anyhow, and there will be evidence enough there too when we've put it together."

The superintendent looked a trifle shocked, but Carrington's sway over him was by this time evidently unbounded. He coughed an official protest but said nothing.

The prisoner only hesitated for a moment. He saw Carrington taking out a cigarette, and then he took out his keys and said:

"This is the key for that drawer. You'll find my pipe and baccy there. I'll tell you the rest." And then he started and exclaimed: "But how the h— did you know I smoked?"

"At five minutes past nine o'clock last night," said Carrington, as he handed him his pipe, "I was within three paces of you."

The prisoner stared at him with a wry face.

"You devil!" he murmured, and then added with some philosophy: "After all, I'd sooner be hanged than stop smoking." And with that he lit his pipe.

"You want to know about old Cromarty," he resumed. "Well, I made my first bad break when I carried on a correspondence with him which Simon had begun, not knowing they had had a talk between whiles cancelling the whole thing. You know about it and about the letter Sir Reginald sent me after I'd written. Well, when I got that letter I admit it rattled me a bit. I've often wondered since whether he had really suspected anything or whether he would have sooner or later. Anyhow I got it into my head that the game was up if something didn't happen. And so it happened."

"You went and killed him?" said Ned.

"That's for you and your glass eye to find out!" snapped the prisoner.

"Take his pipe away," said Carrington quietly.

"Damn it!" cried Rattar, "I'll tell you, only I'm fed up with that man's bullying! I put it in a stocking" (he nodded towards the match box) "just as you guessed and I went out to Keldale that night. My God, what a walk that was in the dark! I'd half forgotten the way down to the house and I thought every other tree was a man watching me. I don't know yet how I got to that library window. I remembered his ways and I thought he'd be sitting up there alone; but it was just a chance, and I'd no idea I'd have the luck to pick a night when he was sleeping in his dressing room. Give me another drink!"

Carrington promptly brought one and again it vanished almost in a gulp.

"Well, I saw him through a gap in the curtains and I risked a tap on the glass. My God, how surprised he was to see me standing there! I grinned at him and he let me in, and then—" He broke off and fell forward in his chair with his face in his hands. "This whisky has gone to my head!" he muttered. "You've mixed it too damned strong!"

Ned Cromarty sprang up, his face working. Carrington caught him by the arm.

"Let's come away," he said quietly. "We've heard everything necessary. You can't touch him now."

Cromarty let him keep his arm through his as they went to the door.

"I'll send a cab up for you in a few minutes," Carrington added to the superintendent.

They left the prisoner still sitting muttering into his hands.

40

THE LAST CHAPTER

On their way down to the hotel Ned Cromarty only spoke once, and that was to exclaim:

"If I'd only known when I had him alone! Why didn't you tell me more before I went in?"

"For your own sake," said Carrington gently. "The law is so devilish undiscriminating. Also, I wasn't absolutely certain then myself."

They said nothing more till they were seated in Carrington's sitting room and his employer had got a cigar between his teeth and pushed away an empty tumbler.

"I'm beginning to feel a bit better," said he. "Fire away now and tell me how you managed this trick. I'd like to see just how derned stupid I've been!"

"My dear fellow, I assure you you haven't! I'm a professional at this game, and I tell you honestly it was at least as much good luck as good guidance that put me on to the truth at last."

"I wonder what you call luck," said Ned. "Seems to me you were up against it all the time! You've told me how you caught Rattar lying at the start. Well, that was pretty smart of you to begin with. Then, what next? How did things come?"

"Well," said Carrington, "I picked up a little something on my first visit to Keldale. From Bisset's description I gathered that the body must have been dragged along the floor and left near the door. Why? Obviously as a blind. Adding that fact to the unfastened window, the broken table, the mud on the floor, and the hearth brush, the odds seemed heavy on entry by the window. I also found that the middle blind had been out of order that night and that it *might* have been quite possible for any one outside to have seen Sir Reginald sitting in the room and known he was alone there. Again, it seemed long odds on his having recognised the man outside and opened the window himself, which, again, pointed to the man being some one he knew quite well and never suspected mischief from."

"Those were always my own ideas, except that I felt bamboozled where you felt clear—which shows the difference between our brains!"

Carrington laughed and shook his head.

"I wish I could think so! No, no, it's merely a case of every man to his own trade. And as a matter of fact I was left just as bamboozled as you were. For who could this mysterious man be? Of the people inside the house, I had struck out Miss Farmond, Bisset, Lady Cromarty, and all the female servants. Only Sir Malcolm was left. I wired for him to come up and was able to score him out too. I also visited you and scored you out. So there I was—with no conceivable criminal!"

"But you'd already begun to suspect Rattar, hadn't you?"

"I knew he had lied about engaging me; I discovered from Lady Cromarty that he had told her of Sir Malcolm's engagement to Miss Farmond—and I suspected he had started her suspicions of them; and I saw that he was set on that theory, in spite of the fact that it was palpably improbable if one actually knew the people. Of course if one didn't, it was plausible enough. When I first came down here it seemed to me a very likely theory and I was prepared to find a guilty couple, but when I met Miss Farmond and told her suddenly that Sir Malcolm was arrested, and she gazed blankly at me and asked 'What for?' well, I simply ran my pencil, so to speak, through her name and there was an end of her! The same with Sir Malcolm when I met him. And yet here was the family lawyer, who knew them both perfectly, so convinced of their guilt that he was obviously stifling investigation in any other direction. And on top of all that, all my natural instincts and intuitions told me that the man was a bad hat."

"But didn't all that make you suspect him?"

"Of what? Of leaving his respectable villa at the dead of night, tramping several miles at his age in the dark, and deliberately murdering his own best client and old friend under circumstances so risky to himself that only a combination of lucky chances saw him safely through the adventure? Nothing—absolutely nothing but homicidal mania could possibly account for such a performance, and the man was obviously as sane as you or I. I felt certain that there was something wrong somewhere, but as for suspecting him of being the principal in the crime, the idea was stark lunacy!"

"By George, it was a tough proposition!" said Ned. "By the way, had you heard of George Rattar at that time?"

"Oh, yes, I heard of him, and knew they resembled one another, but as I was told that he had left the place for years and was now dead, my thoughts never even once ran in that direction until I got into a state of desperation, and then I merely surmised that his misdeeds might have been at the bottom of some difficulty between Simon and Sir Reginald."

"Then how on earth did you ever get on to the right track?"

"I never would have if the man hadn't given himself away. To begin with, he was fool enough to fall in with my perfectly genuine assumption that he was either employing me or acting for my employer. No doubt he stood to score if the bluff had come off, and he banked on your stipulation that your name shouldn't appear. But if he had only been honest in that matter, my suspicions would never have started—not at that point anyhow."

"That was Providence—sure!" said Ned with conviction.

"I'm inclined to think it was," agreed Carrington. "Then again his advice to Sir Malcolm and Miss Farmond was well enough designed to further his own scheme of throwing suspicion on them, but it simply ended in his being bowled out both times, and throwing suspicion on himself. But *the* precaution which actually gave him away was putting in that advertisement about his ring."

"I was just wondering," said Ned, "how that did the trick."

"By the merest fluke. I noticed it when I was making enquiries at the Police Office on quite different lines, but you can imagine that I switched off my other enquiries pretty quick when Superintendent Sutherland calmly advanced the theory that the ring was stolen when Rattar's house was entered by some one unknown on the very night of the murder!"

"This is the first I've heard of that!" cried Ned.

"It was the first I had, but it led me straight to Rattar's house and a long heart to heart talk with his housemaid. That was when I collected that extraordinary mixed bag of information which I was wondering yesterday whether to believe or not. Here are the items, and you can judge for yourself what my state of mind was when I was carrying about the following precious pieces of information."

He ticked the items off on his fingers.

"A mysterious man who entered the garden one night and left his footprints in the gravel, and whose visit had a strange and mysterious effect on Rattar. Funny feelings produced in the bosom of the housemaid by the presence of her master. Doors of unused rooms mysteriously locked and keys taken away; said to be old papers inside. Mysterious visit of mysterious man at dead of night to remove the said papers. A ring that couldn't come off the owner's finger mysteriously lost. Mysterious burglary on night of the murder by mysterious burglar who left all windows and doors locked behind him and took nothing away. Mysterious perambulations of his garden every night at nine o'clock by Mr. Simon Rattar."

"Great Scot!" murmured Cromarty.

"I have given you the items in what turned out to be their order of date, but I got them higgledy-piggledy and served up in a sauce of mystery and trembly sensations that left me utterly flummoxed as to how much—if anything—was sober fact. However, I began by fastening on to two things. The first was the burglary, which of course at once suggested the possibility that the man who had committed the crime at Keldale had returned to Rattar's house and got in by that window. The second was the nightly perambulations, which could easily be tested. When Mr. Rattar emerged at nine that night, I was in the garden before him. And what do you think he did?"

"Had a look at his brother's grave?"

"Smoked two pipes of tobacco! A man who was an anti-tobacco fanatic! The truth hit me straight in the eye—'That man is not Simon Rattar!' And then of course everything dropped into its place. The ex-convict twin brother, the only evidence of whose supposititious death was an announcement in the paper, obviously put in as a blind. The personal resemblance between the two. All the yarns told me by the housemaid, including the strange visitor— George of course arriving; the man who came for the papers— George himself taking out the body; and the vanished ring. Everything fitted in now, and the correspondence between Sir Reginald and Rattar which had beaten me before, gave the clue at once as to motive."

"I guess you felt you had deserved a drink that trip!" said Ned.

"I didn't stop to have my drink. I went straight off to see old Ison and pumped him for the rest of the evening. He wasn't very helpful but everything I could get out of him went to confirm my theory. I found for certain that Simon Rattar had never smoked in his life, and that George used to be a heavy smoker. I also learned that a few recent peculiarities of conduct had struck the not too observant Ison, one being very suggestive. Rattar, it seemed, kept an old pair of kid gloves in his desk which he was in the habit of wearing when he was alone in the office."

"Don't quite see the bearing of that."

"Well, on my hypothesis it was to avoid leaving finger marks. You see George was an ex-convict. It was a very judicious precaution too, and made it extremely difficult to catch him out by that means, for one could scarcely approach a respectable solicitor and ask him for an impression of his fingers! And anyhow, nothing could be definitely proved against him until we had found Simon's body. That was the next problem. Where had he hidden it?"

"And how did you get at that?"

"Guessed it. At first my thoughts went too far afield, but when I went over the times mentioned in the maid's story of the man who took away the papers, and the fact that she heard no sound of a wheeled vehicle, I realised that he must have simply planted it in one of the flower beds. This morning I prodded them all with a stout walking stick and found the spot. Then I talked like a father to old Sutherland and fixed everything up with him. And then I sent my wire to you."

"And you deliberately tell me you got there as much by good luck as good guidance?"

Carrington's eyes thoughtfully followed his smoke rings.

"I can see the luck at every turn," he answered, "and though I'd like to believe in the guidance, I'm hanged if it's quite as distinct!"

"If you are telling me the neat, unvarnished truth, Carrington," said his admiring employer, "I can only say that you've a lot to learn about your own abilities—and I hope to Heaven you'll never learn it!"

"But I assure you there are some people who think me conceited!"

"There are guys of all sorts in the world," said Ned. "For instance there's a girl who has mistaken me for a daisy, and I've got to get back to her now. Good night! I won't say 'Thanks' because I can't shout it loud enough."

When his gig lamps had flashed up the silent street and Carrington had turned back from the pavement into the hotel, he met his friend Miss Peterkin.

"Mr. Cromarty's late to-night," said she. "A fine gentleman that! I always say there are few like Mr. Cromarty of Stanesland."

"That's lucky for me," said Carrington with a smile that puzzled her a little. "My business in life would be gone if there were!"

CARRINGTON'S CASES

This description of Mr. F. T. Carrington, private detective (or "inquiry agent," as he preferred to call himself), appeared in a tale entitled *Simon*, and is culled from that work with its author's permission: "He was a young man, apparently a little over thirty, above middle height, with a round, ingenuous, very agreeable face, smooth fair hair, a little neatly trimmed moustache, and a monocle that lent just the necessary touch of distinction to what might otherwise have been a too good-humoured physiognomy." The following stories were for the most part told by Mr. Carrington himself over a smoking-room fire.

1

A MEDICAL CRIME

"One of the most futile-looking jobs that ever came my way," said Carrington, "was my trip to the royal burgh of Kinbuckie in the Kingdom of Scotland; and yet . . ." he paused and flicked the ash of his cigarette into the fire with a reminiscent smile.

"And yet," echoed one of his audience, "I rather suspect it wasn't as futile as it looked!"

"Why?"

"From your eye."

"I must wear an eyeglass in both eyes," he smiled, "if I'm going to give myself away like that. But I assure you it did honestly seem a pretty hopeless case when I was first asked to take it up. There had been a series of very mysterious burglaries in Kinbuckie and the police were absolutely beaten. The provost of the town, however, was a determined gentleman, and extremely well-to-do; he had heard of me somehow or other—one's sins will find one out, don't you know—and he took it into his head to get me down at his own expense to try and clear the business up. As you'll hear in a moment, there was something particularly unpleasant about it for a man like this provost, who took a keen interest and a great deal of pride in the town, and he was quite resolved to remove the shadow somehow. So I said I'd go down and see him, and I went.

"All the way in the train, the futility of the quest struck me more and more forcibly. It was over a fortnight since the last of these crimes had been committed, and what clues would be likely to be left? Probably none. I couldn't possibly afford the time to spend more than two or three nights in the place at the outside, and it was any odds against another burglary being committed while I was there. And after that I could only advise them from London. Even if it were a provincial town in England, the difficulties of acting effectively would have been enormous, but the fact of its being away up in Scotland added to them infinitely. It wasn't a job for a man like me in the very least; or anyhow, that is what I thought on the way between King's Cross and Kinbuckie. But, as some other great thinker has probably remarked, one never knows one's luck.

"Well, at the end of a long journey I found myself in a greystone, seaboard town, with a small harbour, an old clock tower on the town hall, a couple of church spires, and the Lord knows how many kirks without them. At one end were quite a few modern residential villas, and there were a certain number of solid old-fashioned houses more in the heart of the town, that also looked as if they might have pickings for the enterprising burglar. But the total population was something under ten thousand, and even before I reached the provost's house, the very idea of a series of mysterious crimes in a place as small as this, where everybody must surely know everybody else, began to intrigue me. And when one gets really interested, the mind works a lot more briskly. Though at that moment, mind you, I didn't see a glimmer of how to tackle the problem.

"I found the provost to be a very shrewd sensible man, and we had a long talk together over a glass—or possibly even two glasses—of one of the best whiskies I've ever tasted. All the time I was in Kinbuckie there was a whistling east wind, a bursting grey sea, and exactly one half-hour's blink of sunshine; and with such a climate and such whiskies, why everybody in Scotland doesn't die of drink is a mystery to me.

"What the provost told me of the burglaries was also told me later by the Superintendent of Police, and I'll come to it in a moment. Meantime I'll only say that I quite saw why he was so keen to clear the thing up, and that personally I became very interested and curious indeed. But I got one very nasty jar that seemed, at the moment, to dish any slender chance I had of finding much out.

He had told several people that he was getting up a detective, whereas I had counted on making my inquiries in the guise of a harmless visitor. In fact, I had brought my golf clubs as a blind, and even taken the trouble to turn into a shop on my way up from the station and buy half a dozen balls. And now here was the fat in the fire! However, as I remarked before, one never knows one's luck.

"From his house I went on to the police office, and introduced myself to Superintendent Pringle. He was a tall, stout, square-shouldered man, every inch a bobby, with a face very full below and narrowing towards the top, a red moustache, small but exceedingly alert eyes, and a manner worth a small fortune in this suspicious, credulous, competitive world. It was a manner so confidential, impressive, and genial, that one simply couldn't help feeling that with Superintendent Pringle at one's back things were bound to be all right. And my first glance round his office showed me that he was evidently an enthusiast in his profession, and studied its possibilities and finer points. For I noticed on a shelf three or four volumes of stories of crime, and the reminiscences of great detectives.

"'A most mysterious business, sir,' said he. 'Aye, five separate burglaries in a matter of as mony months. Ye've got the fac's precisely right, sir. It's nae wonder the provost's upset, poor man. There's not been such ongoings in Kinbuckie since the Police Act first came into force. I'm aware, sir, it kin' o' reflects upon me, but if ye kent all the trouble I've taken! I've suspected everybody in this town excep' the provost, and I've been gey near suspecting him!'

"'By Jove, really!' said I. 'You almost suspected the provost, did you? I say! By Jingo!'

"As I've often assured my friends, I really do need an eyeglass in my left eye, and don't in my right. I don't know that they believe me, but anyhow, a monocle comes in very handy when one wants to produce an amateurish impression, and I let the Superintendent have the benefit of it now. I was also as Anglified as possible, for I know the deep-rooted provincial Scot's contempt for the Sassenach. I wanted Mr. Pringle to be quite at his ease, you see. I knew from the provost he had a very interesting theory, and I wished to draw him well out. In a few minutes, when we had become very friendly, and he had obviously set me down as a better listener than a detective, I asked him—

"'What's this the provost tells me about a curious feature that seems to run through all these five crimes?'

"The Superintendent became even more confidential and impressive.

"'Well,' said he, 'in four o' the cases there's a very singular coincidence, and nae doot it would have been in the fifth too had the man been able to find what he found in the ither houses. Mr. Ogilvy—that's the first case—he's a sort of antiquarian gentleman, and there was a lot of auld bones and things in his library—things he'd dug up, ye understand, sir. Well, if this burglar didna tak' some o' thae bones! What was he wanting them for? I rather wondered.'

"He looked at me very wisely, and of course I asked—

"'And what did he want them for?'

"'Wait a wee minute, sir,' said he, and I'll tell you something else. When he broke into Mr. Thomson's he took a medical book—*Advice to Mothers*, it's called. At the Burnets' house there was an auld skull, and he took that. And mind you, sir, these were just in addition to the valuables he lifted, and no worth a brass farthing, one of them.'

"'You think, then,' said I, 'that it points to some one interested in medicine?'

"'In my deleeberate opinion, it does that, sir! And I havena teilt you that in the fourth case—that was Mistress Lindsay's he took anither medical book, *Burton's Anatomy*.'

"I opened my eyes this time pretty wide.

"'Do you mean *Burton's Anatomy of Melancholy?*' I asked.

"'Aye, sir, that was the vera name of it.'

"Sometimes a flash of light will illuminate the dark of the mind from the impact of two things that haven't apparently a spark of luminosity in them, just as the striking of a brown-tipped splinter on a bit of roughened paper will illuminate the dark of the night. Such a flash lit my brain at that instant, but I think I may say my face showed little more evidence of intelligence than before.

"'Then, Superintendent, what is your theory?' I asked.

"He glanced round the office, as though to see that its bareness hid no eavesdroppers.

"'There is only one kind of folk that has any business to be gaun about the toon at a' hours of the night,' said he in a lowered voice. 'Folks, that's to say, sir, that the police would never think of coupling wi' criminal intent; and that's the doctors.'

"He looked at me hard as though to see how I would take this surprising suggestion, and I made no effort to hide the fact that it gave me food for very serious thought indeed. The provost had told me of this theory of the Superintendent's; and you can imagine how upset he was at the idea of the most respectable professional men in the town going in for housebreaking. He hadn't, however, told me all these details.

"'Do you suspect any doctor in particular?' I asked.

"The Superintendent became cautious.

"'Well, sir,' said he, 'there's six doctors in the town, and it's no' for me to say exac'ly which one's to be suspectit without mair positive evidence. There's Dr. Mitchell and Dr. Rattray, and Dr. Smith and Dr. Douglas, and Dr. Hills and Dr. MacTavish. That's the lot, sir.'

"He spoke with an impartial air, but I could see that there were unspoken thoughts behind his words. I lowered my voice and asked him very confidentially—

"'Now, Superintendent, honestly, what's your own private opinion of these six gentlemen?'

"'Well,' said he, 'Dr. Mitchell is a very decent auld gentleman, and it's no' vera likely to be him. Dr. Rattray is a kind o' cousin of the provost's, and they're a' vera decent folk indeed. Smith and Douglas have been in the place a long while, and it's queer if they should tak' to burgling now. But Hills, sir, is an Englishman.'

"The Superintendent looked very grave as he revealed this damning fact, and then suddenly became distinctly embarrassed as he realised that I came of the same predatory race myself.

"'I know them!' I reassured him. 'You are quite right to be suspicious. And what about the last man?'

"'MacTavish?' said the Superintendent in accents which made his opinion of the English seem comparatively flattering—'He's a Hielander.'

"He left it at that, and seemed to think no further comment was necessary. Hitherto I had always imagined that a Scot was a Scot, and that one drappie set them all quoting Robbie Burns like a Gaiety chorus. But it seems that's only when you meet them in London. Go to a Lowland town, especially anywhere near the Highland border, and ask the average inhabitant his opinion of the MacDonalds and the MacTavishes, and you'll see!

"'Have you anything more definite against Dr. Hills and Dr. MacTavish?' I ventured to ask. 'Were they out on the nights of these crimes? Are they in financial difficulties? Have you traced any of the stolen things to their possession?'

"The Superintendent was prepared with a certain number of facts. He pulled out a note-book and gave me some particulars of the movements of all the six doctors on the nights of the crimes, so far as they could be traced. He had also collected some information as to the money they owed, or were said to owe, in the town. Definite evidence connecting any of these men with the stolen property was not to hand, he admitted, but it was a fact that Dr. MacTavish had settled at least two large bills since the series of robberies began.

"'Well, Superintendent,' I said at last, 'I mean to spend the next day or two in Kinbuckie, and I shall devote my attention to these six doctors. The provost is anxious either to have them all cleared, or to find which is the black sheep and get rid of him, so I won't look outside the doctors meanwhile—especially as you don't suspect anybody else.'

"'Vera good, sir,' said he; 'I ca' that a very sensible procedure.'

"I walked out of that office very thoughtfully indeed, and I spent the next hour or two in solid thinking; and then I set to work. I had come by the night train from King's Cross and arrived at Kinbuckie in the forenoon. The rest of that day and the whole of the next I went my own way, and my next meeting with Superintendent Pringle was in the evening. He was clearly all agog to learn what I had been doing, and when I first began to tell him of my methods I am afraid he was considerably disappointed.

"'In a case like this,' I told him, 'where there is next to no real evidence, and the scent has got cold, I depend chiefly on my judgment of the people suspected. I try to size them up and see whether they look like the criminal type; do you see?'

"The Superintendent clearly did not see, and had some difficulty in refraining from telling me what he thought of such unscientific methods.

"'I have had a good look at all the six doctors,' I went on, 'and made the acquaintance of two or three of them, and I am bound to tell you, Superintendent, that I think you have judged very shrewdly in thinking that Hills and MacTavish are the likeliest criminals.'

"At this the Superintendent manifestly quite changed his opinion, and made no effort at all to refrain from indicating his admiration of my judgment.

"'I spent some time with them both,' I said. 'Of course I went to see them professionally, with the remains of a cold for Dr. Hills and a touch of lumbago for Dr. MacTavish, and of course we started talking about the burglaries. You see, everybody knows who I am; I thought it would be a serious handicap at first, but as things turned out I made a foul wind into a fair, and took advantage of their knowing I was a detective to give them a little confidential information.'

"The Superintendent opened his eyes and shook his head at this, but I soothed him with a confidential smile.

"'Wait till you hear what I told them,' said I. 'I informed Dr. Hills in the strictest confidence that I was depending very largely on the new footprint test. It was practically impossible now, I said, for a criminal to avoid detection unless he wore rubber tennis shoes of the largest size, with ribbed soles. Of course this was a dead secret and I trusted him not to breathe a word to a soul.'

"The Superintendent was beginning to look puzzled.

"'I never heard of that test, sir,' said he.

"'Did you ever hear of the olfactory test?' I inquired.

"He shook his head. He was evidently getting extremely mystified.

"'Well,' I said, 'when I went on to see Dr. MacTavish, I told him in equal confidence that the olfactory or smelling test was the very latest thing. A criminal was nailed to an absolute certainty by means of a delicate odour-registering instrument, and the only dodge for defeating it was by burning feathers. Of course this was an equally dead secret.'

"'I looked at him gravely and asked—

"'Now, Superintendent, do you mean to say you haven't heard of either of these tests before?'

He seemed a little troubled.

"'Well, sir, not exactly . . .'

"'No more have I!' I said; 'but these two doctors have, and if there's another burglary in this town and you find traces of large rubber tennis shoes, you'll know the criminal is Hills, and if you find traces of burnt feathers, you'll know it's MacTavish.'

The Superintendent tumbled to the idea.

"'Man, that's fairly champion!' he cried. 'I've read a lot o' smart stories of detectives, in fac' it's ma favourite reading, but I'm bound to say, sir, this is the best dodge I've heard of yet!'

"I warned him very solemnly not to tell a single soul about this scheme, and we parted on the friendliest terms. To the provost I merely said I had laid a mine, which might go off and blow up something or might not, and next morning I took the early train back to town. And that was the last I saw of the burgh of Kinbuckie."

Carrington paused in his tale, and smiled upon the company.

"'Well,' he said, 'that was a pretty good gamble, wasn't it? Fixing on two respectable professional men at sight, without a scrap of evidence against either of them, and not doing a hand's turn to detect anybody else—not much of Sherlock Holmes or Dr. Thorndyke about that; what?'

"But it came off! Within a week I got a wire from Superintendent Pringle to say that a fresh burglary had been committed, and that there were the remains of several burnt feathers, and what he described as a heavy smell, and should he at once arrest Dr. MacTavish? That night the Superintendent was under lock and key himself with six separate burglary charges against him. You see, I hadn't told another living soul but him about the olfactory test!"

"How did I suspect it was the Superintendent? By his unfortunate choice of *Burton's Anatomy of Melancholy*. I realised in a flash that only an ignorant, half-educated man would mistake that classic for a medical treatise, and therefore it was obviously such a man who was clumsily trying to throw suspicion on the doctors. Besides, imagine a doctor taking the trouble to steal *Advice to Mothers!* Then my eye fell on the shelf of detective stories, and I realised further that the Superintendent had his mind well stored with criminal dodges and false clues, and all that sort of thing. Also, leaving out the doctors, whom he was ingenious enough to select as his victims, nobody but himself and his constables had the same opportunities for wandering about the town at night unsuspected. And, by the way, it was found that one of his constables was in the game with him. And finally, the man himself had his character written on his face—a low, cunning, specious, animal type.

"Inside half a minute I had made up my mind that it was a hundred to one on the burglar being Pringle himself. The only question was, how to bowl him out? And, by Jingo, I got the middle stump right enough that time!"

2

MR. SNAKES

"What are you shivering for?" said the man in the slouch hat.

The dilapidated creature in the broken billycock glanced apprehensively over his shoulder, and his voice quavered a little as he answered—

"Coppers ain't much in my line, mate—not that sort, any 'ow."

A thin river-mist blotted out all save the nearest lamps, a short strip of pavement, and a glimpse of oily water. The tall mansions across the road seemed to melt into vapour, and the helmeted figure pausing beside the parapet a short way from their bench loomed up like a gigantic monument erected to the memory of the London police. It was as raw a February night as even the Chelsea Embankment was acquainted with, and the man in the billycock shivered again, even though the monumental policeman had moved on and vanished into the mist.

"What are you shivering for this time?" asked the other.

"It's blinkin' cold," said the man in the bowler (though that was not the adjective he used).

Slouch-hat stared at him apace. There seemed to be a little curiosity in his stare, considerable contempt, and something of another emotion as well—an emotion hard to define precisely, but which might perhaps best be put into the words, "This creature may have his uses after all!" He himself was not much to boast of so far as outward appearances went, just one of those shabby figures who nightly fill the London benches; yet to the attentive eye there was one difference betwixt him and the myriad other benchers. The purposeless, vagrant look was lacking. And either the purpose that animated him, and kept his shoulders braced against the back of the bench, instead of collapsing and leaving him a huddled heap like his friend, was unlikely to be philanthropic, or else his bearded face belied him. When he spoke, his voice was tinged with a twang, never acquired in the islands wherein he sojourned at present.

As for Billycock, a more typical specimen of the average derelict it would be hard to find if one searched all London. He appeared to be still a young man, and if his face had been well scrubbed and carefully shaved, it might have been not ill-looking, while a certain alertness in his Cockney voice seemed to hint at a fall from a height considerably above the Embankment bench level. A dishonest or drunken clerk he might once have been. But he was a miserable specimen now, and when his companion spoke it was always as to an inferior.

"Who are you, anyhow?" he demanded suddenly.

"I told you yesterday; Lumley's my nime," leered the man in the billycock. "Good nime, ain't it? And what's yours, seein' we're standin' on ceremony? You've never told me yours at all."

"Snakes!" said slouch-hat. "That's as near my name as Lumley's near yours! But I ain't wantin' to know your name, especially as it's not your real one. I've taken a fancy for knowin' who you are—not what your name is."

"Sime as I might 'ave taken a fancy about you, Mr. Snakes," grinned the man in the billycock; "and if you tell me your past 'istory, I'll try to remember the most entertaining parts of mine."

Mr. Snakes leant suddenly towards him, and in his voice was a subtle hint of menace.

"My past is no damned business of any one's, and I'm not interested in yours except so far as it shows how far you've got *guts*. You've told me enough to get yourself into trouble if I was one of that sort. And maybe I am!"

The man who called himself Lumley shrank further back towards his own end of the bench.

"My God, d'ye mean that?" he exclaimed.

"You'll see what I mean soon enough. I ain't done anything to bring myself up ag'in your damned laws over here—not *yet* I haven't! So I haven't any short hairs to catch ahold on. But you have!"

"I told you that in confidence, matey," said Mr. Lumley, with as much dignity as his broken billycock permitted.

"Confidence!" scoffed the other. You was boastin' of it! Great hand at gettin' into houses through the back windows and such-like! Only wished you had a pal and you'd show him some sport! That was the way you was goin' on! A damned lot of confidence there was about it!"

"It was m-meant to be in confidence," stammered Mr. Lumley.

The man who called himself Snakes shifted himself along the bench till there was only a matter of inches between the pair. Then he folded his arms, and with his eye fixed unwaveringly on the other and the same dominating note always in his voice, he went on—

"I'm a different sort from you. I'm not out for talkin' but for *doin'* things!"

"Oh, I can see that right enough!" said the man in the billycock.

Mr. Snakes permitted a smile to flicker for an instant across his saturnine countenance.

"Folks that are up ag'in me see it fast enough! There's a man in this town of London who's up ag'in me, and *he's* goin' to see it. I've come right across from the other side of the world after that man, and I'm goin' to make that man sorry he was ever born!"

Lumley dropped his voice.

"Do you 'old a secret over 'im?" he asked eagerly.

"No, I don't; and anyhow, holdin' a secret and squeezin' him would be letting that man off too light. He was my partner across where we both came from, and he let me down, and he took my girl, and here he is rollin' in money and me sittin' on this bench!"

"But if he did all that, and did it crooked, you'd 'ave an 'old over him, wouldn't you?"

"Never mind whether he did it crooked or did it straight," said Mr. Snakes, "he did it, and that's enough for me! What if he has the cursed law on his side? I'm here in London, and he don't know it!"

"Got no idea, hasn't he?"

Snakes laughed, or rather, he gave a short sharp bark that was apparently meant for a laugh.

"I passed him and his wife—*my* girl that oughter be!—passed 'em in the street, not farther off than the length of this bench, and they didn't know me from Adam, not in this rig out!"

"'Ow long ago was that?" asked Lumley.

"Three days ago, it was."

"And you 'aven't done nothin' to him since?"

Mr. Snakes seemed to scent a hint of criticism in this inquiry.

"I can settle with him whenever I want to, just as easy as I could settle with you!"

"Oh, I know that, Mr. Snakes," said the other hastily. "I'm perfectly sure of that! You're just waitin,' I suppose, for a suitable night—bit o' fog like this, per'aps."

Mr. Snakes seemed struck with this observation.

"It *is* a proper night for the job!" said he. "That's one of the wisest things you've said yet. And you and me's goin' to do it together!"

Mr. Lumley's start was so violent, and he had edged away so nearly to the end of the bench, that he almost started himself off on to the pavement. In fact he had to cling to the back of the bench to keep his balance.

"You and me—together!" he exclaimed. "But—but—what 'ave *I* got to do with this 'ere pal o' yours?"

Snakes kept his eye straight and steadily on him, and his voice was that of a man addressing a dog or a servant—the assured voice of one who had sized up his man and knew how to handle him. Nor did he take the trouble to hide the run of his thoughts.

"I don't need to know a man more'n two days to know if he's the man I want," said he, "and I've known you long enough to be sure of several things. One is, that all that talk of yours about housebreakin' and it's bein' a two-man job is right enough. And another is, that I want a man along o' me with a bit of experience. Much better use that experience than mention it to the p'lice; see?"

Again there was an unmistakable hint of a threat, and the huddled form beneath the billycock shivered afresh.

"The one thing I'm doubtful about," continued Mr. Snakes, "is whether you've got the *guts*; but I reckon I've enough for two."

"My eye, you 'ave and no mistake!" murmured Lumley, and once more Mr. Snakes shed him a fleeting smile of approval. The habit of judging of others as they judged of him seemed in fact to be among the most prominent of his virtues.

"You can lift what you like out of the place," he said generously. "My business is with the man."

"Oh, I begin to see!" said Mr. Lumley. "I tike the swag and you tike your friend?"

The other nodded.

"Maybe I'll help myself to a bit of the swag—if there's anything worth my while," he said with engaging candour. "But the man's my game. Hands off him, Mister Lumley!"

Mr. Lumley had already begun to look a little doubtful.

"What your gime?" he inquired.

"You'll see! Come on, it's time we was off."

But the man in the billycock shook his head with more firmness than he had shown yet.

"I've got to know a little more about what we're goin' to do than that!" said he. "Blimey, you're tiking me as your hexpert adviser, ain't you? 'Ow can I advise if I don't know your gime?"

Still maintaining his cool authority, the slouch-hatted man condescended to explain.

"You've got to help me into this man's house. There's no other man in it but himself, and we'll be two to one if it comes to the worst—but it won't. You'll be lifting the stuff and he'll hear you and come down. He won't see me till I've fixed him. Then we'll walk out again."

"What d'you mean by 'fixin'' him?"

"I mean *fixin'* him!"

"So as he can't raise no alarms?"

"So as he'll never raise no alarms in this world again."

Lumley seemed to be reflecting.

"If I wasn't on my blinkin' uppers," he said, "you wouldn't tempt me into a job of this kind—nor frighten me neither! Suppose the man doesn't come down? Suppose he has a telephone and rings up the police instead?"

"He won't," said Snakes with conviction. "I know Bill Barton—" he checked himself and then went on. "Well, that's his name—ever heard of him?"

"No," said Lumley, "I don't keep up quite as much acquaintance with the nobility and gentry as I used to."

"You might have heard of him all the same. Lord, the pile he's brought back to the old country! And half of it oughter be mine!" The thought seemed to spur him. "Come on!" he said. "It's a good step from here."

The other made no further spoken protest, but he shivered afresh as he rose from the bench, and he kept half a pace behind Snakes when they started westward along the Embankment.

"Lucky I've guts for two!" said his leader.

"You're a holy terror, you are!" murmured Lumley, and again he was rewarded by a gleam of Mr. Snakes' teeth.

It was now nearing two o'clock in the morning. In that part of the town the streets were silent as the grave and utterly deserted. Though the mist drifted a little as they drew farther away from the river, it was always foggy enough to hide the opposite pavement, and chilly as the Arctic. Once when they heard measured steps ahead, they had merely to slip across the road and stand till they passed by, invisible as spirits. It was a night made for crime.

"You seem to know your way pretty well, mate, considerin' 'ow you've only lately come to London," remarked Lumley as they turned a fresh corner and still went on unhesitatingly.

"I've learned the way to *his* house! If I was struck blind to-morrow I could find my way to that hound and fix him up! "

The quarter of London they had reached was a region of large houses, detached and semi-detached, standing in strips of garden. The pair were walking cautiously now and in dead silence.

"This is the house!" whispered Snakes. "There oughter be a side door in this wall. Here it is!" He laid his hand on it, and started back. "Hullo! The blank thing's open!"

"Bit o' luck for us!" grinned Lumley.

His leader peered dubiously into the foggy space beyond the door. "I somehow don't half like this door bein' open," he muttered. Lumley laughed softly.

"You ain't used to this job, that's plain enough! If you'd 'ad my experience, you'd know better 'ow people practically invites genelmen like me and you to walk in by leavin' garden doors open. You'd find 'alf of them garden doors along this road was open if you only tried 'em!"

It was curious to see how the man of experience began to take the lead now that they were on the ground, and how cautious was the man of guts. They had tiptoed down a strip of grass and were close under the black windows.

"He's a tough nut is Bill Barton, I'll always say that much for him," whispered Snakes; "we've got to be precious careful till we've planted ourselves so as he's sure to fall into the trap!"

He gazed dubiously at the dark mass of building and added—

"Now the thing is, which window?"

"Lem'me 'ave a look," whispered the expert, and crept on till he was merged into the blackness of the house. In a few moments he had crept back and was whispering again. "There's one of them French windows just made for the purpose! It ain't properly fastened either."

"What! Not the window properly fastened either? I say, this looks to me kind o' queer; don't it to you?"

"It looks to me as if tacklin' this friend o' yours was no job for the likes of us," said Mr. Lumley candidly. "It's not me as wants to get into this 'ouse—not much! I don't pretend to 'ave much guts. And if you're feelin' the same, then let's get out o' this, says I!"

No one who had been there to hear Mr. Lumley's earnest voice and note the fresh access of shivers that accompanied it could doubt that his suggestion was fervently meant; but it was unhappily expressed.

"Feelin' the same!" muttered Mr. Snakes, and topped it with a round of oaths. "Haven't I told you I've guts for two, and that I'm going to fix this chap up now or never? Show me that window!"

"Well," said Lumley, "you goes in first, that's all I say!"

Snakes paused again.

"Who said he was an expert?" he demanded ironically.

"I'm afride," confessed Mr. Lumley, "and you says you ain't."

"Where's the blinkin' window?" snapped Snakes.

He stretched out his hand, the window opened with almost miraculous ease, and he stepped across the threshold. The next instant he felt himself seized from behind, one firm hand grasping his collar, and the other the slack of his trousers. At the same moment the room was suddenly flooded with light, and into it he staggered on a series of jerky steps. Lastly, at the bidding of the unseen hands, he sank upon his knees and confronted three visible people. One was a broad-shouldered man of middle height, with iron-grey hair, a fighting face, and a revolver in his hand. The second was a big young man of the plain-clothes policeman type. The third was a woman, nearer forty than thirty, but still beautiful and with the spirit of a Boadicea in her eye.

"Hands up, Jim Starkey!" commanded the man with the revolver, and the hands of Mr. Starkey alias Snakes went up obediently.

Then the man with the revolver turned with a grim smile towards a fifth occupant of the room.

"Well done, Carrington," said he. "You've brought it off just beautiful!"

The late Mr. Lumley strolled round his victim and joined the group in front of the late Mr. Snakes. His shoulders were straight now, a smile lit his good-humoured face, his accent was gone. It seemed extraordinary that he could ever have been mistaken for anything but an agreeable-looking young man about town very obviously disguised.

"He went for the bait like a hungry pike," said he.

"Meant to do me in?"

"I have his explicit declaration that he meant to 'fix you up,' Mr. Barton. I was very particular to get that out of him. He has confessed, in fact, to having come all the way to London for that express purpose."

Bill Barton's fighting face set hard as he addressed his late partner.

"You swindling, murderous carrion," said he. You thought you could fix me up, did you? When you passed us three days ago, I didn't recognise you, but *she* did."

He nodded towards the lady, and Starkey's eyes followed him, but fell straightway when they met hers. Pride in her husband, contempt and loathing for the creature who had meant to murder him, shone from them like the flash of a beacon.

Barton went on—

"I knew what you had come over for, just as well as if you'd shouted it out loud. I called in this gentleman, and he advised me how to fix *you* up—and now you're fixed! I've given you chance after chance in the old days till I saw that chances were thrown away on such dog's meat. Now I'll give you one chance more, your very last, Jim Starkey! Either you go off in charge of Mr. Carrington and he puts you aboard the boat sailing Wednesday and you never come to this country again, or I give you in charge for burglary with intent to murder—which means penal servitude. Now which do you choose?"

Starkey spoke for the first time since he had entered that room, and there was little of the man of guts left about him now.

"I'll go home," he muttered.

"Take him off, then," commanded Barton.

In company with the late Mr. Lumley and the big young man, Bill Barton's old partner passed out into the misty night.

3
THE MILLIONTH CHANCE

"Surprises?" said Carrington. "By Jingo, I should think I do get some! Fellows like Sherlock Holmes may always have known what was going to happen, but certainly I don't. I remember one case—" He paused, and a reminiscent smile stole over his face as he lit a fresh cigarette.

"Anything you can tell?" asked one of us.

"Ye-es," he drawled. "I don't really see why I shouldn't, provided I don't give you the right names."

We settled ourselves down in our chairs, and he began.

"It was quite early on in the war, when the scare about spies and aliens in our midst and so on was at its height. I had just started my secret service work and was busy over some case or other up at the head office when Livermere walked into the room.

"'I wish you'd come along and help me to interview a lady,' he said.

"'What's it about?' I asked.

"'Her name is Mrs. Schultze,' said he. 'You remember the case of Herman Schultze, the fellow we were going to intern, only he gave us the slip? Well, this is his wife.'

"'German too?'

"'English as they make 'em. Above suspicion one would say, if she hadn't been married to this fellow. But as it is, one never knows. They've got a country place in Norfolk, a little too near the coast to let us run any risks. Now she has discovered she is being watched— some one hasn't been exactly tactful I fancy—and she has come up

257

full of righteous indignation. If we suspect her of anything, then let us out with it and give her a fair trial; if we don't, then why watch her house? That's the line she's taking.'

"'And what do you want me to do?'

"'Hear her talk, ask her a few, questions, and see what you think of her. You call yourself a judge of character, don't you?'

"'It was a risky remark if I did make it!' I replied. 'That's to say, if you mean to put any money on my tips. They don't always come off. However, let me see the lady and I'll give you my impressions for what they are worth.'

"He took me into his room, and I must frankly confess that for a moment my breath was fairly taken away. Livermere had left me deliberately unprepared for what was coming, and I'd naturally enough fancied I. should see an average British matron. Instead, I saw one of the most bewitching creatures I have ever come across in a considerable experience. Slender, dark, piquante, breeding to the tips of her fingers, gowns made in Paris, voice that would have stirred a doormat,—that was the lady I found in Livermere's room. He introduced us, and I bowed as gracefully as nature has permitted me, and smiled within the same limitations. She seemed a trifle surprised at seeing such a peaceful and amiable apparition. Then she drew herself up and became the traduced patriot again—and a more charming and animated patriot I never want to meet. In fact, I was quite near enough being bowled over by this one.

"'I have been telling Captain Livermere,' she said, and her voice had a curious subtle thrill in it, 'that I am either a traitor to my country or I am not. If you think I am, then place your spies openly in my house—read my letters—question my servants frankly—arrest me if anything is suspicious, and try me! If you don't think I am, then leave me alone to do the work I'm trying to do for my country!'

"'What work is that?' I ventured to ask, very politely indeed, I assure you.

"'I have offered my house as a hospital. If the Government will take it, I am willing to scrub my own floors so long as I may work in it! Just now I am helping in another hospital.'

"'Nursing?'

"'I wish I could! At present I am driving my car for them. It's a hospital for wounded officers.'

"Livermere shot a quick glance at me. Of course I knew what was in his mind. A beautiful woman like that could extract a good deal of information from wounded officers in the course of a drive. However, we neither of us dropped the least hint of what we were thinking.

"'And what do you complain of, Mrs. Schultze?' I inquired.

"'I complain of my house being watched surreptitiously, servants being questioned, and letters being tampered with!'

"'But isn't that what you have just been inviting us to do?' said Livermere.

"'I ask you to do it openly and thoroughly—so that you can really *see* whether I am capable of being what you suspect! You are finding out nothing like this—because there is nothing to find out! And yet you keep on suspecting.'

"Livermere is a first-class fellow, but I could see he was only irritating the lady to no purpose, so I tipped him a wink and he left us alone together. I don't mind confessing that I didn't hurry the interview, and by the end of it I was quite smitten—as I often am, though luckily always temporarily so far. As for the lady, I really think she thought me rather a nice sort of fellow. In fact, since I wanted to produce a good impression both for business reasons and because I couldn't help it, and since one gets a little practice in my job in producing the kind of impression one wants, I may even say that she very possibly thought I was a bit carried away by her charms.

"After we had parted on very amicable terms I had a little talk with Livermere.

"'Well, what do you think of her?' said he.

"'Either she's no traitress or else a spy in a million.'

"'So that it's a million to one on her being straight?'

"When it was put to me like that I hesitated for a moment, and then took the plunge.

"'Yes,' I said, 'I think I'd be willing to let it go at that.'

"'And otherwise very charming?' he smiled.

"'Quite delightful. A woman with a temperament, mind you; capable of a devilish lot if the temperament ran away with her. One could tell that by something in the quality of her voice alone. What's Schultze like, by the way?'

"'Stout prosperous party of the commercial type; quite a bit older than she is. He's rolling in money and she hadn't a sou. Hence the marriage, I believe.'

"'Doesn't sound likely to have roused the temperament to the pitch of betraying her country,' I said; 'I think you can risk it, Livermere.'

"Well, three or four weeks passed and I heard nothing more of the matter. And then one day Livermere called me into his room. I could see that something was worrying him pretty seriously.

"'You remember the fair Mrs. Schultze?' he began.

"'I remember the dark Mrs. Schultze,' I said.

"'You were right,' said he, though hardly in the tone in which one usually makes that remark.

"'About her being straight?'

"'No, about taking your tips.'

"I looked as calmly superior as possible, and merely asked—

"'In what way can I assist you this time, Livermere?'

"'We'll come to that in a moment,' said he. 'In the first place here are the facts. I acted on your judgment and stopped doing anything that could annoy her. Of course we kept a general eye on the place, but there was no more regular watching. In a little while rumours began to go about. They came from one of her servants first of all in the form of a ghost story.'

"'A ghost story!' I exclaimed.

"'First of all—Odd sounds in her house and so on. Then a glimpse of a figure was seen in a passage where nobody had any business to be; seen by a fairly reliable witness too. And then came an even more specific tale of mysterious sounds and movements. Finally, I have got hold of a very full and particular description of the house, with a number of plans, from an architect who was employed by Schultze a few years ago to make some alterations, and I find it's an old rambling Tudor place, with secret stairs and passages and priests' hiding-holes, and the Lord knows what all.'

"'And you want me—?' I began.

"'To take the thing up,' said he in his crisp way.

"There seemed to be but four explanations: spooks, rats, men, or lies. Not being a spookist myself, I eliminated that alternative. A very little careful inquiry showed that though there might be exaggeration, the stories were founded on fact of some sort. Sifting the evidence as thoroughly as it could be sifted, rats wouldn't account for everything. Therefore men alone remained. I studied the plans of the house to see how the secret stairs, et-cetera, ran, and I found they were not in the servants' quarters. Their part of the house in fact was comparatively modern. I also inquired into the servants' characters, and found they were under a regular dragon of a housekeeper—a model of all the virtues, especially the more aggressive ones. The very idea of anything improper going on under this elderly virgin's eye made the villagers smile.

"'She has made a fool of me!' I said to myself; and yet I was loth to believe it. In fact, I still declined to believe it until I could find evidence of one thing.

"And here came the most mysterious part of the business. If this lady were harbouring spies, they would have to get in and out, or what good would they be doing? And the one bit of evidence lacking was evidence of any suspicious character entering that house, leaving it, lingering in its neighbourhood, or in fact of being within fifty miles of it. I was having the place watched day and night. My watchers included two or three fellows in corduroys cleaning ditches and clipping hedges, an elderly-looking botanical enthusiast, in short, a really excellent mixed bag of disguises, and first-rate men at their job too; for I tell you I was now on my mettle. Best of all, they included the austere housekeeper, who turned out to have lost two nephews at Mons, and to be as down on Huns as on lapses from virtue. She had a natural suspicion of beautiful women, and had been quietly keeping her eye on her mistress all along.

"And yet something was still going on in that house beyond the shadow of a doubt.

"And then a certain bit of information came to my ears. I made inquiries in quite another direction—in the neighbourhood of the port of Hull this time, and, by Jingo, I sat up! Next morning I was back in town talking it over with Livermere.

"'Are you sure that Herman Schultze ever got out of this country?' I asked him.

"'He was supposed to have,' said he.

"'A man devilish like him was seen at Hull trying to ship himself to Holland,' I told him. 'He was headed off, and after that all traces of him were lost.'

"Livermere whistled.

"'Then the milk has practically never been out of the cocoanut,' said he. 'And the one in a million chance has come off, Carrington.'

"'I said it was a million to one against her being a *spy*,' I corrected. 'This is rather different. What would any devoted wife do?'

"He looked pretty thoughtful for a minute or two, and then he said—

"'The point now is: What are we going to do? Searching the house would be a mere farce if we didn't search every corner of every one of those dashed hiding-holes.'

"'Whatever we search, if we find nothing it will be a good deal worse than a farce,' I argued. 'We'll have given the whole show away, made fools of ourselves, and possibly raised Cain. For there are limits to the patience of the public if they hear of houses being watched for weeks, and then ransacked, with not a scrap of justification to show for it. We'll weaken our hands against the next time.'

"'Do you know the run of these passages and things well enough to make sure of covering them all?'

"I shook my head very decidedly.

"'I've gone into that, and I know a bit about them, but even that architect has only a sketchy idea of them. He says they are the most extraordinary rabbit-warren of that sort to be found in any house in England.'

"'Then how are we to get at the fellow? We can't leave a Hun hiding in his own house within a couple of miles of the North Sea coast.'

"I had been wrestling with the problem pretty well all night, and I put my solution to him now, not as a very pretty one, or the kind of solution that either of us liked—especially myself, who had to do the dirty work—but simply as the only feasible solution I could think of. Its chief merits were that it wouldn't give our hand away if it didn't come off, and that nobody could be blamed but me.

"Well, we made our plans, and proceeded to set our trap; and first of all, I must ask you to believe that I never felt such a swine in my life, and never liked a job less. However, war is war.

"The next afternoon a motor rolled up to the door of the chateau Schultze, and a very smart and fashionable gentleman alighted. That was me. He was driven by a chauffeur whose face was shrouded by a cap with an immense peak. That was Livermere. The housekeeper alone was in the know, and had given us the tip as to the proper hour to call, so as to catch the lady as near napping as we could. I was shown straight into a very charming old-fashioned room used as a sort of boudoir, and as soon as I had disappeared, the chauffeur slipped into the hall and stood ready to do a sprint to my rescue if need be.

"I went slap into that room on the heels of the maid, and if ever a lady was flurried and found a guest unwelcome, it was the fascinating Mrs. Schultze. She was so flurried (though she carried it off marvellously) that she never noticed one little object lying on a small table till I had closed my hand over it and slipped it into my pocket. It was a half-smoked pipe, and by Jingo, it was *warm!* So was the scent, thought I.

"I had picked up enough of the run of the secret passages to feel perfectly certain that one of them opened into this room somehow and somewhere. Looking round it, I at once suspected either a certain old portrait or a section of the bookcase as being the door. Within a couple of minutes I had plumped for the bookcase. I had heard a sound, very faint and gentle, but still an unmistakable sound. And I could see that the lady had heard it too, and was trying to cover it up.

"There was no doubt I was in luck's way, and all seemed to depend on my having enough assurance and brutality to carry the thing through. Lord, how I would have liked to kick myself! However, instead, I went straight at it. I had taken a small nip of raw whisky just before I got out of the car, so as to give my breath a good alcoholic reek, and if I describe my manner as sprightly, I don't exaggerate in the least.

"'My *dear* Mrs. Schultze!' I said, as I squeezed her hand, and breathed at her for all I was worth; 'I say, I hope you're all alone, and all the rest of it, eh? What? I simply couldn't resist the temptation of looking you up—literally couldn't keep away from you. I say, you know, you're even more beautiful than you were last time. You remember last time, eh? What?'

"She was deadly pale, poor creature, but her voice was very quiet, and her dignity perfect. If war hadn't been war, I'd have chucked it, and bolted. However, war being war, I didn't.

"'I remember you, Mr. Carrington,' she said, 'and you were very kind and polite to me—last time.'

"It was a fair hit on the point, but I was prepared for it, and merely beamed the more affectionately.

"'I say, sit down and tell me what you've been doing?' I said, and put out my hand to catch her arm.

"She whisked herself away, but still kept her composure.

"'Will you come into the drawing-room?' she said, and tried to head for the door.

"I was expecting that move, and got in front of her.

"'We're jolly quiet here—nobody to disturb us!' said I, and, of course, I was pitching my voice pretty high. On top of that she gave a smothered cry when she saw my arms opening amorously, and knocked over the small table in getting clear.

"'If that husband was anything but a Hun, this would have brought him out already!' I said to myself, and the next instant I did hear a most distinct sound from the neighbourhood of the bookcase. But he still stayed in his burrow, and there was nothing for it but piling on more insults.

"'I'm in love with you!' I cried, right loud out too.

"'You are drunk!' she said, stinging and low.

"I pretended to get annoyed at this.

"'Drunk!' said I. 'By George, I'll make you pay something for saying that! A kiss! Damn it, I'm going to have a kiss!'

"She made a dive at the bell, but I was ahead of her again, and did catch her by the arm this time. Mind you, I was acting the part of half-sprung ravisher for all I was worth, and though her nerve was good, it gave when I had actually caught hold of her. She gave one piercing cry, and that did the trick. The old bookcase flew open in the middle, and out leapt a most furiously indignant gentleman in khaki!"

"'In khaki!' we cried. "Do you mean that Schultze was disguised as—"

"Unfortunately it wasn't the lady's husband at all," said Carrington.

"Yes," he added a few minutes later, when we had recovered from the shock of this *dénoûment*, "as I said to Livermere driving home, 'If you really want to make sure of winning your money, Livermere, back a wounded officer against an absent Hun as often as you get the chance."

4
COINCIDENCE

I
Mr. Wickley's Story

"If it wasn't for lucky coincidences," said Carrington, "many a gentleman in ginger and broad arrows would be a highly respected citizen. They're done in again and again by the most infernal flukes. The most baffling mystery—yes, I really think I may call it absolutely the most insoluble-looking that has ever come my way—was solved by what seemed like a mere series of extraordinary coincidences."

"Do you mean they weren't really coincidences?" somebody asked.

"There was one real coincidence. The rest was a curious but not at all an unnatural result of quite an ordinary affair—a county dinner, in fact."

After that we simply had to get the story out of him.

"I was asked as a guest to the Devorsetshire Association's Annual Dinner in London (you can guess which county it really was for yourselves). There was nothing very remark able in that, for I get asked out to all sorts of dinners. I had to reply to the toast of the guests, and there was nothing very remarkable in that either, for I'm always getting let in for after-dinner speaking—when they don't want a very serious oration. In consequence everybody—or at all events most of the people there—discovered who I was; which was a very natural consequence.

"Again, it was very natural that natives of Devorsetshire and people connected with the county who hadn't seen each other for years, should happen to meet on such an occasion. And if any one, or any two, or any three of them wanted advice in a ticklish matter, it was extremely natural that they should think of the eloquent gentleman who had replied for the guests.

"If you bear all this in mind, you'll see how things fell out, though on the surface it looked as if some capricious elf had taken over the duties of destiny.

"Well, to come to our muttons. The very next morning a card with the name of 'Mr. R. C. Wickley' was handed in to me, and in a moment Mr. Wickley himself walked into my room. He had reddish hair, a somewhat receding forehead, curiously suspicious eyes, and a prize-fighting jowl. It doesn't sound a very promising description, and yet somehow or other the man was distinctly likeable. For one thing, he had a pleasant smile, and for another, the look of one who has seen a good bit of trouble and yet hasn't let his tail down; also he was unmistakably a gentleman.

"'I saw you last night at the Devorset dinner, Mr. Carrington,' he began, 'and I thought you looked the sort of man who might help me, and who could be trusted.'

"This was not merely pleasantly flattering, but it was said with an air of really meaning it and of badly wanting some one he could trust, that roused my interest at once.

"'What I am going to tell you,' he went on, 'must be *absolutely* confidential. Your business is a purely private agency, isn't it? You don't give things away to the police?'

"You may imagine that this roused my interest still more.

"If you come to me confidentially I give nothing away to anybody.'

"'Not even murder?'

"I tell you frankly I hesitated. I had never had such a question put to me before.

"'It would depend on the circumstances,' I said.

"He looked at me and thought for a moment.

"'I'll risk it,' he said, and plunged into this yarn.

J. STORER CLOUSTON

"'I'm a Devorset man originally,' said he, 'but I've lived a lot abroad and had a pretty mixed career. I'm going to make no bones about anything, and I may tell you candidly that there was one particular part of my life that I want to forget and don't want other people to know. It isn't the part I'm going to tell you about, but it partly accounts for it.

"'Eleven years ago an old uncle of mine died, and as he hadn't left a will I came into his property in Devorset. It included an old manor-house of the smaller type and quite a nice bit of mixed co-vert shooting—rough but good sport, and it suited me down to the ground. I came home, settled down on the place, and hoped my troubles were at an end. Being a hilly, wooded part of the county I hadn't many neighbours—in fact I couldn't raise enough guns to shoot my coverts properly, but that was the only disadvantage. Things being as they had been, I didn't like meeting too many people, for fear some one should turn up who knew what I didn't want known.'

"'Were you married, by the way?' I asked.

"'No. I'm not much of a ladies' man and have never missed a wife. I was quite contented, in fact, till things began to go wrong, and I may tell you absolutely honestly, Mr. Carrington, that why they began to go wrong has always been a complete mystery to me. In fact, as you'll see presently, the whole thing has been more like a nightmare than a bit of ordinary life.

"'My nearest neighbour was a man Spencer, "Toddy" Spencer they called him, a fellow with a handsome wife but no children, pots of money, and quite a big country house. He was a wealthy stockbroker and had bought the place himself, largely for the shoot-ing. As he was always keen for an extra gun and so was I, we struck up quite a friendship to begin with and I saw a good bit of them. The wife was a trifle too go-ahead for my own taste—though most men would probably have been keen about her; but Toddy Spencer himself seemed quite a nice fellow, in spite of being rather a sulky-looking chap and obviously with a devil of a temper. Like a lot of fellows of his type, he did himself a little too well, both in the eating and drinking line; though I never saw him actually the worse for liquor.

"'At first, the Spencers used to come down to Devorsetshire only for part of the year, and then they settled down there for good; though Toddy himself always spent at least two or three days in the week in London on business. He was one of several partners in a very big firm, I may mention.

"'Well, after about two and a half years, during which we had been excellent neighbours, the first mystery began. For some unknown reason Spencer suddenly took a violent dislike to me. In fact, dislike is too mild a term. The man hated me.'

"'How did he show it?' I asked.

"'Wouldn't shoot with me, stopped me and my tenants from using a path through his grounds, blackguarded me behind my back, and insulted me to my face. This low-class swine of a stockbroker! A man without birth or breeding or any connection with the county before he bought the place! A damned *nouveau riche!*'

"It was quite evident that though Mr. Wickley didn't look particularly aristocratic, he was a gentleman with very sensitive family pride. In fact, the mere recollection of Mr. Spencer's behaviour was making him boil afresh.

"'I won't trouble you with all the details, for his final performance made the rest seem almost nothing. I gave him a bit of my own mind, I may mention, which finally put an end to all relations. . . .'

"'What did you say to him?' I asked.

"'What I thought,' he answered briefly, and I guessed that what Mr. Wickley thought had probably made Mr. Spencer sit up pretty sharply. 'Well, anyhow, things had gone like this for months, and we were past speaking terms, when one day I got a note from him. I can't remember the exact words, for I threw the thing straight into the fire, but this was the gist of it. He had discovered the black mark against me, and gave me the choice of exposure, or leaving the county and selling my place to him.'

"'One moment,' I interrupted, for I saw that my visitor wanted to hurry over this part. 'I don't want to press you to tell me anything you prefer not to, but in order to understand this extraordinary ultimatum I must ask you one or two questions. Was this "black mark"—er—pretty serious?'

"He hesitated for an instant, and I saw how suspicious those eyes of his could look. Then he answered, and I saw how doggedly that jowl of his could set.

"'It was nothing I could actually suffer for—by the law, I mean. I had suffered already. But it had an ugly name, and I don't suppose many people would have been keen to speak to me again. You don't need to know the name, do you?'

"'No,' I said. 'In fact I had rather not. I only wanted to be sure that it actually did give him the leverage he seems to have assumed it gave him. How did he find this out?'

"Wickley shook his head.

"'I don't know. He could have found out in one or two ways, if he set to work to find things out about me. And he obviously did.'

"'Why did he want to buy your place?'

"'Simply because he hated me, and knew that was the way to hit me hardest. He didn't want more land or an extra house.'

"'I see,' I said. 'Go ahead.'

"'Well, after that note came I want you to understand, Mr. Carrington, that things happened right on end, one after the other, without giving me time to cool down or think quietly. I had a lot of woodland on my place, and was rather keen about forestry. It was a hobby of Spencer's, and he had started me, and, curiously enough, the pruning-knife I was carrying that afternoon was a present from him. He got one for himself and one for me. I picked it up and took it with me simply automatically, because I had been carrying it every day lately. But I was thinking of nothing but that note.

"'Imagine what it meant for me! To hand over a place my family had owned for four hundred years—hand it over to this unspeakable bounder, lose everything worth having, and clear out of the county—imagine what it meant! As to the other alternative, I felt I would rather shoot myself first. Perhaps I don't express myself very well, Mr. Carrington, but I daresay you can more or less understand.'

"His words may have been restrained, but his face was working and his eyes blazing, just as they must have been when he set out on that walk. I did understand, and I told him so. He seemed pleased, and for a moment almost smiled. And then his face set, and he went on—

"'Without thinking where I was going I wandered about the Lord knows where, but, anyhow, at last I headed for a certain wood where I had been doing some pruning before. It was just on the boundary of the two properties. In fact, the stream that formed the boundary ran through it. It was a winter afternoon, and growing a little dusky by this time. I entered the wood—all the time, mind you, without realising where I was or what I was doing—and then about ten paces from the outer edge of it I pulled up dead. Spencer was standing, half leaning against a tree, with his back to me!'

"Wickley stopped for an instant, and looked at me hard.

"'I am trusting you with everything!' he said.

"'I know you are.'

"He moistened his lips and went on

"'The sound of the running water had drowned my footsteps. It still drowned them as I took three more steps, and then let him have it in the broad of his back with the pruning-knife. I remember striking sort of slanting and downwards so as to give the curved knife a chance. I'm pretty strong, and it did give it a chance. It went in up to the handle and stopped there. He fell on his face without a sound or a struggle. I had seen dead men before, and I knew he was one. And then, suddenly, I realised what I had done.'

"He paused and licked his lips afresh.

"'How long ago was this?'

"'Eight years,' he said.

"'Eight years!' I exclaimed. 'But I never remember hearing—'

"'Wait a bit,' said he. 'The interesting part of the story hasn't begun yet.'

"I wondered what his idea of an uninteresting story was, but I said nothing, and he went on—

"'I don't mind confessing that I lost my head—or anyhow my nerve utterly. I remember I could only say one thing to myself—"I didn't know what I was doing!" I hurried home and made no attempt to seem cool. I got out my car, drove it myself at break-neck speed to the station, and simply left it standing outside. I took the first train to London, and made so little effort to hide what I was feeling, that everybody who saw me stared. I got to London late in the evening, and wandered about the streets all night. In the morning I still kept wandering, trying to avoid newspapers and posters. Then I suddenly got desperate and bought a paper. There was nothing about the murder in it. So I bought another and then another, till I had bought six papers, but still there was nothing. And then I got reckless. I went straight off to the Hotel Metropole in Northumberland Avenue, the place where both Spencer and I generally stayed when we wanted an hotel in London, ordered a room and went straight to bed.'

"He paused for a moment again, and I couldn't help observing—

"'Your story is interesting enough now, Mr. Wickley.'

"'Wait!' he said. 'I haven't come to the interesting part yet.'

"I really began to think the man was off his head.

"'I slept almost all day,' he continued, 'and when I woke up in the late afternoon my head was pretty clear again. And, heavens! I was afraid now! I dressed very quickly, and then sat in my room waiting for some one to come for me. And then I suddenly got reckless again, walked out into the corridor, and boldly went down by the lift. I stepped out of the lift, and was crossing the hall, when out of the corner of my eye I seemed to see some one I knew. I looked round, and as I'm a living sinner, Carrington, there was Toddy Spencer sitting in an arm chair looking at me!'

"He stopped abruptly and added—

"'*That's* the interesting part.'

"And I had to confess he was right.

"'What did you do?' I asked.

"'Simply stared at him, just as he was staring at me, only he wasn't staring quite so hard. And then he suddenly spoke to me in quite a friendly voice, almost nervously in fact. I answered him in just the same tone, and there we were talking together in the hall of the Metropole as if nothing had happened at all.'

"'What did you talk about?'

"'The weather, I think, and we each made the pretty obvious remark that the other seemed to have come up from Devorsetshire.

We exchanged about half a dozen sentences or so, and then we each nodded, and I went out.'

"'"I'm not a murderer after all!" was my first thought, and for half an hour I was happy as a boy.

"'And then the whole thing began to come back to me—Spencer standing in the wood the way he fell—everything. I simply *couldn't* have imagined it! And yet equally I couldn't have imagined talking to Spencer in the Metropole. I stayed three days in London hesitating, and then I simply had to go back and see for myself.'

"Again he stopped abruptly and asked—'Now what's your impression so far, Mr. Carrington?'

"'That you were overwrought, and imagined—or else dreamt—the murder scene.'

"Wickley's voice sank.

"'I went back to that wood, very cautiously, and taking care that nobody was about—and there was a freshly filled-in grave there! Some one had been buried, very roughly and hurriedly, and not very deep. Who was it?'

"I thought he was going to answer the question himself, but instead he waited for me to speak.

"'Do you mean to say you never discovered?'

"He shook his head.

"'It's an absolute mystery to me! Nobody in the neighbourhood apparently was missing. Nothing was ever said, or whispered, or rumoured, of a murder. Nothing more ever happened. I couldn't possibly live on in that place. I let the house, but not the shooting—because I didn't want people to be going through that wood, and I've been a wanderer for eight years. Last week I came to London and met a cousin who persuaded me to go to the Devorset dinner last night. And there I saw Spencer again, for the first time since we parted in the Metropole. That started the whole thing again in my mind. And then when I heard you were a private inquiry agent, I suddenly decided to end the suspense and come to you. I want you to find out what happened—who that man was.'

"I thought for a minute or two.

"'You have only mentioned three people,' I said. 'It obviously wasn't yourself, and it wasn't Spencer. The third was his wife.'

"'It certainly wasn't her. It was a man. Besides, she is still alive.'

"'Then I have absolutely nothing to start upon. What made you think it was Spencer?'

"'I knew his overcoat and his felt hat.'

"'That was all you had to go upon?'

"'It was a man of the same height. Besides, who else would be in that spot wearing Spencer's coat and hat?'

"'Or a coat and hat like them.'

"'Identically the same! I can still see them quite distinctly.'

"'You say it was getting dark?'

"'Dusky; but then I was within a yard of him.'

"I was silent for a little longer, and then I said—

"'I must think it over, Mr. Wickley. Leave me your address.'

"He left me thinking very hard, I can assure you."

II

THE STOCKBROKER'S WIFE

Carrington lit a fresh cigarette and began the second part of his story.

"Wickley left my office only a little before my usual lunch hour, and I sat on over my fire for some time, thinking, but not seeing a ray of light. That made me rather late in getting back after lunch, and when I came in my clerk handed me a card and told me a gentleman was waiting in my room. On the card I read the name, 'Mr. A. D. Spencer.'

"When I glanced up from it and caught my clerk's eye, I could see that he evidently thought I had done myself too well at lunch. I suppose I had been standing for the whole of five minutes gazing at that card. The appearance of Mr. Spencer immediately on top of Mr. Wickley seemed a thing hardly in the course of nature. I began to wonder whether there was some sort of a conspiracy between the two men. I tried to see in advance what line this man Spencer was going to take. And then I recovered my wits and walked into my room.

"I found a heavy-looking man of rather above middle height, clean-shaved, with a blue chin, baggy eyes, and very black hair. He had the skin of a man who, as Wickley said, did himself a little too well, and I could also quite believe that he could be a sulky ill-tempered devil if things went wrong.

"'We didn't exactly meet last night, Mr. Carrington,' he began, and there was quite a dash of geniality about the man when he made the effort, 'but I was at the Devorset dinner and heard you speak. I also came across an old acquaintance there. Meeting him set me worrying about an old problem, and seeing you put it into my head to come and consult you on the matter.'

"And then I realised that there was no conspiracy at all, nor even any very extraordinary coincidence, but, as I told you at the start, just a series of quite natural events that had produced this startling result. My second thought was—'What a bit of luck! The solution to the insoluble problem walks into my office!' However, you'll see how far out I was there.

"'Of course you'll understand that this is strictly confidential,' said he.

"'Naturally,' I said; and I noted that though he was evidently keen on secrecy, he didn't show the same extreme anxiety as Wickley.

"'Well,' he said, 'I'll begin my story eleven years back. Or perhaps I should first mention that some years before that I had purchased an estate in Devorset. I'm a stockbroker, by the way: Spencer, Spencer, & Luderman is my firm, and I'm the senior partner. Eleven years ago an old fellow in the neighbourhood called Wickley died, and his nephew came into the property and settled down next door to me. By next door I mean rather under a couple of miles away; but we had no other neighbours—of that class, I mean—within six or seven miles, and we didn't know them either. Consequently Wickley and I saw a lot of one another and became very friendly.'

"'What sort of a fellow was he?' I inquired, with my most truth-seeking expression.

"'I wish you had noticed him at the dinner last night,' said he, 'and you'd have understood better what kind of a proposition he was. A reddish-haired, heavy-chinned sort of fellow, with queer eyes, and the word "past" stamped all over him.'

"'What do you mean exactly?'

"'Well, I mean that he *had* a past, and I soon began to guess as much from his very appearance and manner, though at first I only felt vaguely that there was something unusual about him. I may mention that he isn't the kind of person one would naturally suspect of a shady record, for the Wickleys are a very good old Devorset family, and if family pride would keep people straight, well, it ought to have kept him. He didn't show that feature either to begin with, but you'll see in a minute the sort of too-good-for-a-damned-stock-broker gentleman he was. My place was about twice the size of his, I may add, and he was deuced glad to have as many days shooting with me as he could get. Some precious rotten days he gave me in exchange; but of course shooting with a two-penny halfpenny squire was always an honour!'

"This speech naturally didn't prejudice me much in favour of Mr. Spencer. Little though he realised it, he was making me look at things more and more from Wickley's point of view—bad hat though Mr. W. may have been, and respectable as Mr. S. no doubt was.

"'I am coming to a very painful part of my story now, Mr. Carrington,' he continued. 'In fact it's so infernally unpleasant that it has kept me from telling the facts to a living soul up to this moment. I had a wife, in fact she's legally my wife still, and I was very fond of her. I can assure you on that point—I was desperately fond of her! She was an uncommonly beautiful girl. She was on the stage at one time, I may say, and might have gone very far on her looks alone, but I married her and took her away from it. She was a lady by birth, but she hadn't a penny, and it was a love marriage pure and simple—love marriage on my part at least, for I don't believe she ever really loved me. We had no children either, and that was a fatal mistake.'

"He paused and stared moodily at my fire. I was much more in sympathy with Mr. Spencer now.

"'Well, to get over an unpleasant business as quickly as possible, we began to drift apart pretty fast. I still loved her to distraction—in a way; but we both had tempers and she led me the devil of a dance, and it was cat and dog half the time. When I bought this place in Devorset she kicked at living there permanently—too slow for her. She'd stay for some months and we'd have house parties and so on, and then back to town again. And then all of a sudden she quite changed round. Perfectly agreeable to living all the year in the country she became now, so we gave up our flat in town and settled in Devorset; even though it meant her being quite a good bit by herself, for I generally had to spend part of my week in town for business reasons.'

"'Then, like a thunderclap, came the suspicion that there was something behind this change of tune. One needn't go into all the details, but several little things made me morally certain that Elise was being unfaithful to me. We were having worse rows than usual at that time, and in one shindy I charged her with it. In order to hit me back hard she actually admitted it!'

"'In order to hit you hard?' I interrupted. 'Are you sure she meant it?'

"'Perfectly, because she got in a funk afterwards, when her temper cooled, and tried to unsay it and back out. Besides, the little things on which I had based my suspicions had convinced me already. And now I had her word for it!'

"Spencer was quite carried away by his own story by this time, and I could judge exactly the kind of dangerous revengeful man he was.

"'The only question was, who was the man? And there couldn't be any question about that either. Wickley was the only possibility!'

"'Ah!' I exclaimed, and he looked at me sharply. 'Go on,' I said, 'I begin to see the position now.'

"I saw it a lot clearer than he had any notion of. This of course accounted for Wickley's first mystery—the sudden hatred of Spencer for his neighbour.

"'There could be no doubt about it,' said he. 'He was the only man in the neighbourhood of our own position in life whom we knew in the very least intimately. And he lived inside of two miles from us. Six miles away there was a fat fellow of fifty with a wife and large family—a dull bore of a fellow. Seven miles away were two maiden ladies. Nine miles away was an invalid of seventy.

Those were the only alternatives, and we scarcely ever saw any of them. Besides, I had grown more and more convinced that Wickley had something shady in the background. I knew him now to be a blackguard!'

"'Knew?' I repeated. 'But had you any proof?'

"'When there are no possible alternatives, that's proof enough! Besides, I soon got proof of his character. I made inquiries about him—set an agency on to his track, and I discovered'—he paused and hesitated for an instant—'well, I need only say that he would never have been received in any decent society if people knew what I found out. It had happened abroad—he had done ti—.' Again he broke off and the scowl lifted a little from his face. 'But the man had suffered for his sins, and it had really nothing to do with my story except that it gave me a hold over him. I was mad with anger and I determined to use it.'

"'Had nothing else passed between you?' I ventured to ask, for I remembered Wickley's version and I suspected Spencer was skipping a bit.

"'Oh, well,' he admitted, 'I may as well allow that I had shown him pretty plainly that I didn't want to have anything more to do with him. We had one open row, and that was when he showed me what a damned high and mighty aristocratic snob he was. "Gentlemen aren't grown in two days out of dirty stockbroking mushrooms!" Those were his actual words!'

"I must confess that I had scarcely given Mr. Wickley credit for such powers of invective, and I realised now to what a pitch of fury the two of them had roused one another.

"'As I was saying,' he went on, 'I was quite beside myself with rage by this time, and I did a damned silly thing. I wrote to him threatening to show him up if he didn't clear out of the place. I even went the length of telling him he must sell me his property. That was simply to crush his pride, of course.'

"'You called it *silly*,' I said. 'That seems hardly the adjective.'

"'Wait a bit and you'll see why,' said he. 'I must tell you first that I was trying hard to catch my wife all this time. Having to go up to town two or three days a week and leave her to play the devil with that fellow nearly drove me demented. On the other hand, it gave me a chance of catching her napping. One of my servants was watching her for me, but I think Elise must have suspected him. . . .'

"'Him'? I said. 'Do you mean your butler?'

"'It was my chauffeur as a matter of fact; a smart young fellow. He came to me one day and told me he suspected what was up and offered to watch her. I paid him well for it, but though he said Wickley was often hanging round my place, he never found anything definite against my wife. I tried my own hand at it too, by coming back from town when she didn't expect me, but they were cunning as Satan. I never caught them.

"But to come to the climax of the affair: I wrote that letter to Wickley from my London office, and then the sudden thought struck me that I would come straight home myself. He wouldn't expect me, seeing the address on the letter, and he would probably see my wife at once about it. That's how I argued. When I got home my wife was out, nobody knew where. My suspicions became a practical certainty. I took my gun and I set out in the direction of his house. I'm telling you everything quite candidly, Mr. Carrington. I was just approaching the boundary of the two properties when I saw him coming towards me, as I thought. I slipped behind a tree and watched him. He turned into a wood that lies just on the boundary, and I stood for a short while like a man in hell!'

"Mr. Spencer took out his handkerchief and passed it across his face. As for me, I never was more fascinated in my life. To think of hearing the other half of Wickley's story like this! In a moment Spencer went on—

"'I yielded to temptation, Mr. Carrington. I felt sure that he and my wife were in that wood, and I meant to kill one or both— Wickley certainly. I made a little detour, entered the wood, crossed a stream that forms the boundary, and suddenly I saw him. He was lying dead on his face, with a huge blood stain all over his back!'

"'Wickley was?' I exclaimed.

"'I had just seen him go into the wood. Who else could it be? But I didn't go near the body. I simply turned tail and hurried home as fast as I could walk. It took me all my time to keep at a walk and not to run! And now do you see what a silly performance that threatening letter was? It had come on top of other foolishness, for I had used my tongue pretty freely about the fellow. And now he was lying murdered and I had been seen leaving my house with a gun, and probably had been seen going in that very direction! Also, I knew in my heart I had meant to kill him. Lord, what a shock I got! You may think me a fool to have felt like that. . . .'

"'I don't in the very least,' I assured him in all sincerity.

"'Well, that's how I did feel. I may add as some excuse for my next performance that this trouble had been leading me to drink a bit too much, and my nerve wasn't at its best. Anyhow when I got home I didn't wait in the house longer than to order the car; and then as a finishing touch, the chauffeur couldn't be found, and so I couldn't get to the station in time to catch the last train that evening! I had hired from the station when I arrived, so as to give no warning of my coming, but the car had gone back, and there I was landed. However, I didn't wait in my house—I simply couldn't do it. I tramped off to a little local pub, slept the night there, and went back to town in the morning. And now comes a bit of the story that you probably won't believe, Mr. Carrington.'

"'I believe everything you tell me,' I said.

"'I had a room at the Hotel Metropole at that time. On the same afternoon, soon after I had got back to London, I was sitting in the hall with a bundle of evening papers, looking for some news of Wickley's murder, when what do you think? Wickley himself stepped out of the lift and walked across the hall under my nose!'

"He looked at me expectantly, and I tried to seem dumfounded. I must have succeeded pretty well, for he seemed quite satisfied.

"'It is absolute gospel truth,' he said. 'Just as he was passing, he spotted me, and do you know, the extraordinary thing was that all signs of enmity seemed to have left the man! As for me, I was so thankful to see him alive, I could have embraced him. We exchanged a few ordinary remarks in a perfectly friendly way, and then he walked out of the hotel. I haven't seen him from that moment till last night at the dinner, and it was meeting him again that tuned me up to doing what of course I always should have done. I want this mystery cleared up, Mr. Carrington. I want to know who that man was I saw lying dead in the wood.'

"He stopped, and I realised with a shock that Spencer's story had done absolutely nothing to solve Wickley's mystery. I had counted confidently on its cracking the nut, but instead it simply presented me with the same mystery over again.

"'You never discovered who it was?'

"He shook his head.

"'Never to this day. I can only tell you that nobody is known to have been murdered, or even missing, in Devorset at that time. But I'm afraid that won't help you very much.'

"'Tell me what you did, and your wife did, immediately afterwards.'

"'I funked going back for three or four days. My nerves were utterly rattled. When I got home, my wife had left, cleared right out, and we have never lived together again since. Before leaving she told our housekeeper that she sacked Martin, the chauffeur—no, Marwell, that was his name. Presumably she sacked him because she had discovered he had been spying on her. Of course she had no business to do it on her own account, but I didn't care by that time. In fact I was rather glad to be rid of him. He knew too much about the miserable business. She left a short note for me, only a line or two. I can remember it by heart. "This is absolutely the end of it. We must never meet again. I have done my best for you. Be grateful to me for that."'

"'What did she mean?' I asked.

"He shook his head.

"'I haven't the least idea. A woman's way of getting in the last word and claiming to be in the right, I suppose.'

"'And have you ever met again?'

"'Never.'

"I fell very thoughtful. Dim ideas were beginning to float across my mind, but very mistily and tentatively.

"'Have you lived there at all since then?'

"'No. I let the place at once. And Wickley let his too. Neither of us have lived in Devorset since.'

"'Did you by any chance lose an overcoat about that time?'

"Spencer stared at me very hard.

"'Lose an overcoat?' he repeated. 'No—or rather yes, now I come to think of it. I used to have rather a nice burberry, which must have gone missing just about that time. I remember wondering what had become of it, though such trifles didn't worry me much then.'

"'And a felt hat?'

"He stared again and then thought again.

"'Possibly; but I had several felt hats, and one might have gone astray without my noticing it, especially in the state of mind I was in. Why do you ask?'

"'Just a vague idea I had. It was getting towards dusk, you say, when you saw the body in the wood?'

"'I don't think I said so, but it was.'

"'Well, I'll think over the whole story,' I told him, and Mr. Spencer shook hands and walked off."

III

THE LOST ENGINEER

"Now," said Carrington, "we come to the one really remarkable coincidence. There was present at that Devorset dinner a man with an unsolved riddle lying on a dusty shelf at the back of his memory, and he wasn't a Devorset man either, but a guest like myself. He was a fellow Tuke, a London solicitor; he knew the man who was acting as my own host that night, and so I made his acquaintance at the dinner and had quite a yarn with him. Furthermore, Tuke's host knew Spencer and introduced Tuke to him. It was Tuke's two meetings with Spencer and myself that brought him to my office a couple of days later, and one can trace cause and effect just as in the cases of Wickley's and of Spencer's visits to me. But it was an extraordinary chance that Tuke, with that riddle on the dusty shelf, should have happened to be at the dinner at all. Here you get the work of the sprite who seemed to be acting for Destiny."

"He was a nice, gentlemanly, solid-looking man was Tuke, and didn't suggest anything very exciting when he sat down and told me he had come to see me professionally. But when he said that it was the meeting with Spencer which had reminded him of an un-solved, half-forgotten mystery, I assure you I pricked up my ears.

"'About nine years ago,' he began, 'a poor girl came to me with a very queer story, and a very sad story too it was. She was a Mrs. Borham, or thought she was—a pretty slender young thing of barely twenty-one, full of pluck, but with the marks of pain and worry stamped too clearly on her face for any one with any observation to miss. And this was the story she told me.

"'She was the daughter of an impecunious half-pay Naval Officer and was staying with some relatives at Dover when she met Reginald Borham, if that was his real name, which I should think is very doubtful. He was a man of about twenty-five or twenty-six, a mechanical engineer by profession, remarkably good-looking, with the manners and address of a gentleman, and a most romantic tale of high-born relations who had disowned him owing to his refusal to marry an heiress whom he did not love. It was a cock-and-bull story if ever there was one, but as he professed to having fallen in love with this poor girl, and as she certainly fell in love with him, she swallowed it whole, and to make a long story short, married him.

"'Reading between the lines of her story, and interpreting it by what I was able to pick up about the man, he seems to have married her simply because she wouldn't succumb to his advances otherwise. She was unusually attractive, and he was evidently carried away by her for the moment very completely, for it wasn't his usual procedure with women by any means. As a rule he specialised in married ladies, and lived either on their bounty or on blackmail. In fact he was the worst type of animal that goes about on two legs, a creature vicious to the core, without a rag of honour to cover him or an ounce of compunction in his heart. Such animals ought to be shot at sight!

"'He actually had an engineer's training, plenty of brains, and considerable aptitude for mechanical work, and at the moment was connected with some Admiralty job at Dover, but within three months of his marriage he deserted his work and his wife and vanished into space. I traced another woman in connection with his flight, but she lost sight of him too, and as his employers strongly suspected his honesty, they didn't make any effort to trace him. In fact every man he has been connected with has been thankful to see the last of him, and every woman has bitterly regretted she ever met him.

"'The poor young wife came up to London and determined to make her own living. She had no money, her people had strongly disapproved of the marriage, and things weren't pleasant at home. Having no business training of any kind and being passionately fond of children, she took on the job of nursemaid in the house of some people she knew, and there she was in a dark-blue uniform and bonnet, wheeling a perambulator about the Park and the streets of Bayswater when I made her acquaintance.

"'Well, now I'm coming to the part where I want your detective mind to follow me very closely, Mr. Carrington. Just ask any questions you like if things don't seem clear. It was about a year after her marriage, and she had been nearly nine months on this job, when she was wheeling her pram one day along a quiet street in the neighbourhood of the Edgware Road. Suddenly on the opposite pavement she spied her husband walking rather quickly in the opposite direction, with a lady at his side! They never glanced across the street, and of course it would never have entered the blackguard's head to suspect that a nursemaid wheeling a pram could be his wife; but she, on the other hand, studied them carefully and described them to me exactly.

"'Borham himself was got up immaculately as the young man about town,—silk hat fashionably tilted backwards, morning coat, black and white striped trousers, patent boots with yellow tops, and all the rest of it. The lady had extremely golden hair, a face which even her rival admitted was remarkably pretty, with long eyelashes and very red lips, decidedly of the actress type, Mrs. Borham described her; and as for her dress and hat, she portrayed those so exactly that we were able to identify the lady afterwards through them alone. Of course I can't remember a single item, but anyhow she was very smartly and extremely expensively rigged out.

"'Mrs. Borham stopped short on the opposite pavement and bent over her charge as a nurse might naturally do, but her eyes were following the couple across the way, and she was prepared to wheel round and follow them when they were safely past. However, they didn't go very much farther. There was a quiet hotel in this street, one of that type which probably does a pretty mixed sort of business, but with a very large smart-looking motor-car standing in front of it. She was struck at once, she said, with the contrast between the car and the hotel. Borham and the lady glanced over their shoulders as if to see that the coast was clear, and then turned into the hotel.

"'Imagine the poor girl's feelings as she watched this performance! Fortunately she had heaps of pluck and resource and she determined to see the affair through, so she crossed the street and paced backwards and forwards for about half an hour, taking care never to come near enough to the hotel to be seen from the windows. Unfortunately she was just about at the farther end of her beat when the lady reappeared, and she didn't even see her actually come out of the hotel. In fact, when Mrs. Borham looked round, the lady was on the pavement just about to get into the car that was standing by the kerb, and the only person with her was the chauffeur, who was just at her back. He opened the door of the car, she got in, and then off they went.'

"'And Borham himself?' I asked.

"'Never came out at all. His wife waited and waited in that street, but there was not a sign of him.'

"'Could he have come out before the lady, while his wife happened to be walking away from the hotel?'

"'She declared it was quite impossible, for she kept constantly glancing over her shoulder. No; for some reason or other he must have remained in the hotel till after his wife went away. Conceivably he had spotted her.'

"'Was the chauffeur with the car before the lady came out?'

"'It seemed a curious thing, but Mrs. Borham declared that there was no one with the car. Presumably the man was in the hotel having a drink. You see he would have a long wait, and his mistress would hardly be in a position to wig him for it, considering that he could scarcely help seeing what she was up to.'

"'I see. Well, what happened next?'

"'Just before leaving, Mrs. Borham wheeled her pram right past the hotel, and when she was passing the door her eye was caught by an envelope lying in the gutter immediately opposite. On the off-chance that the lady had dropped it while getting into the car, she picked it up. It turned out to be empty, but on the outside was written, "Mr. J. Marwell, c/o A. D. Spencer, Esq.," and then followed an address at some well-known Kensington flats. Next morning she came to me with her story and the envelope.'

"'Dropped by the chauffeur, I suppose?'

"'By Jove, you're quite right! I put the matter into the hands of an inquiry agent, and found that Mrs. Spencer corresponded to the account of the mysterious lady, and one of her costumes tallied exactly with Mrs. Borham's description. Also Spencer's chauffeur was named Marwell.'

"'And Borham?'

"'Ah, now we come to the most mysterious and extraordinary part of the whole business. Not a single trace was ever seen or heard of Borham again! I admit there were difficulties in the way of tracing him. There was obviously no use in tackling Mrs. Spencer direct, for she would simply have denied everything. We might have threatened her with exposure, but Mrs. Borham wouldn't hear of a public scandal, for in all probability exposure would have meant the Divorce Court for Mrs. Spencer, with Borham's name and history brought into the business. The people at the hotel denied all knowledge of the whole affair. It was that sort of an hotel, you see. My agent tried Marwell, but he was like a clam. And nobody connected with the Spencers, whom we could get hold of, seemed to have even heard of Mr. Borham.

"'As a final and complete checkmate, the Spencers very shortly afterwards gave up their flat in town, and settled down on an estate he had purchased in Devorset.

"'Our only remaining chance of getting at Borham had been by watching Mrs. Spencer, and now, of course, that was gone.'

"'Has Mrs. Borham never heard anything of her husband again?'

"'Not from that day to this. I heard from her about six months ago. Apparently some other man was wanting to marry her, but that vanished blackguard, Borham, stood in the way. She asked what I should advise? Well, I gave her the best advice I could, but

I had to confess that the man had beaten us completely. And now, Mr. Carrington, can you suggest any possible step that might be taken?'

"I thought for a minute or two, and then I said—

"'You can tell Mrs. Borham that her husband has been dead for eight years.'

"Tuke stared at me very hard indeed.

"'But—how do you know?' he exclaimed.

"'Borham was Marwell,' I said, 'and Marwell met the fate he deserved—very suddenly.'"

"After Tuke left me I made certain other inquiries, and here's the true history of the vanished Borham, *alias* Marwell, from the time he went down to Devorset with the Spencers.

"Mrs. Spencer was infatuated with the scoundrel, and the scoundrel had Mrs. Spencer under his thumb. His latest enterprise, just before he first met her, had been in connection with a fraudulent motor company. You'll remember, of course, that he was a useful engineer, and he was a man who would stoop to anything, and stick at nothing. He applied for the job of Spencer's chauffeur, and Mrs. S. saw that he got the billet, without raising the faintest suspicion in her husband's mind. Then he started this double life of young blood and chauffeur, always changing clothes at that hotel.

"The next thing was the warning given them by the efforts of Tuke's agent (who must have been a bit of an ass) to bribe Marwell to give away Borham! Hence the move to Devorset, where they thought they would have an absolutely free hand, and in a very short time the scoundrel found himself in clover. Mrs. Spencer had her scene with her husband, and knew he suspected Wickley. She told Marwell alias Borham, whereupon the man—without telling her hit upon the ingenious device of going to Spencer and offering to shadow his wife. He thus had three sources of income: his pay as chauffeur, together with various perquisites that he didn't stick at picking up—honestly or otherwise, his payments from Spencer for acting as spy, and any amount of odd sums from the infatuated woman. Also he lived in comfort, and had a beautiful woman devoted to him. And with Spencer's suspicions all directed at the wrong man (and Marwell assisted in this) the game seemed safe as houses.

"After a time, however, one small fly got into the ointment—though it seemed only a trifle. Under yet a third name, he started an intrigue with the daughter of a respectable farmer some miles away, and then began to get in a funk of driving his mistress about in the car more than he could help. He belonged to that class of man who seems able to tell an infatuated woman anything without breaking the spell, and he actually had the audacity to tell her this, and suggest meetings in the woods about the place, instead of taking her afield. She provided him with a coat and hat of her husband's, so that he might pass as Spencer himself if any one caught a glimpse of them; for Spencer was known to come and go constantly between London and his country house, and was also known to be often wandering about his woods when he was at home. And now Destiny prepared at last to clear the earth of this pest."

Carrington rose and planted himself before the fire, looking down upon the three of us who were listening to him; and suddenly and very impressively came to the *dénoûment* of his tale.

"One evening at dusk she came a little late to a rendezvous in a certain wood. It was just across the boundary, so as to add to the chances of not being interrupted,—Destiny had seen to that. There she found him stark dead on his face, with the handle of a pruning-knife sticking out of his back. She had thought her husband was in town, but guessed instantly he had come back—and guessed rightly. She thought she recognised his pruning-knife (he had bought two, and given one to Wickley, you'll remember)—and this time she guessed wrong.

"She hurried back to the house half demented, and found her husband had actually been home, and now had fled. And then she was quite certain who had done the deed. What should she do? Hide her own shame, save her husband's neck, and smother the scandal! That woman actually took a spade, and in the dark, in that lonely wood, found a bit of loose soil, and got the body hidden somehow. The next evening, she had the nerve to go down again and pile more earth on top, and meanwhile she told the housekeeper that Marwell had been sacked. Nobody else in the house had liked him, and nobody worried what had become of him. And then she wrote that note to her husband—'I have done my best for you. Be grateful to me for that,' and left the house and him for ever."

"How did you find all those details?" we asked.

"Well, to begin by giving myself a little pat on the back, I came to a pretty correct conclusion at the end of Spencer's story. One man alone had disappeared from the neighbourhood, and that was the chauffeur Marwell. He was said to have been sacked within the next day or two, but he couldn't be found immediately after the murder when his master wanted the car. I judged him to be an obvious rascal from his offer to spy upon the wife. Also I knew that there was nobody in her own station of life who could possibly have been Mrs. Spencer's lover. Finally, I had learnt that one of Spencer's coats had been abstracted, which not only accounted for the unknown victim being mistaken for Spencer, but pointed to his having been a member of the household. I suspected something very like the truth, but of course one needed more facts.

"Then came Tuke with his story which confirmed my suspicion, and told me almost everything. And finally, I hunted down Mrs. Spencer, and made her tell me the rest of the story."

"And did you tell any of them the whole truth?"

"Only Wickley. I couldn't give his secret away to anybody else. But I told him everything. Whether it consoled the poor devil or not I don't know, but I assured him he was simply the instrument selected by Fate to rid the world of an unspeakable blackguard."

"Are women much use as detectives?" one of us asked.

"Rather!" said Carrington; "for certain things, and within their limits, they are first-rate. And, of course, the same qualifications apply to men. Women don't generalise as well as men, but then very few men have the habit of observing small things as well developed as most women. Also, their boldness in jumping to conclusions often takes them straight to the bull's-eye, where the more logical male would regard the connection of ideas as too fanciful to be treated seriously. On the other hand, they constantly jump to the wrong conclusions, where a bit of stern reasoning would have kept them straight."

"Have you had much personal experience of them?" some one else inquired.

The reminiscent smile we knew so well stole across Carrington's ingenuous-looking face.

"I once had a lady partner," said he.

"Was she a success?"

"As long as the partnership lasted, a great success."

We began to scent a yarn.

"What ended the partnership?" I asked.

"A ghost," said he.

Whereupon we insisted on hearing that yarn.

"The lady in question was a Miss Marsh," Carrington began, "Miss Hermione Veronica Staveley Marsh, and in some roundabout way, I think by marriage, she was connected with my sister. Hence, presumably, she was connected with me, but, personally, I had never so much as heard of her till one day my sister asked me to dinner, gave me the port I like best, and then informed me that Hermione Marsh was taking up lady-detecting, and would I put some work in her way, and how nice it would be if we could work together, and wouldn't it be so convenient to employ her on jobs specially suitable to a lady such as running down female murderesses, &c., &c. Any of you who have met my sister probably know how persuasive she is. She herself says it's a family characteristic.

"Well, it ended, of course, in my committing myself to interview Miss Marsh, and see what I thought of her. She came to my office, I interviewed her, and, by Jove, I did think! First I thought that my dear sister had been playing a trick on me, for instead of the sharp-featured, alert-looking female I had expected, in sailed as pretty a girl as you want to meet—brown hair and eyes, pale complexion, but not a bit too pale, a heart-winning smile, and a costume apparently designed to settle my hash in case the eyes and smile didn't quite succeed.

"'It's so good of you to let me come and see you, Mr. Carrington!' she began in a most moving voice, but even as she was gushing, I noticed her brown eyes sweeping up everything about me and my office, and my second thoughts were more hopeful.

"After we had been talking for ten minutes I began to think my sister had builded better than she knew, and in the course of an hour we were practically partners. It turned out that she had had quite a bit of experience—how she got it is another story, too long to tell now—a little money of her own, and a real enthusiasm for the job. Her eyes were like needles, her feelings were well under control, and after the preliminary bit of fascination (which she employed most judiciously) she came to business and stayed there.

"The next few months were the pleasantest of my whole scandal-ferreting, crime-detecting career. Why didn't I fall in love with her? I'm hanged if I really know; in fact, I've often wondered since. I suppose it was partly that I was very busy for a spell just then, and we were chiefly talking shop; and partly because I didn't feel quite equal to the strain of sitting opposite a lady detective every morning at breakfast. After dinner one might have played guessing games with her and kept her mind distracted, but imagine being penetrated to your back-strap at 8.30 A.M. by a pair of eyes specially trained to detect rascality! No, when I marry, the lady will be picked for her blessed innocence. And that's a tip I pass on to you fellows.

"Nevertheless, I frankly confess I enjoyed the society of Hermione Veronica immensely, and I enjoyed her capacity even more. Observant, very quick, and wonderfully correct in her decisions, and entirely fearless—that was Miss Marsh, and I drink to my late partner! Her pluck was really splendid—so splendid that it bust up our partnership in the end; but that's anticipating. She had handled five or six delicate jobs quite extraordinarily well, and as a combination we were getting along like a Welsh three-quarter line, when one morning Mr. Locker-Gavelston and his sister walked into my office.

"Old L-G, as his friends called him, was a bit of a character. He had a place in Hampshire, plenty of money, a strong streak of crusted obstinacy, and a number of fads. One of his fads, combined with his obstinacy, caused a bust-up with his eldest son; the son was cut off with a shilling, went abroad, and disappeared. Another fad was a notion that thieves were always going to burgle him. He had a rambling old-fashioned house in a lonely pine-wooded part of the country, and a year or two before the burglar-mania got so strong that he came to consult me. That was my first acquaintance with him, but after I had satisfactorily accounted for some footsteps in a flower-bed as being made by his gardener, and a missing trinket of his wife's as having been absent-mindedly pocketed by himself, he felt such confidence in my powers that he came back and asked me to trace his missing son. As he wasn't disposed to pay my expenses out to Mexico to look for him, that task beat me, and I saw no more of him till this said fatal morning.

"The old boy had brought his sister, Mrs. Wimpole, with him. She was an impecunious widow who lived most of the time with the Locker-Gavelstons, and I noticed that both she and he were dressed in mourning. I should add, by the way, that Miss Marsh was not in the office when they turned up.

"'I have come to you this morning, Mr. Carrington,' said he, 'on a very bothersome, perplexing bit of business. I make little doubt that your powers of—shall I say putting two and one together, and presenting your clients with four' (he was a bit of a humourist, was the old squire), 'I have no doubt that this magical gift will very easily solve the mystery. But I assure you my wife and sister and I have very nearly parted company, and gone in three several directions over the business.'

"'Come to the point, John,' said the lady rather stiffly.

"Old L-G turned on her like a terrier, and I could see that recent events, whatever they were, had ruffled him not a little.

"'Allow me to tell my story my own way, Anne,' said he; but he, nevertheless, did come to the point. 'We are troubled with very mysterious noises in the house, Mr. Carrington. The thing is getting to be so bad that we can hardly keep our servants. I say that they are caused by some human agency, and the only person who can possibly be supposed to be in another man's house at night is a thief!'

"'Has anything been stolen?' I inquired.

"'Nothing so far,' he admitted. 'And in consequence my wife contends that the place is haunted. It's an old house, and it is quite true that there are ghost stories connected with it, but I am no believer in the supernatural, and I tell her the idea is absurd.'

"Nevertheless he didn't quite look as if he believed it to be absurd. In fact there was a kind of haunted look about the man. Something was badly on his nerves; so much was plain enough.

"'I say it is rats,' Mrs. Wimpole cut in. 'I want them to try a new rat poison that would very quickly put a stop to these noises, only my sister-in-law has a decrepit old pet dog which eats everything it shouldn't, and so she won't let me try poison.'

"'Rubbish!' said the squire testily. 'My wife very properly refuses to have her dog poisoned in order to kill non-existent rats. My house is not a sanctuary for vermin. It isn't rats!'

"In connection with another case I think I told you my four alternatives to account for a haunted house. Here were three of them in the field already—spooks, men, and rats. The fourth was lies, and the witnesses seemed too numerous and too respectable to admit of that possibility. I tried to be as judicial and as tactful as I could.

"'If it were thieves,' I said, 'one would certainly expect them to have stolen something by this time. If it were ghosts, one would think that after all the centuries the house has been in existence, ghosts would hardly begin their nightly perambulations now; unless there were a new ghost. . . .'

"I had meant this suggestion as a small joke to cheer things up a little, but I stopped short when I saw the effect on Mr. Locker-Gavelston. He started palpably and seemed to turn a trifle pale, and then he indicated his clothes and said simply—

"'We are in mourning, Mr. Carrington.'

"As he didn't tell me, I scarcely liked to ask who had died, and for a moment there was an awkward pause. And then, radiant and looking her very best, in walked Miss Hermione Marsh.

"'Oh, I beg your pardon,' she began, and was going out again, but the fates had decided otherwise and unscrupulously used me as their instrument. In fact they put into my head what seemed the brilliant idea of handing the whole case over to my lady partner. She was a sensible girl, I thought, and very tactful, and would soon make an end of any little imaginary trouble that was worrying these good people.

"'Come in,' I said, 'I'd like to have your opinion,' and thereupon I introduced her to my visitors.

"I could see that old L-G was simply charmed with her from the very start, and even Mrs. Wimpole—a bit of a stick with none too angelic a temper—forgot her indignation with the pet dog and became quite amiable.

"But imagine my own feelings when my sensible partner whom I'd counted on either to back the rat theory or think of something equally prosaic and probable, suddenly revealed herself as a keen spookologist! Of course she would have been excessively indignant to hear it put like that. She took an intelligent interest in the occult; she had imagination; she despised people who denied the existence of anything simply because they had never seen it themselves; and so on and so forth. That's how she put it to me afterwards.

"Anyhow, what actually happened was that her interest and sympathy drew old Locker-Gavelston into a practical confession that he more than half agreed with his wife. And then at last he told us who he was in mourning for. Word had come from Mexico that his eldest son was dead. He didn't actually say what spirit he feared in that lonely old house, but both she and I knew.

"Within half an hour it had been arranged that Miss Marsh was to go down to Hampshire with them and spend as many nights in the ancient mansion as should prove necessary. The old gentleman was quite carried away by her, and money was evidently going to be no object with him. So I wished her luck, and off she went.

"The house was large, rambling, mellow with age, and crusted with tradition. It lay low in the midst of old-fashioned gardens full of huge clipped yews and hollies. One particular walk with a high yew hedge on either side was a place to be avoided towards dusk and to be fled from after dark,—unless some very circumstantial tales were quite untrue. And indeed the whole place, with its background of dense pine woods, and its centuries of strange happenings, was a stage set for a story, tragic or ghostly.

"It required considerable nerve in one who believed not a little of these stories to sleep in the blue room at Amley Court, a high square apartment with furniture vast as a herd of elephants and one of those dark old-fashioned wall-papers that reflect not a ray of light and make six candles look like mere stars in the gloom. Here was the haunted room *par excellence*, and yet Hermione Marsh, though she did half believe in these stories, had the nerve to insist on sleeping there her first night.

"She told me afterwards that when she had blown five of those candles out, and the sixth was a mere glimmer in the darkness, and when at that very moment she heard the faintest rustling somewhere seemingly not far away, she felt frankly a little shaken. However, she quietly opened the door and flashed her candle up and down the passage, flashed it all round the room, and then stoutly got into bed and blew it out.

"There was not much sleep for her, that night, for all her courage. Thrice at least she was up with a lit candle, and she says the sounds she heard were quite enough to stampede a nervous visitor straightway from the house. She didn't actually see anything however—not that night.

"At breakfast the others looked at her curiously, but she held her head high, talked cheerily, and declared she was going to sleep in that room another night. And then, after breakfast, she set about making a thorough search of the house. How many family portraits, mostly very grim and looking quite ready to walk out of their frames on a dark night, and dusty cupboards and odd stairs and passages, she made the acquaintance of she couldn't tell; but-anyhow she put in a very busy day's exploring, and by the afternoon felt in need of a little fresh air.

"The other three had all gone out in the car to tea at a house some miles away, so when she came back from her walk she knew she had the place all to herself. She entered by a side door opening into the garden, closed it quietly behind her (we get into the way of closing doors quietly in our job) and turned into a long passage. And as she turned into it she caught one swift glimpse of a man's back disappearing round a corner at the farther end.

"She stood stock-still, and she afterwards confessed that for a moment she hesitated. That sleepless night in the blue room had shaken her nerve more than she realised. The man had been too distinctly seen to be a figment of her fancy. He certainly wasn't the butler or the footman, for he was wearing a light tweed suit, and there were no other men in the house. And he could scarcely be a robber strolling quietly about at that hour in the afternoon. She almost funked it, and then took her courage in both hands and followed him down the passage and round the corner.

"Ahead was a half-open door. She pushed it right open and found herself in a smoking-room. At one side of the fire was a large easy-chair, and in that chair sat a figure she recognised in an instant. She had seen his portrait among the others. It was the long-lost eldest son, whose death had lately been announced to his father, whose spirit the father feared.

"She gave her nerve no time to leave her, but walked straight towards that starting figure, and actually had the astounding courage to sit boldly down in that easy-chair! And that was the end of my lady partner."

Carrington paused to blow a cloud of smoke reminiscently towards the ceiling.

"But what happened to her?" we cried.

"Well, the fact was she didn't really quite reach the chair. The gentleman's knees were in the way—and the next moment the gentleman's arms were round her. Possibly he even kissed her, but I never quite liked to ask her that. And there she was, hoist by her own pluck—on to a gentleman's lap.

"Well, the moral is, don't believe that everybody you hear has died is actually dead. The long-lost son had turned up that afternoon and been in the house only half an hour when he and Hermione met their fates. She married him in six months and I lost my lady partner.

"What actually caused the noises? I can only tell you that shortly afterwards the long-lost son took his turn of sitting in a chair which he thought was empty. This time it was the pet dog that had got there first, and as he weighed thirteen stone and the dog had just finished dinner, he left no argument remaining against using the rat poison. And certainly the noises ceased."

8

A PHOTOGRAPH

"I don't believe there is any business in the world in which a man gets more puzzlers as to what is his duty, than in mine," said Carrington. "With the official detective his duty is plain. He has got to arrest if he thinks a man guilty and there is evidence to support his belief. There's no choice. Or if he begins an investigation of any kind, he can't break off because it's going to cause pain and do some moral injustice. I'd blame him if he took any other view of his job.

"But in the kind of private work I do, I'm constantly up against the nastiest snags. One generally has to toughen one's hide and go ahead, or a very deserving young man would starve. On the other hand, there are cases where he stands to score by putting his telescope to the blind eye when it ought to be at the other. And there are certain occasions on which he simply doesn't know which way the finger of duty points. I remember one in particular. Anybody got a cigarette to lend me?"

He lit the cigarette, leaned back in his chair and told this story.

"It was only a few years ago," said he, "when a man walked into my office one afternoon and began in a most promising fashion—

"'I've come to you on a very queer bit of business, Mr. Carrington,' said he, and I noticed at once that he spoke with a distinct bit of American accent, yet not really strong, only sort of half-and-half American it seemed to me.

"'You've lived some years in the States, my friend, but you come from this side of the Atlantic,' I said to myself, though I didn't Sherlock-Holmes him by shooting it at him aloud. In fact I rather believe in looking as sympathetic and encouraging as possible and not interrupting more than I can help.

"'I want you to find out who I am,' he went on; and at that I sat up and had a very good look at him indeed.

"He seemed about forty, and allowing for the strenuous life of the States, which I could see he lived, from the business-like way he had and other little signs, I put him down as actually round about thirty-five. He was quite a good-looking chap, but with a mouth and chin that didn't suggest sticking at much if it came to a tight corner and he had to get out of it. However, ninety per cent of successful business men in the States look like that—possibly owing to the climate—so at the moment I didn't let myself make too much of it. In fact the first thing I really wanted to be sure of was that he wasn't either a practical joker or a lunatic. And there was certainly no sign of either about him.

"'If I guess right what do I win?' I couldn't resist asking.

"He was the strenuous sort and no humourist, for he promptly pulled out a pocket-book.

"'Name your fee, Mr. Carrington, and I'll pay you in advance if that's your custom,' said he.

"'It isn't,' I said, but all the same I named the kind of terms on which I do business.

"'I'll double that if you'll crack this nut for me,' said he.

"'Sit down and fire away,' I told him.

"'Well,' said he, 'for all practical purposes I came into this world just ten years ago, Mr. Carrington.'

"'Ten?' I repeated, for I thought I surely must have misunderstood him.

"'Yes,' he said with a thoughtful, serious air, 'I guess that's just about the size of it. For practical purposes I entered this world ten years ago in a hospital in Chicago. They *told* me I'd been picked up in front of a street car and that it looked almost like suicide, but I didn't know. My memory was clean gone, and it has never come back yet.'

"Of course I had often heard of such cases, and I was able to follow him quite sympathetically now; and very keenly too, for such a thing makes a curiously strong appeal to one's imagination.

"'If it really was a fact that I had been in some bad trouble previously,' he went on, 'Providence seemed determined to make up for it, for the man who picked me up from under that street car was a regular good Samaritan. Leslie his name was, and his first name was Bennett, and as I couldn't remember my own name and there was nothing to track me by, he suggested I should take his names, only change them round about. So since then my name has been Leslie Bennett.'

"'You mean there was no clue at all as to your previous identity?' I asked.

"He shook his head decisively.

"'None. I was ill a long while, and I guess that made the scent some cold; but Leslie said it almost looked as if I'd been trying to hide my tracks for some reason, there was so little to be learned about me. My pockets were practically empty, and my clothes had evidently been bought ready made in some dry-goods store after I came to the States; for I should mention that everybody said from my voice I was an Englishman, and hadn't been long out either.'

"'And that was ten years ago?'

"'Yep,' said he. 'Well then, after I was cured Leslie found me a job in his business; a printing and publishing business in a small way it was then. But once I settled down to work I showed a kind of aptitude for the job, and especially a knowledge of the financial side of things that showed I must have been a business man of some capacity and with a more than average good education. Leslie and I used to puzzle ourselves a lot how a fellow who seemed so able to take care of himself and make his way in the world had come to be wandering penniless in Chicago, and perhaps even thrown himself under a street car. However, as there was no answer to the puzzle we soon gave it up, and in fact we hadn't much time for wondering. Gee! but I've been a busy man these ten years, Mr. Carrington. Leslie very soon took me into partnership, and then the business began to boom till it's quite a big thing now. I hadn't time to wonder, I hadn't time to puzzle, I hadn't time to marry, many days I'd hardly time to eat! And then quite suddenly four months ago Leslie was taken ill, and inside a week he was dead.

The business was now mine and I was well on my way to being a rich man, but that didn't comfort me much. I was sort of half stunned at losing him. And then a very extraordinary thing happened to rouse me up. It was the finger of Providence once more, Mr. Carrington!'

"He paused for a moment and began to take out his pocket-book again. I was so fascinated by his yarn that I said nothing, but just waited for him to go on.

"'It was just about a month after poor Leslie's death that his widow sent for me. "Something of great importance to tell you," she said in her note. Well, I went right straight off to see her, and do you know what she had found among her husband's letters and things when she had been going over them? An old pocket-book which had been in one of the pockets of the coat I was wearing when I was taken to hospital. Leslie had mentioned it to me, but as nothing had been found in it I wasn't interested and didn't even know he'd kept it. His widow, however, had looked more carefully, and tucked into the lining through a slit made with a knife, as if it had been to hide something extra precious, she found this.'

"He handed me a photograph. It showed a young man and a young girl standing side by side, and at the first glance it was evident who the young man was. It was my client, Mr. Leslie Bennett, just as he must have looked ten or twelve years ago, and a very presentable young man he was. As for the girl, she was uncommonly attractive; distinctly pretty, but even better than pretty, a face that kept you looking at it. I did look. I simply stared, in fact, and then I tore my eyes away and watched him as he talked.

"'Who's that girl?' he was saying (and his voice was beginning to get a little agitated now), 'What was she to me or I to her? What has become of her? Who or what was I when that photo was taken? Those are the things I want you to find out for me, Mr. Carrington.'

"He saw me turning the photograph to look for the photographer's name on the back.

"'It was taken by Atkinson, Taunton, Somerset,' said he, 'as you can see for yourself. That's the only clue I've got for you, and I want you to follow it up for me.'

"'You prefer me to do it, rather than take the matter up your-self?' I asked.

"I was staring at the portraits of that man and girl again, and I really wanted to make a little time to think.

"'Yes,' said he. 'I guess I feel kind of—' he hesitated—'well, kind of shy about butting right in myself. Might be embarrassing, or— well, one never knows; and, anyhow, you'd make a better job of it.'

"I didn't answer for a moment or two, and when I looked up at him I could see that he seemed a bit surprised at my absentmind-edness.

"'All right,' I said, 'I'll take the thing up and let you know the result.'

"He went out, and I was left with a pretty problem to tackle. The reason I stared so hard at that photograph was that I had seen it before—not more than three or four weeks ago. And the place where I had seen it was Scotland Yard, when I happened to be look-ing through a collection of photographs. And the people whose photographs are kept at Scotland Yard are not usually the people who come to me and ask me to identify them!

"What was I to do? When I saw the photograph before, I had been running through a pile of them for a specific purpose of my own, and hadn't stopped to inquire who all the people were, so that I knew nothing whatever about the young couple. Mr. Ben-nett's problem could be solved in a moment by going to Scotland Yard; but with what consequences to Mr. Bennett? He was my pri-vate client, and had left his interests in my hands. Also, what kind of a horrid moral dilemma might I not land myself in if I knew too much? I thought, and better thought, and finally decided to run down to Taunton, and follow the clue of the photographer's name, just as though it were my only means of information.

"Down to Taunton I went the very next morning, found Atkin-sons the photographers, and showed them the photograph of the *girl*—the girl only, mark you! I managed it quite easily by bending the photograph across the middle, and only showing the half with her on it; and to obviate any chance of suspicion, I played the part of the kindly genial fellow who tracked down his distant cousins through their photographs, in order to send them Christmas presents and leave 'em money in his will, but who didn't want his left hand to know what his right hand was doing—hence the little touch of eccentric secrecy in the matter of bending the photograph over.

"I managed the business rather creditably, if I say so myself, and Atkinsons took considerable trouble to help me, without smelling so much as the whiskers of a rat.

"Forty-eight hours later I was ringing the bell of a small house in a long row of ditto, ditto, ditto, most of 'em with Venetian blinds and apartment notices in the window. The town wasn't Taunton this time, but I can't give its name away, and the lady I asked for may as well be called Mrs. Morris as anything else.

"I was shown into just the sort of parlour one would expect, by just the sort of little skivvy one would expect, and presently Mrs. Morris entered. She hadn't changed so much as one would have expected in the ten years since the photograph was taken. A very graceful, taking-looking young woman of thirty-two she was now, refined, a little sad looking, and with a pleasant low voice.

"I felt that anything Nature may have endowed me with in the shape of tact and courtesy was required for this interview, and I began as politely as I knew how—

"'You don't know me, Mrs. Morris,' I said, 'and just for the moment I need merely explain that I am acting professionally on behalf of somebody you did once know. Forgive me if I am doing anything that gives you any worry or recalls any trouble, and stop me if you like. I am merely going to show you a photograph, and ask you if you know anything about it.'

"I handed it to her, and for a few moments looked out of the window. One glance had been enough to see that the photograph had recalled trouble with a vengeance, and I kept my back to her till she was ready for me.

"'How did you get this?' she asked, and her voice was so low now that I could hardly hear it.

"'From the gentleman for whom I am acting.'

"'Who is he? Where is he?' she asked quickly.

"I had to blend firmness with kindness now.

"'I am very sorry, Mrs. Morris,' I said, but I am afraid I must ask you for information first. You see I am acting on his behalf, and he is trusting himself to my judgment and discretion. You can speak perfectly freely and frankly.'

"She stared at the photograph, and she hesitated. And then she spoke—

"'He was my husband,' she said.

"'Husband!' I exclaimed, for somehow or other I had only reckoned on her being his sweetheart. 'Was his name Morris, then?'

"For a moment she hesitated, and a look of pure fear came into her eyes. Then she took her courage in both hands and murmured

"'Yes.'

"'He left you, I believe, about ten years ago?' I suggested.

"Again she only breathed one word—'Yes.'

"'Under what circumstances?'

"There was a moment's pause, and then she made up her mind to go through with it.

"'A man was found dead,' she said, 'and my husband was suspected.'

"'What man?'

"'His name was Harper—a very bad man!'

"The thing came back to me in a flash. It had happened before I took up this sort of job, but I always had a morbid interest in crime, especially mysterious crime and undiscovered criminals, and I remember reading about the Harper case quite distinctly.

"'He was a sort of third-rate lawyer who did a bit of money-lending, wasn't he?' I asked.

"'Yes,' she said, and began to look frightened afresh.

"'I am only recalling what I read in the papers years ago,' I assured her. 'Was your husband the young man to whom he had been lending money, and who afterwards disappeared?'

"'Yes,' she said again. 'He had got my poor Jack into his toils— he was trying to ruin him—he—he said he admired me. But Jack was innocent!'

"The last sentence suddenly rang out like the blast of a trumpet, defiant, fervent, loving—every splendid thing, in fact, except convincing.

"'You are quite sure of that?'

"'Absolutely!'

"'Then who did murder Harper?'

"'Nobody ever knew.'

"'Didn't you suspect anybody else?'

"'He had many enemies.'

"'Did the police suspect anybody else?'

"'They never made proper inquiries about anybody else. But Jack was innocent!'

"'Then you never lost your love for your husband, or your confidence in him, or anything?'

"'Never! Never for one moment! I feel exactly the same to-day as I felt when I married him.' She paused, and then suddenly cried, 'Is he alive? What do you know? What are you hiding? Tell me!'

"Here was a nice problem to be settled off-hand, shut up in a room twelve feet square, with a pleading, tearful, charming woman, who wanted her answer within a matter of seconds! It seemed any odds on the man being guilty, and if he was, there was no doubt about its being a deliberate premeditated affair with the intention simply of getting out of a very tight place (and I now recalled vividly my first impression of Mr. Bennett's mouth and chin). Harper may have been a bad lot, but a murderer is a murderer. And if I wasn't simply going to class myself among the dirty rank and file of private inquiry agents who do what they are paid for and swallow their consciences, what was my duty in the case of a man badly wanted by the police on a capital charge?

"On the other hand, to try the man and convict him now that his memory had gone, would be like trying any one of us in this world for unremembered sins, committed in another life on another planet. Also he had come to me, trusted me, and employed me. Finally, there was this poor woman hanging between hope and fear.

"'I'll tell you the whole story,' I said, and I told her exactly what Mr. Bennett *alias* Morris had told me in my office. At the end of my tale I remember vividly how she cried—

"'Then Jack won't know me!'

"'If he is any judge at all, he'll be jolly glad to have the chance!' I assured her, and I also remember very distinctly how charmingly she blushed.

"Quarter of an hour later I was sending off a wire to Mr. Leslie Bennett to meet us at Paddington Station, and the last I saw of 'em was getting into a taxi together. He *was* jolly glad, there was no doubt about that."

"Supposing he ever recovers his memory?" said one of us when we were discussing the problem afterwards.

"God forbid!" said Carrington.

9

DUPLICATES

"The advantages of booming to the actor, author, politician, and society climber are obvious," said Carrington, "but for a fellow engaged in my business it's the very devil and all. Imagine a cat circulating her photograph and record of kills among the mice! I once had a brief boom myself, and I know."

"That was after some jewel case, wasn't it?"

Carrington nodded at the fire.

"That was the time. A small but remarkably select and efficient gang—Flash Dick, Gentleman Charlie, & Co. had been working the whole country between Bond Street and the City, and made a very lucrative trip to Birmingham too. I happened to know old Rogerson in Regent Street, who was one of their victims; he asked my advice, and I chanced to be lucky. Gentleman Charlie we couldn't lay hands on; he really was a most superior person, I may mention, a credit to his public school. Also another minor light got off, but we bagged the rest, and then my photograph got into the papers, and like an ass I allowed a polished creature with braid round his coat to interview me for two minutes, and read next morning a solid column of rubbish purporting to be the opinions of Mr. F. T. Carrington. Lord, how I wished that young man would commit an indictable offence, and let me at him!

"On the other hand, I quite admit that it brought grist to the mill, and for some time thereafter I was rather in request, especially if any jewelry came into the case. I don't mean necessarily when a crime had been committed, but human beings being the queer mortals they are, a baby would swallow a necklace, and Daddy would say, 'Oh, isn't there a man called Carrington who's an expert at recovering jewelry?' Or the family would squabble over Aunt Maria's legacy, and some genius would remember Carrington, the expert, and call him in to value the paste diamonds and the cairngorms.

"Quite seriously, I did get some rum jobs about that time, but of course a few interesting cases too. One that presented a curious little problem was brought me by Mr. Headlam, of Headlam, Stonewall, & Jennings, the well-known solicitors. He called one day with his client, Sir Walter Basebroke, an elderly baronet, with a place about an hour's run out from Paddington. We had only a short talk then, but Headlam and I arranged to go down together a couple of days later, and go into the thing carefully. Briefly, the facts were that Lady Basebroke had a lot of jewelry, some of it very valuable, and including among other things an extraordinarily fine turquoise and diamond necklace and an almost equally fine diamond tiara. Two of the diamonds from the tiara had been stolen, and a servant was suspected. Compared with some of the cases I had lately been engaged upon, it was quite an interesting little conundrum. I was distinctly intrigued with it and keen to go.

"Well, Headlam and I had arranged to meet at Paddington, and catch a train starting shortly before eleven in the morning, and I went round to my office first just to glance through my letters before making for the station. I found a telegram waiting for me as well as a few letters, but as the top letter was marked 'urgent' I began with that, and I can tell you it made me stare. The address was Waven Hall, near Biggleswade, Beds., and the signature seemed to read R. E. Merryweather, but I had never heard of the gentleman before, nor of Waven Hall. As far as I can remember it, the letter ran—

'Dear Sir,—You will remember that you promised to return my wife's emerald necklace by the end of the week at latest, when you said your examination of it for the purpose of comparing it with the imitation would be completed. It is now Tuesday, and the

necklace has not yet reached me. Kindly return it by
first post after receipt of this, of course registering
the parcel.—Yours truly,
   'R. E. Merryweather.'

"I never was more completely and absolutely mystified in my
life than I was by my first reading of that letter. The second reading, however, suggested several possibilities—a practical joke, a
letter put in the wrong envelope (for the writer hadn't added my
name on the letter itself), another Carrington—presumably a jew-
eler or a connoisseur, or a lunatic. The last solution quite took my
fancy, and I pictured Waven Hall as a private asylum, and Mr.
Merryweather as an inmate with a delusion about jewels who had
seen my name in the papers, and I imagined the doctor's annoyance when he discovered what his patient had been about.

"However, I had no time to deal with the letter that morning,
so I laid it aside and opened the telegram. And again I got a bit of
a jar, but this time of a different kind. It was from Headlam saying
it was quite impossible for him to get away that day, and asking
me, or rather commanding me—for it was couched in somewhat
peremptory terms—to go down with him to-morrow instead.

"I glanced at my engagement book and saw that to-morrow was
quite impossible. In fact I was booked up everyday for the rest of
the week. I had left this day free at Basebroke's particular request,
and I was keen to go on my own account, because I was interested
in what I had heard of the case. And finally, I was a little nettled at
Headlam's dictatorial tone. So at last, after a few minutes' debate,
I decided I would go without him and try to smooth matters afterwards by a tactful explanation. Headlam's presence wasn't in the
least essential, but he was scarcely the kind of gentleman to see
that himself, and if he had been on the telephone I should have
rung him up and tried to persuade him to come after all; only unfortunately his was an old-fashioned firm, and at that time no telephone was installed in their office.

"The consideration of that telegram and letter, and a run
through the rest of my correspondence, exhausted all the time I
dared spend in the office, so I put off writing to Headlam till I came

back, had a taxi called up, and set straight off for Paddington. However, it happened that the streets were clear, and the booking-office window likewise, so that eventually I found myself sitting in a first-class smoking carriage with nearly quarter of an hour to spare. I had bought a paper, and just before settling down to read it, I cast my eyes out of the window in the instinctive way one does when one is sitting with only a sheet of glass between oneself and a bustling platform. And I assure you my two previous surprises were mere nothings to the surprise I got now.

"A young man, carrying a brown leather attaché case, was strolling along the platform with his eye glancing at the train, evidently selecting a compartment. For an instant he seemed extraordinarily, almost shockingly, familiar, and yet unplaceable in my memory. And then I recognised my own sinful self! He had the eyeglass, the light spats, the felt hat, everything most characteristic that I was wearing. His face, whether by nature alone or nature reinforced by art, was mine, or at all events near enough it to deceive any ordinary acquaintance; and as far as I could judge of my own walk, he seemed to have either inherited or borrowed that too. In fact he was simply me.

"You have no idea what an extraordinary sensation it is to see one's own self casually strolling along a railway platform. It must be experienced to be appreciated. For a moment or two I sat absolutely fascinated. I didn't *think*, in any proper sense of the term. Vaguely I accepted the conclusion that I had a double in the world, like people you sometimes read of in stories—and in real life police reports too. And then the man half turned round to look at a pretty girl who was passing. Whether that is also one of my characteristics, is not for me to say, but if he intended it for one he overshot the mark. For as he turned, the brown leather attaché case swung round and for a instant showed its side to me. And there I read the legend painted in very fresh staring black letters, 'F. T. CARRINGTON.' And then in a flash I knew he was no genuine double, no mere freak of nature. The man was impersonating me.

"Thank the Lord, I can generally think quick and also move quick when the emergency prods me up. Almost in the instant that realisation came home, I was on my feet, crouching a bit, and backing away from the window. I saw the duplicate Mr. F. T. C.'s eye leave the lady and turn again to the train, and then when he was nearly opposite, I *knew* he had selected my own compartment. How did I know? I saw him glance at the label 'smoking' on the window and his eye suddenly became satisfied. The next moment he had opened the door—and I was safely under the seat.

"I think it was Napoleon who said that his happiest inspirations were frequently only a recollection, or words to that effect. My own dive beneath that seat was founded on a mixture of my experience of falling on the ball to stop a forward rush, and of my recollection of seeing a rabbit go down a hole. The combination worked excellently. I didn't even bump my head, and I had the wit, moreover, to remember to take my paper with me. And then on top of that, or perhaps I should rather say on top of me, I had a slice of luck. My duplicate fortunately selected the seat under which I was stretched, so that I was absolutely safe from observation.

"Though I was quite invisible to him, I could see his feet and recognise the spats, and I knew the right man had actually got into the carriage. And then, hardly daring to breathe, I waited for the train to start. But before it did start the door opened again and I heard the collector punching the ticket of the gentleman above me. I rather grudged now having bought a ticket myself. I may add that I hadn't a shadow of doubt that, like the two Mr. Carringtons, the tickets were twins.

"How I longed for that train to start! Something was tickling my nose and one foot was precious near catching cramp, but I dared not move a muscle till the rattle and thud had begun. At last, however, we were off, and I very gently eased my nose and foot, and gradually, inch by inch, stretched myself out as comfortably as I could. But it was devilish hard lying all the same. I very soon began to feel extremely indignant with the gentleman who was occupying my cushioned seat. The only consolation was that I felt pretty certain he would thankfully change places with me before many hours had passed.

"At Westbourne Park we stopped, and again the door opened. This time another passenger got in, and I could see a pair of nailed shoes and hear the rattle of a bag of golf-clubs being laid on the rack. I knew the golf-courses on the line, and felt sure he would leave us before we reached the other Mr. Carrington's destination. This was all to the good, for I had no wish to have any one else in the carriage when I emerged from my lair. For a few minutes after we started there was silence in the carriage, and then I heard a familiar voice say—

"'Good morning, Carrington.'

"For a horrible instant I thought I was ignominiously spotted, and then I realised the situation and chuckled silently. There was a rustle of paper and I could feel the man overhead distinctly start. Then, cool as a cucumber, he answered—

"'By Jingo, I'm sorry I didn't recognise you for a moment. Good morning. How are you? Going to play golf?'

"It was quite brilliantly done. And what is more, the man imitated my voice and expression and way of putting things with extraordinary fidelity; at least so far as I could judge. He had evidently been seeing me, hearing me, and making a most careful study of me. I began to have a very high respect indeed for my duplicate.

"'Yes,' said the other man. 'And you, I suppose, are on your usual lay. Going crime-detecting; what?'

"I knew him from his voice as a fellow Bodley-Brown, a man with whom I had a sort of familiar slight acquaintance. Luckily for my duplicate he didn't know me at all intimately.

"'That's it,' said the duplicate coolly, 'more exciting than golf, too.'

"'And more paying likewise,' said Bodley-Brown. 'You are getting quite famous now, Carrington. I've seen your portrait in several papers.'

"'So have I,' replied the duplicate in a nonchalant voice. 'Quite gratifying to find oneself famous, but a damned bore. And now, old chap, if you'll excuse me I'll get on with these papers. I've got to read up this case a bit before I get down to the ground.'

"Again he was brilliant. In the friendliest way, without giving offence or exciting suspicion, he had choked off Bodley-Brown and avoided any further risk of falling into conversational pitfalls. He must even have come provided with papers of some kind in preparation for such a contingency. I really admired the fellow immensely.

"A station or two farther on Bodley-Brown said good-bye, and he and his golf-clubs got out. The two Carringtons were alone now, and the next stop was the station marked on my ticket. I was ready to lay all my money on its being the station on the other fellow's ticket too, and very stealthily I completed my preparations. Going through every tunnel and under every bridge, roaring past every train we crossed, whenever in fact there was noise enough to drown my movements, I had been getting ready. And now I added the finishing touches.

"The train slowed down, and for the first time a horrid doubt assailed me. Could I by any chance be wrong in my calculations? Had I made a bad guess after all? And then the man rose to his feet and I knew I was right. I heard him putting the papers back into his attaché case, and then the click of the lock. The train thumped to a standstill. The light spats moved along the carriage. The door opened.

"Out of a first-class carriage stepped an immaculate young man with an eyeglass, a smart felt hat rather on the side of his head, and beautiful spats. He marched down the platform and turned through the booking-hall out of the station. Out of the same first-class compartment a minute or two later slipped a deboshed-looking wreck with a bandage round his head, a lot of stamp paper stuck all over his face, as though he had stood a fusilade of broken bottles, the brim of his hat turned down all round, no eyeglass, and his spats in his pocket. The first F. T. Carrington jumped into a smart dog-cart beside a horsey-looking driver and rattled off down the village street. The second F. T. Carrington perceived that his duplicate was only being propelled by a horse, and beneath his stamp-paper smiled freely at last."

"That highly respected baronet, Sir Walter Basebroke, was somewhat surprised this same morning to receive a telegram from Mr. Carrington asking him not to send a conveyance to the station, as the train he would arrive by was uncertain. However, the boomed detective did turn up in the morning, and explained that he had managed to catch the 10 something-or-other train after all. He regretted, however, that Mr. Headlam had not been able to accompany him, and conveyed that gentleman's humble apologies to the baronet.

"And then Mr. Carrington very briskly got to work. He wanted to see the diamond tiara, and examined it with extreme interest and intelligence. Then he asked if he might see the turquoise and diamond necklace, and he examined this with equal intelligence. In fact, he exhibited if possible even more acumen, for in a minute or two he made the startling announcement that three or four of the stones were paste substitutes and that the originals had been stolen.

"'You don't say so!' exclaimed Sir Walter, looking very grave. 'But how can you prove that?'

"'Well, really, Sir Walter,' said the famous detective, 'I begin to think the best thing will be for me to take them both back with me and subject them to such a searching expert test as I'm afraid I can't very well give them out here. Of course you will seal them up very carefully and I shall give you a receipt. In fact, it would per- haps be as well if you accompanied me yourself up to London. That's to say, if you feel the least doubt as to their safety.'

"'We feel none,' remarked the other Mr. Carrington, emerging from behind the window curtains. 'But the game is up, Gentleman Charles, and your pal is sitting in the hall with a horse-girth round his elbows at this moment.'

"Gentleman Charles carried it off as brilliantly as ever.

"'Arrest that impostor, Sir Walter!' he commanded, throwing me a friendly wink.

"Even the dignified and very nearly swindled baronet couldn't help smiling, and I felt my admiration for my duplicate turning into something devilish like affection.

"'I see you are still keeping up your form in the train,' I said to him.

"That fairly shook the rascal up.

"'What the—blank—do you mean?' he exclaimed.

"'I'll tell you,' I said, 'if you will first kindly explain the one mystery that has puzzled me. Why did you wire to say you didn't want to be met at the station?'

"Charlie looked a bit nasty at this.

"'That blank blighter with the girth round him wouldn't trust me,' said he. 'The blanker insisted on driving me himself.'

"'Well,' I said, 'that let you down badly. Did you notice a car passing you at fifty miles an hour on the road from the station?'

"He had recovered his composure now.

"'Oh, and so you were in it?' said he. 'I see the game now. But what about me in the train?'

"'You were sitting on top of the other F. T. Carrington,' I explained, and I had the last laugh there.

"Gentleman Charlie spent the next few years extremely quietly, and his costume didn't include spats or an eyeglass. But the rogue had had an uncommon good run for his money while it lasted. The way in which he impersonated me at Waven Hall and did the unfortunate Mr. Merryweather was a first-class effort of its kind, and he would very likely have done Sir Walter too if his luck hadn't turned.

"He took infinite pains. I found afterwards that he had sent a duplicate wire to my rooms in case I didn't go to my office that morning, and of course he had also wired to Headlam in my name commanding him to postpone our trip. But he overdid his cleverness twice, first in making that bogus wire from Headlam so peremptory, for that merely made me disinclined to consult Headlam's susceptibilities; and secondly, in painting my name on his bag, for that roused me to a realisation of his game. All the same, I think he was theoretically right in both instances, and luck was simply against him.

"In fact, to be perfectly candid, Gentleman Charlie had distinctly the best of the play, and the final score against him in that match between the two Carringtons didn't indicate their respective merits in the least."

10
THE TRUTHFUL LADY

We had got Carrington well on the talk one night on top of an exceedingly good dinner, when one of us suddenly asked him—

"By the way, Carrington, did you ever come across Sherlock Holmes?"

He shook his head.

"I've often wanted to, but unfortunately he was before my time. I've met Dr. Watson though."

"What, *the* Dr. Watson, Holmes's pal?"

Carrington nodded.

"The very fellow. He came to consult me once. It was his case, not mine, so I don't know whether I really ought to tell you the yarn."

He paused, but there was a twinkle in his eye that encouraged a little pressure. We pressed and he succumbed.

"When he sent in his card," he began, "I didn't in the least grasp who he was, but the moment I saw him I began to have a dim suspicion that there couldn't be two Dr. Watsons with such a preternaturally wooden-looking head, and his very first words settled the question.

"'You have no doubt heard of my distinguished friend Mr. Sherlock Holmes,' said he. 'And possibly you may also be aware that in many of his little investigations he was assisted by a certain Dr. Watson. *I* am that Dr. Watson.'

"He spoke exactly like his books, and looked on the whole like most of the illustrations, only of course by that time he was a good bit older.

"I told him of course how delighted I was to see him, and how honoured a young man should feel at a visit from such a well-known, et-cetera, et-cetera. The old boy lapped it up cheerfully and was quite human for a few minutes, and then he became extremely serious, and that extraordinary woodenness settled down over his bluff countenance like a cloud over a mountain.

"'I have come to ask you, Mr. Carrington,' said he, 'if you would be good enough to give me the benefit of your opinion in a little matter on which I have recently been consulted.'

"'I'll be charmed,' I said, 'though I'm afraid you won't find my opinion of much weight compared with the kind of opinion you've been accustomed to.'

"'We cannot all have the ability of my distinguished friend,' he answered in a kindly voice.

"It was no doubt a well-intentioned effort, and I let it go at that.

"'What's the problem?' I asked.

"'Well,' he began, 'the fact is that since the retirement of my distinguished friend, one or two of his old clients have occasionally approached me and asked me to assist them in the investigation of any little problems and difficulties that may be troubling them. The not unknown connection between my distinguished friend and myself had led them to take this course, as you will no doubt understand.'

"'Perfectly,' I murmured.

"'In the present instance the client of my distinguished friend who has taken this course is no less exalted a person than Lord Algernon Fitzpatrick, younger son of his late grace the Duke of Munster, so you will see that the matter is one requiring the greatest delicacy and circumspection.'

"He paused to let this sink in, and I endeavoured to look sufficiently impressed.

"'The matter,' he continued, 'is of a peculiarly private and painful nature. It is concerned, in fact, with no less grave and serious a matter than the disappearance of his late grace's will!'

"'By Jingo!' I murmured.

"'By this will, which Lord Fitzpatrick assures me he has seen—'

"'Excuse me,' I ventured to interrupt, 'but do you mean Lord Algernon Fitzpatrick?'

"'Certainly,' said he, 'I *said* Lord Fitzpatrick!'

"'Yes,' said I; 'but which do you *mean?*'

"He looked a trifle pained.

"'My distinguished friend used to have no difficulty in following my meaning,' he said severely.

"'He probably knew your habits,' I said soothingly, and seeing that the old boy evidently did mean Lord Algernon and Lord Fitzpatrick to be taken as the same person, I let him go ahead.

"'As I was saying, Lord Fitzpatrick has seen this will . . .' he stopped suddenly with a slight start, hauled a small paper bag out of his pocket, and took out of it a large pink globule. This he put into his mouth and sucked vigorously. Then he glanced for an instant at his watch and went on with his tale.

"'Lord Algernon Fitzpatrick has seen this will and assures me that the seven world-famous old masters, the fourteen priceless Agra topazes, and that historic heirloom the battle-axe of the first Duke, were all bequeathed to him. When, however, his grace died and his effects came to be examined, this will had disappeared. The only will that could be found was an earlier one by which these articles of vertu were left to his lordship's sister, Lady Diana Mountfalcon, and his lordship has no doubt whatever that her ladyship has abstracted the second document. He now wishes me to recover it for him.'

"The doctor looked at me very gravely, and I looked at the doctor with, I hope, an equally serious expression.

"'Well,' I said, 'what strikes me in the first place is that if Lady Diana has actually abstracted this document she is not likely to have preserved it.'

"'Ah!' exclaimed Dr. Watson with an air of profound admiration. 'That had not occurred to me! This quite reminds me of my distinguished friend! How on earth did you arrive at that conclusion, Mr. Carrington?'

"'It isn't a conclusion,' I hastened to say, 'it is only a suggestion, but it is certainly worth considering somewhat seriously.'

"'I shall look into this little point at once!' said the doctor. 'Possibly his lordship may throw some light on it.'

"He took up his hat and hurried off, with his cheek much less distended by this time. The pink globule had apparently been sucked just about to a finish.

"About an hour later Dr. Watson was again announced, and marched in with one side of his face the size of a balloon. He had evidently just tackled another globule.

"'I am glad to say that your suggestion has been met, Mr. Carrington,' said he. 'His lordship is quite convinced that the will is still in existence.'

"'Why?' I inquired.

"Dr. Watson coughed as it were delicately.

"'I almost hesitate to quote his lordship's precise words,' he said. 'My distinguished friend was not a swearing man and I got out of the habit of hearing it. With your permission I shall substitute the word "blank" for his lordship's adjectives.'

"I granted my permission, and he went on—

"'Lord Fitzpatrick says that his blank sister is a blank superstitious red-haired blanker. She will do any blank dirty trick, but she won't tell a blank lie for fear of losing her blank soul. And she has sworn that she hasn't destroyed the will and won't destroy it. Also she is in such a blank funk of consequences that she wouldn't dare to. Under those circumstances, Mr. Carrington, I feel almost justified in assuming that my distinguished friend would deduce that the will is hidden but still in existence.'

"'In that case,' I suggested, 'I should think the best thing would be to take advantage of her ladyship's truthful nature and simply ask her where the will is.'

"Dr. Watson was evidently beginning to regard me by this time as a bit of detecting phenomenon.

"'Your powers of inference do indeed somewhat remind me of my distinguished friend!' he exclaimed. 'I shall convey your suggestion to his lordship immediately.'

"Apparently his lordship was paying for the doctor's taxies, for he was back again well within an hour. His cheek seemed just as distended, and I ventured once more to imitate his distinguished friend by deducing that he had recently inserted a fresh globule.

"'His lordship informs me,' said he, 'that his blank sister tells him that I ought to know as much about the whereabouts of the blank will as she does. Apart from this ambiguous statement she refuses to say anything more.'

"'You don't know anything, do you?' I asked.

"Dr. Watson seemed a little ruffled.

"'My distinguished friend would never have asked me such a question!' he said with some asperity. 'His marvellous intellect was always aware of what I didn't know.'

"'I am gradually picking up the same knowledge of your capacity,' I assured him in a soothing voice, 'but it will take me a little time before I get anything like as good at it as he was.'

"The globule seemed to have got under his tongue, and for a moment he couldn't say anything very distinctly, but as far as I could judge from such a glassy eye, he seemed appeased.

"'What are your own deductions, Mr. Carrington?' he asked, as soon as the line was clear.

"'What are your facts, Dr. Watson? So far I really know nothing about the case.'

"'Your method,' said Dr. Watson with cordial approval, 'is steadily developing a greater and greater resemblance to that of my distinguished friend. Facts first; that was always his rule. My confidence in your judgment has increased very much indeed since you asked me that question.'

"I saw that he was already beginning to consider very seriously the advisability of writing me up, and as the afternoon was wearing on I ventured to rouse him from his reverie.

"'What are your facts?' I asked again.

"He put his hand into his pocket and drew out first the paper bag. This was evidently an accident, but it seemed to remind him of some duty, for he glanced suddenly at his watch. However, it can't have been quite time to take another globule, for he put the bag back and produced a note-book instead.

"'I have been most careful to note everything of importance,' said he. 'My distinguished friend always began with measurements, and so have I. His lordship's dining-room is 32 feet long and 19 feet wide. There is a discoloration of the wall-paper within 1 3/16 inches from the bell. The front stairs—' he paused to put on his spectacles, and I managed to get in a question.

"'Have you got any note of the date when this will was made?'

"He wet his thumb and began turning over the leaves.

"'No,' said he, 'I don't seem to have any note of that.'

"'Or of the names of the people who witnessed it? Or whether it was holograph? Or of anybody except Lord Algernon who saw it?'

"'I can't make notes of *everything*,' he replied with a touch of rebuke. 'I do not profess to resemble my distinguished friend exactly and in every point; but I have made very full notes of all the measurements in his late grace's house, and of every footprint that I could find, and of the hour at which the clock stopped—'

"'Hullo!' I exclaimed. 'This is new. You say the clock stopped?'

"'Certainly,' said Dr. Watson. 'I stopped it. My distinguished friend always noted that fact, and the only way of observing it on this occasion was by stopping the clock myself.' He suddenly gave a little start, and pulled out his watch once more. 'Just time,' he said. 'Talking of the clock reminded me,' and thereupon he took out the paper bag and put another immense pink globule into his mouth. It was the last, and he threw the paper bag into my waste-paper basket.

"By this time I was getting extremely curious to know what disease the doctor could be suffering from that required such terrific dosing. He seemed to me to be as fit as a fiddle.

"'I hope it isn't asking a very rude question, doctor,' I ventured to say, 'but I really should like to know what those pink pills are.'

"'They aren't pills,' said he, 'they are a new form of digestive bon-bon.'

"'Where did you come by them?' I asked.

"'Well,' said he, 'it is a rather singular story. In fact, it would have interested my distinguished friend very much indeed. This afternoon, just after lunch, and shortly before I set out to see you, a lady called upon me and said that she had so enjoyed reading about my distinguished friend, that she wanted to make some return to his biographer. So she had brought me a special form of bon bon, invented and manufactured by herself. She called them digestive bon-bons, because she said they were particularly suited to people with very strong digestions. She was so affable, and said such nice things both about me and my distinguished friend, that I couldn't possibly refuse her request.'

"'Her request?' I repeated.

"'Yes, she begged me to take one of these every quarter of an hour till the bag was finished, so that she could feel sure her tribute to my talents had really touched the spot. I wasn't sure what spot she meant, but I promised her I would do as she desired.'

"A sudden idea had hit me in the eye as he was speaking.

"'Had this lady by any chance red hair?' I asked.

"'Marvellous!' he exclaimed. 'This is really like my distinguished friend at his very best. Yes, she *had* red hair. However did you deduce that?'

"'And did she seem a particularly truthful lady—the sort of blank lady who wouldn't lose her blank soul by telling a blank lie?'

"His glassy eyes were positively glaring at me.

"'You are a perfect magician! This beats anything my distinguished friend ever deduced! Yes, she told me herself in recommending the bon-bons only for extra strong digestions that she never deviated from the truth. She didn't call it the blank truth, but otherwise your deduction is perfectly correct! How did you—'

"But I interrupted him this time.

"'Take that bon-bon out of your mouth, and let me have a look at it!' I commanded.

"He looked extremely surprised, but fortunately his distinguished friend had acclimatised him to strange commands. The globule had been sucked white by this time, but otherwise it was still intact. I cracked it with my office ruler—and took out the last fragment of the missing will.

"'You can just see the signature, *Munster*,' I pointed out to him.

"You should have seen the doctor sprint for the nearest chemist's. Everything possible was done, I believe, but the truthful lady had sized up his digestion only too correctly. It had done its work."

"Is that story literally true?" asked a sceptical member of our party.

"Ask Dr. Watson when you next meet him," said Carrington.

11

THE MISSING HUSBAND

"Fortunately for society," said Carrington, "the membership of the Stick-at-nothing-to-get-what-you-want brigade is strictly limited. Outside the frankly criminal class, jolly few men—so far as my own experience goes—will really stick at nothing. Unless, by Jingo, a woman is the thing they want. In that case the membership of the brigade is vastly increased. In fact one never knows who won't join it next. I remember one case . . ."

"Well, if you insist upon listening to scandal, I'll begin by explaining—no, I'll begin with Gerald Hathway's visit to my office one October morning. I hadn't heard of him before, but we have kept up our acquaintance—unprofessionally—ever since. A real good chap he was, I could see at a glance, about twenty-nine or thirty, with a cheery smile, but a shrewd eye, and immaculately turned out as the young man about town. He was a barrister with some private means, and at that time a good deal of leisure; but he is getting quite a few briefs now, I believe.

"'I'm a cousin of Lady Powell's,' he began; 'you may remember helping her in rather an awkward bit of business about a year ago.' I said I remembered the lady quite well, and he went on, 'It's her sister, Mrs. Escourt, who wants your assistance this time. The whole business is rather curious, and I'm beginning to fear it may turn out to be serious. Her husband has clean and absolutely disappeared.'

"And then he gave me an outline of the case. The Escourts had a place in Westmoreland, quite a big country house, I gathered, and Tony Escourt—as he was always called—lived the life of a country gentleman; bit of hunting, bit of shooting, bit of county business, the usual sort of round that enables a man to say he is too busy to do anything he feels disinclined to do, but doesn't prevent him from accepting an amusing invitation, or running up to town whenever he has a fancy.

"Well, just six days before, Tony Escourt had set out from home to spend a week in town. There was a special meeting of his club he wanted to attend, and he also wanted to see his stockbroker about selling some shares, and look up an old pal who had come home from East Africa, and forgather with one or two other fellows—he actually mentioned Gerald Hathway's name as being one of them. He went in his car to the local station, where he was going to take a slow train as far as Carnforth and pick up the London express there.

"His wife never expected to get a letter from Tony himself while he was away for such a short visit, but quite unbeknown to him she happened to have written to her cousin Gerald Hathway, and mentioned that her husband was arriving at Euston by such and such a train. Gerald wanted to see Escourt rather particularly, and so he went to Euston to meet the train, but no Tony Escourt arrived by it. He therefore sent a line to his cousin Lydia (that's Mrs. E.) and said that her husband hadn't turned up. Whereupon came an urgent note by return of post giving Tony's plans and telling Hathway to find out what had become of him.

"Hathway, being a great friend of both husband and wife, and the most obliging of fellows, thereupon made inquiries, and these revealed the startling facts that Tony Escourt had never attended the meeting of his club, never seen his stockbroker, and never looked up the old pal or any of his other friends. And then, at last, Mrs. Escourt had written commissioning him to employ me to trace the missing gentleman. That, in brief, was Hathway's story as he told it to me in my office, and as I watched his face I felt sure that he, at least, was keeping back nothing.

"'What sort of a man is Escourt?' I asked, for that's the funda-
mental thing to get at—the nature and character of the people of
the drama. It is far from easy to discover at second hand, but, fortunately, Hathway had a shrewd eye for human nature, and a tol-
erable gift for expressing himself.

"'A thorough good sort,' he said, 'popular with everybody. He
has lived a pretty easy life, not much of the curb has ever been
applied to Tony, and he had a bit of a splash before he married;
but nothing serious, mind you. Since he married, I've noticed that
he still likes dancing, and still chooses the prettiest partners in
the room, and as he's an uncommon good-looking chap, the pretty
girls still like him. But I know him very well indeed, and I can answer
for it that there has not been a breath of scandal in connection
with his name or his conduct since he married my cousin Lydia.'

"'Yet I notice,' I said with a smile, 'that you begin with that
aspect of Mr. Escourt's character.'

"'Well, hang it,' said he, 'when a fellow disappears like that,
one naturally thinks first thing of a woman. *Cherchez la femme* is
said to be rather a sound rule, isn't it?'

"'It has its exceptions,' I replied. 'Do you know if he had any
money troubles—or business worries—anything of that kind? Think
carefully.'

"He thought for a moment, and then shook his head decidedly.

"'Of course, one can't be certain,' said he. 'His affairs were beginning to get a little mixed up before he married; but that put everything right, and I've never known of any money difficulties since.'

"Then I gather that he married money?'

"'Yes, his wife was the eldest sister, and there were no brothers, so she came into the place; and a tidy lot of money besides.'

"'Oh,' I said, 'the place is hers then?'

"He nodded.

"'The place and most of the income.'

"'How old is he, and how old is she?'

"He is thirty-two. Lydia wouldn't thank me for telling you, but
between ourselves, forty must be pretty imminent.'

"'Is she at all like Lady Powell?' I asked,

"He shot me a shrewd humorous smile.

"'Lady Powell was considered the pretty sister.'

"'And in character?'

"'Much alike, but there again Gladys Powell has it.'

"I knew Lady Powell—no beauty, and a masterful rather suspicious woman; and I began to visualise more distinctly this fortunate couple, with their big place in the north, and their tidy lot of money.

"'And now to come to Mr. Escourt's visit to town. He wanted to see his stockbroker. That suggests possibilities of business troubles. Did he speculate?'

"'On horses a bit, but never in stocks and shares so far as I know. In fact I'd have been almost sure to have known, for if he had anything in the nature of business he always discussed it with me.'

"'What about this meeting of his club?' I asked. 'Was it important?'

"'It was about making some addition to the club house.'

"'Is he on the committee—or particularly interested in any way?'

"He shook his head.

"'He isn't on the committee. And the whole thing was only a small scheme to add some extra bedrooms. As he never stayed at that particular club, I can't honestly see what there was to interest him.'

"'He also wanted to see an old pal just home from East Africa.'

"'Yes, Jack Burton, Tony's very oldest and dearest friend. A bit of a rogue in his day too, but an excellent chap.'

"'Is Burton only in town for a short visit?'

"'No, he has settled down again in his old rooms for the next year anyhow.'

"I thought over all this information for a few minutes, while Hathway watched me in silence.

"'Well,' he asked at length, 'what do you think of the conundrum?'

"Yet though he expressed it lightly, I could see that he was anxious.

"'I was wondering,' I said, 'where exactly one should start the inquiry.'

"I had hardly spoken the words before that question was answered in a very surprising fashion. There came a knock at my door and a telegram was handed in. I opened it, and then opened my eyes.

"'It is from Mrs. Escourt,' I said, 'and this is what she says: "Mysterious discovery here come immediately."'

"'Mysterious discovery *here*,' repeated Hathway. 'Does that mean at their own place?'

"'Looks like it,' I said; and I added, 'It's lucky you turned up first, or this peremptory summons would have struck me as quite as mysterious as the discovery.'

"'Lydia might have said "please come",' he observed; 'however, I'm afraid that's rather her way. But all the same you'll go I hope.'

"'When is the first train?'

"'Good man!' said he. 'I say, you know, I'm really awfully re-lieved that you've taken this thing up. It was beginning to rather worry me. And yet, I'd like to see the thing through. Would you mind if I came with you?'

"'I'd very much sooner have you,' I said, and thereupon we fell to on a timetable. Five minutes later we were both hurrying off to pack our bags, and we met again at Euston in time to catch the two o'clock train.

"It was long after dark when we arrived at the Escourts' place, and I could see nothing of the outside of the house, except that every here and there along the front a lighted window glowing in the night showed that it must be an extensive mansion. Inside, the hall was imposing, the butler was the proper size and girth a but-ler should be, and there was also a liveried footman. Evidently Mr. Tony Escourt had done himself well when he married, I perceived; anyhow in matters material.

"We were taken straight to Mrs. Escourt's own sitting-room, and there I found a middle-sized lady, inclining to grow stout but well laced in, with a nose on the hooky side of dead straight, a pair of chilly eyes, and a manner that couldn't exactly be called bad, but certainly wasn't very happy. One made allowances for her present state of mind, yet when I pictured a popular, dashing, good-looking man of two-and-thirty attached to this dame, I couldn't help sympathising with his desire to spend a week in town now and then. At the same time, disappearing into space—assuming he had done it voluntarily—was rather a different matter. And then too there was always the chance of foul play; so that in spite of her manner I tried to be as sympathetic as I knew how.

"'My cousin has no doubt told you about my husband's unaccountable disappearance,' she began.

"'I assure you I was very sorry indeed to hear of it,' said I.

"She looked at me rather as though sorrow was unbecoming in a paid hand, and I resolved to be strictly business-like.

"'It is very extraordinary,' she said, 'and this morning one of my housemaids found something that makes it look extremely mysterious.'

"She turned to her writing bureau, opened a drawer, and took out a glove.

"'This is one of my husband's gloves.'

"'Indeed?' said I, examining it, I am afraid not very attentively.

"'It was one of a pair he took away with him,' she added.

"I pricked up my ears now and looked at the glove very closely indeed. It was an ordinary man's dogskin glove, size 8, such as are sold in tens of thousands.

"'Are you quite sure it is his?' I asked.

"'Quite,' she said in the same dry, chilly, emphatic voice she used all the time. 'You will see that it is scorched just there by the end of a cigar. Also the button is a little loose. I came down to the front door to see my husband off and noticed that he had forgotten his gloves. I picked them up myself and handed them to the butler, and I noticed the burnt mark and the loose button. In fact I was with him about a week before when he burnt his glove.'

"'And he certainly took the gloves away with him?'

"'Yes, certainly. I saw him slip them into his overcoat pocket as he was getting into the car.'

"'By Jove,' murmured Hathway. 'This is most extraordinary!'

"'It is more than extraordinary, Gerald,' said his cousin; 'I cannot understand it in the least.'

"'Where was this glove picked up?' I said.

"'Just inside a door leading out to the garden.'

"'This morning, you say?'

"'Yes, early this morning. The housemaid found it first thing when she was beginning her work.'

"'Is that the garden door in the old wing, near the foot of the back stairs?' asked Hathway.

"'Yes,' she said, 'and it seems a very curious place to find it. Don't you think so, Mr. Carrington?'

"'Finding it at all seems to me extremely curious,' I said.

"'What do you make of it?'

"'I shall have to think about it a little longer, I'm afraid,' I said cautiously.

"She turned to her cousin and said—

"'I have had some dinner kept for you, Gerald. You can show Mr. Carrington the way.'

"Gerald and I went to the door together. Something was probably the matter with the handle, for the catch hadn't caught and so he opened the door for me without a sound. I went out first and almost ran into a girl who might have been merely passing the door, but who certainly seemed rather to have only just started to move when she saw it open. She was a slender girl, dressed in dead black—all save a dainty apron—a lady's-maid obviously, and for an instant she looked at me and I saw her face distinctly. It was an uncommonly pretty face too, with large, brilliant dark eyes, rather petite features, pale skin and red lips; a type you'll meet every now and then, and a very fascinating type when you do meet it. But the expression in her eyes as they shot that single swift glance at me was not the fascinator's twinkle in the least.

"'Who is that girl?' I asked in a casual voice.

"Hathway looked at her departing back.

"'Oh, that's Elliot, my cousin's maid; a jolly pretty girl too.'

"'Jolly,' I agreed.

"We ate our belated dinner, had a smoke, and turned in, for I saw my way to doing nothing more that night.

"Next morning came an exceedingly surprising development—a regular rouser in fact. On the breakfast table Mrs. Escourt found lying a letter from her husband, dated the day before from his old pal Burton's rooms in Jermyn Street, conveying his love, the news that he was having a pleasant visit to London, and the information that he would be home in a few days' time. You can imagine how we stared at one another as she read this epistle aloud.

"'Great Scot!' cried Gerald. 'Then he has been in town all the— But dash it, how can he have been? I made inquiries—' he broke off again, and looked at me.

"'What do *you* say, Mr. Carrington?' the lady asked.

"'Did you tell anybody, except Mr. Hathway, that Mr. Escourt was missing?' I inquired.

"'Not a soul,' she said emphatically.

"'Nobody in the house—even in the strictest confidence—a confidential maid, for instance?'

"'I should never dream of telling any of my servants!' she answered with some indignation. 'I have told nobody.'

"'And the glove was found early yesterday morning. I suppose all the servants would know about it at once?'

"'I'm afraid they would,' she admitted. 'But that was all they knew.'

"'Can one post a letter in this neighbourhood early in the morning?'

"'One can post at the station before eight o'clock.'

"'Have any of your servants got bicycles?'

"This shower of apparently irrelevant questions seemed to annoy the lady.

"'A few of them,' she answered very coldly; 'the footman I believe has one, and my own maid, and one or two of the others. But may I ask what that has to do with it?'

"'You have hired a dog, Mrs. Escourt,' I smiled, 'and you must let him bark after his own manner. I have only one or two more questions left. At what o'clock were you told of the glove?'

"'When I came down to breakfast.'

"'And that would be?'

"'I was rather late yesterday morning. There was some stupid misunderstanding. I only began breakfast at half-past nine.'

"She was getting very nettled now, and I said soothingly—

"'Only one last question. How far away is the station?'

"'We call it three-quarters of a mile.'

"'Thank you,' I said. 'And now, Mrs. Escourt, are you satisfied with this letter of your husband's, and will you just wait now till he comes home?'

"'Certainly not!' she said emphatically. 'I know that he didn't go straight to London, and didn't do the things he said he was going to do. But he evidently doesn't know that I know.'

"Hathway and I glanced at one another. 'Evidently!' I said softly.

"'Ah!' she exclaimed, 'you quite see how suspicious it all is! I want you to go to London at once, Mr. Carrington, and find out what he has been doing.'

"'You are quite determined to pursue this matter?'

"'Absolutely!'

"'Well,' I said, 'I'll do what I can. But I first want to make some inquiries in this neighbourhood. I want, for instance, to speak to the officials at the station who saw him depart.'

"'There is no need,' she said. 'He certainly did leave by that train. I found that out at once.'

"'Better let Carrington follow out his own ideas,' said Hathway. 'You let him have one of the cars for the day, Lydia, and I'll guarantee he will do honest work.'

"As we went to the smoking-room, he lowered his voice and said to me—

"'I have a sort of dim idea of what's in your mind, but for the life of me I can't follow you all the way.'

"'I want to feel sure I'm right before I say anything more,' said I, 'but I'll tell you as soon as I do feel sure. Let's come for a stroll outside.'

"It was a fine morning, and we strolled and smoked on the terrace. I now saw the whole lie of the house. It was a rambling place, built at different dates, one whole wing being very old indeed.

"'You say that glove was found just inside the garden door of the old wing,' I said. 'Is that the old wing?'

"'Yes, and that's the door,' said he.

"'And the back stairs are close by?'

"'One of the back stairs. This staircase is really in the old wing, but you can get from it into each floor of the modern house.'

"'Including the servants' quarters at the top?'

"'Yes,' said he.

"'What is in the top of the old wing?'

"'Only a vast collection of attics.'

"'Suppose we go and have a look at the place where the glove was found,' I suggested.

"We looked at the place, and then we went up the old back staircase, and even poked our noses into the attics. And then I set off by myself in the car, and only got back at six o'clock.

"Gerald Hathway met me in the hall.

"'Discovered anything?' he asked in a whisper.

"'Where is Mrs. Escourt?' said I.

"'Lying down. She always has a rest between tea and dinner.'

"'Then now's our chance!' said I. 'Can you raise a couple of pairs of tennis shoes? Fetch them as quick as you can, like a good chap, and I'll tell you what I am after as we're on our way.'

"He dashed off for the tennis shoes, and five minutes later we were going up those old back stairs like a couple of burglars, except that I whispered enough to let him understand the game, so long as it was safe. But we were still as mice by the time we reached the top flight—and so we surprised her again.

"It was the same slim, dark-eyed girl, only now she wasn't wearing an apron, and the expression in her eyes as we caught her slipping along from the servants' quarters to the unused attics was even more vivid than before. It was fear before—and that was what first put me on the proper scent; but it was terror now.

"'Take us straight to Mr. Escourt,' I said quietly.

"'To—to—Mr. —?' she stammered.

"'Mr. Escourt. We want to keep the whole affair dark, and we shall if you'll help us. Otherwise there may be a scandal.'

"She said not another word, but led us through those dusty attics, getting pretty dim now that the evening was falling, till we found the infatuated Tony Escourt skulking under the slates of his own house. For a solid week that man had been surreptitiously enjoying the society of this girl whom he had fallen head over ears in love with, with his jealous wife down below trying to find him in

London. There was one of your stick-at-nothing brigade. But it was a woman he wanted, you see."

"And what happened to them?" demanded one of his audience.

"Oh, we got him safely off that night, and coached him up in a plausible yarn about meeting an old friend who had persuaded him to run up to Scotland and look at a salmon fishing before he went to London. Mrs. Escourt gulped a little but swallowed it all right. As for Miss Elliot, she gave up her situation suddenly—mother very ill, and passed into the unknown, at least so far as I am concerned.

"How had he managed the thing? Why, he had only gone as far as Carnforth junction, melted away out of the station while waiting for the express, lain low till night, and then come home by car. The glove? He used to slip out at nights for a breath of air. That particular night he was wearing his overcoat with the gloves still in the pocket, and one of them fell out. The girl told him it was discovered first thing in the morning, whereupon he scribbled that note to his wife, enclosed it in another note to his old pal Burton, and asked him to post it in London instantly. Only unfortunately neither he nor the girl knew that he had been reported missing and was being searched for. The girl rushed with the letter to the station on her bicycle, and got back a trifle late; hence the 'misunderstanding' which caused her mistress to breakfast at 9.30.

"As for my own part in the show, well, the glove found in the house, the glimpse of that eavesdropping girl with stark fear in her eye, and my knowledge of the characters and circumstances of Escourt and his wife, gave me an inkling of what might *possibly* be the truth. Then my questions about the letter showed me how that *might* be accounted for. The presence of the old attics, with the glove at the foot of the stair, added to the chances of my being right. And, finally, I went in that car to the station and found that Miss Elliot actually had posted a letter in the early morning, and then I traced Escourt's whole movements at Carnforth; I even interviewed the man he hired his car from.

"And the moral is, don't marry for money!"

12

THE PRICE

Three men were lingering over their coffee and cigars at a small table in the almost deserted restaurant. They had sat down late and by this time most of the other diners had gone, and the supper parties were not yet arrived. It was a wild November night, and now that the room was silent, the dirge of the wind and the platter of rain rose insistent.

"Lord, how sepulchral this place is tonight," said one of them, "with no band, no company, half the lights out, and a gale on the windows. It isn't the same place at all!"

"Except that we shall pay exactly the same for our entertainment," added another.

The third man said nothing. He was gazing hard across the room, and the others, following his eyes, caught a glimpse of two ladies passing from an inner room across this in which they sat, and then vanishing through the door into the hall. One of the ladies was old and frail, the other was still young, and still had beauty despite her extreme pallor and the drooping sadness of her air. Both were in dead black, and neither threw a single glance across to where the three men sat.

"There goes a poor girl who has paid for her entertainment," said the third man. "Our bill will be a trifle compared with hers!"

One of his friends looked at him keenly.

"A story, Carrington?" he asked. "Come on! We need something to cheer us up!"

"It won't cheer you," said Carrington. "However, if you like to hear it . . ."

"I can remember Rosie Gavin almost as early as I can remember any one outside my own family. Her mother (that's the frail old lady you saw) and mine were both widows, both badly off, and both by way of being well connected, and a little critical of most of their suburban neighbours. We lived in the same quiet road as the Gavins, in the same kind of semi-detached villa, with the same sort of regimental and Indian trophies and faded photographs of people in uniform on our walls. In the course of time the two families became more like cousins than mere friends, and Rose and I more like brother and sister than cousins. We should probably have become a good deal more like lovers than either, only just as that stage was beginning, fate sent me out into the world, and very shortly afterwards threw her across the path of Edward Kirchell.

"It was looked upon as a splendid match for her, and I remember sighing enviously to think of a fellow not much older than myself, with £10,000 a year put into his pocket by destiny, a fine old country place in the Midlands, and Rose Gavin as his bride. They seemed to me an extraordinary lucky couple of mortals.

"A few months after their wedding I spent part of a holiday with my people, and one night my mother grew confidential. And then I got my first hint of the price Rose Gavin had paid. Kirchell was handsome, charming, clever, and well-born; a first-class man on a horse, and even wealthier than I had heard—*but!* My mother whispered the secret of that *But.* There was a taint in the blood. His father had died by his own hand, and Edward Kirchell himself had been drinking too much before he was twenty. Also, poor Rose was more flattered and dazzled than really in love; and she knew all about that *But.*

"It is easy to be critical now, and wise on her behalf too late. But the man was very attractive, she loved nobody else, he had sworn reformation, and the difference between penniless suburban obscurity and a country seat with all that money can buy, can only be realised by those who have tried the one and sighed for the other. And then there was that chorus of 'Lucky girl!' that made refusal seem a form of lunacy. So she ran the risk and took him.

"Four or five years later we met by chance at a dance, and had a long talk. Her husband wasn't there, and I noticed that she hardly spoke of him. Considering the larger life she lived, and all the new interests that ought to have filled it, she seemed to me pathetically eager to talk of old times, and recall our ancient intimacy and the days that were gone. She had become more beautiful than ever, and yet, even in her looks there was something that made me uneasy. Unless I were very much mistaken, she was a woman who knew what fear meant. It was my second hint of the price.

"Still more years went by—some six or seven this time—when I was told one morning that a lady wanted to see me very urgently. She gave no name, and when Rose Kirchell walked into my office, glad though I was to see her again in one sense, I got about as unpleasant a shock as I have often received. People who walk into my office in business hours are not the happy ones of this earth, and Rose looked one of the least happy.

"'Fred,' she began, and there was something almost unbearably touching in that re-use of my Christian name, spoken as she spoke it, 'have you heard anything lately about my married life—and my husband?'

"I confessed then I had; but only rumours.

"'They are quite true,' she said in a low voice, without even troubling to ask me what the rumours were. 'Fred, it's horrible! For more than a year Edward has been drinking worse than ever. He isn't responsible for his actions now in the least. I am afraid of him!'

"I could see that without her telling me, and I scarcely knew what to say in answer.

"'You have never seen him, have you?' she asked.

"'Never.'

"'That makes it so difficult to explain things!' she said. 'If you only knew how charming he can be when he likes, and how dreadfully clever he is, and what an extraordinary mixture of strong and weak points he has, you might understand. Dr. Jourdain says he is certainly insane, and getting worse and worse through drink, and yet he is so cunning and suspicious that he won't give himself away before a doctor—and certainly not before two doctors. So we can't get him certified and put under restraint. And yet, before me alone, he lets himself go freely. He thinks he has some mission from Heaven! He talks about God wanting him to rid the earth of people—but the moment a doctor appears, he pulls himself together instantly, and discusses horses and books and the ordinary things he used to be interested in. Perhaps you can't believe me, but Dr. Jourdain can assure you it is true!'

"'I can believe you,' I answered her; 'I have heard of such cases before.'

"She seemed greatly relieved.

"'Then you will help me, Fred!' she cried. 'Dr. Jourdain has been constantly about the house. He has even slept there once or twice. He would do anything he could to protect me and save Ned from himself, but Ned is getting horribly suspicious of him, and we have simply *got* to take stronger measures!'

"'Who is Dr. Jourdain?' I asked. 'A specialist?'

"'Oh no,' she said, 'he is our local doctor.'

"'Young man or old?'

"'Oh, quite a young man—but very clever. I don't know what I'd have done without him!'

"Couldn't his wife put you up at their house when your husband has his bad turns?' I asked.

"'Oh, but Dr. Jourdain isn't married.'

"It was merely to find this out that I made my suggestion. Her answer did nothing to make the situation seem any the more promising.

"'And your husband is of a very—did you say of a jealous nature?' I ventured to ask.

"Her colour rose a little.

"'I told you he is not himself,' she said; and then she went on quickly, 'but we have decided to take steps now. Dr. Jourdain is getting Sir James Normanton down tomorrow; he's the great mental specialist, you know.'

"'Ah!' I said emphatically. 'That's much better, Rose. But how are you going to get your husband to give himself away?'

"'Dr. Jourdain and I have arranged that,' she said. The two doctors are going to be behind curtains in my sitting-room so that they'll hear Ned talking to me as he talks when we are alone.'

"'You'll have to make your plans very carefully,' said I. 'A trap like that is easier to arrange in theory than practice. Still it should be quite possible. . . .'

"'Will you help, Fred?' she cried. 'That's why I've come to you this morning. I've persuaded Dr. Jourdain to let me get you.' She lowered her voice and added, 'But really I want you even more to help Dr. Jourdain—and Sir James too, of course—in case my husband gets violent when he discovers what we have done. If Ned got desperate . . .'

"She broke off and gave a little shiver. It spoke such volumes for the life of terror she lived and the real possibility of danger, that I never hesitated a moment.

"'All right, I'll come down too,' I said.

"Her grateful smile and her moving faltered thanks were ample reward, and yet her last words stirred once more a fresh sensation of uneasiness.

"'Dr. Jourdain is planning everything,' she said, 'but I am sure he will be very glad of your suggestions.'

"'There seems to be a trifle too much of Dr. Jourdain in this business,' I said to myself.

"Next morning I met Sir James Normanton at St. Pancras and we traveled down together. I found him an extremely interesting shrewd man of the world, with a host of anecdotes of similar situations. He seemed quite glad to have my company, for, like me, he distrusted amateur attempts to arrange and bait a trap such as Jourdain proposed to set.

"'The really cunning lunatic is often extraordinarily difficult to trap,' said he. 'I only hope our friend Jourdain realises the difficulties.'

"'Do you know Dr. Jourdain?' I asked.

"'Not personally,' he said, 'but I remember his name in connection with the Hospitals football cup. He was a very well-known athlete in his day, and I believe a smart fellow too.'

"'He seems to be taking a very energetic part in assisting poor Mrs. Kirchell,' I remarked with my most innocent air.

"Sir James shot me an exceedingly shrewd glance.

"'Very,' he said, a trifle drily; 'I trust he has been as judicious as he has been energetic.'

"It was a fast train, and the second stop was our destination. We had been told that Dr. Jourdain would meet us at the station, and sure enough a very well dressed youngish man picked us out on the platform and greeted us extremely courteously, but—it struck me—with rather a marked touch of formality.

"'I am Dr. Jourdain,' he said. 'You, I suppose, are Sir James Normanton and Mr. Carrington?'

"We said we were, and both of us looked at this energetic young doctor with some curiosity. There was no doubt about his being of the strapping athletic type, and of his being a smart fellow. His manner was remarkable for its decision and its intelligence, and was equally remarkably well-bred and gentlemanly. And yet there was *something* I didn't quite take to, but what my feeling was I had no time to analyse, for he took us in hand and gave us our directions briskly and instantly.

"'Mrs. Kirchell's car is not yet at the station,' he said, 'but it will come for you, Sir James, in a few minutes. Meanwhile I shall drive Mr. Carrington up to the house in my dogcart.'

"As he led us towards the exit, Sir James and I exchanged glances. His raised grey eyebrows seemed to say, 'Energetic—yes! Judicious—well . . . ?'

"An extremely well-turned-out four-wheeled dogcart stood outside the station, and into this Dr. Jourdain jumped as quickly as he had done everything else, and I followed him, while Sir James nodded farewell from the pavement. One of the station cabmen had been standing by the horse's head, and as he stepped aside to let us start, he cried—

"'Your 'orse would have been on his way 'ome, sir, if I hadn't 'ave left my cab to stand by him!'

"But instead of pausing to give the man a tip, Jourdain muttered something uncommonly like an oath, cracked his whip, and sent that horse out of the station yard and into the street like a flash of greased lightning. The way in which he took the sharp turn at the corner showed him to be a first-class whip, but apart from that, the incident impressed me anything but favourably. A man whose thirst for instant action led him to leaving his horse unwatched in the station yard and then to ignoring the cabman's assistance, seemed to me singularly ill-fitted to conduct such a delicate affair as we were engaged on. 'Judicious?' The question seemed answered now.

"Through the streets of that market town we sped like the foul fiend himself, and personally I was much too interested in wondering whether the inhabitants were all going to survive our whirlwind passage, to indulge in any conversation. However, they fortunately got out of the way in time, and presently we were safely spanking along a country lane. For a few minutes I waited for the explanations that I thought my companion would surely give me, but never a single word did he say; so at last I asked—

"'How is Mr. Kirchell to-day?'

"'Mr. Kirchell is very well, thank you,' he answered politely enough, but very briefly.

"'He is at home, I hope,' I inquired.

"'He is at home,' he repeated in the same tone.

"'I presume you have made all your arrangements,' I said next.

"'I have made them all,' he replied very definitely and with a certain curious emphasis.

"I felt snubbed, but I determined not to notice it, so in as friendly a tone as ever I asked—

"'And how is Mrs. Kirchell?'

"He threw me a sudden sidelong glance, and if ever a single gleam of an eye could daunt a man, his would have done it then. Daunted or not, I was conscious of a shiver running through me from scalp to knee.

"'Mrs. Kirchell be damned,' he said, not violently or loudly, but in a low, quiet, malicious voice, and as if he meant every syllable.

"For a moment my heart froze within me. Was this the man whose devotion to poor Rose had made me fear lest her husband's jealousy should be too dangerously roused? Was this expert whip, with his distant, coldly courteous manner, his air of dominating authority, and these extraordinary answers for questions on professional matters, actually the brisk young doctor building up a country practice? Out of the corner of my eye I looked him up and down, and the answer to those questions seemed to spring out of him and shout itself at me. And for some long, long minutes that I don't want to live through again, that answer kept my heart frozen. For who was it then who was driving me at break-neck speed through an utterly deserted country lane? And why was he driving me?

"We had turned into this lane almost as soon as we were clear of the town. It wound between high hedges, so that I could see nothing beyond, and in dead silence we wound our way with it; not a house or a soul in sight. And then there suddenly flashed into sight on the right-hand side a pair of ancient pillars with a closed gate between them and a grass-grown drive beyond. The lane widened into a semi-circle before this gateway, and into this my companion swung the dogcart and pulled the horse up on his haunches with his nose almost touching the gate.

"'Hold the reins,' he said abruptly, and before I realised what was happening I had taken them from his hand and he had leapt out on to the ground. Naturally I had imagined he was going to open the gate, and I have no doubt at all he had counted on this and selected the spot deliberately. But, instead, he drew himself up within a yard of the wheel, and the next instant I was looking down the muzzle of a revolver—a terribly steady revolver too.

"'You have ten seconds more to live, Carrington,' he said, in the same even, malicious voice, and with the same dreadful glint in his eye. 'Make your peace with your Maker! He has delivered you into my hands, and I am commanded to slay and not to spare. My damned wife and that damned doctor are with their Maker already. I discovered their infernal plot against me, and I sent them to Him before you. Normanton will follow in half an hour. When I say "Three" I shall shoot you as dead as the other carrion. One . . .'

"I never was quite as near death. The man was a homicidal maniac without compunction in his heart or any way of rousing it. And his hand was steady as a rock.

"'One moment, Mr. Kirchell,' I said very quietly, rising to my feet as I spoke.

"'Two!' he cried.

"'I have a message from our Maker,' I went on, still quite quietly, and I could see that his interest was aroused, for the word "Three" still hung on his lips. 'He wishes my body to fall upon the ground, and not to defile your dogcart. If you will kindly wait for the fraction of a second I shall move, so that I shall fall out on to the road.'

"He said not a word, nor did he move a single muscle while I stepped across, and stood with one foot on the very edge of the trap. And then, suddenly, I looked right over his head, and opened my eyes with an expression of extreme surprise.

"'Hullo!' I said, as if to some one behind him, 'How did you get here?'

"It came off even better than I had dared to hope. He gave a violent start, and turned his head right round, but even as it began to turn I had jumped. Luckily, I weigh a good bit more than I look, and the next instant Mr. Kirchell had thirteen stone descend upon his shoulders. Heavens, what a smash we came down! But I was up first, and the revolver was safely in my hand when he struggled up on to his knees.

"'Get into that dogcart,' I commanded, 'and drive me straight to your house!'

"He stared at me in bewildered silence for a moment, and then obeyed like a lamb. I was taking no more risks, and so I let down the foot-board of the back seat, and sat there on the near side of the trap, with the revolver ready in my hand, and in that order we drove to his house of mourning.

"The only words he said the whole way were—'I must see my wife!' But he has never seen her yet. She was at death's door when we got to his house, and it was many a day before she was out of the wood. But poor Jourdain had gone beyond recall. As for Kirchell himself, he is confined during His Majesty's pleasure, hopelessly and permanently insane; but still Rose's husband until our merciless divorce law is altered.

"And that is the price the poor girl paid."

13
THE ENVELOPE

[PUBLISHER'S NOTE: *Technically, this case does not involve Carrington, but it was included with the original stories, and certainly has that Carrington quality . . .*]

"By Gad!" exclaimed the General, "this is deuced different from traveling on the Highland line before the war!"

"Very, sir," the young Guardsman agreed.

"You know this country then?"

"I sometimes used to shoot at a place in Sutherlandshire, sir."

"Well," said the General, a stout affable warrior with a row of ribbons on his broad chest, "except when I was in India, I've shot and fished in Scotland every year since I was a boy. How many times I've been up and down this Highland line I'd be afraid to say; and, by Jove, what a contrast now!"

"Just what I was thinking, sir," smiled the young officer.

"Not a lady to be seen!" continued the General. "Not a keeper, not a dog; not a gun or a rod or any other mortal thing one used to see here. Everybody's in uniform; and by Gad, even then you've got to get a pass like a ticket-of-leave man! The piping days of peace seem far enough away; what?"

One of the two young Australians at the other end of the carriage took his cigar out of his mouth and joined in the conversation. There was none of the Guardsman's well-drilled air of deference about this young man. His manner was engagingly frank and direct.

346

"This is my first trip to the Highlands of Scotland," said he, "and a mighty nice country to go fishing and shooting in it looks. I suppose the whole place used just to be crawling with tourists and sportsmen and guys collecting butterflies and birds' eggs. Not much Prohibited Area about it then, I guess!"

"The rummiest thing about the whole show," put in the R.N.R. Lieutenant, "is not being able to get a drink whenever you want. Just fancy being in the home of whisky and having to wet your whistle with tea!"

There were these five officers in the carriage: the burly conversational General; the two young Australians—one, who had just spoken, tall and thin with very black hair and a long nose; the other, a quieter young man, of the fair, blue-eyed, stolid type; the R.N.R. Lieutenant, a plain-looking freckled man with a wide mouth; and the young Guardsman, with a captain's stars and the Grenadier's cap-band, spruce and slender, a type of the "pukka" army officer. And there was also one civilian, a quiet-looking man with a beard, who had begun by joining in the general conversation, mentioning incidentally that he was an official of the Board of Agriculture traveling on business, and then had put on a pair of spectacles and become deeply immersed in a mass of papers, apparently official correspondence. A small blotting-pad lay on his knee, and every now and then he seemed to be scribbling notes with a fountain pen.

The six had found themselves together in this first-class compartment after passengers from the South had changed trains at Inverness and passed the barrier at the southern limit of the Military Area.

"What's the use in this Prohibited Area anyhow?" demanded the tall Australian. "Seems to me it gives a peaceful fighting man a lot of trouble for no particular object I can see."

The General laughed in his bluff way. "They evidently don't think all fighting men are peaceful," said he.

"Yes, but see here, sir," argued the R.N. R. Lieutenant, "it seems to me all very well for civilians to have passports, but isn't the King's uniform a good enough passport?"

The General coughed discreetly, pursed his lips, and then, like one revealing a little more than he had any business to, said—

"I may tell you I had a talk with a somewhat important police official in Edinburgh, and he says that the King's uniform has more than once been the passport for quite the wrong sort of gentleman."

"Black sheep in wolf's clothing," suggested the tall Australian.

The others laughed, all except the civilian, who still seemed absorbed in his papers, and the Guardsman, who murmured—

"What a beastly idea! I didn't know that game was being played in this country."

"I assure you it is," said the General emphatically. "At least, I have the very best authority possible. That's why they're so damned particular about these passports. By Jove, they looked at mine so long, I began to think they were going to arrest me!" He turned to the civilian and inquired, "I suppose even Government officials have got to go through the same thing?"

The man with the beard looked up and nodded.

"They don't let any of us off," said he. "In fact, a civilian's pass-port—even if he be an official—is a much more complicated affair than a soldier's."

"In other words," said the General shrewdly, "a soldier's pass-port is probably easier to fake."

Again the Board of Agriculture official nodded.

"In all probability that's an added advantage of traveling in uniform," said he.

"Meaning if one is the kind of black sheep we were speaking of!" said the sailor. "Well, I suppose there's something in that."

The General was evidently an optimist at heart.

"There's such an infernal lot of exaggeration in everything one hears nowadays," he declared, "that personally I take what my friend in the police told me with a grain of salt. Forging a passport and all the rest of it isn't such an easy game. Gad, I wouldn't like to play it myself!"

"And what is there to be learned when one does get into this Military Area place?" asked the fair Australian. "It doesn't look to me as though there was much to be seen so far."

"Two naval bases—Cromarty and Scapa," said the Guardsman.

"And the north-west corner of Scotland is said to have possibilities for the undesirable visitor," added the Government official, looking up quickly from his papers.

The fair Australian stretched himself, and laughed.

"I thought there were only mountains and stags out that way!"

"So there are—inland," said the General. "Grand deer-stalking country too!"

He turned to the Guardsman and launched forth into sporting reminiscences, while the young officers listened, and the civilian went on jotting down notes, till at last, at one of the incessant stations, the breezy General jumped up and cried—

"Hullo! I ought to get out here!"

It was an old-fashioned carriage, with no corridor, and, besides the six passengers, its contents seemed to be chiefly the General's belongings. Two of his bags were on the seats, and more loaded the rack. The Grenadier Captain lent a hand in clearing this collection on to the platform, and, to make room, the civilian stepped out, strolled a few paces along the train, and stood by waiting. A couple of minutes later they were off again.

"We've got a little more room now," said the civilian, pulling a small suitcase from under the seat and placing it beside him.

"Our friend, the brass-hat, pretty well filled the whole place," laughed the tall Australian; "I guess I'll make myself a little more comfortable too."

There was a general movement in the carriage, each of the five either shifting his seat or moving his belongings. The Grenadier and the two Australians put on their overcoats, and the Government official took a rug from a bundle and threw it over his knees. As they all settled down at last, the tall Australian remarked—

"Well, thank God, one can stretch one's legs at—"

He meant, it seemed, to have added "last," but his speech was arrested in the midst. He caught the Grenadier's eye and then the civilian's. Each had seen the same thing. It was the Australian who picked it up from the floor—a torn and crumpled envelope, but the writing on it singularly legible.

"Here's a queer address to find in the Prohibited Area!" said he with a short laugh.

The civilian and the Grenadier were now sitting in corners opposite to one another, and he held out the envelope so that both could read it. Over his shoulder the fair Australian and the R.N.R. Lieutenant were reading it too. Of the name, only the last syllable "stein" remained, and below it was the address, "Konigstrasse 13, Köln."

For a moment nobody spoke, and then the sailor asked—

"Anybody here claim this pretty thing?"

But nobody answered him.

"Gee!" exclaimed the tall Australian suddenly, "it must have been dropped by old brass-hat!"

The Grenadier answered quickly and warmly—

"Never! That was General Fawkes-Turing! He didn't know me, of course, but I knew him well enough. He's absolutely above suspicion!"

"Suspicion!" said the fair Australian. "You really call this suspicious then?"

"Don't you?"

Again nobody spoke for a moment, and then in a quiet, rather hesitating voice, the civilian said—

"I suppose, perhaps, the fact that nobody acknowledges it, does—er—seem a little odd."

"There's nothing inside the envelope," said the fair Australian; "it's just a dirty scrap of paper."

"That's what started us into this war, my son!" said his friend. "Scraps of paper have taken a new lease of life since August 1914. Still, there'd be nothing so very much in this scrap to incriminate a fellow—if it wasn't, as this gentleman remarked, that nobody is willing to acknowledge it."

"Couldn't it have been in the carriage all the time?" suggested the R. N. R. Lieutenant—"under the seat, for instance?"

The tall Australian looked round the carriage at each in turn, and then at the envelope.

"I suppose it's quite possible," said he slowly.

"But you mean we can hardly take it for granted?" asked the civilian in the same diffident voice.

The other gave a short laugh.

"Well, if you put it like that—"

"Oh, I only supposed you meant that!" said the civilian hurriedly.

There was another pause, and then the Grenadier said—

"We were all moving about the carriage. It's quite clear we can't tell who dropped this thing."

"Assuming any of us did," added the fair Australian.

"My son," said his tall friend, "that's the only derned assumption we can go on, just at present anyhow, till we get things cleared up a bit."

He looked round the company, and then as the others seemed to be waiting instinctively for his opinion, he went on—

"There are just three possible solutions, seems to me. Either old brass-hat did drop this, whatever his name is—"

"Impossible!" reiterated the Guardsman warmly.

"Excuse me, my friend," said the other soothingly, "there's no point in getting gingery. The old boy may have had something wrapped up in it. It says nothing against him, seeing that he hasn't denied owning it. We've got to reckon on the chance of this being a mare's nest, just as we've got to reckon on the chance of the other thing."

"Hear, hear!" said the sailor, beginning to fill a pipe.

"I see," agreed the Guardsman. "Yes, of course that's possible. Still—"

"I'm coming to that 'still,'" smiled the Australian. "Well now, that's the first solution. The second is, that it was in the carriage before any of us got in at Inverness. And the third is, that one of us dropped it and won't own up. Well now, with those three solutions all open, what can we damned well do?"

"I quite see," said the civilian. "Yes, that puts the matter very well. And so you say you propose to go on the only assumption possible?"

"I'm just putting the case to the company. It's not for me to propose."

"Oh, I was only thinking of what you said before," said the Board of Agriculture official hurriedly. "But of course if you think we ought to go on any other assumption—well—er—certainly suggest one."

"I certainly don't suggest anything different from what I said before," replied the Australian emphatically.

"And what did you suggest before?" asked the sailor.

"This gentleman seems to be taking down my remarks in short-hand," said the Australian, nodding towards the Agricultural official, with a pleasantly ironical smile, and yet with something significant in his eye as it rested on the civilian's papers and writing-pad.

"Oh no, I assure you this is merely a little official correspondence," said the civilian with what seemed meant for a laugh. "I speak merely from recollection of this officer's remarks. They seemed to be very reasonable."

The Grenadier cut in abruptly—

"I say that we must obviously all regard ourselves as under suspicion."

"Precisely," said the tall Australian, "that's exactly my point. I say that's the only safe assumption in the meanwhile. The question is—what are we to do?"

"Supposing I arrest you, and this gentleman arrests me, and so on till we all arrest each other?" suggested the R. N. R. Lieutenant.

There was only half a laugh from the Australians and the civilian, and the Grenadier never even smiled. Evidently the situation struck them all as having passed the jesting stage. Their eyes wandered furtively from one to another of their companions, and—so far as their expressions revealed their minds—the same thought seemed to be equally behind each glance—"There is probably a spy in this carriage."

Once again the tall Australian broke the silence.

"Some one's got to speak out," said he, "and I'll begin. What do we know of each other? That's the first question. Well, my name's Mackay and my friend here is called Sutherland; or at least he says he is. We only met at King's Cross Station, but he says he knows some of my folk out in Sydney and I happen to know some of his—

that's to say, if they are the Sutherlands he says they are. *If* his tale is a true bill, I can answer for his people being as good citizens and fine folk as any in Australia. While if his tale isn't true, well, all I can say is he's a kind of magician, for what he doesn't seem to know about Sydney and the Sydney Sutherlands isn't worth knowing."

He looked towards his fellow Australian, who nodded and said—

"That's all right. That's just what I told him, and of course you've only my word that it's true. And all I can say about him is pretty much the same thing. I know his Mackay people out at home—or some of them anyhow, and better folk don't breathe. And we've talked lots since we left King's Cross, and nothing he has said has contradicted anything I know."

"And I may just add," put in the other, "that both our folks came originally from this part of the world—as you can tell by our names— and we are both on leave and going to look up some of the old people. There's a cousin of my father, an old minister up in Sutherlandshire. And he's got far out relations there too, I understand."

"That's right," nodded the fair man. "They are farming folk of some kind."

The sailor took up the tale next.

"My name's Matthews," said he, "and I'm going up to join a ship at Scapa. I'd tell you her name, only it's against the regulations; and in fact, looking to the present situation and seeing that *some one* is under suspicion, I can't break through them on this occasion. I've no pals to bear me out, but that's my sworn statement—for what it's worth."

"I'm in the same boat," said the Guardsman. "I can only say that my name's Hillary, and that I'm in the Grenadier Guards. I'm going up to Scapa too, to put in a week's leave in my cousin's ship, but for the same reasons I can't very well even mention her name."

The civilian spoke last.

"My name's Walters," said he, "and as I mentioned before, I'm an official of the Board of Agriculture for Scotland traveling on official business. Like the last two gentlemen who spoke, I am without witnesses to my identity."

Again there was a pause, and again it was broken by the tall Australian.

"Well," he said, "here we are all together, and if one of us *is* a spy, well, he can't do much spying just for the moment!"

"Yes, I quite see what you mean," agreed the civilian; "I suppose it really wouldn't do to part company till we make sure."

"He didn't quite say that!" exclaimed the sailor. "Damn it, how could we manage it, all going to different places?"

"Oh, I only thought that was the suggestion," said Mr. Walters hurriedly.

"It's the only thing to be done," said Captain Hillary abruptly.

"Precisely," agreed the tall Australian. "The only difficulty is, how are we to arrange?"

"Where do you get out?" asked the Guardsman.

"Place called Lairg." The tall Australian turned to his companion and added, "You meant to stop not far off there, didn't you?"

"One station beyond," said the fair man, "but getting out at Lairg would make no odds. I can manage that."

"As I was saying, I'm bound for Scapa," said Matthews, "but I can't ask you chaps to go on all that way, and if they don't like my turning up a day late, well, they'll just have to lump it! It's a good enough excuse, I reckon. I'll stop at Lairg too."

"So will I," said the Guardsman briefly. There was a moment's pause while they all looked at Walters.

"Oh, I think I can manage to go on to Lairg," he said after an instant's reflection. "But what do you propose to do when we get there?"

"Well," said Mackay, the tall man, "I suppose we'd better wire the situation to Inverness or somewhere, and just wait at Lairg for instructions."

"That's it," said Matthews, and Hillary nodded approval.

The civilian also nodded, but more thoughtfully, and almost— it seemed—a trifle absently; and he said nothing. The other Australian seemed satisfied also, and now that the arrangement was made, silence fell upon the carriage.

It had been a day of heavy clouds with a gusty wind, and the short afternoon merged early into evening; while, in the spell of absolute silence, the gusts seemed to have risen into squalls, and filled the carriage with constant little sounds. Lieutenant Matthews sucked at his pipe, the two Australians seemed immersed in illustrated papers, Mr. Walters continued to glance through his official correspondence, and the Guardsman smoked a cigarette and stared out of the window. None of the five so much as looked at one another.

Suddenly Mr. Walters looked up from his papers and exclaimed—

"I am very sorry, gentlemen, to seem to back out of what we have arranged, but I have just realised that my official duties really won't permit of my going through to Lairg to-night. I am afraid I must get out at Tain. I can give you, however, every assurance that no suspicion can possibly attach to me. As I told you, I am a Government official, and surely that should be a pretty good guarantee."

He looked towards the Australians as he spoke, and then—a little anxiously one would think—at the R. N. R. Lieutenant. These three exchanged glances, and all seemed to hesitate for a moment. The tall Australian spoke first.

"Well," he said, "if you are really traveling on Government business, Mr. Walters—and mind you I don't doubt it!—I think that perhaps we might make an exception and raise no objection under the circumstances."

"If the gentleman gives us his word, I'd be quite willing to agree with you," said Matthews.

Sutherland, the fair Australian, nodded, and added—

"I'd feel quite satisfied to risk it."

"Thank you, gentlemen, thank you very much," said the civilian gratefully, and turned towards Hillary.

The Guardsman shook his head suddenly and firmly.

"I'm very sorry," he said shortly, "and please don't think I suggest any suspicion, but we've made this arrangement, and I'm afraid I

shall have to call the guard at once if anyone leaves the train before Lairg—just as I should expect you to do if I tried to leave."

For a moment there was an awkward pause, and then Matthews
began—

"This seems a bit hard on the gentleman if he has really got
business—"

Mr. Walters interrupted hastily—

"Not a bit; not at all; I quite see Captain Hillary's point. It will
be a little awkward for me, but rather than raise any difficulty I
shall certainly go on with you to Lairg—certainly."

Matthews seemed about to speak again, but the tall Australian
cut in quickly—

"Well, that's settled then. I apologise for my share in putting
you about—"

"And I apologise too," put in Hillary, "but I really think you
must see our position yourself."

"Quite, quite, I see it perfectly," said the Government official.
"Don't trouble to apologise."

The spell of silence that followed was even more strained than
the last. At one station the lamps were lit and the blinds drawn
down, and just after starting again Mr. Walters made the first remark.

"Our next stop is Bonar Bridge," said he. "As that is the only
place where one can get refreshments, and as I have already passed
my intended destination, I think we might all, perhaps, arrange to
leave the carriage for a few minutes, and then any of us who want
it could get a cup of tea. We would, of course, all keep within sight
of one another."

He looked at Hillary as he spoke, and the Guardsman at once
nodded a brief assent.

"I am quite agreeable to that," said he.

"And I—and I," added the others.

It was getting pretty dark when the doors were opened all down
the train, and a crowd in blue and khaki poured across the platform to the refreshment-room. The more dignified demeanour
demanded of an officer handicapped the five in this race, and for

two or three minutes they were passing slowly through the back of the crowd, waiting their turn. The Grenadier was a little apart from the other three officers, and the civilian was pushing close at his shoulder. For one single instant Hillary seemed to start, and it looked as though he were going to turn his head and then refrained. He stood quite still, however, with all expression vanished from his face, and then in a minute slipped forward between two pairs of shoulders to the buffet.

The four officers each returned to the carriage carrying a cup of tea and took their seats. On the platform the crowd was breaking up and scattering back to the train, and the guard was shouting something and waving a lantern.

"Hullo!" exclaimed Lieutenant Matthews, "the Board of Agriculture chap hasn't turned up!"

"Is he going to give us the slip after all?" cried Sutherland, and there was more than a trace of excitement as he gazed through the window.

"Oh, surely not!" murmured Hillary, and yet there was a trifle of anxiety in his eye.

This time the tall Australian said nothing, but his brow was knitted, and in his eye wonder was manifest, and also a trace of excitement held on the curb. And then he spoke in rather a curious voice.

"Ah, here he is!" he said.

The civilian apologised for his delay as he rejoined the four officers.

"I'm afraid you must have thought I was going to back out," said he, "but the fact is I thought I was never going to get my cup of tea!"

"That's all right!" said Mackay, quite cheerfully again, "we're used to getting our nerves rattled!"

"Part of our business!" laughed Matthews.

The tension seemed a little relieved now.

The Australians, Lieutenant Matthews, and the Government official all began to talk in a desultory fashion, and yet with some air of friendliness and less restraint. The Guardsman alone kept silent, and picking up a paper studied it apparently with great attention, for it was noticeable that he only turned over a page once in every ten minutes or so.

Outside, over the empty moor and somber seas of pines, the darkness deepened till night had fallen quite. At one station and then another the train stopped and waited interminably. They were off again and had run for only a few minutes when once more the carriage began to jolt and slacken speed, and then in a moment ceased to move at all. On the instant the tall Australian sprang to his feet and sent the blind flying up and the window down. He looked for a second into the night, and then with a note of agitation cried—

"There's some sort of accident! Tumble out quick, you chaps!"

As he spoke his hand was on the door handle, but before he could even turn it, the voice of the civilian rang out sharp and loud—very differently from the voice they had heard before—

"Drop that handle or I fire! Hands up, all of you!" And then to Hillary he cried, "Knock now! Loud as you can!"

The tall Australian stood looking down the barrel of Mr. Walters' revolver, his muscles paralysed, his face a study in mixed emotions—Sutherland and Matthews each made a movement, and on the instant the revolver made a triangular sweep across the three of them. And meanwhile the Guardsman was hammering on the partition. All this happened within the space of some five or ten seconds, and then the door was flung open from the outside and a square-shouldered man in plain clothes mounted into the carriage. Behind him was another in plain clothes, and behind him again three or four figures in khaki.

"Arrest these three men!" commanded the late representative of the Board of Agriculture.

The tall Australian found his voice at last.

"What the hell's all this about?" he demanded coolly enough. "What do you take us for?"

"Spies," said the detective quietly.

"Come on; game's up, out with your hands," said the plain-clothes man stolidly.

The handcuffs clinked on the wrists first of the tall man and then of the fair man and then of the R.N.R. Lieutenant. A couple of minutes later the civilian and Captain Hillary were alone in the carriage.

"I still can't take it all in," said Hillary. "When you whispered in my ear at the buffet that you were a detective and told me to knock on the partition when you gave me the tip, you dashed near flattened me out on the spot! I had honestly thought that either you were the spy, or that there was some mistake and nobody was!"

The detective smiled.

"I had only made up my own mind a few minutes before that."

"What! Didn't you know who were the spies all the time?"

"Not for certain. I don't mind telling you now, Captain Hillary, that we had information which led us to suspect very strongly that a spy—or possibly more than one spy—was probably going to try and get through on this train. Also we suspected that the uniform of a colonial officer would probably be the disguise. But that was all I had to start on, and I didn't know my man by sight—or whether there would be more than one—or even whether there would be anybody on this train at all."

"Then how did you get on their track?"

"Well, luckily there was a very small selection of Overseas officers starting from King's Cross, and only these two went north of Inverness. I'd fastened on to that tall chap from the start, simply by kind of instinct and experience, but I wasn't a bit sure that the other fellow mightn't have been the genuine article. As for the naval lieutenant, he was a complete surprise packet. He took me in fairly for a long while. In fact, if they hadn't been fools enough to travel all three in the same carriage, he'd have got through to Lairg or Cromarty, or wherever he was going, safe enough."

"He said he was going to Scapa."

The detective shook his head.

"He might have been, but I don't quite see how he'd have got into Scapa and out again without being spotted. Lairg's the centre for striking off for the north-west corner of Scotland. That's more likely, or else Cromarty. However, he won't get to either place now."

"Then when did you know that the whole three were spies?"

"I'd been noticing a few little things—looks passed between them and so on; but what settled it was when I pretended I wanted to get out at Tain and all three of them agreed to it. And that was when you cleared your own character, Captain Hillary!"

Hillary laughed.

"Lucky for me I was rude to you!"

"And unlucky for them they didn't take the same line. They might have kept me wondering a bit longer. But they all three jumped a little too quickly at the chance of being left with only one man to deal with." The detective's face lit up with a smile of reminiscent admiration. "I must say, though, that tall fellow was a clever chap! When I let him in for that arrangement of all keeping together, he played the innocent manly sort of game uncommon well!"

"He took me in completely," said Hillary, "but then, of course, I'm an innocent fat-head in these matters." He paused and looked across at the other. "By Jove, now one comes to think of it, that was a fat-headed sort of thing one of those fellows did—carrying about that envelope with a German address on it! What on earth was he doing with it?"

The detective seemed to look at him rather oddly.

"It almost seemed as though it had been dropped just to provide an excuse for keeping the company from separating," he suggested drily.

The young officer laughed.

"Great idea, bringing an envelope from Germany for that purpose!"

"That envelope was addressed in this carriage," said the detective gravely.

Hillary stared at him.

"What! But it was torn and dirty! Besides, how—"

"It was torn by the fat-headed chap who addressed it. He tore it because it hadn't a German stamp and postmark on it, and the whole envelope would have given the show away. As for when he did the tearing, it was when the old General got out and he jumped out too. And he dirtied it by putting the piece he meant to drop under his foot while he was standing on the platform."

"By Jove!" murmured Hillary, and then suddenly burst into a roar of laughter. "How those three must have wondered which of his pals had done such a damned silly thing!"

Coachwhip Publications
CoachwhipBooks.com

THE COMPLETE ADVENTURES OF
ROMNEY PRINGLE

R. Austin Freeman &
John J. Pitcairn
(as by Clifford Ashdown)

COACHWHIP PUBLICATIONS
COACHWHIPBOOKS.COM

VULTURES
IN THE SKY
A HUGH RENNERT MYSTERY

TODD DOWNING